The
SOUL
THIEF

BOOKS BY CECELIA HOLLAND

The Soul Thief
The Angel and the Sword
Lily Nevada
An Ordinary Woman
Railroad Schemes
Valley of the Kings
Jerusalem
Pacific Street
The Bear Flag
The Lords of Vaumartin
Pillar of the Sky
The Belt of Gold
The Sea Beggars
Home Ground
City of God
Two Ravens
Floating Worlds
Great Maria
The Death of Attila
The Earl
Antichrist
Until the Sun Falls
The Kings in Winter
Rakossy
The Firedrake

FOR CHILDREN

The King's Road
Ghost on the Steppe

A TOM DOHERTY ASSOCIATES BOOK
New York

The
SOUL
THIEF

CECELIA HOLLAND

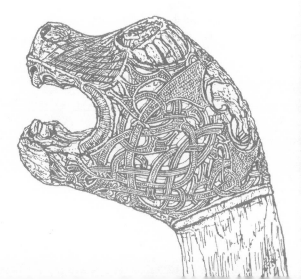

THE SOUL THIEF

Copyright © 2002 by Cecelia Holland

Design by Heidi Eriksen

A Forge Book
Published by Tom Doherty Associates, LLC
175 Fifth Avenue
New York, NY 10010

www.tor.com

Forge® is a registered trademark of Tom Doherty Associates, LLC.

Library of Congress Cataloging-in-Publication Data

Holland, Cecelia.
    The soul thief / Cecelia Holland.—1st ed.
      p. cm.
    ISBN 0-312-84885-4
    1. Brothers and sisters—Fiction. 2. Kidnapping—Fiction.
  3. Vikings—Fiction. 4. Ireland—Fiction. 5. Twins—Fiction. I. Title.

PS3558.O348 S68   2002
813'.54—dc21

                                    2001055571

First Edition: April 2002

Printed in the United States of America

0 9 8 7 6 5 4 3 2 1

for Bob and Jackie Batjer,
most excellent friends

The
SOUL
THIEF

"You coward, Corban. Loose-strife! Changeling! No-Son! So I call you! You do no good, you only cause me trouble!"

Corban stood, his jaw clenched, silent, enduring the pounding of his father's wrath. He felt all their eyes on him—his mother, hunched at his towering father's side, his brother like a mouse down by the table, his little sister and his grandmother at the hearth—but no one spoke out for him. They kept still, out of the way, while his father roared.

"For the sake of your family, I order you to go! Find some shred of manhood in you and take up a sword with the High King!"

"No," Corban said.

He stood fast, staring at the floor, unable even to look his father in the face. If he obeyed he was nothing. If he went to the High King he would stand under the King as here he stood under his father, he would never have what he wanted.

He had no idea what he wanted.

"Damn you! You are not my son!"

"Father, please!"

That clear voice rang through the hall. Corban lifted his head. Behind him his sister Mav had come in the door. She walked swiftly up, her head high, and went by him and stood before their father, and laid her hand on his arm.

"Sir, don't speak so. Don't say what cannot be unsaid."

The old man turned his gaze on her, his shaggy grey hair wild around his head like the bursting of a sun, and smiled, as he always smiled for her. He said, "I wish you were the male, and he the female. I would have no doubt of you."

"Father," she said. "I beg you. Make peace with him."

He swung his gaze toward Corban, who lowered his eyes, unwilling to look his father in the face. "Peace? He gets no peace from me! You will do as I bid you, Corban, and go offer your service to the High King. Or leave this place and this family forever!" At the last word his voice cracked like a whip.

Corban clenched his fist. "You give me no choice," he said, low, and turned, and went toward the door.

Now suddenly his mother cried out, not words, not even his name, but a wail, rising above the sudden low rumble of voices. He caught a glimpse of his little sister, watching him open-mouthed. He reached the door and went out into the bright sunshine, and stood there, surprised at his own calm, looking around him at the farm yard, the stone wall of the byre, the mound of cut turf, the bondsmen walking away down toward the green meadow, where the cows were already grazing. Past everything the glitter of the sea dazzled his eyes. He drew a deep breath. He turned, and his gaze found the long path that led past the byre, past the bake oven and the pigsty, up over the hill and away.

He started off. This part was easy enough, he had been going this way all his life. When he came to the place where the path turned up the hill Mav caught up with him. They walked along together a while, climbing the grassy treeless hill. He glanced at her, striding along beside him, with the wind blowing her long black hair back, her cheeks ruddy.

She murmured as she walked, and turned, looking back, her lips moving. He went along a step ahead of her, toward the top of the hill. He began to think of the way ahead but could not. He was just going away. He had his cloak, and his sling in his belt, nothing else. His heart sank.

He said, suddenly, "I'm not a coward."

"What are you, then?" she said.

Beside him she strode along, her long skirts whipping around her legs. Her words rang in his ears. He had no answer; he knew nothing of himself save what he would not be. She was watching him, her eyebrows raised, as if he might say something, but he could not.

Her gaze jerked suddenly off around past him, back the way they had come, and a low moan burst from her.

He looked; he saw nothing. They had come to the top of the hill, where a grey rock thrust up through the green sod, its surface rough with patches of lichen. He said, "What's wrong, Mav?"

She gave a shudder, as if something shook her from top to bottom, and lowered her eyes. She did not answer. From the belly of her cloak she drew forth a loaf of bread and a jug.

"Take these."

"You are good," he said, grateful, and took them, and set them on the rock. He took hold of her hand and looked into her face. "What is it?"

"Ah, I don't know," she said. She was staring away toward the sea. With her free hand she drew the cloak tight around her again, the wind buffeting her, plucking at her hair. The linen hem of her gown fluttered. "I think only that something is coming. Someone." Her long cold fingers tightened around his.

He looked away back down the path, toward the farm. He doubted her somewhat. They saw few travellers, out here at the edge of the world. Still, what she said impressed him. She was long-sighted, his sister. She knew what happened before it did, she could find what was lost, she could see what was hidden. Whenever before he had seen her this way, generally then something did happen, not always evil, but often evil; he remembered especially how she had twitched and murmured like this for two days before a sudden storm off the sea wrecked their fishing boats and killed half their cattle.

Some said she made the evil happen.

He held tight to her hand. He knew that was not so. She was good, she was true as steel; his father was right about her.

He wondered if she foresaw his banishment. He said, "Father will let me come back, maybe tomorrow. You know how he is." But he was not sure. The fury that had stiffened him had melted away and he knew nowhere to go. Off to the west the land rose toward the low hills in the distance, all turning brown now as the winter crept toward them. Suddenly his homefire seemed the only warm place in the world, his family the only people who would ever love him.

Mav drew her hand from his grip; she gripped the cloak in her fist, her face staring fixed at the sea. "I will try, Corban. I will talk to him." She raked her hair away from her face. Then suddenly she flung her arms around his neck.

"Corban. I'll make him let you back, or we'll go away together. Now, go into the woods and wait, and meet me here tomorrow, when the sun is well up." She pushed abruptly away from him.

"Will you be hungry? Did I bring you enough?" Her eyes turned steadily away from him, toward the sea.

He thought she looked beautiful, her hair flying in the wind, and her cheeks red and her eyes bright. He knew she would not leave their home, even to go with him.

He said, "Tomorrow then."

She came around to him again, leaning on him, and kissed his cheek. She looked deep into his eyes, their noses almost touching.

"I think I shall bring you home again, Corban," she said. "But better it would be if you came home yourself, alone, and faced him, and made him take you as you are." She kissed him again and stood back, frowning, her gaze running suddenly over him, and she made as if to pull off her cloak and give it him.

He laughed at that; he caught her hand. "No, no, I am warm enough." And she shrugged. Without a word, she turned, and went off back down the path to the farm.

He watched her go, his mirth fading.

They had been born on the same day, one-two out of the womb; folk said they were as alike in their looks as two eggs, and yet he saw nothing of himself in her. Mav was straight and clean, she thought long on everything, she had no fear, and cared for all of them. Corban was neither wise nor brave, his father wanted him to be wise and brave, and so, clutching always to himself that part of himself his father could not touch, he was foolish and slack. Whatever else he would be, whenever he began to form a thought of that, he saw his father there ahead of him.

He took the bread from his wallet, and ate it. He went away over the hill, and down through the oak wood, hunting squirrels with his sling. Against them he was a brawny man, he knew their ways as they coiled around the oaks, and waited patiently and struck when they grew too curious or bold.

He worked his way so along the edge of the great wood, where the going was easier, following the line of meadows and bogs where the red deer grazed. He watched for the bright splashes of nut trees and for berries. He flushed a covey of little marsh hens that fluttered up and away across the meadow, their wings buzzing. The grass was turning yellow, dying back for the winter, yet the day was warm and he had no use for his cloak and wore his shirt down around his waist. Going down a long brushy hill he came on fresh bear droppings full of seeds. Twice he killed squirrels in his hunting and hung the stripped bodies from his belt.

The sun rolled away into the west and he was far from home. Ahead of him the forest lay thick and shadowy, and to his right, to the north, the hills sloped down and he could see the sheen of water in the distance and knew it to be the long lake. He walked that way across a bog, following an old path marked with stones, and went down a steep long slope toward the water. Coming around the flank of a hill, he reached the shore.

Afar he could see men in a boat on the lake fishing. The curling water of the lake rippled along the shore. The sun was sinking down and he was tired suddenly and cold, and he pulled his shirt up, and wrapped his cloak around him. Against the face of a pocky grey boulder he made a little fire and spitted his squirrels.

At home they would be gathered to eat, his father and mother sitting together, and his younger brother taking them their meat and bread and filling the cup between them. His sisters next beside them, waiting until they were done, and then the bondsmen and their wives and children, all around in a ring. His spirits drooped. He wished suddenly he were among them, in their shared warmth, waiting for the common meat, telling some joke to make them laugh. He remembered his little sister, how she had looked when his father cast him out, her eyes round, her head twisted on her neck to watch him go; she had been sitting by the hearth, with his grandmother roasting apples, and her eyes followed him the whole way across the room to the door.

He would never go back. He did not need them, he would go on by himself. He needed nobody. He thought of the great inland farm, Dun Maire, where a girl lived who had looked on him well, and more, the last time he was there. He could go there. He might never go back again to his home.

He thought of Mav, and his mind faltered; he loved his sister best, alone, of all of them. Certainly, in a flash, he hated them all, all but Mav: his father, his mother who had said nothing, his brother Finn, who mumbled and bowed and prayed like a madman to convince his father he would make the priest the old man wanted.

He loved Mav. He would go back, for his sister's sake. A prickle of uneasiness passed through him. Surely he would go back.

The sun set; while it sank down to its rest it swept a wash of color over the sky above and over the lake below, until all the world streamed with the strong ruddy light. The rosy hue faded at once. On the lake, the little boat rowed slowly away. Corban felt the dark settle over him, fitting down around the glow of his fire. He felt his aloneness like the cold air all around him, the singleness of his being, untouched.

He shuddered off that feeling. In the morning he would go back to the rock above the farm, and Mav would have won their father over, and they would let him go home again. He ate the squirrels, sucking the bones empty. He would work harder than usual for a while, to make up for it all, and soon enough there would be another quarrel.

He flung the bones into the trees. Wrapping himself up in his cloak, he said an old charm against fairies, even though his father wasn't there to hear it, and lay down to sleep. His father was a stout Christian, and they had pounded the Cross and the Trinity into him all his life, but it was no use to him, any of it. Mav went her own way, and some of the bonders, while praying loudly to his father's face, made offerings to the old folk; but he put no more faith in the sidhe than he did in Christ, since they had let Christ defeat them.

There was no place for him, the world was not of a piece with him. He was outside everything, belonging not even to his own family, not to anywhere or anyone. Lying there, watching the fire die down to glowing ash, he felt empty as the hollow of a beggar's hand.

The fire darkened, showing a single dull red eye under the weight of ash. The lake glimmered under the moon, and he slept.

—⚬—

"Mav," her father said, "don't talk to me anymore about Corban. I want nothing more to do with him. Damn him, I hope he never comes home."

"Ah," she said, "what are you saying?" She flung her hands

up. They were standing in the center of the hall, with all the family gathered for the evening meal; the chatter and laughter of the other people smothered their talk. She took her father by the arm. "Once more, Papa. Forgive him, just once more."

"Bah." He shrugged her hand off. Under the great wooly ridges of his brows his eyes burned hot. He gripped her by the arm, hard, but his voice was gentle.

"For you, my dear one, my darling, I would do almost anything, but this time—no." He bent and put his lips against her forehead, and went off down the long room.

She stayed where she stood. Around her the bondsmen and their wives and children stuffed themselves with bread and fish. By the fire somebody was telling a story. The room was smoky from the fire, and too hot. All her nerves rippled again. Everything in her was churning. Her mind strained toward her brother, off in the wilderness.

Her father was wrong. Corban was unformed as a chick in the egg, but in him there was a rare goodness: not what their father wanted, but finer still. She had to bring him home again. But some cold dread dragged her down. For an instant, she thought of something else, something terrible, but it was gone before she could lay her mind on it.

She went away from the fire, to the cool by the door. Her mother sat at the table still, picking at a piece of meat, her head-dress all undone and hanging around her ears. Mav's little sister came running up, holding out her hands, and their mother took her and lifted her onto her lap. The two heads bowed together, the child's cheek smooth and the mother's rough, the child's hair black and the mother's grey.

Her younger brother Finn came up. "What did Papa say?"

"You should hope he lets Corban come back," Mav said, with an edge in her voice. She thought he sometimes steered their father against their brother. "Or next he will be wanting you to go off to King Brian's court."

"Not me," Finn said. He was eating nuts by the handful; he spoke through a mush of filberts. "I shall go to be a priest, and make sermons all over Ireland."

"I hope not spitting on people as you do it," she said, brushing bits of nut off her sleeve.

Finn snorted at her. "When I am a bishop you will like me better."

"When you are a bishop, I will fall over speechless with surprise."

Again in her mind, some great wave rose, like the breast of the sea, as if to break up and drown all her thinking. She shut her eyes, queasy in her stomach, struggling against that feeling of dread.

When she looked up again Finn was gone. She folded her arms over her chest, looking out over the hall. Without Corban there it felt only half-real to her.

He had to come home. She would make sure that he came home. Over there by the hearth, one of the women began to sing in a high, light voice, an old song of Saint Brendan, and all around the room, others joined in, a seamless cloak of voices. She leaned against the wall behind her, shivering in the draft. She had a song to sing, but they would not hear it; and she bit her lips to keep them silenced, and hugged her arms around herself and waited.

⟶⟶⟵

Corban slept without dreams. When he came awake finally in the morning, he thought again of not going home at all, but of walking on, along the margin of the lake, and finding somewhere else to live. Dun Maire, or O'Banlon's homestead farther north. O'Banlon with his great flocks and herds always needed men. But he thought of Mav and suddenly a fierce wild yearning arose in him to see her. He remembered how she had been the day before, uneasy and restless. He thought suddenly that he should have gone back with her to the farm, as she had said, and challenged his father.

What would he have said? He knew he was no hero. What his father wanted of him he could not do. To strut and shout as he had seen such men do, to fight not to save himself and his own but merely to further the wishes of the high king—another man's wishes—

"You coward, Corban."

He felt the words still like a whip, even in his memory, like a lash across his face. He wondered if he were in fact such an empty man as his father said. He climbed up along the steep hillside, against the margin of the oaky wood, the going harder this way, mostly uphill, when the day before he had gone so easily down. Crossing the bog, he cut through the forest toward his home. The leaves of the trees were turning and falling and underfoot he trod on carpets of thick damp forest rot, hard to keep a firm footing on. He was hungry. He reached the top of the hill and looked out toward the sea, and saw there a column of smoke rising up, black and rolling.

For an instant, he thought, What are they cooking, to make so great a smoke?

Then he began to run, his heart pounding, straight down into the glen. Thick billows of smoke rolled off across the sky. He sobbed as he ran. The downward hill gave him long, long strides. It seemed so far still. His lungs were bursting. He flew by the rock where the day before he had met his sister and turned down onto the path.

The glen opened up before him. The smoke rose from the house, from the byre, from the cookhouse, black billows of smoke blown down low by the wind. As he ran he saw people scurrying across the open ground between the buildings and the home pasture. Beyond the drifting smoke, through it, he could see the dragon-headed ships drawn up along the beach.

He screamed. He stretched his legs to giant strides, hurtling down the path. Now among the rushing and scurrying of the people he could see bodies sprawled on the ground, and heard shouts and shrieks. He rushed down the last stretch of the path to the back of the farm, past the midden heap, toward the blazing pigsty and the byre.

They were driving off the cattle. Already most of the herd was shuffling away down toward the beach. Just past the byre he came on a big man with a long braided beard waving a stick at a brindle cow and her calf, and Corban without pausing in his long strides leapt on him from the side.

The bearded man went down under him with a yell. Corban

hit the ground so hard all the breath left him. He clutched at the
body under him, struggling to get air. The man under him roared,
and rolled over, throwing him off.

Corban scrambled away; he looked around quickly and saw,
surprised, that he and this other were the only people he could see.
Somewhere though, a woman was screaming. Flame crackled. The
bearded man raised his stick and came at him.

Corban dodged, all his hair standing up on end. He stooped,
groping over the ground, and felt a rock under one hand, and leapt
up, breathless, just as the other man swung his stick. The blow
struck him glancing on the shoulder but still knocked him to his
knees. The bearded man let out a howl of triumph. Swung the long
stick high. Corban reeled away from the stroke, snatching the sling
from his belt, but he had no chance to load the stone. The stick
cracked him across the head and he went down cold.

—◦—

He woke in the dark, and thought he was blind.

He blinked. For a moment he had no memory. He could smell
smoke, and he pushed himself up on his arms and looked around,
and saw it was night, deep in the night. His head hurt. Above him,
above the stone wall of the cattle byre, the thatch was gone; he
saw the rough line of the top of the wall against a strange red haze
in the dark.

He leapt up, all his memory flooding back, the smoke, the
bearded man, the ships on the beach. He screamed, "Mav!" His
heart thundered under his ribs, painfully hard.

Standing, he could see past the stone wall of the byre. The
house beyond was mostly gone now, the fire low and crackling
along the last of the walls, casting up a red blur into the air. He
blinked again, looking around him. The brindle cow and her calf
were gone, the bearded man was gone.

He groaned. His belly heaved, and his legs sagged at the knees.
"Mav!" He staggered out toward the fire.

The light grew stronger as he passed the byre wall. The whole
of the long meadow down to the sea was filled with a faint orange
flicker of light from the burning house. He saw a dark shape

stretched on the ground and went down and knelt by it, and put a hand on it, and saw it was one of the bondsmen. His head was smashed in, his brains like a red pudding on the ground. Corban was sick to his stomach; he lurched off away from the body and threw up.

From there he saw another, right in front of the doorway to the house—what had been the doorway to the house—and that one he knew at once. His knees gave out and he fell. He stood and staggered over and fell again to his knees by his father, but he dared not touch him.

He should have come, she was right, he should have come down. His father lay with his face turned away, the harsh line of cheekbone and jaw fuzzy with dried blood. Corban sobbed; his eyes stung from the smoke. He croaked out something, a call to God, and shut his lips again. God had not saved his father. He shambled off toward the next dead, two more of the bondsmen, sprawled in a heap.

He straightened. The dawn was coming, the sky turning paler. He screamed, "Mav!" and there was no answer.

He wheeled around, looking for the others. His mother, his grandmother, his sisters, his brother Finn. He went from one heaped corpse to the next, rushing back and forth across the meadow. Too few.

At first he found mostly the bondsmen: they would have come out to defend the farm. Then where the edge of the pasture ridged out over the sloping sandy beach, out in front of them all, he came on his brother, lying sprawled face down with a club still in his hands, his back carved open in a great red wound.

"Finn."

He had fought them, his brother, slight and young, always praying. It seemed he had led the fight. Corban's chest throbbed, some hard hot lump lodged in his chest refusing to come up or go down; he stood beside his brother a long while. Better to have died so than be Corban now, he thought, and the great lump in his chest choked off his breath.

He drew back from Finn, his heart pounding, afraid. He had seen no sign of his mother. He stumbled on, following the trampled bloody trail down onto the beach. He remembered seeing the ships drawn up on the beach; now they were gone, even the family's fishing boats were gone. Along the sea's edge were heaps of bones, and piles of guts and heads and hoofs, slick drying puddles of blood. They had slaughtered the cattle here. The stench made him gag; his legs wobbled. Beyond the slaughterground a row of black buzzards flapped and lumbered awkwardly away from him down the beach, too heavy with feasting to fly.

His heart clenched in his chest. Ahead he saw a woman's shape, but it was his mother's old spinning woman, crumpled on the grass. Nearer the water lay a baby, its head horribly flattened. By the very edge of the waves he found his little sister, four years old. Her eyes were open. Her hair floated on the little lapping waves. There was a horrible wound in her chest, a gash that seemed bigger than she was, a great mouth come out of the sea to eat her up. He sank over her, rocking back and forth, gasping for air again. His hands moved over her, not touching, as if he could somehow smooth together the hole in her chest.

Mav.

He stood. He turned and looked back at the burning house. His heart was a drum, a thunder in his ears. This girl, and the old woman, the baby—where were the other women? He bent to gather the little girl up in his arms and trudged up toward the house again.

The day was breaking over him, clear and cool. Going back up he saw now the tracks where the old woman had been dragged along—that was why they had killed her, he thought in a flash, because she was too weak to keep up. Why they had killed the baby, and this child in his arms. They wanted strong young people. Strong young women. Mav. His legs wobbled. He went on back toward the house, and laid down his little sister in the dooryard where his father lay. Grimly he went around between the house and the cookhouse, and there at last he found his mother, crumpled in a heap near the cookhouse door.

He lifted her in his arms; she was stiffening, her hands flexed like claws. She had fought them, then, like Finn. No use, but she had fought them. A surge of pride struck him unawares, that his family should have struggled so against their doom. He took her to his father, lying before his doorstep, and laid her down beside him. Tears streamed down his face. He tried to say words but nothing would come. His mouth worked, but his mind was empty. He buried his face in his hands.

He thought of Mav. He knew she was taken. He went back down to the sea's edge, where the surf broke, and stretched his gaze out across the water, as if she might have left a track on the waves. The water rose and fell away from him. Before he realized it he had walked out into the waves, into the sea, reaching with his gaze as far as he could over the water. Toward the horizon, where they had taken her.

The sea lifted him, as if it would carry him away after her.

He shivered in the cold. He backed away, back up onto the beach. In his mind he heard her calling out to him. He knew she was alive, that she was out there, somewhere.

He should have come back with her. He bent his head and wept.

The rest of the day he gathered them up, all the dead, and laid them in the dooryard around his father. He could not bury them, there were too many of them. It cost him all his strength to drag them, cold and stiff, some from the far edge of the meadow. Overhead, ravens and buzzards circled and he kept them up there with his sling. Off by the edge of the meadow, he saw a long grey shape skulking, too far away to shoot.

The raiders had left one of the pigs in the sty, where it had burned along with the buildings, so Corban ate of fine roast pork all day long. But it choked him to swallow the flesh.

All the while, he thought of what he could do to find Mav, and by afternoon he had resolved to go to a place called the Black Pond, which was down on the coast a little, on a river there. He knew that the foreigners kept a market there and perhaps the men who had done this would take what they had stolen there, to sell.

He thought he might also find the men who had done this. What he could do then he had no way to know. He bundled up all his rage and hate and stuffed it away in a black corner of his mind, down out of reach.

He went all over the farm, making sure he had discovered everybody. By the ruined byre he caught sight of another wolf, slinking into the brush behind the midden, and back by the field of corpses the birds were lighting on the ground. The wolves and buzzards would get them all in the end, anyway. His mind was clogged, he could feel nothing, think nothing, and he was weary to his bones.

When he had at last done, and all his people were gathered in the dooryard, he stood there, and thought he should say something over them. He had lost all sense of them as horrible, from the custom of handling them, and now saw them as the people they had been, and still were, for a little while, in some way. Many still had their eyes open, which made it seem all the more that they lived, inside: some little warm life still there, inside. Others lay in strange poses, curled up, or stretched sideways, one arm awkwardly out, clutching the air. The smell of them made him sick to his stomach.

He had to get out of here, out of this place of death, where he couldn't even breathe. When he left, he knew, the scavengers would come, and tear them apart.

Now suddenly words leapt from his tongue.

"I can't help you any more than this. I'm sorry I was not here to die with you, but I shall find Mav." He was weeping again, like a woman, he felt himself pitiful and frail, useless in this huge task before him, and yet he dared not turn from it, because what else could he do? He stretched his hands out toward them. "Good-bye. Good-bye."

He turned, and made ready to go. He had put some of the roasted pig into a sack, and he slung that on his shoulder. He found a stout stick to lean on. He filled his waterskin with water, took the stick, and walked across the farm, weeping as he walked.

He went down along the seam between the pasture and the sandy beach, and crossed the little stream that ran down to the sea. On the far bank he climbed up the narrow path to the top of the sea cliff. There he looked ahead and saw the land rolling away before him, vanishing into the haze of the distance, and he quailed from it.

As he stood there, unsure how to go on, he realized he was not alone after all.

They had all come with him. He saw nothing, and yet he sensed them all around him. They spoke, their voices jumbled, complaining, reproachful, and sad. They tugged on his arm, and poked him, they breathed down his neck and draped themselves across his shoulder. They made the air thick, so that he went along stiff-legged, his hair on end. He heard the deep rumble of his father's voice; and his mother's sigh; and low and terrible, the baby's hopeless wailing; and all the while, the many others, muttering and weeping and trudging along with him. He went forward as stiff as wood, his breath stuck like a fire in his throat.

So he traveled in a great cloud of souls along the top of the cliff, where the path ran bare as a scar through the high yellow grass all bent down by the harsh wind off the sea. But as he went along, he realized that those around him were becoming fewer, their voices hushed. They touched him less and less. One by one they were falling behind, going back to the farm again.

Now he was afraid of losing them. He began to listen for them, as the voices died away. In the thinning braid of their voices he could no longer find the baby's crying, and then his little sister was gone, then Finn and his mother, until at last he heard only his father, and that fainter and more seldom. Corban crept along the path, bent under the weight of this, his ears straining, until he had gone a long, long way and heard nothing.

Then he sat down by the road and wept again, until his eyes were dry. He sat slumped by the road, his hands dangling over his knees. He felt thin and flat as a winding sheet. He had thought he was alone before, he had thought he was no part of them, but he had always been part of them, he had measured himself against them, needed them always to set himself against. Now he knew better, too late now he knew what it meant to be alone.

His head hurt where the stick had struck him. His belly churned. His feet were sore already. The ordinary world settled down around him, the twittering of birds, the long grass bending and hissing under the wind. The sky was enormous, stippled with thin cloud, traced with long-gliding gulls. He had thought two nights before that he might leave them. He remembered that with an agony like a white-hot iron through his mind. He had brought this on himself. He had made this happen. Grimly he rose, and put his legs under him, and set off down the road to find his sister.

Mav thought she might die; she might float up from her body and sail away across the stars, back to the farm. She had seen her father killed, her sister killed; shackled together with the other women, she had been flung down in the wooden belly of a ship. She had thought then of climbing up and throwing herself over the side of the ship, but the chains held her fast to the other women around her and she could not rise.

Then they came quickly to some other place, and they were dragged off the ship and thrown down on the sand, and all the men made use of them. The men made a big fire somewhere near and roasted meat and drank and all the while one after another they had the women. Mav lay still, her eyes shut, while they hollowed her out like a hole in the ground.

The woman next to her was from the farm; once, as they lay there, somehow, her head turned, their eyes met, and she saw death there, in her bondswoman's eyes. A moment later they dragged her body away.

She stared up at the sun, then the moon, then the sun again. More women came, from other places. "Our men will come," one shouted, over and over. Mav lay still, thinking: All our men are dead.

When she thought of her mother and father, her sister and her brothers, from deep in her belly a wave of such feeling rose into her head and her eyes and her mouth that would drown her if she let it break.

She could die, somehow, and be safe from this. She knew if she lived on, that worse would come, that her soul might die, wink out like a candle in the rain.

"Our men will come—"

Dead. All but one. She kept her eyes shut, and thought of her brother Corban, and her ruined body throbbed, quickening again.

Around her as her senses sharpened she could make out the other women, groaning and crying, some of them, but many only lying there on the rocky shore. She felt them around her and in her, all their terrors and pain, and gritted her teeth. It was too much, it was too hard. She would die. She saw her mother and her father hovering around her, and talked to them, and saw her brother Finn smiling at her, although he was dead, and the stars shone through him.

Farther away, she saw her brother Corban, coming toward her.

"Worthless boy," her father said.

No. He was still there, he was coming after her. No, she said, to the starry sky. Her father floated around her, her mother, summoning her. She could go back to them, to the farm.

"Damn Corban," her father said. "No son of mine."

No. She saw Corban coming after her. She saw him stagger on the long road.

She forced herself back into her body, down into her fingers and toes, even into the bloody ruin of her woman's place, which no man had known until so many of them did. She took up the pain, even the pain and the fear of the other women. She would live. Corban was coming.

Beside her someone was weeping, low and wretched. She turned, as much as she could with the ropes around her, and moved her arm and touched the unseen, unknown girl there. That girl jumped, afraid. Mav whispered, "I am here." At the sound of her voice the girl stilled, and crept a little toward her, and Mav slid her bound arm around her and comforted her. "I am here," she said, into the girl's filthy, sea-smelling hair. "I am here."

CHAPTER TWO

Wrapped in his cloak, Corban slept that night at the foot of an ancient stone standing beside the road; in the morning he lay snug in the warmth of the cloak and could not make himself rise. There seemed no reason to do anything at all. A heaviness lay on him like the shadow of the stone. Some vague dream pricked at his memory, of being helpless among great birds who stabbed him with their beaks. Above him the sky stretched enormous and empty to nowhere.

Eventually he got up because he was hungry. With his sling ready he went along the road south, watching for hares and birds. The road led through bracken and forest, bracken and forest, endlessly over the low rolling hills; he walked and walked but never seemed to get anywhere. He thought of Mav, as she had looked the last time he saw her, with the wind blowing her hair back. The rush of memory gripped him; there seemed so much behind him, and yet nothing in front of him.

When he came to the Black Pond, if she was not there, what then? He would have walked all this way for nothing. He began to calculate when he could give up searching without feeling bad. Nobody would know, if he gave up. There was nobody now to tell him what to do. Nobody who cared what he did. Nothing he did was going to matter anyway.

In his mind, he saw her, with the wind blowing her hair back, staring out to sea, waiting. He realized he had come to a stop, he was standing in the middle of the road, staring away into the empty air.

Help me, he thought, but there was no one to ask.

He shuddered. His father's curse was following him. Yet he stood a long while, miserable, seeing nothing, missing again the voices of his people, all gone now, gone.

He could not stand there in the road like a stone; he had to do something, and so he started on again. He found some berries and nuts and drank from a cold spring and began to feel better. He went down through the lane under the branches of the old trees, shutting out the sun, and watched for something to kill and eat.

The dream caught at him again, the beaks of the birds.

Hungry, he made a better hunter, and he killed a hare, and dug some wild onions, and that night ate by a little fire in the open, on the cliff overlooking the sea. The sun went down and he drew his cloak around him against the sudden sharp wind. The stars came out like thousands of cold, fiery eyes opening. He thought about going on in the morning and saved some of the hare to eat then.

He realized, with a start, that he had not given up. He could have given up and no one would have known. He would have known, he would have carried that knowledge along with him, together with his father's curse and the memory of his mother dead and his home burning and his sister standing by the grey rock, her hair blown like a flag in the wind, feeling the approach of something evil. He was pleased with himself suddenly, that he was not a man who gave up without even trying.

In the morning, walking on through thick woods, he came before the middle of the day to a road worn and rutted from the wheels of carts, and that road led him on over the hill to the edge of the forest. He came out of the trees above a river and looked down and saw a settlement there on the far side of the river like a great gall stuck onto the side of a watery oak.

The green water ran in from his right hand, and went away toward his left, toward the sea in the distance; opposite where he was standing, another little stream came in from the south. Just before it met the river's smooth rush it widened out into a still pool fringed with the stalky brown rushes of dead cattails. Dubh Linn, the Black Pond: there it was.

The settlement was much greater than his farm, or even Dun Maire; it was the largest place he had ever seen. On the land between the converging waters stood two rows of well-made houses, with thatched roofs. The land on that southern bank sloped up away from the river and on the rise was another, larger building; a hall, maybe.

Past that were people working on a wall of mounded dirt and stakes, carrying baskets back and forth, and digging. Two big piles of stakes stood at the foot of the earthen wall. There was one who watched and did not work, and when a digging man suddenly flung down his shovel and sat down on the ground, that watcher went over and kicked him back to work. Corban shivered, and drew his eyes away.

Closer to the river, around the houses, were a lot more people, most of them not working. They stood or sat in groups and talked, or wandered up and down through the open ground below the rows of houses. They kept to the walkways of planks that ran all over the open ground, and he guessed the ground there was wet; a goat was browsing on the reeds near the river's sloped bank and Corban saw how the goat with every step had to pull up its feet out of the muck.

A little way along the river bank was firmer ground, where several people sat with baskets while others strolled slowly by. He had seen markets before and knew this was one, but he also saw they were selling no people there. He saw nowhere that his sister could be.

Just upstream of the market, a long wooden wharf walked out over the river on stilt-piers. A round-bellied ship was tied up to it. Three other ships, smaller, were hauled up on the riverbank. None of them looked like the ships he had seen through the smoke of the burning farm, with their great serpent heads: these were smaller and rounder.

From down in his memory the sound of screams rose, again, and the wafting of the smoke, and the smell of the smoke, and the fire's roar. He pushed all that away; that did not bear thinking about.

He went down the slope toward the river. A little upstream from the wharf was a plank bridge, where people were crossing into the settlement, and he made for that.

The slope was high in bracken. The path cut sideways across the steep pitch of the hillside. A whiff of the stink of a cess pit reached him. Mav was not here, and yet he was eager to see this place. He had to go somewhere and this place drew him like a fly. He went over the bridge, following a hunter carrying marsh hens by their feet and an old man with a load of firewood on his back. Garbage littered the edge of the water. Just below the bridge, a broken hurdle of withies was rotting in a green scum in the shallow water.

When he came to the far side of the bridge, two men sitting there leapt up and stopped him, their hands stretched out to hold him back, a barrage of words he did not know. He stood on the very end of the bridge, looking from one to the other: an old man and a young one. He said, uncertainly, "Why can I not go in?"

The young man frowned, and grumbled something, giving him a harsh look, but the old one stepped forward, and suddenly spoke so that Corban could understand him.

"What's your name? You're Irish?"

"My name is Corban Mac—" He stopped. He could not use his father's name. "Corban. I came from up the road."

The younger man had lost all interest and was walking back to his place on the river bank. The old man watched Corban keenly. His head was bald as a buzzard's, his cheeks and jowls hanging from it in folds and sags, his jut of a nose like a buzzard's beak. He said, "What do you want here?"

"I'm looking for my sister," Corban said. "She was taken by the—the foreigners, yesterday morning, and I was thinking she might be here."

The old man's sparse white eyebrows wobbled up and down. "I don't think so. We've had no slaves here since the summer. Most likely they'll have carried her off to Jorvik."

All this way for nothing, Corban thought. A cold despair dragged at his mind. His gaze lifted past the old man to the wattle houses, the crowds of people, and returned to the keen old buzzard face before him.

"Where is Jorvik?"

"Across the sea. It's a long way."

"Can I come in here?"

"To Dubh Linn?" The white eyebrows jerked up and down again. "Do you have anything to sell?"

"No," he said, startled.

"Are you buying anything?"

"No."

"Do you have any weapons?"

Corban put his hand to the sling in his belt. "Only this."

"Pagh," the old man snorted. "Squirrel-killer. Go in, then."

Gladly, Corban went the last few steps off the bridge into the city; the old man was going back to the river bank, and his voice rose, incomprehensible again. Corban realized he was speaking the foreigners' language, what he had heard called the dansk tongue. His skin tingled with panic. But no one stopped him or even looked curiously at him; he went into the settlement without attracting any attention at all.

The boardwalks were crowded and he had to worm his way through. Everybody here now was speaking that other language. They filled the boardwalk, too close for his comfort, and stepping down onto the ground he picked his way carefully through the mucky swamp. He passed a crowd of men shouting and waving their arms at each other. Carelessly he stepped into a wet patch and drew his shoe free with a loud squelch. A naked child ran past him, laughing, its mother racing afterward, her hands outstretched and her mouth open. Across the bare mucky ground were dog prints and goat prints in every direction.

He went down along the river, past a row of frames made of poles, where nets hung to dry; in front of them an old man sat mending a net, the shuttle flying back and forth in his hand. Somewhere up on the higher ground a hammer began to rang out a steady metal rhythm—he knew that sound. There was a smith here, as there was at Dun Maire.

There would be many things here he had only heard of, until now. He kept his eyes moving, looking at everything. The place stank, not just of the marsh; the air was streaked with the flavor of cess pits, and middens, and ovens and brewing beer. He moved carefully along the edge of the river, stalky with the bent and broken reeds that grew up through the litter of garbage—shells, old bones, a rotting cat carcass—until he came to the market.

Here were only two old women dozing over their goods. He thieved a handful of nuts from one and went on along the river cracking the nuts in his fingers and eating the meats. He told himself that now he would have to steal to live. Just past the wharf, where the ships were drawn up on the bank, a dozen men had gathered, talking and arguing; he could not make out a single word of their speech. They were watching two other men who sat with a board on their knees, bending over it, intent. A dog began to bark, and all around the place other dogs took up the yowling.

He remembered what the old man had said: They would have taken her to Jorvik. He had heard that name, another great settlement like this one, far across the eastern sea. He went off along the river again, past the wooden wharf, where people were loading sacks and bundles onto one of the fat-bellied boats, and walked on a little farther, until looking down the river, toward a rising headland there, he thought he saw the glimmering of the sea.

That was all, then; he could not cross the sea. He had to give up now.

He stood a long while, staring out past the headland to the distant strip of water. No idea came to him how he might cross it. Yet he felt no release from the task. He told himself again the search was over, he could stop looking now. He turned, and walked up through the settlement, toward the houses.

Here there were women working, and he looked closely at them, thinking by some wild chance she had gotten among them. The houses had little yards around them, fenced off with woven withies. Behind one such, a girl was pulling turnips.

He stood a while, hoping she would look up and notice him. If he could make friends with someone here, anyone, he could stay. She was pulling turnips, her arm moving rhythmically back and forth, her head bowed; a white cloth hid her hair, but enough escaped away from the headcloth that he saw how fair she was. After a moment, as if she felt his gaze on her, she lifted her head and their eyes caught.

He jerked a smile onto his face. She frowned, a little, and glanced away, and then looked back at him. Her frown melted into a little smile, and she started to get up off her knees.

Gladdened, he started forward, to meet her by the withy fence. Then behind her someone shouted, a man's voice, harsh. Her face went red as a berry. She wheeled and ran back into the turnip patch, her back to him, and Corban went quickly off again.

A little way off, he turned to look back, and saw her watching him, her head turned over her shoulder. When she caught him watching her she whipped her head forward again.

He laughed. He felt much better, suddenly, as if the sun had just come out; he thought, I can get along here, if the women like me. He went back toward the river bank, hungry again, watching for a chance to steal something more to eat.

The crowd there had grown. The two men with their game-board had gotten up and moved away; one of them still stood nearby, the board dangling from his fingers, watching a man with a stocky, smooth-coated brindle dog, who stood in the middle of the crowd, talking loudly in the strange foreign speech. Corban went along the edge of the mass of bodies. A slat-sided boy was coming up, dragged along on a rope by an eager black dog that lunged and bulled at the lead. They were going to have a dog fight.

The swarm of men drew back, clamoring. Among them, one in a long cloak trimmed with red fox fur plucked a fat bag from inside his cloak and dug into it with his fingers and took out a bit of something that flashed in the sun; he tossed it up into the air.

In the crowd all the heads turned, and tipped up, all eyes following that flashing bit. Corban eased into the crowd. He saw how all the others watched the man in the fox cloak and his bag and the shiny bit he had taken out of it, which now he stuffed back into the bag, and stuck into his belt. He spoke in a hard, loud voice.

The crowd backed suddenly away from the dogs. The brindle dog was growling and standing up on its hind feet against its lead, and the man with it squatted down beside it and spoke to it, stroking its dusty striped shoulder. The slat-sided boy brought up his dog lunging and snarling. The dogs faced each other. The other men yelped and laughed and cried out, giving the dogs room to fight, circling around them. The man in the fox fur cloak stood with his hands on his hips.

The dogs began to lunge at each other, growling and slavering; the two men held them back a moment. The brindle dog had burst into a sweat that darkened its coat almost black. The watchers crowded in closer, elbowing each other and shoving to get a better view. Corban hung back a little, wary, to the left of the man in the fox fur cloak; all these people seemed as fierce as the dogs, and he reminded himself that the men who had murdered his family were foreigners, danskers, like these.

His gaze snagged on the fat little sack in the belt of the man with the fox fur cloak, like a fine red apple, just waiting to be plucked.

With a yell, the slat-sided boy loosed his dog, and in two leaps it jumped on the brindle. Howling and whining, the two dogs tangled. Clods of mud flew up around them. Strings of bloody foam spun through the air. The men watching screamed and howled, their arms driving up and down, and Corban backed up, unwilling to get into their midst. One of the dogs let out a terrible scream.

The crowd surged closer. Behind them all, Corban could see nothing of the dog fight; he was trying to work up the courage to grab for the fat sack, there on the big man's belt, still right in front of him. Abruptly, as if his wish had made it happen, through the corner of his vision somebody else's hand darted out toward the bag.

Corban gave no thought to what he did, but reached out and caught the outstretched hand by the wrist just as it closed on the bag. The owner of the hand jerked back, trying to yank free, flexing his arm up; Corban grappled with him, which brought them face to face. Corban saw sleek black eyes, a mouthful of crooked yellow teeth. He clutched the man's wrist, although the man wrenched at him, silently, the bag tight in his fingers; then abruptly from behind a hand fell on Corban's shoulder, and a voice roared incomprehensibly in his ear.

Startled, Corban stepped back and let the thief go. The thief wheeled, already running, but the big man in the fur cloak, his hand still on Corban's shoulder, thrust one foot out, and tripped the thief headlong and put his foot down firmly on his back.

On the far side of the crowd the dogs were yelping and screaming and the men roaring. The big man turned to Corban. He had a broad face above a thicket of fair beard. For a moment, Corban felt the glare of his eyes on him and his skin crawled; he would think Corban a thief, too, how could he know what had happened? Then the big man said something in dansker and thrust out his hand, smiling.

Behind him, unknowing of any of this, the crowd gave up a blast of noise, waving their arms. The dogfight was over. Relieved, Corban put his hand out and took the big man's. When the foreigner spoke again, Corban shook his head, and shrugged.

"I don't . . ." He shook his head again, letting go of the other man's hand, and taking a step back. The crowd was turning toward them. The slab-sided boy was trudging away, tears running down his face, the black body of his dog in his arms. The foreigner in his fancy coat shouted something to the now curious crowd and waved his arm, and several of the men from the crowd launched themselves at the thief, still pinned under the big man's foot, and hauled him up.

The big man's blond eyebrows jerked up and down. He was still staring at Corban and now suddenly he spoke Irish. "Quick hands yourself." He ground the Irish words slowly out, all growls, like a southern man. "I am to thank you. You saved me a quantity of money, or at least the trouble of recovering it. Who are you?"

"Nobody," Corban said, smiling, but wanting to get away from this attention; he edged backward a step, seeing everybody looking at him. "I am only just come here."

"Maybe so you still see everything sharp," said the big man. He turned, and said something in his foreign tongue to the men holding the thief, and they carried him away up the slope from the river. Corban took another step away, but the big man put out his hand.

"Wait." He took the fat bag from his belt, opened it, and shook out a scatter of the flashing silver bits. "If you decide to stay here, come to me. I can always use good men." He held out the silver, and when Corban held back, wary, took his hand and put the buttons in his palm. "Einar Ship-Farmann, I am." He put his purse away, still very fat, and held out his hand to Corban to shake.

Corban put the silver into his left hand and gave Einar his right. A few of the crowd had stayed to watch them, and these let up a cheer.

Startled, Corban looked down at the silver in his hand. He remembered how the other men had watched just one piece of it, in the air, as if it were an angel messenger. Now he himself had some—thinking back, he hastily smoothed away how he had thought to steal the purse himself—now, he saw, he had cleverly only seen it could be done. And look what he had won for that. And it seemed Einar Ship-Farmann was offering him more. The silver held his eyes; the surfaces had figures on them, a cross, lettering. His chest swelled with a deep, gut-full pleasure.

Then, suddenly, there was another man in front of him, talking.

It was the old bald buzzard of a man, from the gate. "Well," he said, "I found you a ship to England."

"What?" Corban said, startled.

The man's gaze stuck, goggling at the silver. "Where did you get that?"

"From—" Corban nodded happily over his shoulder. Big Einar Ship-Farmann was already walking away, putting on his hat.

The bald man counted the money with his finger. "Tenpence. You could buy your way to England." He reached out as if to take one of the buttons and Corban closed his fist on them. He was wondering what Einar would want him to do, to get more of these.

"Well?" said Grod, impatiently. "Do you want to go to England or not? That's the way to Jorvik, you know. First you have to go to England."

Corban stared at him. Mav might be in Jorvik. He did want to go to England, or he had, before he got this handful of silver, which now suddenly seemed larger and brighter than anything else, and more of it for the having, if he went after Einar.

"Who are you?" he asked the old man.

"My name's Grod. I found a boat leaving for England, and you can get on it, if you want." His eyes flicked down Corban's fist. "You could give me a little of that, too, for doing so. If you want."

Corban closed his fist tighter on the silver. He turned and looked after Einar, walking away down the slope toward the river. Then he turned to Grod.

"How?" he said. "What is this, I might go to England?"

"That merchant boat, down at the wharf. It's leaving tonight, when the tide goes out, and they need rowers. He came up to the gate, to see if we knew anybody—I thought about you. He will take you to the other side of the sea if you row."

Corban grunted at him. England was far away. Mav might not even be there. He felt the silver in his hand, safe in his hand.

His mind divided; one half of him stood there, wanting not to go to England, but to stay here, where so much was going well, and the other half stepped back, and saw himself in the grip of the silver.

That pushed him along, recoiling at that, to be under anything. He nodded to Grod. "Take me to the boat."

"Good." The bald man led him away. His head turned, looking over his shoulder, not into Corban's face but at his fist. "Are you going to give me some of that?"

Corban laughed. The silver felt warm in his hand. He began to think where he might hide it, to protect it. With some difficulty he pulled his mind from the contemplation of it and thought of England, and Mav.

He remembered his sister, the last time he had seen her, as she had told him she would bring him home. He thought how she would think of him, if she knew he stopped looking for her.

He and Grod were walking down toward the wharf, now, and he heard the loud voices ahead of him, speaking nothing he understood. He drew in a deep breath. In England they would all speak that other tongue. If he was going to look for Mav, he had to have help.

He said, "Grod, have you been to England?"

"Oh, yes," Grod said. "I have been everywhere." His eyes followed Corban's fist with the silver. "I'm not Irish, you know."

Corban laughed again. He felt the tug of the silver's power over him and knew Grod felt that too. He said, "I will give you all this silver."

"Ah!"

"But you must come with me to England."

Grod's bald head wrinkled; he tore his gaze from Corban's fist and looked up into his face. "What?"

"As I said. I need you to come to England with me, and help me find my sister." He stopped; they were nearly to the wharf again, where men were carrying folded hides, stiff as planks, into the round wooden belly of the boat. Already the space there was stuffed with goods. His boat, he guessed. He faced Grod, opened his hand, and held it out to him.

Grod's face flushed. He reached for the silver, and Corban closed his hand again. "When we find my sister."

Grod snorted at him. "She may be dead. We may never find her."

"In England, then. When we reach Jorvik, and you have helped me look."

Grod's mouth worked. His eyes looked past Corban, seeing someone else. Somewhere else. He nodded abruptly.

"I will take you to Jorvik. Then you give me the silver." He pulled his cloak up over his shoulder. His mouth curled. "I have been here long enough, I will go to Jorvik gladly, and then maybe I will go home again, who knows?"

"Good," Corban said, and opened his hand and took two of the silver bits and handed them to him. Grod seized them, and smiled; he had a wide mouth that smiled like a snake.

"Jorvik," he said again, and tucked the silver away in his shirt.

CHAPTER THREE

Mav felt stretched out long and thin; it seemed to her that she was leaving herself behind with every step, and yet she was going on, also, down the long road. They had come across the sea and now were walking, walking endlessly through fields, a forest of oaks, toward low, lumpy hills.

They had been bundled along from place to place now so much she had lost track of the days and the places. Now they seemed to be in another country. Only three men guarded them. At first they kept the women tied together, a rope looped from neck to neck. The men rode horses and as they rode they whipped the women along with long switches of willow. At night they stopped by the rutted path, and the men gave them pieces of flat bread and let them pass a jug of water, and they slept together like eggs in a nest, curled up.

They passed a few people on the road, who stared and whispered as they went by; Mav could see there was no hope of help from them, who didn't even speak her language. During the first night, when she thought the men weren't watching, she tried to untie the rope around her neck, but the knot was tight, and she could not wiggle the loop up over her head. The rope wore her neck sore. She saw that, too, on the other women, the red ring like a mark of their slavery, and her spirits sank as low as the road.

They passed through a village, a string of huts with a squat mill at the edge of a river. The men on their horses, with their long willow switches, kept them moving at a quick pace along the little row of houses. A woman stood in her dooryard, but she turned her back rather than see them go by. With their switches the riders harried out of their way an old man hauling a load of sticks on his back. A child stared at her, as she walked along, but then its mother came and snatched it up and went inside.

Passing by the mill, with its yard half-full of sacks, and the slow grinding of its turning wheel, she smelled the fresh flour and

her stomach growled. Soon they were walking through the lonely
countryside again, toward the hills.

Two days later, in the distance, she saw smoke rising. As they
drew closer the road swerved, and on her right hand, to the south,
she could see a great hall behind a fence with other buildings
around it, just a little walk off the road. Sheep dotted the rising
green hillside beyond. That place seemed as good as home to her,
but the men whipped them on with their switches and they did not
stop.

Now they were climbing the hills. The bread was stale, and
they had to soak it in the water to make it soft enough to eat. They
saw no more people on the road, and the men stopped tying the
women together. That night, a tall skinny girl ran away.

When the men woke, and discovered this, they cursed and beat
the women who remained, and tied them together again. One stayed
with them, and the other two on their horses went after the tall girl,
and brought her back quickly enough. Then they laid her down on
her back in front of the other women and possessed her, one after
the other, over and over, until around Mav the bound women were
sobbing and covering their faces and trying to turn away.

Mav only shut her eyes. She could escape nothing. She knew
not only the moaning women and the endless road, but all that lay
behind them, the wild forest and the moors, and the sea that ringed
it, as if her great floppy self reached all across the world. Voices
sounded in her ears, speaking words she did not know, and wild
singing, and screams and laughter, some in the distance and some
right in her ears. She thought she had ripped, maybe when they
raped her, and spilled herself out of her skin.

She yearned for her home, but she saw the flames, she saw the
dead, she knew she had nowhere to go back to. Only, ahead of her,
she could make out nothing but a cold gray fog, into which she
walked and walked.

The men untied the women again, and drove them on. They
straggled along the worn little path, one of the men leading the
way and the other two coming after, with their willow sticks har-
rying anybody too weary and sick to keep up. The tall skinny girl
stumbled along, her thighs streaming blood. Mav put an arm around

her waist and helped her walk. She could feel the girl shaking with every step.

They trudged through the forest. At night they stopped and ate bread and crouched miserably around the fire trying to get warm. The men were tight with the bread, breaking the loaves into quarters, a piece for each of the women; the men themselves each ate a whole loaf.

All day long they plodded along on the road. Mav had no trouble keeping up, and easily stayed close behind the lead rider, but when the other women began to fall behind, she slowed her steps, falling back among them, and the other women slowed even more, until the lead rider disappeared around the curve ahead of them, and the two men herding them along were yelling and whipping at all of them.

Mav stopped. One of the men came up screaming at her to go on and lashing at her legs with his long willow wand, leaning awkwardly from his saddle. He was a boy, who always shouted; she knew he was lowly among them, and kept her eyes on the road, waiting. Soon the lead rider came galloping back around the curve, his cloak flying out behind him.

The boy stopped yelling. His face was red, and he lowered his eyes and pulled his horse around and back. The rider galloped up and stopped. He glared at Mav and looked down the road again and bellowed a stream of words she did not bother to understand. She started forward again, swinging around his horse, and the other women with her; she took as easy a pace as she could keep step to.

The women bunched behind her, murmuring. From horse to horse the men were shouting at each other over their heads. The lead rider swung around, and came close by her; he snarled something at her. She braced herself, knowing what was coming, and took the lash of his willow wand across her shoulders. She gathered the rags of her clothes around her and walked on. Soon the skinny girl was beside her again. Her thin hand crept into the curve of Mav's arm.

Walking, she felt herself enormous, reaching backward to the edge of the world, where in her mind she saw a little figure toiling along. That was Corban, her brother, she realized, with a gladness like a surge of warmth all through her body. That was where she was stretched to, wherever her brother was.

She longed for him; she remembered what her mother had said once, that maybe in their shared womb some piece of him had grown in her by mistake, so that she had more of everything, and he had less. That explained why she longed so for him, even more than she mourned the rest of them dead, and why now everything seemed to whirl around her all in bits and shreds, nothing fitting together, nothing making sense.

Always before, at her family's home, she had known where she ended, but now she flowed everywhere, borderless. She was walking on this road, and at the same time she was creeping over the branches of trees, sprouting up through mold, she was whirling in the air like a blown leaf, she splashed over rocks, she ran crab-wise under the curling edge of the sea, she buzzed in the hollows and soared over the sky.

Her head whirled, lost in the middle of it all. There seemed so much more going on now, more all the time. She saw her mother, as she had been, an old woman, and also as a young wife, her belly round with her first baby. She saw her father laughing and her brother Finn trying to play the harp. They seemed around her and she called out to them but they never answered, they never noticed her, they floated away from her into the woods and disappeared. Then it seemed all around her was the deep fog that let no sun through, and clung cold and wet to her skin, and she longed to sink down and weep until she turned all her self into salt water.

The road went over a little wooden bridge and the posts and planks of the bridge groaned and sighed under her feet, mourning the trees they had been once.

She walked fast and then slow. The lead rider came back twice more and lashed her, to make her go faster, but she ignored him. The men gave them bread and now and again sips of water. They made a game of that, taunting the women with food and water, so that they had to beg. Mav would not do it; when they offered her food and then, laughing, pulled it away, she only shrugged and sat down.

She found other things to eat, mushrooms and nuts, gathering them up as she went along. When she was thirsty, she turned off the little track they were following, cutting across the stony hillside, although the men came and tried to drive her back. The trees hampered them, and they and the other women came crying and complaining after her. Down in a gully she found a spring and drank, as did the others around her.

The men watched from their horses but let them all drink their fill. That night they pulled her away, off behind the bushes, yanking her hair and rubbing themselves on her, and while they did as they pleased with her, she let her mind go into the fog, where she felt nothing. Afterward for a long while she felt as gray and blank as the fog, all through herself.

Other times she walked along and saw the broad sky and the wide moor, all covered with heather, and some strange random joy took her like wings and her heart flew up. She sang, and strode along so fast she once found herself passing the lead rider, the women croaking after her to wait, to slow, and she all unheeding, singing at full voice.

One day on the long declining side of the hills she felt the vast envelope of herself shaking and quivering and her belly rolled and she could smell rain in the wind. The wind was rising and the sky, although still blue, was beginning to go milky. She could sense in the air a great tightening and twisting, as if some tremendous force knotted up, ready to spring free. Then she turned and spread her arms, gathered them all, sweeping up the riders with her, led them all off into the bed of the river and found a place where a south-facing bank beetled over; the riders screamed and fussed and would not get down and crowd into shelter with them, but all the women did. Then the storm broke over them with the wild hammers banging and the laughter of the great smith and the howling of his dogs, and the huge lightning as if the air itself split apart; the bitter stench of lightning, the annihilating blasts of thunder like fists of air in her ears. And the horses reared and shrilled in terror, and the riders left their saddles and burrowed in among the women and they clutched one another and watched a tree across from them explode in a blinding white flame.

Through sheets of rain they watched the tree blaze. The heat scalded her; she could feel the burning all through her, pure and wild. A moment later another terrific crack sounded above them

and the whole world turned white. Mav with her arms around the
skinny girl knew she was singing because she felt her lungs fill
and empty but she could hear nothing. The lowly boy was next to
her huddling against her and she put her arm around him too. The
rain sluiced down over them. Whistling down, yet another great
stroke of the hammer fell, a little farther on. The smith had pounded
directly over them. She began to hear her own singing again, and
she laughed, rejoicing, strained her voice, trying to outsing the
wind. The skinny girl clutched her, laughing. They walked out of
the shelter of the river bank and up to the road; half a tree was
down across the road but they climbed over it and set off still to
the east.

The men looked for their horses all the rest of the day but
could not find them. Thereafter they walked among the women,
and everybody went at Mav's pace. They had lost the bread, too,
which the horses carried, so they chewed grass and drank water
and starved.

They walked out of the forest, and went down a long winding
slope; they crossed another road, where stood a great wooden table,
and on that table a whole feast was, but it was holy meat, food for
the sky and the ravens, and no one dared to eat of it. They plodded
along, too hungry even to speak anymore.

But the next day they descended down onto the broad windy
flatland along a river, and ahead they could see smoke in the air,
a great smudge like a hundred cooking fires. The men began to
yell, and walked around lashing at the women with sticks to keep
them together. All day long they walked toward the smoke. By
nightfall they could see ahead of them a great earthworks. Beyond
it, Mav knew, lay a thick clot of buildings, larger than any farm
she had ever seen.

Many of the women were stumbling and weaving now as they
walked, and the men let them stop and rest. Two remained with the
women and the other went on, trudging away down the road, and
around moonrise he came back with bread and horses. Even in the
middle of the night they woke the women and gave them bread, all
they wanted, now, and the bread was fresh and good. Then in the
morning they walked on and came to the great settlement.

They crossed by a wooden bridge over a little water, and came down on the far side into a place full of people waiting to get through the gate in the earthworks. The air was smoky and foul. All the people stared at the women and Mav put her head down to keep from meeting their eyes. After a while, they went on through the gate into a street filthy with rotten stuff, fallen leaves, horse shit. A big black pig snuffled at them and one of the riders drove it off.

On either side were houses so close together the ground between them was dark with the shade of their pitched roofs. An old woman wrapped in a shawl stood in a doorway and spat at them as they passed. Little boys ran by and hit out with sticks at their legs, screaming to see them shy and skip. The riders shouted at them and the boys dodged away into a lane. The constant noise startled Mav's ears; she lowered her head, her gaze on the ground, drowned in the flood of sights and sounds and smells. In all the clamor of voices she heard no word of her own language.

A wagon lumbered toward them and they all had to stand against one side of the street to let it go past. Mav smelled a delicious aroma of cooked meat, and then right behind it the stink of shit. From a window over her head a voice came screaming. The church bells rang. Two women were arguing somewhere through a window. A rooster crowed. The little boys ran by again, and the riders chased them off. Her mind ached as if all these doings pounded on her like fists.

They trudged along a lane between open stalls crowded with people, where she saw hanging braids of garlic and onions on the walls, the limp featherless bodies of ducks. A wave of a stench of burnt hair made her gag. In front of a stall full of long silvery shapes two dogs were fighting over a bloody fishhead. At the edge of the street were stacks of clay bowls and she stumbled over them and knocked them spinning and rolling. The land tilted under her and she followed the way downward. Ahead was a broad stream, the ground sucking and damp along it, and rows of long dragon ships drawn up among the broken stems of reeds.

Her heart turned over: such ships as those brought the men to burn her home and kill her family, such a ship took her away. Her legs quivered and she nearly sat down in the street. Around her the

other women were wailing and crying. They were driven into a
pen of withies and the gate swung shut on them.

She went down, to where the pen met the water; a little filthy
edge of the river trickled in under the fence. Kneeling down, she
dug out part of the bank to make a pool, and when it filled she
washed her face and hands. Her stomach rolled again. The pressure
of the people around her seemed like a great weight on all sides.
Her ears ached from the sound of them. Suddenly she was too tired
even to sit up.

She wanted only to be home again. To be among her family
again. That would never happen. Everything she had known was
torn to pieces, and the pieces whirled around her now in a rising
storm.

Soon, though, the men were shouting and crushing through the
penned women toward her, and one got her by the arm and dragged
her forward. She was making ready to go into the fog again when
they thrust her out the gate, in front of a row of people staring at
her and talking, and she realized they were not going to rape her
this time. She lifted her head, dazed, and saw directly before her
a fat man with a thick dark yellow beard streaked with white, his
cold wicked eyes like two blue stones lying in the rolls and bulges
of his face.

A shock went through her. She remembered him. Wave on
wave of hurt and fear went through her. All in an instant she remembered the flames, the sword that struck down her father, the
hand hauling her off, and then over her, shutting out the starry sky,
that same face over her, groaning and drooling on her. She felt him
all along her body, in her body, a harsh fierce force crushing her
down and piercing her like a living sword.

The other men were talking to him. His eyes were fixed on her
but she saw that his ears heard what the men who had brought her
were telling him, and although they spoke the evil tongue she read
in their gestures of the great storm and how she had hidden them
from it and how she had sung while the storm raged. Then one
lifted his hand and looked at her intently and drew his finger over
his throat.

Her breath stilled. They would kill her. She looked into the

stony eyes of the fat man while the others told him to kill her, and
she saw no mercy there.

Nor interest. He laughed, a thick grunt from his gut, and
shrugged, and said something joking. One big hand rose and waved
her away.

Then from behind him another stepped forward, one Mav saw
only now, a tall woman, wrapped in a long shawl. Mav thought
she did not even see her now, really; that some veil hung around
her. She blinked, trying to clear her eyes of the sudden hazy shape
before her.

The woman approached her. Her eyes were sharp and they
stuck Mav like points of steel. She said something and the men
stilled, respectful. The fat man with the stony eyes turned. He
growled at her, and the woman in the shawl answered but without
taking her eyes from Mav. She was a blur to Mav, she had no
outline, no solid shape. The old man said something questioning
and the woman nodded and raised one hand and waved it at him.
Her hand was old, the skin wrinkled and the fingers knobbed. Mav
forced herself to see through the veils and the blur and saw that
this woman was indeed very old, although it seemed not so at first.

Mav hunched her shoulders. The strange woman sent shivers
through her. The woman's long gray shawl had slipped away from
one shoulder and beneath she wore a gown all sewn with emblems
of trees and flowers and herbs, or perhaps they were real herbs and
flowers woven into the cloth. Mav thought she saw eyes and
mouths in the cloth, looking at her, and whispering. The woman's
face was soft and light as a girl's but beneath it like the shadow
under a tree was that other face, very old. She smiled at something
the fat man said but behind the girl's smile was the old one's sneer.

The fat man turned, and bellowed; his voice ran cold through
Mav like a dashing of cold water and she gave a shudder. The
woman in the shawl nodded. She reached out one hand to Mav,
and said, startlingly, "Come with me, girl."

The sound of her own language fell on Mav's ears like a blessing. All her body went soft, and she let out a low cry. She could
not help but stretch her hand out to the woman's. Their fingers
touched and the woman's long fingers wrapped around Mav's, cool
and strong.

"You speak my home-tongue," Mav said.

"I speak all tongues," said the woman. "I am the Lady of Hedeby." With Mav's hand in her grip she led her away.

⊸

"Where did she come from?" Gunnhild said.

They were sitting in the High Seat of their hall, King and Queen of Jorvik, and yet no one looked at them. No one paid them any heed; all eyes were on the tall figure in the center of the room, drawing flames, jewels and showers of money out of the air. Gunnhild twisted a lock of her hair around her finger, and never took her eyes from the Lady of Hedeby, and she frowned.

"Her ship came in last night from Hedeby," Eric said. He put one boot up against the edge of the table. Since he had gotten back from his last raid he had shown interest only in drinking and being amused. Gunnhild wound the tress in sleek loops and knots through her fingers, fretting.

Down in the center of the room the Lady of Hedeby turned slowly in the torchlight, and waves of color flowed from her fingertips. The crowded men on either side let out their breath in a long rapt gasp. The lights flickered and swam in streams up toward the smoke hole, drawing all eyes, except Gunnhild's.

"What is she doing here?"

Eric shrugged. He had no interest in anything but his ale and the magic tricks. "She bought a load of slaves from me."

Gunnhild pressed her lips together. The Lady beguiled these silly men with tricks any street magician could perform. Yet she did it well, Gunnhild had to admit; there was a shower of gold, a loud bang, and then the Lady was simply gone, under Gunnhild's own eyes.

Gunnhild shifted in the High Seat. The Lady had to be in Jorvik for some hidden reason. She was the richest merchant of Hedeby, buying and selling from Dublin to Ladoga. She was Bluetooth's shadow. Such a one did not go sailing over the sea just for a load of slaves.

Eric clapped his hands, and shouted for the skalds. He turned to her, smiling, and caught hold of her arm.

"Why do you fret over her? She gave us such pretty presents."

"If we had a greater kingdom it would have been more," Gunnhild burst out. She pushed at the jumble of sheer red Cathay cloth on the edge of the High Seat, so that it slithered sleekly away to the floor. Against her will she admitted it was wonderful fabric.

Eric said, "Jorvik is fine with me." He raised his cup. Gunnhild reached down and picked the Cathay cloth off the floor, and ran her fingers over it, frowning.

In the morning she stood on the bank over the river with her eldest son Gimle, a stripling of eleven, and watched the Lady of Hedeby pull off downstream in her fine ship, which was fully as large as any of Eric's warships, twenty oarsmen to a side, hammered gold shining on the great dragon heads at prow and stern and all along the gunwales. Over the forecastle was a purple awning, under which the Lady sat. The wretched slaves huddled on the deck by the mast.

"She could not have come simply to buy slaves."

Her son wound his arm through hers. "You are more beautiful than she is, Mother."

Gunnhild snorted; she squeezed his arm against her, glad of his stout loyalty. She was Queen of Jorvik. Why should she worry about a mere trader, however rich? Yet she was remembering, reluctantly, how one whose wisdom she respected above all others whispered to her to beware the Lady of Hedeby. That she was older than them all, no true woman, not from here. That she had the power to steal souls.

She was going now, the gilded ship sliding off around the bend in the river below Jorvik. The air seemed brighter for it. Relieved, with Gimle at her side Gunnhild turned back up the embankment toward her own hall, to her own High Seat, her husband and her power.

CHAPTER FOUR

Corban's hands hurt; he could not take hold of the oar in any way that did not hurt. On the back stroke he glanced at Grod, sitting behind him in a crevice between two piles of hides. Grod somehow had talked his way on board without having to row. Maybe he had given up his silver coins. Corban grit his teeth. He could have given the boatman money, and gone without rowing himself, but then there would have been nothing to pay Grod.

He needed Grod, he told himself. In England, across the water, he would need someone who knew his way, who spoke the language, who could get him to Jorvik. But his hands were already raw and bleeding, and past the high stern of the boat the long low shape of his homeland still stretched like a denser mist above the edge of the sea, with the humped back of the northern headland even closer on his right. He would be rowing like this for days and days.

He had worked on his father's fishing boats, he knew how to use the oar. There was no great art to it anyway. Ahead of him, five other men bent forward, and he bent forward, dipped the blade of his oar into the sea, and leaned back with his feet braced on one of the boat's ribs and pulled, drew the oar back through his aching hands, back toward his chest. Then forward again, a relentless rhythm. Along the other side of the boat sat another six men, doing the same thing. Behind them all, even behind Grod, the captain sat in the stern, his hand on the steering board, and guided them along. The packs of hides, the sacks and barrels that were their cargo took up all the rest of the space.

Corban felt the sweat gather between his shoulder blades and spill down his sides. Grod slid closer to him, and held a flask to his lips. "Draw hard," he said, low. "There is no wind, yet, soon there will be wind, and you can rest then. Now draw hard."

Corban set his teeth together. Grod was full of advice. Tucked into the cargo he looked dry and comfortable as a king. The boat groaned as they pulled it through the rippled surface of the sea.

Corban stretched his legs out, up to the bench in front of him; with each stroke of the oars a little trickle of filthy water ran forward past his shoes, pooling in the bottom of the boat. Now his back hurt, also, and each stroke made it worse.

Across the gunwale of the boat he looked out over the flat water. It rose and fell in a long slow rhythm, as if the sea breathed. The land had slipped away down over the horizon, the gulls had given up on them, they were alone on the bulging sleek surface of the vast water. He began to think of wrapping his cloak around the oar, to save his hands, but the cloak was behind him, where Grod sat, and he would have to get up to get it; he knew the other men would howl at that. He had already seen them scream and spit at a man who stood up suddenly to piss over the side, leaving his oar to swing idly. They all had to pull together, to keep the boat moving straight.

Corban made a silent curse against Grod, who had gotten him into this. A new pain began, this one in his upper arm. His shirt stuck to him. His hair was plastered to his cheeks.

They rowed and rowed across the flat sea. The land slid away behind them over the horizon. Corban had never been out of sight of land before and he began to think of the deep cold water under them, full of monsters. He yanked his mind off to other things: his sister, his silver, what he would do to Grod if they got to the dry land and he no longer needed him.

The sun burned through a high mist. Once the boatman stopped them and let them stretch, drink, piss. Corban swiftly pulled his shirt down around his waist and tucked the sleeves under his belt. But soon the captain was shouting them back to the work again, and making the boat move forward again was twice as hard. The men groaned and called out as they rowed, and the captain swore at them. Corban fixed his eyes on the back of the man in front of him, dark from the sun.

In the midafternoon, they halted again. There was a sharp breeze kicking up and Corban thought it might rain; he imagined being in the boat, in the open, in a hard rain, and he shivered. He slumped against the gunwale, exhausted, and drank water from Grod's jug, waiting to be driven back to the work.

The boatman called something out, and Grod leaned toward him. "Ship the oar."

"Hah."

"Bring the oar on board," Grod said.

The other men lifted their oars up vertical and then laid them down inside the craft; Corban did what they did. The boatman came up from the stern. Corban sank back down against the gunwale, his bleeding hands limp before him, and watched the boatman and three of the rowers pull a long peeled tree trunk up from beside the keelboard. They stood it upright in the center of the boat, where there was a block of wood with a hole in it, and sank the butt of the tree down into the hole. The boatman kicked home another chunk of wood to hold it; ropes dangled from the top of this mast and the boatman fastened one to the bow and one to the stern of the boat. Then from the belly of the boat he took another pole, this one wrapped in striped cloth, and hung it crosswise on the upright tree, and fastened a rope to it, and hauled on the rope. Two of the rowers sprang to help him, and they raised the top of the cloth up into the air.

Even before they had made the ropes fast Corban could feel the boat moving, the striped cloth catching the wind. Relief washed over him. This was obviously a better way of doing things. The boat felt different suddenly, alive, sidling like a snake through the waves. The water warbled happily against the hull. The boatman scrambled back to the stern and took the steering board in his hand again, and the rowers all lay or sat down among the heaps of hides and jugs and fell asleep.

Corban woke with Grod shaking him, and got a chunk of bread and a piece of dried fish and ate them in three bites. His belly heaved. The boat was sliding rapidly through the water. Night was falling, the far low edge of the sky pink and pale above the dark water. He stood, stretching the stiffness out of his arms and back; a great twinge of pain shot down through his back and he gasped. All around was nothing but water. He had to brace his legs against the rolling of the boat as it worked up and down the waves.

The wind struck his face. The bow went up against a long wave and skidded down again. His lips were salty and the skin of his face felt stretched and stiff with salt.

"Sit," Grod said. "Sleep some more, we won't row until morning, even if the wind stops."

"You haven't rowed a stroke," Corban said. He felt in his shirt for the silver, tied up in the cloth of one sleeve, and sat down again. The wind was raking across the boat, bearing rain drops. A wave chopped up over the gunwale and soaked his arm and thigh.

The boatman shouted something, and threw a bucket at him. Corban took it, wondering, and Grod nudged him again.

"Bail."

Corban cursed him for an idiot old man. Another wave broke over the gunwale and he felt the water sloshing around his ankles, and bending down he scooped up a bucketful and flung it overboard. Up near the bow another man was bailing also. The boat rolled and lunged over the sea, its timbers creaking. He stooped and sloshed and flung water overboard, the salt eating into his numbed hands. Grod gave him fresh water to drink and he drained the whole jug.

After a while other men began to bail and Corban lay down, soaked and shivering. Grod handed him his cloak and he wrapped himself into it and slept at once.

In the morning, in the red dawn, the wind died. Groaning and cursing the men struggled up from sleep, lifted their oars out over the gunwales, and set to rowing again. Corban's hands were numb for a few strokes but then as if the skin burst they began to hurt all the way up to his elbows, and his back throbbed. His hands began to stick to the oar. He realized he was holding his breath with each stroke and made himself take in the air as he reached out and give it up again as he drew back. He thought of Mav. He thought of beating Grod to a bloody puddle. Grimly he kept on flailing the calm flat sea with the oar. The naked back of the man in front of him had a long scar on it; it began to annoy him to the point of rage that the scar was off center. One of the men suddenly started to whistle, and the others yelled at him and swore until he stopped.

Grod said, "They think it's bad luck."

"Let it bring the wind," Corban said. Somehow Grod had found more water, and gave it to him, pure and cool, delicious in his throat.

All day long they rowed, until near nightfall when at last the breeze came up again and they raised the striped sail again and the boat slid away under the wind, as if it too suffered in the calms, died under the beating of the oars, woke only when the wind came to carry it off in its arms. The bread had gotten soaked with seawater and they ate it anyway. Along the rim of the world the color ran, pink and gold below the lowering sky.

In the night rain fell; Corban huddled under his cloak, Grod snug beside him, and slept fitfully, waking it seemed every few moments from strange gloomy dreams. Grod against him murmured and twitched in his sleep. Corban pressed close to the warmth of his body.

In the morning, the brisk wind blew them eastward, and now, far ahead of them, a faint blue hump of land stuck up above the level sea. The oarsmen all cheered but the captain grunted, shaded his eyes to look around them, and spat over the side. Corban spread out his cloak to dry. His hands were still raw and stiff. Grod was twitching and looking around; he said, abruptly, under his breath, "I hate this boat."

Corban understood that. The boat felt like a coffin, jamming them all together, smothering him with other bodies, as if he could not take a breath without drawing in the foul breath of the other men. He stared away over the side, across the curling waves. The wind broke the tops off into white foam. The boat leaned over, rushing through the water; under his feet he could feel the slap of the waves against the hull. He twisted again, to see the land ahead of them.

He gave a low cry, and stood up. Somebody shouted at him and Grod tugged at his shirt; Corban ignored them, straining his eyes to see toward the land. Then the captain bellowed. He had seen what Corban had seen: the two little boats speeding across the waves toward them, the rise and fall of paddles like the legs of beetles, scuttling over the water.

One of the oarsmen wailed. The captain shouted orders, lashed the steeringboard down, and jumped toward the sail and the mast. The oarsmen were scrambling around in the hull of the boat for their oars. Corban lifted his oar up and swung it over the gunwale.

With a glance over his shoulder he saw the two boats much closer, bounding through the white-crested waves.

The captain shouted again, and Grod, crouched down behind Corban, said into his ear, "Pull. Pull. We have to get away. They're pirates for sure."

Corban did not know the word pirate but he saw deadly purpose in the oncoming boats; he leaned his back into the oar. The men in the row ahead of him bent and drew, part of his rhythm. One of them was crying out, "God help us—God help us—" Corban's heart was pounding. The captain swung the boat around to the north, away from the land. Corban twisted to look back again and saw the boats nearly on them.

The captain screamed again; Grod did not have to translate this. Corban planted his feet on the bench before him and swung the oar and wrenched it through the water, and then from behind him came a whistling, a whining, like a flock of vicious birds, and a flight of arrows pelted into the boat. An arrow struck the naked back in front of Corban and went in up to the feathers, missing the long scar entirely. As that man slumped forward, his oar flopping, the boat wobbled off course. Corban looked around and saw the captain slumped against the gunwale, an arrow through his neck.

The other men were shrieking and leaping up from their oars. One crouched down, his arms over his head, but the others rushed forward, scrambling over the cargo toward the bow of the ship. Corban swore under his breath. Stooped low, he wheeled around him, looking for a weapon. Grod, half-buried in the piles of hides, had his hand up over his mouth, his eyes bulging and slick with fear. The boatman was slumped down over a pile of hides, the arrow jutting up past his ear. Corban wheeled, looking around again.

The two boats swept up toward them, one ahead of the other, full of men standing up now, waving spears and bows. From the first of these, which was swiftly approaching the merchant boat, a rope snaked through the air; the hook on the end landed inside the boat, and the pirate holding the other end began to haul the line in. The hook bounced on the hull and then caught fast on the gunwale.

Corban grabbed for the bench, just as the rope tightened with a snap. The boat rocked under him. In the bow the oarsmen had gotten swords and clubs out of the forecastle and now, clambering around on the barrels and bales of hides, they were leaping to meet the attack; one lifted his sword and hacked through the line that hooked them to the pirate boat.

Too late. The pirates were already leaping across the narrow strip of water between them and the cargo ship. Close behind them the second of the pirate boats was paddling furiously up toward the merchant, half a dozen men yelling and waving spears. Corban crouched down, burrowed deep down into the mass of the cargo, out of the way.

The boat rocked violently again, as two of the oncoming pirates leapt over the shrinking space of water into the merchant boat and launched themselves at the fighting oarsmen. Flattened between the rowing benches Corban pretended to be dead, as a stream of men followed the others across the gunwale.

The boat heaved and pitched under their feet. They rushed on past him. Corban popped up again. At the bow end of the boat men were scrambling over the heaps of cargo, stabbing with spears, but all he saw were their backs; no one was watching him. He stood up, panting, knowing he had to do something quickly, and then started and shrank at something moving just behind him.

An empty pirate boat was bumping down alongside, its cut line trailing along. He reached down and grabbed the floating rope and reeled the boat in closer. It was light as a walnut shell; it bounced on the surface of the sea like a skipping rock. He twisted around, grabbed hold of Grod, down in the cargo, by the front of his shirt, and heaved him over the gunwale and into the little boat. Grod wailed. Corban dove overboard.

The cold sea took him in. He swam strongly upward, seeing the hulls of the boats above him hanging down from the light-filled surface of the water. The cut line from the little boat trailed past him. His head broke the surface; he swam to the boat and shoved it away from the others. When he stretched up as far as he could he was able to see over the Goat's leather-bound rim, to where Grod sat, clutching the round gunwale with both hands, his eyes white. Corban leaned his weight against the boat, got it moving, and drove it on with strong kicking of his legs.

Salt water splashed into his mouth. He could see nothing, only the boat's hull before him—a boat of hide, it was, leather and wax. He laid his hands on it and kicked hard with his feet, driving it through the water away from the merchant boat. He stayed down as low as he could in the water, so they would think back there that the boat was just drifting away. He shoved and muscled the little boat over a wave; on the far side it got away from him and slid down into the trough.

Corban rode up on the crest of the wave, and looked back. The other men were still fighting on the merchant boat. He could hear the thin howling of their voices, and the sunlight glinted off a raised blade, and a body splashed into the sea. He turned back to the work of widening the stretch of water between the hide boat and the merchant.

He began to feel the cold of the water. He stopped a moment, panting, took the gunwale of the boat with both hands, pushed it hard up and away from him so that the boat rocked, and then rocked it toward him and flung himself over the edge and in.

The boat bounced and rolled wildly, and Grod, clutching the gunwale, let out a wail. "I can't swim—Don't throw me in—"

Corban sat upright in the bottom of the boat. "Hang on, Grod. You're all right." He looked around for a paddle. He had used such boats as this since he was a boy, he understood them better than the merchant boat. In its bowl-shaped belly were wooden paddles, and he took one up, knelt down, and dug the blade into the water and sent them whirling away.

The wave carried them up and he looked over his shoulder; from the peak of the wave he could see the merchant boat, the men chopping and hacking at each other. No one paid any heed to Grod and Corban. The wave carried them down again out of sight. With all his strength he paddled them off to the east and the last of the screaming and yelling died away behind them.

Grod was watching him, pop-eyed. "You did it. You saved us."

"Maybe." Corban slowed his pace, his strength fading. His cloak was gone, but he still wore his shirt, with the money tied into the corner of the sleeve. He felt at his belt; he had lost his sling. But his knife was still there. And Grod was there, sitting upright as a little priest, his eyes still huge with fear, clinging to the gunwales. Corban laughed to see him. He gave another quick look behind.

For a moment he saw nothing, only the rolling sea, and then a wave lifted the boat and he saw the merchant boat, far behind. Nobody seemed to be fighting anymore. The wave carried it down again out of sight. He turned forward again, watching for the land he had seen; it was well to the south now, but he could see a dark line of hills behind it, curving deeply around in front of him. He paddled on eastward. His chest felt tight. He was soaked and shivering.

But he laughed, quavery with relief. They had gotten away, they had escaped.

Grod said, "They would have killed us. They killed everybody else." His eyes were wide with shock and admiration. Corban laughed again, triumphant.

He struggled to keep hold of the good feeling. He was so cold his teeth began to bang together. Among the gear in the belly of the hide boat was a blanket, soaked through, and he wrung it out and wrapped himself in it. Grod shook off his terror and went through the gear and found a jug of water but nothing to eat. Corban set himself to paddling. The boat moved well; by the look of the water around them he thought they had gotten into a current, and he tried to paddle the same way as the current ran, although it took them away from the head of land now rising to the south. Grod gave him water. Gulls floated by them, their white wings curled to the wind.

He thought again and again about how they had escaped. The first hot rush of triumph would not stay with him. He thought he had not actually done so great a deed. He remembered huddling down in the hold, while the others fought to defend themselves and their boat. Probably Grod was right and they had died for their bravery. He began to wish he could find some reason in it, that he should live and they should die—that they should fight and die so that he should live.

He knew no reason. He was not a good enough man, that a dozen men should die for him. He felt uneasy, as if some charge now lay upon him.

He paddled all day. He was so hungry by nightfall he could have eaten the blanket, or Grod. Now they were floating past a shore, with hills behind it, vague in the distance. He pointed.

"We should go in. We have to find something to eat."

Grod shook his head. "Keep going."

"I'm starving!"

"That's where the pirates came from," Grod said. "Do you want to give us back to them, now that we're saved? Keep going east."

Corban groaned and set to work again with the paddle. When darkness fell he rolled himself into the blanket and lay down and slept, and Grod curled up next to him and the warmth of his body was like a little fire. Halfway through the night rain began to fall, and Corban woke, cold, huddled up against Grod. His belly was a knot of hunger.

He thought about his sister, about his home, and the warm hearth and the people there, now gone, forever gone. A deep raw grief took him, as if all the world had died, and left him here floating in this leaf of a boat, freezing. His father's curse swam up to the surface of his mind. He was Corban Loosestrife, who brought only trouble, who did nothing well or right.

With the desperation of a drowning man he thought of Mav, and that gave him some heart. It came to him that he was sure that Mav was alive, somewhere; as he thought of this, the feeling grew stronger in him, as if she spoke to him from somewhere over the horizon. Surely she was alive. And he was not alone; against his chest Grod murmured in his sleep, and shivered. Corban pressed himself against him, to warm them both, and put his head down again. The rain had stopped, at least. He laid his cheek against Grod's shoulder and tried to sleep.

⟶⟨∘⟩⟵

When the dawn came, they were floating along, much closer to the land; he saw a long pale beach, dark trees behind it, behind that the blue loom of mountains.

"Let's go in," he said. "We have to find something to eat."

"Not here," Grod said, and pointed to some rocks in the water.

"I can steer between them," Corban said, picking up the paddle.

"How do you think they got there?" Grod said. "Giants live here. They throw rocks at any boat that comes ashore. When they sink one they wade out and pick up the bodies of the drowned people and eat them."

Corban stared at him, startled, and turned and gave a long look at the shore. All he saw was a long thin pale beach, with trees behind it, and then the lofting crags of the mountains. "How do you know this? Have you been here before?"

"I've been everywhere," Grod said.

Corban bent to the paddle, keeping them out to sea, away from the rocks and the shore and the giants. "Where did you begin?"

Grod said something he could not understand. "The danskers call it Gardarik. It's way to the east of here, where the sea ends."

Corban bent steadily to the paddling. "The sea never ends. The sea is everywhere."

"Hah," Grod said. "So little as you know. East of here the sea does end, and the land goes on forever. That's where I came from."

"Why did you leave?"

Grod shrugged. On his cheeks a glinting stubble of beard showed, strange beneath his shiny bald head. "I wanted to see what lay out here. I wanted to see how far I could go." He scratched his cheek. "Young men have strange notions. If I had known there was nothing out here but rocks and water and savages I'd never have come."

Corban laughed. "Then where you were—what was it—"

"Gardarik."

"Is a better place?"

"Oh, certainly. There even ordinary people live in palaces, and everybody eats whenever he wants, eggs and cream and wonderful golden bread. Everybody wears fur robes and boots, even the beggars. At night in the summer the sun stays in the sky all day long, and we dance and sing for the wonder of it."

Corban's belly was cramped and his back aching. He stroked steadily along with the paddle, the long shore off to his right. "The summer sun stays long above my home, too. You have a family there, to go back to?"

Grod looked at him a moment, his wide mouth soft. "Yes," he

said. "I suppose they're still there—my mother and my brothers. My father died when I was a little one."

Corban thought unwillingly of his family, of the burning farm, and the bodies. The piles of bloody bones by the shore. Abruptly his throat tightened, and his vision swam. He drew a long breath, forcing himself cold again.

Grod reached out and touched his arm.

"I'm sorry."

Corban shook his head. "I have to find my sister."

"Maybe she will be in Jorvik," Grod said. "And you can take her and go back again to your home."

Corban felt a sudden rush of affection for the old man. He was glad not to be alone, maybe that was it. And he had saved Grod; now Grod belonged to him. He collected himself. The day was clear, the sky cloudless, and the sun beat on him. He felt this all in a new way, as if he had just awakened.

Toward noon, he could see land ahead of them, too, and he straightened, resting his throbbing arms.

"Now tell me why we can't go in there," he said, pointing.

Grod peered over the gunwale, putting his hand up to shade his eyes. "Over there," he said. "See where that river comes in? Go there."

Corban paddled. Ahead, the land bent around to the north, but he could see where a wide river mouth opened into it, and as they drew closer he saw other boats sprinkled across the broad reach of water, and men fishing from them with nets. He began to think of baked fish, and warm bread. His arms trembled with weariness but he bent his back and paddled them on.

Grod said, "Keep going. What's the matter with you? We're almost there, don't give up now."

Corban set his teeth together. He paddled them in past a fishing boat, and then another, until the land loomed all around them, the heights dark with trees; he saw the regular lines of buildings, on the ground above the shore.

He was paddling now up the narrowing mouth of the river, the long waves of the sea fallen behind them. He had to pull hard against the outrush of the river and the boat kept trying to turn. On the shore along the northern edge of the river were other boats drawn up on the beach. Beyond them, on rising land, houses stood. "Look, there—we're coming to some place important."

Grod twisted to look over the gunwale of the boat, holding on with both hands. "Yes," he said. "Go in there."

"Is that Jorvik?" Corban asked. He plied the paddle strongly on one side, sending the little boat skimming across a stretch of placid water, toward the shore.

Grod laughed. "No, no. Jorvik is far away still. But we can probably get something to eat here, and we can sell the boat and go on by land."

Corban nudged the boat into the shallows and stepped out. Grod bounded past him. "Wait here," he said, and went running off.

Corban stretched; it felt so good to be on solid land again that he bent down and put his hands on the sandy beach. He thought he should give a prayer of thanks, but he did not know to whom. He dragged the boat up high above the tidal wrack and sat down to wait for Grod.

Almost at once several boys appeared, wandering around as if they didn't even notice him, but watching through the corners of their eyes. He ignored them, turning his gaze out over the river. Although he was sitting on solid ground now, he still seemed to feel the rise and fall of the sea under him, and his hands ached. He had come a long way, he realized, with a sudden, tardy amazement. A few days ago he would never have dreamt he could do this.

He wondered if Christ were here, and if not, what gods watched over this country; he wished he knew some charms against them. The memory of the fighting clung to his mind, and he could not shake off the feeling that he owed something to those other men, who had died while he escaped.

One of the boys said something. Corban did not understand him, and therefore he kept on staring at the river, thinking about gods and spirits, and wondering when Grod would come back with food.

The boy came closer, moving in front of him, into his line of vision, speaking. Corban shook his head at him. Then Grod came up beside him.

"Here." He held out a round loaf, smelling strongly of rye.

All Corban's thoughts shrank down to this wheel of bread. He seized it with both hands and ripped it apart and stuffed the pieces into his mouth. The taste made him groan. It was still warm, strong and sour, delicious on his tongue. Grod stood beside him, and spoke to the boys.

"What do they want?" Corban said. "Is there more bread? Where did you get it?"

Grod produced another loaf. "They say this is a Cymryc boat and they're wondering if we're Cymryc. I told them no."

"Tell them to go away." Corban ate the second loaf as fast as the first. "Give me some water."

Grod held out a jug of water. "We need to pay for this."

Corban nodded; he drained the jug. "What's Cymryc?"

"That boat," Grod said. His eyebrows went up and down. "I need money, to pay for the bread, and then I will bring you more."

Corban unknotted the corner of his sleeve; the salt water had hardened the knot in the cloth and he had to tug it apart with his teeth. He gave Grod a silver bit, but the old man shook his head.

"Too much. Cut it in half, that's plenty. Then I'll bring you meat." He straightened; the boys were still watching them. He spoke to them in a long rattle of words. Corban laid the bit down on a stone by his knee, drew his belt knife, and sawed the coin in half. The cut edge was brighter than the rest.

Grod said, "I told them you are a prince from beyond the sea and we took the boat away from pirates, killing many."

Corban gave him the half piece. "That's not smart—maybe they're kin of those people."

"No no no. They hate the Cymry. That's why we have to keep telling them we aren't." Grod took the bit and went away.

Corban was still hungry but the bread made him feel much better. He sat there ignoring the boys, drinking from the jug. The boys clustered together in front of him, their eyes thoughtful. The boldest, not the biggest, a half-naked black-haired boy, came a step forward and pointed to the boat and said something, rising at the end into a question.

Corban shrugged, shook his head, spread his hands to show he didn't understand. The black-haired boy came another step closer and squatted down, watching him steadily; he licked his lips. Corban could see he was trying to find a way to talk to him. He smiled, and the boy smiled back, brushing away his thick black hair.

Grod came back; he had a dish of meat in his hand, and a piece of a savory pie. Corban said, "What does he want? We should get out of here."

"Don't be so jittery," Grod said. "Eat this."

"Don't you want any?"

"I've eaten. Here."

Corban took the food. Grod stood with his hands on his hips, throwing his puny chest out, and looking down his long nose at the boys. He said something, and the black-haired boy, ducking his head humbly, answered and pointed to the boat and to Corban. It seemed to Corban now that he could make out some words: one word that sounded over and over could have been boat. With his belly full and his feet on dry land, he felt much better about everything.

Grod spoke at length to the boys, and then turned. "I told them we defeated the pirates in a huge battle out to sea, and everybody was killed but us and so we came here."

"Oh, well," Corban said. "Tell them whole packs of lies, I don't care." He wiped his mouth.

The black-haired boy's face was wistful. He spoke again, trying once more to speak directly to Corban, and Corban smiled at him and nodded at Grod. The boy gave Grod a sideways glance.

"He likes the boat," Grod said.

"Tell him he can have it, then," Corban said. "We have no use for it any more."

Grod's jaw dropped open, and he goggled at him. "What kind of fool are you, anyway? You'd just give it to him?"

"What use is it to me?" Corban said. Suddenly this felt like a good way to get rid of it all: the fight, the boat, the bad feeling. He faced the boy and said the word he thought meant boat and pointed to him. In his own language, he said, "It's yours. Take it."

Grod said, "Don't be a fool! You could sell it to somebody!"

The boy bounded forward, his face shining. Corban pointed to the boat again and nodded, and the boy let out a shriek of delight.

Grod began to protest, shaking his head, arguing with the boy, and Corban got him by the arm and pulled him off.

"Leave him alone. Let him have the boat. You said Jorvik was overland from here. What are we going to do, sail it on dry land?" He turned, scanning the higher ground above the shore where thick tangles of brush grew, and some old crooked trees, their leaves gone for the winter. That reminded him that it would be cold tonight. "Let's go find someplace to sleep."

Grod moaned. "You're mad, Corban. We could have gotten something valuable for the boat."

Corban snorted at him. "You're always trying to get something." The boy was still standing there, balancing on his toes, his face flaming with desire and eagerness, and Corban said the boat word again and pointed to the boat and to him, and nodded. The boy sprang toward the boat and the other boys, whooping, joined him; circling the boat, they gripped it by the gunwales and bore it away in a rush toward the river. Corban laughed.

Grod said, "I don't know why I am staying with you. You're a madman, giving away everything we own. You'll never get anywhere if you give everything away. I thought you were cleverer than that but I guess I was wrong."

"You're staying with me because you want what I have," Corban said, and jingled the sleeve full of silver at him. He walked away, not bothering to see if Grod would come after him, up across the shore toward the brushy slope. The food in his belly felt good, and he knew Grod would come along. In fact Grod trotted along beside him.

"It's a long way to Jorvik. We could have gotten more silver."

"Boys don't have silver," Corban said. "Boys have nothing. Now they have something, that's good, leave it at that." He climbed the bank, going into the edge of the wood, and began looking for something to build a shelter with. The wind was rising, rustling the brush and banging the dry limbs of the trees together; soon it would be dark. The more he thought about giving the boat away the better he felt about it.

Grod was still grumbling. "This is why you need me with you. You are an innocent."

They gathered branches and built a lean-to, and started a little fire. The cold wind prowled up the river and set its teeth into Corban's bones. He huddled close to the fire, thinking of sending Grod out for more food; the sun was going down, and he was getting hungry again. Then suddenly the black-haired boy appeared, running up the beach toward him.

The boy's face shone; his black eyes snapped. He stopped in front of the little shelter and held out his arms, full of heavy cloth. He said a long string of words, put the cloth down, backed up a step, and made an awkward bow.

Grod said, "Well, that's fine."

"What?" Corban said.

"He says he sees you need a cloak, and he needs the boat, and so this is fair."

Corban grunted. He stepped forward around the fire and picked up the mass of cloth. He remembered other words he thought he understood, and said them. "Thank you." The cloak was old and worn, but very heavy and thick, big enough to wrap around him for a blanket, and supple as a braid of woman's hair. Red color ran one way of it, and blue the other.

He said, again, "Thank you," and the boy nodded, smiling. Corban put his hand out, and the boy came forward and shook his hand. Then, with a jump and a skip of his skinny legs, he was running away.

Grod said, "Sometimes you are just lucky, Corban."

Corban shook the cloak out and wrapped it around him. "I hope so," he said. He sat down again by the fire, no longer cold.

CHAPTER FIVE

Grod had not been this way in a long while—he had forgotten how many years—but he still knew the road to Jorvik. He led Corban inland from the river, following the beaten road eastward, first along the tree-shaded riverbank, and through a village; at the mill in the village several men were hauling the wheel up out of the race, to keep it safe through the worst of the winter storms.

Corban had spent the other half of the cut penny for more bread, and they slept that night beside the road, and ate of the flat round loaves and drank the river water. Halfway through the night a burst of rain swept over them; they crawled into the shelter of a tree but in the morning they were both drenched.

Grod felt the damp and the cold in his knees. He had lived soft in Dublin and now was paying for it. The burning pain in his knees made him grumpy and he told Corban how silly and stupid he was to think they were ever going to find his sister. Corban only walked along, not looking at him. Grod wondered if he even heard him.

All the next day they walked along, climbing the road steadily into the hills, now and then passing other travelers, and slept again in the open. The day following, just before sundown, they saw a great farmstead, set back off the road, and went cautiously toward it, to beg some food and shelter.

A wall of brush and earth surrounded the farmstead. The double wooden gate stood open; as they came up to it, the sound drifted out of many voices chanting, long drawn-out words in another language.

Grod said, relieved, "It's a monastery. We'll get a welcome here."

"A monastery," Corban said. "There was one such near where I lived, but it was not like this."

They went in through the gate, and came directly before a church with a bell tower; the slow eerie music of the chanting drifted out the open doors. A lay porter came yawning up from just inside the gate, waved to them to stay where they were, and went off toward the church. Grod and Corban stood uncertainly there in the gateyard, listening to the clear voices of the monks in the church, and looking around them.

Corban said, "The monastery at home was just a crowd of little huts. This is a very great place."

"You know nothing," Grod said. "There were such in Ireland once but the Vikings took it all."

Corban was looking all around them, his eyes probing. Low-voiced, he said, "Maybe we should leave. I don't think we belong here."

"Ssssh!" Grod said, and cast a look around them. "They'll take us in, here, it's part of their duty. Don't be a great fool, now. If they ask you if you are a Christian, say yes."

Right away, looking around beyond the church, he had noticed the storehouses built against the inside of the wall, the sacks of wool piled outside as if there were no more room within for all this wealth. Off behind the hall was a long three-sided building; along the open front the rumps of oxen showed, and a plow with a huge curved iron blade was drawn up in the shelter of the over-hanging eave. The church was stoutly made, and large, and the other buildings as well, strong and well-kept. They would have bread here in plenty, and a warm dry place to sleep.

The service was soon over. Another monk came to them, very courteous, and took them to the guest house, brought them a cup of beer there, and invited them to dinner in the refectory. As he took them to the sleeping room he asked them a few questions, too—who they were, where they had come from, where they were going—which seemed easy enough to Grod. Corban of course said nothing, having no dansker. Grod let the monk know Corban was a bit of a fool.

He himself, he let the monk know, was not a fool at all, but a wide-traveled man, and very rich and well-known in his own country; even, perhaps, a prince, but traveling humbly, to avoid thieves.

When they went over to the refectory and sat down, the monastery's only guests, the abbot himself came in and sat with them. He was a younger man than Grod had expected, his hair bristling around his tonsure, and a red glow high in his cheeks. Sitting across the table from them with his hands clasped before him, he hardly

let them get a first bite of the mutton and bread before he began
to question them again.

"You told my young fellow you are from Gardarik? I have
scarcely heard of that place. What prince is there?"

"Igor Olafson, when I left, a man's whole lifetime ago."

"Is he the Emperor's man?"

Grod's chest swelled, and he stuck his chin out. "My prince
bows to no one, not even to Miklagard, which is the center of the
world."

"Miklagard!" The abbot lifted his head, his eyes shining. "We
speak of different emperors—your homeland is farther even than I
thought. Where you come from, then, are you Christian men?"

Grod cleared his throat, and made the sign of the cross. "In
God's holy name, I am."

The abbot's eyes narrowed, although he smiled still. He raised
his left hand, on which a carved seal ring gleamed, to touch his
shaven chin. "God's holy name be praised. In Gardarik, do they
customarily make the sign of the cross backward?"

"Unh—" Grod hastily did the sign the other way, but the abbot
was turning to Corban.

"And you, are you also come from far across the world?"

Corban was eating, his elbows on the table, and his jaws grind-
ing away. He shrugged, his gaze drifting toward Grod. "He is
Irish," Grod said. "He cannot speak the dansk tongue, not a word.
He is very dull of mind."

The abbot's gaze remained on Corban, and he spoke Irish.
"Blessed Ireland is full of saints. Are you a Christian man?"

Grod rammed his elbow into Corban's side, hoping he would
remember what to say. Corban glanced at him and back to the
abbot. "Christ was my father's god. But my father is dead, and
Christ did not save him."

Grod hissed his breath out; the boy would not learn. But the
abbot's smile only broadened. "Not that you know, anyway. Can
you see into the next world?"

Corban sat up straighter. "No, that I cannot. But when the
Vikings came to our farmstead no god stood between their swords
and my family."

The abbot nodded. "God have mercy on them."

"When?" The word burst from Corban, and his whole upper body jerked forward, his hands rising. "When will this mercy come for them?"

"Only God sees enough to know," the abbot said. To Grod's relief none of this pagan talk seemed to bother him. He was, Grod thought, looking over his well-kept hands, his fine woolen robe, a worldly man for a monk. "And would you then follow the Viking gods?"

Corban let out an oath. "I would die first."

The abbot nodded, looking pleased. He said, "Then you are on the road to Christ. May you make the right decision before you meet your father again. My young fellow said you are going to Jorvik—there you may find some need of God's love."

Grod said, "Is Eric Haraldsson the King there still?"

"Yes, he is still king. There is none to cast him out, and Jorvik, you know, has long preferred a dansker king, when they can get one."

"Eric was king there before, though, and he could not hold it."

"Yes, indeed, I see you know the situation there well. It's true, as you say, Aethelstan called him to be King in Jorvik, when the men in Norway threw him out, but when Aethelstan died and Edmund came to the throne, we saw Eric cast out of Jorvik also. But now that our good King Edmund is dead, and all we have is our not-so-good King Edred, here comes Fairhair's son, Eric of the Bloody Ax, to try on Jorvik's crown again."

Grod scratched his jaw. In Dublin he had kept himself neatly shaven, like this monk, but now his beard was growing out, and it itched. "What about the priest in Jorvik? That Archbishop. He stood mightily against the King, always, and spoke out in councils. Him it was who sought out Eric in the first place, I had heard."

The abbot leaned on the table. It occurred to Grod that he enjoyed this worldly talk for its own sake. "Wulfstan the Archbishop is locked up in Jedburh, where he can do no harm, as Edred thinks. It seems to me Wulfstan could do him some good, if he were set free to counter Eric, but Edred pays little heed to any churchman's advice, and much heed to men who whisper against Wulfstan. As for the other powers hereabouts, the King of Scots is old and tired, and the Orkney Earl is busy in the northern islands, and so Eric Haraldsson goes where he wishes and does as he wants."

"Does he keep order?"

The abbot snorted. "Order is not what Bloodaxe is interested in. He lives for plunder and ease. I have heard many a story of some thievery or other, there and on the road to there, and casual murders done, and I know getting in the gate of Jorvik can be a matter of considerable risk. The road to Jorvik is always risky. You should travel in company. Unfortunately no one else is here right now. Perhaps you should wait."

Corban said, "Do you know anything of the slave market there?"

The abbot crossed himself. "God have mercy on those captive souls. What interest have you in slave markets?"

"I am looking for my sister, who was stolen away when the Vikings attacked my farm."

"God help you find her." The abbot nodded. "The slave markets in Jorvik are very busy. I shall pray for your sister. And for you."

"I need no prayers," Corban said.

The abbot's smile widened again, his eyes direct and bright. "Well, you shall have them anyway. Now, eat all you wish, I see you are weary. Thank you for your talk." He rose and left them there.

Grod leaned toward Corban. "Will you learn? Be Christian here. It smoothes the way."

Corban was reaching for another piece of bread. "You talk too much," he said. Grod opened his mouth, to argue more, and Corban stuck a piece of bread into it. "Now, use your mouth for its better purpose, Grod. I didn't see that lying got you much at all."

⁘

They went on the next day, still following the river, now small and thin. The monks had given them some bread to take along with them, and two handsful of apples, but Corban began to wish he had his sling again. The world was slowing down, cooling into winter, and although he kept watch for tracks and droppings of

animals, he saw few. The food they had would not last them more
than a few days. He began looking also for nut trees.

They went over the river on a little wooden bridge that creaked
under their footsteps, and climbed higher into the hills.

Grod, as he walked, delivered himself of some advice. "You
should tell people here you are Christian. Christ is very strong here,
and you may need some of his help. And these people here will
treat you better.

"Of course," he went on, pensively, "that will change in Jorvik."

"That priest knew you were lying," Corban said. "I don't think
it does much good to lie. The god would know you are lying."

"I've gotten out of practice, is all," Grod said. "Being around
a great fool like yourself, on whom the pretty art of lying well is
utterly wasted."

Corban thought this was so. He remembered that he had not
cared much about the truth, before his family died. Now it seemed
to him that he had better be more careful of it; if he started lying,
the way Grod did, he could get lost. He could forget what was
really true.

He said, "Jorvik sounds very bad."

Grod harumphed at him. They were trudging up a steep part
of the road. "All Viking cities are hard places. Dublin was not so
easy. You were lucky there. Jorvik is much bigger and Eric Bloodaxe is an evil man."

"My poor sister," Corban said.

Grod gave him a sharp look. "You are just now realizing this?
You'll need a quicker wit than that, in Jorvik."

Late in the day they saw, ahead of them on the road, a crowd
of other people traveling in the same direction. Until nightfall they
walked along behind them, making no effort to catch up, but the
following day the other folk set off very slowly, and Corban and
Grod drew even with the stragglers of their band not long after
they started off for the day's journey. The two men they caught up
with were young, and had packs on their backs. They walked along
nearly side by side with Corban and Grod for more than a mile,
not talking at all, but exchanging sideways looks.

Then suddenly one of the men spoke in dansker to Grod, and

Grod answered back, and before Corban took another step they
were standing in the middle of the road, passing around a leather
water bag. Corban had the last of their bread wrapped up in a
corner of his cloak and he took it out and broke it and they stood
there eating the bread and drinking water. After that they walked
along as if they had known each other always, Grod chattering
away in their midst.

Corban was thinking about gods; it bothered him that there
were so many of them. With all the world divided up among them,
how could any one of them have any real power? And yet each
god pretended to be all-powerful, as Christ did. It seemed to him
a misdirection at the heart of the whole idea. In his ears the dansker
chatter was like a drone. He wanted to ask Grod about the gods in
his homeland, since Grod clearly was no Christian, but the rapid
garble of the other speech fenced him out.

He felt suddenly as if he walked along invisible to these other
men. He began listening to the sounds of the forest; the path was
leading them steadily higher into the peaked hills. The oak trees
around them stirred in the wind, rubbed and banged their branches
together, and let go showers of their leaves. From far up in the sky
he heard the sad skirling cry of a hawk.

His heart flew upward like the hawk. He felt around him the
seamlessness, the one-ness of the world, alive everywhere; only
people, with their different words for things, their different little
gods, broke it all to pieces. He began thinking again of Mav, and
wishing he knew whom he might pray to for her sake, if any god
at all could help her.

He remembered the abbot, smooth and smiling, who had as-
sumed there were only two kinds of gods: his and the Vikings',
good and bad, true and false. He did not think anything of the
world was so clean as that.

They went by a patch of wood all blackened and charred in a
fire, and climbed over a great tree that had fallen over the path. By
night they had caught up with the rest of the travelers, a big group
of people, men and women, and made camp with them in a clearing
in the middle of a beech wood. Moldering leaves and prickly burs
littered the ground under the trees. The main group of travelers,
who were obviously a single family, built a great fire in the middle

of the clearing and crowded out everybody else. Grod and Corban made their own little camp back in the grove; Grod fussed around, sweeping back the burs and leaves and looking for kernels of the nuts.

The two men they had been walking with called them back to the fire, and gave them bread. They stood there by the roaring, leaping fire, on which the children of the camp were heaping every branch they could find, and broke pieces off flat loaves and dunked them in water and gnawed them down.

Grod was talking to the other two men; Corban stepped off a little by himself. The women all around him drew his eyes. He tried not to look at any of them too long; he knew each of them had men to watch out for her. After a while, he turned his gaze to the fire.

Grod tapped his arm. "This woman here says she will give you three loaves, and a jar of honey, and all those apples for your cloak."

Corban looked where he was nodding. A large, heavy-fleshed woman sat by the fire, a child on her knee, and when she saw him looking smiled at him; yet he did not like her looks.

"No," he said. The cloak was wrapped around him, the end thrown over his shoulder; he gripped it with his fist. He had come to love it, and something in her put his back up. He saw the woman read his answer in his looks, and lose her smile.

She pushed the child impatiently out of her lap and spoke again, more sharply. Grod answered, shaking his head, not even bothering to translate for Corban. Listening, Corban picked out some words—he realized the old woman was offering him more bread, more apples. Grod kept shaking his head. Around them other people were watching. A lanky young man came up beside the woman and squatted beside her, as if to be ready for an order.

Corban saw they were getting into trouble; he thought of giving her the cloak, to avoid that, but the idea rankled with him. He thought: I am a match for them, surely. He said, "Tell her I will never trade away my cloak, and she can stop asking."

When Grod said that, the woman spat to one side. The man squatting beside her reached out and touched her arm, and she glanced at him and their eyes met and she said nothing more. Corban glanced at the people around them, who were watching with interest, and then went away from the fire, back to their camp.

There he wrapped himself up in his cloak and lay down for the night, Grod beside him. The blaze of the fire cast a flickering orange light everywhere through the grove, making all the trees seem to dance. Other people were going to sleep, however, especially the children, and the fire began to die.

Corban did not sleep. He watched the darkness creep back under the trees and he heard the grove around him fall silent. The night grew cold around him. When he thought the whole camp slept, he got up and woke Grod, and made him move off deeper into the darkness, dragging him by the arm when he stumbled.

There, in the dark, Grod went back to sleep at once, but still Corban did not sleep, but looked back toward the fire, and the place where he had lain. So he saw a lanky man creep up through the dark, two others on his heels, with clubs in their hands.

He put his feet under him, and stood. He watched the men steal through the dark trees to the place where he and Grod had lain down to sleep, and suddenly pounce, the clubs swinging down. He shook Grod quickly out of his blanket and made him run. Behind him the men were kicking and striking furiously at the ground, their voices rising, as if they had been cheated. Corban with one hand on Grod's shoulder steered him back into the trees and down a bank. There they waited, sleeping fitfully, until the dawn.

When they came carefully up toward the road again Corban saw that the great crowd of travelers was ahead of them, already moving off to the east. He and Grod waited for a long while to let them get far ahead of them. Grod searched through the litter under the trees and found a few whole beechnuts.

Soon after they set out, they left the forest and came out onto a broad and treeless moor, tilting downward in long soft slopes. Far ahead of them they could see the other travelers straggled out along the road. Corban was relieved; now in the open he could see easier if anybody lay in wait for them.

Far down on the moor, just off the road, he saw some loose horses.

The thronging travelers had seen them too. Some of the men chased them, crashing through the heather, but the horses galloped away. As they drew closer Corban saw that two of the horses wore saddles, and all three had bridles on their heads. When the travelers had gotten tired of chasing the horses and gone back to the road, he set off after the horses, walking steadily toward them.

The horses moved away from him and he walked after them, following the paths they made through the waist-high brush. All the morning he followed, until at last he walked one of the horses down. When he laid hands on it, it was quiet at once and stood while he freed it of the saddle and bridle. There was a sack of moldy bread tied to the cantle of the saddle and he threw it away for the winter birds. The saddle and the horse he left where they were, but the bridle he took back with him to the road, where he caught up with Grod, who was sitting on the side of the road, dozing.

"What a fool," Grod cried. "Why didn't you bring back the horse, you big lout?"

"I don't need a horse," Corban said, surprised. He was cutting the leather of the bridle into narrow strips. "Do you think I would eat it, like a dansker?"

"I could have ridden it! My legs hurt! I'm tired! I'm old! Did you think of me?"

Corban laughed. "No," he said, and braided together the leather into a cord. They were well behind the crowd now, and the sun was near the western edge of the world; he was hoping the people in front of him would stop soon for the night. He doubted they were finished with him, and he was afraid of catching up to them in the dark. His belly hurt with hunger, but now he had a long springy leather cord. He had carefully saved out a wide bit of the leather for the socket of the sling and this he fit to the middle of the cord, and got up to look for stones. Grod watched him, morose, but no longer whining.

Before sundown the crowd made their camp on the open road. Corban and Grod loitered behind them, Corban practicing with his new sling, hurling stones off into the heather; but he saw nothing to kill. When the dark fell they circled cautiously around the camp, fighting their way through the close-growing tangling brush.

This took them nearly half the night, and they found nothing to eat. Grod moaned and begged to stop and sleep but Corban dragged him on. At last they reached the road again, well ahead of the travelers' camp, and then he let Grod sleep, and slept himself, the sling and some stones in his hand.

—⚬—

In the morning they went on, but they had not outdistanced the others, and Corban, looking back, saw several men striding out after them. It was just after dawn and there were hares and birds fluttering in the brush. He made some casts at them but missed. With the men stalking them he could not be patient enough to kill anything.

"I have to stop," Grod said. "I'm worn out. I can't go on any more."

Corban swung an arm around him and helped him walk along. When they came over the brow of a low hill, he looked back along the road, winding away over the heathery moor, and saw the lanky man and several others coming after them. They were not gaining ground; he thought they walked slower, now, as if they were giving up.

He doubted they had given up.

"Stay here, then." He let Grod sink down to the ground. "They won't hurt you, it's the cloak they're after." He wound the cloak around him and went off through the heather, and rambling away from the road came eventually to a meadow by a spring. There he waited a while, still and patient, until some little birds with bobbles on their heads came to the water, and he killed three of them with stones from his sling.

When he reached the road again, the lanky man and his friends were just climbing up the hill toward Grod. Seeing them come, the old man had stood up, and found a piece of wood somewhere, which he had cocked back over his shoulder like a club. He was shouting at the lanky man to stay away, and did not see Corban until the first stone flew by him and hit the lanky man in the arm.

The three men stopped in their tracks, their heads swiveling around toward Corban. Stopping to pick up stones as he went, Corban ran up the road toward them, and cast three or four more times at them; he saw a fat stone bounce off a shoulder and another hit smack above an ear. The three men wheeled and ran hastily back the way they had come. Behind them, Grod stood yelling insults and taunts at them.

"I'd have killed them all," he said, when Corban reached him. "I once killed four men just like them, down in England. They're just lucky you came along."

"So are you," Corban said, and showed him the three little birds. Grod gave a cry of pleasure.

"We'll make a fire. There's plenty of brush."

"Wait," Corban said. "Not here." Down the road, the lanky man had stopped, back there, out of range of the sling, and was watching them. "They haven't quit. They'll wait until we camp, and then steal up on us. We have to find someplace safe."

Grod gave a wail. "I'm tired. And I'm so hungry I can't even walk. Give them the cloak."

"I won't give them my cloak," Corban said, through his teeth. The cloak was his, and too good for these base crooked people. He helped Grod hobble along, the old man leaning on him, his breath short and loud. After a little while, Corban picked him up on his back and carried him. The lanky man and his friends trailed after them, staying well out of the sling's range.

As he went along, bent under Grod's weight, Corban looked for some place he could defend. There seemed no refuge anywhere along this road. There were no trees, not even a steep hillside, or a big rock. The way bent down along the cheek of a long low hill, and as the sun was setting, they came on a great stone cross, where another road ran in from the north.

There, opposite the stone cross, a gallows had been raised, and on the gallows hung three dead men. Corban stopped, thinking this over.

The bodies were very old, and stank powerfully. Scraps of cloth still clung to them and the birds had eaten most of their flesh, so that the bones of their legs and feet dangled down from the rags of their clothes. Corban went in directly beneath them and lowered Grod down to the ground.

The old man had been asleep; now, lying on the grass, he lifted his head and looked around like a startled bird. Corban put stones in a ring for a fire.

Down on the road, the lanky man had stopped too, and was arguing with his friends.

"You can't be camping here!" Grod cried. He scrambled to his feet, staring up at the gallows.

Corban was laying out the fire. "No one will bother us here, will they? Sit down, you'll get used to them soon enough." He straightened to look down the road, and laughed. The lanky man was walking back forlornly along the road, following after his friends, who were running.

Grod sank down on his haunches, but he could not help tipping his head every few minutes to look up at the bodies dangling from the crossbar of the gallows. "Better we should hide in the forest."

"There is no forest." Corban spitted the birds and put them over the fire to roast. "And I have to stop, I can't walk much farther. We are close to this city, which you say is so wicked, and certainly this tree here proves that, so tomorrow we can go there, but tonight we have to sleep. Just sit still, and don't let it bother you."

Grod came around to sit next to him. "Likely their spirits are still here somewhere."

In fact now the wind blew up suddenly, and the three bodies dangling down began to shift and move, as if they were trying to walk in the air. Corban remembered gathering up the dead of his family, back at his home; he thought no corpse would ever frighten him again. The dark was falling around them like a soft blanket of moving night. Bats twittered and dashed through the air above the gallows. Grod huddled close, but he was falling asleep again; Corban had to waken him to give him his dinner.

"You're mad," Grod said. "I can feel ghosts all around here. They'll kill us in our sleep."

"Pagh," Corban said. "They are just lonely, hanging up there in the air all this while, and cold, too. I think I'll bring them down and let them sit by the fire and get warm."

At that Grod gave him such a look that he burst out laughing. Corban ate all the meat on his bird, crunched up the bones, and devoured everything that Grod left also. His belly wasn't full but he felt stronger, and now very sleepy. He wrapped himself in his cloak, and slept.

The night turned around them. Corban woke once, and saw the moon overhead, a thin white sail ghosting through the stars. He slept again, and dreamt that one of the corpses called to him—the middle one—and tried to tell him something, but he could not understand because the corpse spoke dansker.

Just before dawn hoofbeats woke him up.

He opened his eyes. There on the road a troop of men was trotting up from the direction of the city. The watery, pale, pre-dawn light gleamed on the studs of their leather breastplates and the swords hanging from their belts. Corban did not rise, but under his cloak he took hold of his knife. Beside him Grod slept on.

The leader of the band called out sharply, and his troop slowed and stopped in the crossroads. The leader had seen Corban and Grod lying there, and he reined his horse around, and drew his sword. From his troop someone called, pointing to the gallows.

From the edge of the world the wind rose, and the hanged men swayed; their leg bones clattered together, and their bony arms swung. The leader of the little army flinched back from the sound, sheathed his sword and wheeled his horse and galloped off. His men rushed after him.

Corban let go of his knife. Under his breath he said a little thanks to the hanged men. He shut his eyes and went back to sleep, and Grod never woke at all until the morning sun was fierce in his eyes.

—⸘—

Hedeby.

Of the voyage that had brought her here Mav remembered almost nothing: salt spray, a steep sea before the wind. She had spent most of the journey in the far, gray, cold place. Now that they were here she felt the city all around her, a puzzle of wooden walls and walks up and down, forward and backward, of canals and dikes, morning fog and afternoon wind; a jumble of people, all talking at once. She lay in the bed the Lady had given her, shut up and away from everything else, and was sick in the belly as if she had drunk up the sea.

The Lady herself came, and sat by her. Fed her broth and dry bread. Her hand stroked Mav's hair. "Never mind, girl. Never mind."

Mav shut her eyes, sick. She wondered how she knew the name of this place. All around her she felt it, chamber after chamber, boxes of wood filled with people, and the sea around it like a cold chain. Even that chain could not hold her. She could feel herself stretched out now to the edge of the world, thin and feeble, streaked with failing light.

She felt the bloodknot in her body, smaller than a fingernail, that was not her, but only within her, waiting. She was sick again, and threw up into a basin.

The Lady sent that off with one of her servants. There were many other people in this house, all gray and afraid, going up and down, scrubbing and scouring, bending and lifting, talking to no one. In the middle of it was the Lady, who knew all, who alone had no fear.

Her face floated in a mist of faces, many-eyed, not all of them smiling. Mav saw her several times at once, young and old, ugly and beautiful, happy and raging. She wondered which was the true woman. She wondered if any of them were true, and shuddered.

Yet the Lady, toward Mav at least, was kind. Stroking Mav's hair. "Is he still there, girl?"

Mav's mouth tasted foul. The Lady fed her sips of a clear spicy wine. She laid her head in the Lady's lap and kept her eyes closed. At first she had spoken her heart, grateful for the tenderness, for the warm food and the gentle hand on her hair, but now she could sense the fear all around her and she was afraid to talk. She had said too much already. She had given away too much.

She felt this begin, a long struggle, whose end she could not imagine. She was too weak even to move, much less give battle.

"Is he there? Is he still coming?"

Off at the edge of the world, yes, that was her brother, walking toward her. She was glad of him; weak and thoughtless she said, "Yes." The Lady fed her sips of broth. Her whole being yearned toward her brother, creeping over the curve of the world toward her. Light wrapped him, red and blue. She said, "Corban."

The Lady said, "Sleep, girl. Don't worry about the baby. We'll get rid of it, don't worry."

She folded her arms over her belly, where the little alien knot pulsed. She shut her eyes and sent her mind to Corban. He was not alone, he walked with others, but he was in danger. She could feel anger all around him like thorny brambles; she saw great pits opening up before his feet, that he could disappear in. The red and blue light shone warm around him. He walked with a long step, his head up, his eyes forward. Her heart gladdened to see him strong.

Later the Lady brought her a goblet of green water, but when she looked into it, she saw worms in it, coiling and uncoiling in the green, and would not drink it.

Hedeby. Lying in the warm bed, the blankets around her, she half-drowned in its jumble, the voices of men and of seagulls, the barking of dogs, the heavy lumbering of feet, coming and going. Some people cried here. Women and children, taken away, penned and sold like cattle. A strange harsh voice sounded close, inside this same house: a man's voice, a royal voice. She flinched from it.

Outside. Everywhere arguing. The clink of gold and silver. The slice of a blade into flesh. The stink of smoke, rising into the still cold air, of cesspots and rot. Always, like music, the tramp of feet on wooden walks, and the rush of the sea past the keels of boats, heavy laden.

She knew the Lady walked through her house, her servants quailing and bowing away from her, as if she walked in a coat of winds that blew them down. The Lady nodded and men quaked. Not all men. That harsh voice sounded again, in this house; he sat somewhere nearby, stinking of swords and blood.

"I will have it all, or my sons. Then let Fairhair sleep deep and cold in his howe, and his sons come with tribute to me and mine."

That voice made her shiver; it went through her like a knife of ice. A name came to her, out of nowhere, not even really a name: Bluetooth.

Another goblet came, this one red, with a smell like fish blood, and she would not drink it.

"If you drink this, girl, you will not have to bear this brat. Drink, drink."

She drank only the good broth, ate the dry bread, and threw

most of that up again anyway. Her head floated, a great soft empty haze, above her ruined body. She was dying.

The Lady laughed. "No, no, not dying. You are safe here, and most precious. Come, come, don't you understand me yet? Trust me. I love you. I shall not let you die."

The hand stroking on her hair lulled her. She found herself talking again, of her home, her family, her brother.

"He comes."

"Yes," said the Lady. "Where is he now?"

"He walks." She shuddered. She knew that bridge, those trees. He was following the way she had come. There she had walked on the road. There the men had dragged her off and thrown her down and made use of her as if she were nothing. Quarried a nothing out of the middle of her. All around him walked men with knives in their hands and their eyes. She wept, and the hand on her hair soothed her.

"You are safe now. Only, drink this, and the baby will be gone. Do you want it? Foolish girl, they raped you, it has no father, why should you want to bear it? Such pain as that is, even for a wanted child."

She would not drink. She held her arms over her belly, where the little life grew, filling up the nothing, and clenched her teeth against the rising wave of nausea.

"She seems half dead to me." That was the cold bloody voice, right before her. She lifted her eyes to narrow eyes pale as water beneath his crow's wing of an eyebrow. In his eyes she saw a fathomless hunger like a black pit in the center of the world.

The Lady spoke. "She has a great power. It comes also from the brother. When I have both of them, I shall have something to watch. You said you wanted a spy, to go to Jorvik and see what Eric does, and maybe twist him a little. This is the chance."

"Bah. She is a waif, and dying."

"You know nothing of this. What you know, you know, but of this you are ignorant."

Mav shut her eyes, to keep from seeing his hunger, but she could not shut the eyes of her mind. Within her, the little life beat. She wondered which of the many men had planted that seed in her belly. Yet she would protect it, hers to love, hers alone. Around her the wooden city clamored, a thousand pounding feet, a thousand bawling voices. And somewhere, in the distance, Corban, coming toward her.

CHAPTER SIX

Just before midday the road led them over a bridge and down toward a great stone bar, a gateway through the overgrown earthworks of the city wall; beyond the ragged upper line of the wall Grod could see the wooden finger of a steeple, and in the distance some roofs. The stink and uproar of the city reached his nose, and all along his arms the flesh pebbled up: he could not wait to get in there, to the crowds and the bustle and the food and excitement. He wondered why he had ever taken to the road.

Of course there was Corban. He gripped the young man by the arm and drew him off the road, into the shadow of a tree, where they could talk. Down the road past them came a steady parade of people going into the town and from it, and Grod kept watch on the gateway while he talked.

"Now, you remember what the abbot said, back there. That getting into Jorvik can be hard."

Corban turned toward him, his eyes sharp. "Yes. What should we do?"

Grod stroked his chin, bristling with his new beard. "You see those men in the bar?"

Corban lifted his head and looked. "Yes. They are stopping people."

"I saw that." Grod shifted his weight from one foot to the other, uneasy. Corban had sharp eyes; Grod hadn't even really seen the guards there, among the clog of people by the bar. "They're looking for the King's enemies, and for people who are coming in to sell and buy—he gets a tax from those. We should go in separately." He looked down at himself. "We don't look like much— we look even less, one at a time. Good. I'll go first, you watch me, and do as I do. Meet me at the church by nightfall."

Corban's head bobbed up and down. He fumbled with his sleeve. To Grod's amazement he saw the boy was taking out some of his silver money. His heart swelled. Corban was as good as sunrise. He reached out his hand and Corban put four pennies into it.

"Meet me at the church," Grod said again. "I'll be there by the time the sun goes down, certainly. And stay out of trouble." He closed his fist over the money. "Be careful, Corban, will you?" Now suddenly he could not bring himself to part from the young man, although the stream of people walking by, the open gate, and the city beyond called him like a sinner to his luxuries. He nodded to Corban. "Be careful. Watch me."

Grod turned back toward the road, saw a woman passing with a bundle on her arm and a baby on her back, and went after her. He fell into step with her, a pace behind, close enough to see the eggs in her basket. They stood a while, among a dozen other people, until a big wagon in the gateway passed on through, and then in the midst of the crowd entered the gate.

The dark air of the stone passageway fell over him, cold and dank. The gate was deep, ten feet from outside to inside, paved with square stones. Off to one side, two men in iron-studded leather shirts were watching people go in and out of the city; another, redheaded, slumped with his back to the inside wall of the gate, dozing. King Eric's men stopped the woman with the basket. Grod kept on walking, and was out the bar, and into the narrowing street leading into the city.

He felt suddenly much lighter. He knew this place, somewhat. He had been to Jorvik once before, years ago; then he had known people here, and maybe some of them remained. He went on into a narrow planked street that wound between buildings, closer together than in Dublin. Within a few steps he was closed in, the city crowding around him. He turned and looked back, toward the bar, thinking about Corban.

His heart lurched in his chest. He reminded himself he had always meant to slip free of Corban, somewhere.

That had been before. He could not remember exactly when his notion about that had changed, whether it was when Corban tossed him into the Cymric boat, or when he brought him the fat tender birds when he was starving, or drove off the men attacking him on the road. Somewhere everything had changed. He wandered deeper into the city, aching for his missing friend.

The sun was still high in the sky, and the shops and markets of the town were full of people. He ducked beneath the great hanging shoe sign of a cobbler's shop, and went by a candlemaker's, stinking of tallow. He realized he was hungry and began looking for something to eat. He stowed the silver pennies carefully away in his clothes, too precious to waste on simple things like food, and watched for the chance to steal something. He tried to forget about Corban.

The road dipped, going down a short slope, and he saw the river in the distance, smoothly flowing under the thin winter daylight. A bell began to ring, off to his right somewhere, up on the higher bank. The street was full of garbage, the center of it a string of puddles, and he kept to the side. Abruptly a woman stepped out of a doorway right in front of him and upended a bucket of slops; he bounded away, and she laughed at him, a harsh, croaking cry like a bird.

A pieman strolled toward him, calling out in a long mournful voice. Grod licked his lips, his belly rumbling. He remembered that the market street lay just ahead, and turned into it, looking for a familiar face. It all seemed changed; he did not remember these bakeries, three of them all in a row, crowded around with people; the smell of the bread almost led him to take out some of his money.

Silly to spend good silver on bread, which was eaten and gone right away. He hurried off, looking around him. Near the foot of the street was a big spreading oak tree; he remembered that—a market tree—and there were people under it now, buying and selling. Across the way from that, on the corner, a small woman in a white headcloth sat among an array of pots, bent over something she was doing with her hands. A boy with a stick drove three scrawny pigs up the street toward him and Grod drifted out of the way, around into the next street.

That put him almost in the doorway of a house; he sniffed and drew in a long savory aroma of onions and pork. His mouth filled with water. He glanced around, saw nobody watching him, and went around the side of the house, chasing the aroma.

Halfway down the house was a little open window, and on the ledge sat a fat pie, cooling. Steam rose from its thick brown crust.

He slid his hands up into his sleeves, and with his fingers thus protected, lifted the pie neatly up off the ledge and continued on down the side of the house, toward the darkness of trees he saw just beyond.

The steaming pie was still too hot to eat. He came to a thick hedge, set the pie down, stooped, and squeezed himself in through the spiny trunks at the bottom. That took him out to a dark lane, smelling of piss and garbage. The high steep bank of the earthworks rose just beyond. He reached back through the hedge and found the warm and crusty pie. He sat down and ate the pie, delicious with gravy and the sweet bite of the onions, and licked the sauce off his fingers.

Now he drifted back toward the center of the city. He wished Corban were there; he felt small and unsure, and everything about Jorvik seemed to have changed since he had been here last. There had been a fire, he remembered. Maybe the pest had come through here. In any case he recognized none of the buildings. Everywhere he looked he saw Eric's men, brawny danskers with leather shirts and swords in their belts, doing no work; walking idly up the street, or standing around, watching everything. In a doorway, as he passed, he saw a girl sitting, her red skirt drawn up to her knees. She caught his eye, and stared boldly at him, and pulled down on her dress, showing him her breasts.

He slowed, an old practiced lust stirring in him, and thought of the silver, again, and turned and went on. He told himself a woman like that was the same as a bite of bread, nothing to spend money on. He did not remember such a thing before in Jorvik and at the corner he turned to look back at her. She was sitting well back inside the doorway; only her red skirt showed against the wall. He hurried on.

He came into a narrow lane stinking of blood. The center of the street was a rotten running stream, clogged with mats of feathers and hair and crawling with flies. On either side were pens floored thick in manure, with here and there a cow or a sheep. Between the pens stood houses, their heavy thatches leaning over the street. In paying so much heed to keeping his feet tidy, he nearly brained himself on an iron meat hook dangling from the projecting eave.

This was the shambles, he realized, and now suddenly he knew where he was in the town, and went on more confidently, past a little herd of doomed swine waddling down the street, to where the way suddenly widened into a square, and the high front of the church loomed.

Now he was certain he knew where he was. He drifted around the edge of the square and down a lane between the church and another house; between the two high walls the lane was dark even in broad daylight, and halfway down the church wall he came on several men throwing dice.

Grod's neck tingled. He suddenly felt very lucky. He went into the ring of men watching the game. The shadow of the church lay deep over them here and he had to look sharp to see. One of the men took the little bones and rattled them in his hand.

"Doubles! Give me doubles!"

Beside Grod, somebody bawled, "A farthing he makes it!"

"Taken," Grod said, mindful of his silver.

The player cast, bent over the dice, and let out a wail. Grod turned to the man beside him, his hand out.

"Another," this man said. "Double or nothing."

He was tall, with a grizzled beard. Grod squinted at him in the bad light. "Edbert?"

The broad face turned toward him, mouth falling open. With the light on him Grod was sure now, and he said, "It's me, Grod, remember me? We came here together from London, after King Aethelstan died. Remember?"

Edbert's mouth sagged. Abruptly he was wheeling back to the dice game, where the players stooped to see the bones roll, and screamed and cried. "Damn," he said.

"That's a halfpenny," Grod said.

Edbert swung toward him again. "Yes, damn you, I remember you now." He made no move toward his purse. "What are you doing in Jorvik again?"

"I was in Dublin. I thought I'd get on my way home." Grod nudged him. "You owe me half a penny."

"Bah," said Edbert. "Put it on his next throw. Landy! Make this one a good one, hey?"

The man with the dice said something muffled. Across the way somebody else was calling out a bet. Grod poked Edbert with his elbow again. "I'm looking for a place to sleep. How about taking me in?"

Edbert craned his neck, watching the dice. Then he threw his arms up, triumphant. "There! Yes!" All around, the crowd laughed and cheered, and the man with the dice leapt up and danced.

Grod wiped his mouth. He should have collected the halfpenny. Now Edbert was pushing away. Grod followed after him.

"I'll sleep on the floor."

Edbert grunted. "There's no—" His head rose, his gaze sliding past Grod, and he hissed, "Beat it, lads! Eric's men!" Wheeling, he fled away.

The rest of the dice players scattered. Grod shrank back against the wall of the church; from the head of the lane came a hoarse cry, and two danskers came running down past him. He shrank against the wall, hunching his shoulders, his arms against his chest. Down where the lane met the square somebody screamed. Grod wheeled away from the wall and dashed the other way, around the church, and dodged inside.

Here he would be safe. Yet his heart galloped rabbity in his chest. The place was dim and empty. It smelled of mildew; the bare earthen floor was slick under his feet. At the opposite end of the building, above a narrow table, hung an image of the Hanged God. He went to the side wall and sat down, to wait for Corban.

He wondered why he had ever taken to traveling again. It was mad to think he would go back where he began, to his birthplace in Gardarik. He could hardly remember the place; he had been wandering all his life, all he could ever recall clearly was the last place he had been. Of his homeland he remembered the heavy mounded snow bulging over the riverbank, the black water racing by. He remembered the mosquitoes in the summer, the backbreaking work, and the curses and the blows of his mother's fist. His family had been fishermen and boatmen, but since his father died, he and his brothers had only the scraps, the leavings of his uncles and cousins. As soon as he could, he had escaped on a boat, when danskers came by.

He had gone to Birka, and to Nid, to London and Hedeby and Dublin. He had seen much but he had left nothing behind, not even a friend he could count on. His spirits sank down. It seemed to him he had lived all his life like a grasshopper one leap ahead of the plow.

He leaned his back against the wall, and dozed. When he woke, people were moving into the church, carrying candles, and he started up onto his feet, afraid. But they only walked down toward the far end, where the flat table was, and began to light the candles there.

Corban had not come. He shivered a little; the air was cold, the night seeping in, dark and pestilent. He could not stay here, and he went out the door and into the city.

The square in front of the church was empty. Somewhere a dog was barking. The air was cold and still, and a haze of smoke hid the stars. He went uncertainly away down the long street that led down toward the river. On the right rose the steep embankment where the King's Hall stood, and he saw lights there and knew to stay far away. He had to find somewhere to sleep. Along the street stood a row of houses, but every one was shuttered and dark. He stopped in front of the last one, thinking of climbing over the withy fence and crawling into the lean-to tipped against its wall, but a dog started barking inside and he went hastily away.

He was hungry. The savory pie seemed days behind him. He huddled his arms around himself and went on down to the river-bank; off to his right, downstream, several ships were drawn up on the shore, and a fire glowed in among them. He thought of going down there, of begging and whining his way in with those men, but there was risk in that, especially if they were drunk. He turned upstream, walking along the flat beaten path along the shore of the river, following the way that led up the bank and back into the city's heart.

Down this path someone was toiling along, a woman, small and slight, struggling with a handcart. He gave her a keen look, wondering if she had anything to steal, and saw it was the little potter woman he had seen earlier, in the Coppergate marketplace. She would have nothing worth stealing. He started by her, his shoulders hunched up, cold.

She rolled the barrow on toward the river; he could hear the grunt of her breath as she wrestled with the weight of it. Then she gave a cry of exasperation, and the handcart thudded over. With a loud clatter everything inside fell out.

He stopped, looking back. For a moment the woman stood still, her arms hanging, staring at the upset cart. She lived here, he thought, she was going somewhere. Suddenly he remembered how he had fallen in with Corban; if he helped her, or seemed to, maybe she would give him a place to sleep. He went back over toward the upturned handcart, which she was now struggling to right.

"Here," he said, "I'll help you." He took hold of the side of the cart.

She started, her head flying up, and he saw he had frightened her. She gave him a wild stare. She was much younger than he had thought, only a girl. He said, "I'm just trying to help."

"Thank you," she said, and wrenched the cart up onto its wheel. "I can do it—" Quickly she knelt, gathering up pots. "Thank you, I'll do it."

"I'll help you," he said, again, and hurried to pick something up before she got it all. Then, on the far side of the river, there was a yell.

The potter woman straightened, looking across the water, and shouted, "I'm here!" She gave Grod a sideways look and dumped her armload of pots into the handcart. "Thank you," she said, sending him off, her voice clipped.

Grod dusted his hands together. From the other side of the river, a girl came running toward them, bounding lightly across the surface of the water. As she came up, even in the darkness Grod could see her smile. She walked up beside the potter woman and slipped her arm around her waist, saying, "Where were you, Benna? I came at sundown, you weren't here."

"I was doing something," the potter woman said. "I'm sorry, I didn't see how late it was getting." She glanced at Grod, and said, again, insistently, "Thank you."

"Please," Grod said. "I need a place to sleep—"

"Oh, no," the potter woman said.

The other girl gave him a keen look. "Who is he?"

"I spilled out the pots—he just stopped—"

"Please," Grod said. "I'm cold."

The other girl said, "You can stay with us. We don't have very much—"

The potter woman, Benna, tossed her hands up. "We have nothing. And what we do have, Arre, you give away to strangers."

"We can give him shelter, and lose nothing ourselves." Arre smiled at him. "My name is Arre, and this is my sister Benna, who is much kinder than she's seeming right now."

"Thank you," Grod said. "I'm cold, I wouldn't ask—"

"Hah," Benna said. "Well, then, come along, I suppose." She grabbed the handles of the cart.

"I'll help," Grod said, gladdened. He could tell Benna was glaring at him in the dark but he ignored her. He took one of the handles of the cart, and she took the other, and they started over the river; there were stones laid down in the river here, which was how Arre had seemed to skip across the surface. The wind bit cold, but he kept his groans to himself. It was amazing how a few words from a woman made everything seem better. Now he was thinking that Corban had just gotten lost somewhere, and he would find him in the morning. Happily he struggled getting the handcart across the river.

⟶⟨⟶

Corban waited a little while, after he saw Grod get through the gate, and fell in behind a stream of people, as he had seen the old man do. As he came near the gate he fumbled up into his mind all the dansker he could remember, which was almost nothing, and then he was going in behind a cart full of firewood, into the shade of the gate. The cart rolled on, past the three men in their iron studded jackets, standing to one side watching.

Corban's face heated. He tried not to look at them, but he felt as if he gave off some glow of alarm, and suddenly one of them was shouting, and stepping forward, pointing at him.

He stopped, his palms suddenly greasy. The three men came toward him; the one in front, who had shouted, wore a leather cap, his red hair sticking out in bunches all around the lower edge.

He said something in dansker. The teeth in the front of his mouth were missing, and when he spoke his lips flapped around this hole in his face; Corban could understand nothing of what he said.

"I only speak Irish. I'm Irish."

"Irish." The redheaded man wiped the back of his hand over his mouth. "I speak Irish. You are?"

"Corban Mac—" He would not say that name. "Corban Loose-strife. I came from—"

"Why you wear Kenneth's colors, hah?" The Viking reached out and pulled at Corban's cloak.

"I don't wear anybody's color," Corban said, startled; he glanced around; the other two danskers were behind him, now, watching him steadily, keeping him in the middle. He turned back toward the man with the hole in his face. "I don't know any Kenneth." But he had heard the name, at the monastery: the King of the Scots. "I'm not Scot."

The redheaded man was looking him over, even pulling the cloak away so he could see what Corban carried on his belt. "How you know Scot if not Kenneth? No weapon?"

"My sling," Corban said. "My belt knife."

"Money?"

Corban stared at him, confused, wondering if this meant he had to pay money to get into the city; the redhead rubbed his fingers together. "Money money money!"

"I have some money." He gave the redheaded man his four pennies.

The Viking took the coins and went over to the sunlight and stared at them. Corban glanced at the other men, who were beginning to look bored; he thought suddenly he would get by them soon, and be out of this.

"Hah!" The redhead strode back to him. "Jedburh!" He waved a coin under Corban's nose. "Jedburh! Explain that one, hah?" He gripped Corban's arm and held him. "We're taking you to see the King."

—⊱—

Corban thought of running, of jumping one of these men and knocking him down and bolting, but they were watching him; one on either side, and one behind him. On their belts they carried swords. They went down a crowded narrow street, past a big wooden shoe hanging from an eave, through a delicious wafting aroma of baking bread. He had told the truth and this was what it had gotten him. As he went along he saw people in the street turning to see him, and the back of his neck heated.

Off past a row of thatched roofs he saw the wooden tower of the church. Grod might be there waiting for him. His stomach fluttered. They walked down a broad street, littered with cow shit; the street turned downhill and they came into sight of the river, green and slow between its high banks. From the street a broad path led up the last stretch of the embankment, toward the height, where there were two or three large thatched wooden halls.

They led him to the middle hall, the largest. The yard was trampled dust, and the front door into the hall stood wide open; a dog lay over the threshold. When they went in the place was empty. It was a fair hall, Corban thought, wide and long, with benches on either side, two big hearths, and a great carved highseat at one end; he wished he were anywhere else. The danskers led him down to the end, and made him sit on a bench there, and got a chain and shackled him to the bench by one leg, and left him there.

He tried the shackle with his hands and could not budge it. The chain let him stand up but go nowhere. He sat there a while, watching. A woman came into the hall with a load of firewood but left at once. Two little white-headed boys ran in and out again. No one came down toward his end of the place. There was a bearskin on the bench, and he pulled it over and lay down on it, and went to sleep.

—⚬—

He woke in the half-dark to a rising babble of noise. Cautiously he lifted his head. Up there in the middle of the hall, in the light of a string of torches, people were dragging tables out before the benches, talking all the while. More men kept coming in the door, lifting their voices to be heard over the uproar, laughing, and strutting around. He smelled roasted meat and hot bread. Sitting up, he drew himself as far back into the shadows as the chain would let him go.

Up there the people crowded to the tables and sat down. He saw a man in a long blue coat come in, surrounded by people who never took their eyes off him, and thought, That is the King. He was cold, and his empty stomach hurt. In the door two men rolled a great cask, which the others saw, and greeted with a roar and a clapping of hands. They heaved the cask up onto the nearest table and people gathered around it. Then suddenly through the milling crowd the redheaded man with the hole in his mouth was striding down the hall toward Corban.

Corban licked his lips. The redheaded man squatted down and undid the shackle. A scrawny yellow-haired boy had come along with him, and stood watching. The Viking straightened.

"Come, Irish."

Corban followed him up the hall and into the light, the delicious aromas of roast meat, the stares of these men. On either side they lined the opposite edges of the tables, chunks of meat in their fingers, or passing a cup. They watched him, rows of men in leather jackets, their hair braided and clasped with gold. He went straight ahead, up between the tables, toward the High Seat, where the King sat.

Who was not the man in the blue coat. That man sat at that front table, but on the King's right hand. In the High Seat was a great fat man, his tawny beard hanging down over a red shirt stitched with gleaming gold. In front of him on the table was a litter of gnawed bones, and fresh meat juice stained the front of his fine red shirt where it bulged over his belly. He sat slumped in the High Seat, one foot up on the edge of the table, his arm hung over the side of the chair; it was as if he disdained everything, even being King of Jorvik.

The redhead was speaking to him, gesturing with both hands. He spoke so fast and mush-mouthed that Corban could not understand what he said. In the High Seat next to the King, a woman stirred around, looking to see what was happening, and let her gaze fall on Corban.

Corban met her eyes; a shock passed through him. Her look vas hard and direct as a man's, and more, as if she saw down into him. She was beautiful, younger than the King, with hair brighter than the gold in his shirt. Around her neck hung a collar set with pale purple stones, and as she looked at Corban she touched her fingers to the stones. Her gaze held his a moment but she did not smile, or nod, or speak, but searched him, and then dropped him, uninterested.

The redhead said, "The King says who you are."

Corban guessed at what this meant; he spoke his name again, feeling as if he climbed a slippery hill. "I am from Ireland. I know no Kenneth. I am not Scot."

The King grunted at him, and turned to the Viking and said something about the money. Corban understood him much better than the redhead. Leaning across the table, the Viking gave him two silver pennies. Abruptly the woman bent forward, and spoke, pointing one long forefinger at Corban, demanding to see his cloak.

The redhead took hold of his cloak. Corban fisted his hands in the cloth, unwilling to lose this too. The Viking gave him a narrow grin. "Give or not," he said; his hand went to the sword hanging by his thigh, and Corban slowly lowered his hands, feeling cold, and shed the cloak. The redhead passed it over the table to the woman. The fat King twisted his head to look at her, and she bundled the cloth in her hands, put her face against it, and then tossed it down onto the table.

Her voice high and clear and indifferent, she said, "He is nothing. Nobody." She sank back into the High Seat, her eyes half-closing. Corban reached for the cloak. The redheaded man slammed down his hand and pinned it against the table, and the King spoke.

Corban understood all of it, even before the redhead's translation. "Queen Gunnhild makes you innocent, but the King says maybe you hang anyway."

"No," Corban said. His belly gave a sickening lurch. His hand was trapped still under the Viking's. "Why?"

The fat King watched him with a glint in his pale eyes. He drew some little amusement from this, Corban saw, like a bite of something sweet. They would kill him to pass the time between servings of the meat. The Queen was looking off, her chin on her fist, caring nothing anymore, innocent or not. The redheaded man

"You poor for money—how you get money except steal?"
"No," Corban said.

"So thief," the redhead said. "So hang." In the High Seat the
ng smiled, pleased.

"No," Corban said. "I got the money in Ireland, it belongs to
e. I got it fairly." A name swam up into his mind, and he caught
it. "I got it from Einar Ship-Farmann."

That reached them. The Viking lifted his hand, and stepped
ack. The King's eyes widened, and his smile vanished, his lips
drawing together thoughtfully; he jerked his head around to look
down to his right. There the man in the blue coat was turning
around, his eyes sharp, paying attention to this for the first time.
He gave the King a single intent look and sat back, his hands before
him on the table, his gaze on Corban.

Corban straightened; quickly he gathered up his cloak. The
redheaded man said to him, "You are Einar's man? Why you only
ever said this now?"

"I'm nobody's man. I did something for Einar in Dublin and
he gave me the money."

The King waved his fingers at him, and said, "Tell him he can
go free. As a favor to my friend Arinbjorn, here, who is Einar's
friend." He reached for his cup again. The redhead said, "The King
says go. Since you Einar's man."

The man in the blue coat snorted, and looked away. Corban
stepped back, his chest swelling, as if until now he had been locked
in tight iron bands. The itch to be out of this place was like a rash
on his skin. He said, "May I have my money, then?"

The redhead gave a roar of laughter, and the King also, not
waiting for the dansker of it; Corban had suspected he spoke Irish.
The redhead said, "I think you pay King Eric new tax, two pence,
no hang tax." He laughed again, glancing at the King.

"Well, then," Corban said, "I should get not hung twice, since
I gave you four pence." He bowed to the King, and to the woman
in the High Seat with him, and turned and went fast away down
the hall.

Behind him the King's voice rose in a yell. "Sweyn! Where's
the rest of my money?" Corban strode quickly out the door.

It was full night now. He walked down the path across the lip of the embankment, above the dark cavern of the river, and turned uphill on the street. The church's steeple showed dim and dark against the night sky. He was tired; he had eaten nothing all day, and his legs dragged. Grod was nowhere around the church, not inside, where some people slept on the floor at the back and other people prayed by the light of candles in the front, and nowhere around it. He drank long from a fountain, just down the street, and came back.

He was too tired to look any more. He had escaped being hanged but he felt halfway dead anyway. The church at least was warmer than the street, and he wrapped himself up in his cloak and lay down in the company at the back. To the murmuring of other people's prayers he passed into a fitful sleep.

CHAPTER SEVEN

Coming awake, Grod opened his eyes and looked quickly around. He was lying in the back of a hut, under the slope of the tilted wall. A dim light came in through the chimney hole in the roof; day was breaking. He was warmly wrapped in a tattered cloak and felt no need to stir. Somewhere just beyond his head a chicken was clucking. As the light grew stronger the room around him began to appear: the pile of jugs by the stone ring of the hearth, the thatchy inside of the overarching roof, dripping spider webs. His belly rumbled with hunger. In the middle of the hut, under the peak of the roof, a girl with a mass of wild curly yellow hair was sitting on the floor stuffing straw into a shoe.

Her voice rang out. "I will have to go far with the goats today, there is no browse at all between here and Highcross."

From the other side of the hut the potter woman Benna came, small and slight, leading an old man along. "If it looks like snow, stay close." The old man walked stooped down, plodding, one hand out before him, the other in the girl's hand; Grod saw that he was blind. Benna led him tenderly to the door and out.

"I have to find browse for my goats," the wild-haired girl Gifu said. She put the shoe on and laced it.

Arre came in the door, carrying firewood. Grod had not seen her in the light before and recognized her first by her smile. Her dark-red hair flew loose around her shoulders; she was taller than Benna. She wore a long apron, dirty where she had knelt on it in the mud. "We can peel bark for the goats. It's going to snow." She dumped the wood down and knelt to feed the fire.

Somewhere off in the distance a bell tolled. At once the two girls straightened up on their knees, and put their hands together in prayer. Grod looked from one to the other. Arre squeezed her eyes shut, lifting her smiling face up, deep in her prayer, but Gifu barely nodded her head down, and then peeked around her hands, saw her sister gave her no heed, and went back to putting on her shoe.

In the open door came Benna, with the old man by the hand, and brought him to the fire and sat him down. She hung a blanket around his shoulders; he shrugged it off again at once, impatient.

Arre crossed herself and turned again to the fire. She said to Gifu, "Let the goats starve a day, if it's going to snow."

"I can help," Grod said, eagerly. He sat up in the wrapping of the cloak.

Gifu gave him a quick, unfocussed look, seeing him without seeing him. She turned back to Arre. "Who is that?"

"He helped Benna, last night, with the pots. We let him come in to sleep for the night."

Grod said, "I can help find food for the goats."

Benna lifted her head and glared at him. Covering her hand with the hem of her skirt, she took a little crock from the fire, popped the lid off, and wrapped the crock in a cloth and put it into the old man's hands. Into his ear she shouted, as if he were miles away, "Gruel, Papa! Eat!"

Arre reached into a pocket of her apron and produced a lump of cheese, wrapped in cloth. Grod could smell the cheese, and his hunger drove like a sharp knife through his belly; but they did not call him in. Arre broke the lump in half, and gave half to Gifu.

"I wish there were some bread." Gifu bit off a great chunk of the cheese.

Grod wanted to lie down again and go back to sleep. They were feeding a useless old man and ignoring him, who could work, and was starving. He watched the old man slurp down the gruel, his thick hands wrapped around the crock and his dead moist eyes staring at nothing. Grod wanted to be one of them, in their company, even as much as he wanted food, but they shut him out, their backs to him, their eyes elsewhere, their voices pitched away from him.

He had to get moving. He thrust himself up out of the old rag he was wrapped in and stumbled out the door.

A cold wind blew into his face and he shivered. It had snowed a little during the night, turning the ground thinly white; against the snow the leafless trees around him stood out dark and rough. The peaked hut stood in their shelter, only a few steps above the riverbank. There were branches heaped around it, to keep in the warmth of the fire, so that the hut looked like a great nest. Off to one side of it stood a rough lean-to of poles and woven withy, with a blackened brickwork oven beside it: the potter woman's workshop.

Half a dozen brown and white goats nosed around under the trees, crunching the dead leaves under their hoofs, and as he stood there considering it all, the girl Gifu came out and started away. She gave a high call, and the goats bunched together and skittered after her, their tails up. Grod went behind a tree and made water.

Uncertainly he went back to the hut, where Arre was sweeping the floor with a handful of twigs. She sang as she worked, her voice high and strong. The old man dozed by the fire. Benna brushed past Grod out the door, into the watery sunlight.

He said, "I'll help. I'll bring wood."

Benna shook her head. She was wiping her hands on her skirts. Between her teeth, she said, "You don't understand. We have nothing. It doesn't matter how much you can do for us, we can do nothing for you." She turned and went off, toward the workshop.

Grod still stood at the threshold of the hut; just beyond it, Arre straightened, hung the broom of twigs on the sloping wall, and took a heavy cloak down. "I will walk with you over to the river, Grod," she said.

Defeated, he let her shoo him along ahead of him. The sun was rising, stronger now, glinting on the patches of snow; the tracks of the goats led up like ribbons of shadow across the white meadow, where already the snow was shrinking away into the air. Arre walked along beside him, smiling, her cloak slung around her. Her long loose hair showed russet in the sunlight. Some way up the river were other huts, larger and better made than Arre's; the smoke from their chimney holes blew out in a flat fuzz over the river.

She said, "Don't be wrong about Benna. She has a great heart, but she's the oldest, she has us all on her back now."

They had come to the top of the riverbank; a notched log tipped up against it led down to the shore. He remembered getting the pots up this ladder the night before, and wondered again how the girls ever did it by themselves. The handcart still stood down on the shore where they had left it. He looked across at the city, climbing above the far side of the river in layers of wood and thatch, the church steeple overtopping it all.

"Euan!" Arre cried. She flung her arm up, waving.

On the far bank, a tall thin boy was walking across the pebble shoal toward the stepping stones. He lifted one hand to answer her. Arre said, "Euan is my friend."

Grod gathered himself to go back into the city. He said, "Thank you for letting me stay here."

She smiled at him. Her friend was walking across the river on the stepping stones. She took the lump of cheese from her apron pocket, unwrapped it, and broke it in half. She held one half out to Grod.

"Thank you." He seized it, his mouth watering. "You are good, Arre."

She laughed. She turned back to watch the long lean boy Euan climb up the riverbank. Euan gave Grod a suspicious look, got Arre by the arm, and drew her away. Grod heard her sunny laughter rise. He went down the log ladder to the shore of the river and crossed into the city.

⟜⟝

At daybreak Corban woke and realized Grod had not come. More even than the cold, that brought him up out of his slumber.

He went out of the church, found the fountain again, and washed his face and hands in the icy water. The church bell began to ring, right overhead, and he stood with the bell's brassy shivers passing over him and wondered what he should do now.

Look for Mav. He collected himself, and went away down a sloping road, toward the river in the distance.

The day was breaking, fine and cold. As he went by, a few of the shops along the street were opening, a candlemaker already in his waxy apron pushing out the shutter on his stall, two old women hanging sprigs of herbs from a string. He smelled bread baking, somewhere in the general reek of the place, and ached for food.

On his right now loomed the long thatched rooftree of the King's Hall, and he went clear of that. In the cold clear air, his steps boomed on the wooden planking of the street. Ahead in the middle of the street a pack of dogs was fighting over something, and he walked wide of them also. He could hear the high whiny voice of a peddlar calling.

In the first sunlight the town seemed caught in a drowse, only coming awake. On the thatch of a big house he passed, a rooster with a high-arched russet tail cocked its head back, gaped its pointed beak and ripped out a raucous blast of noise. The road dropped away before him, leading down toward the river, broad and brown, and the ships drawn up on this side, where a gravel bar made a broad shore below the bank.

His heart started to pound. Those ships—those ships—he stopped still, his hands opening and closing into fists at his sides, and his throat dry. He had seen them before, he had seen them drawn up on the beach of his burning farm.

He shook himself, and blinked his eyes clear of the smoke of memory. Not the same ships. They just all looked the same. He went on down the road, willing his heart to slow. Nothing he could do now anyway. He closed his mind over it and pushed it down, out of the reach of memory, and went in along the pebbly river bar, past the high deep-breasted prows of the ships, all carved with twining serpents. Ahead he saw a string of pens made of withies.

His steps quickened. But they were empty.

He drew near them, square black-willow shapes laid against the water's edge. Through the screen of the withies he could see that there was nothing in any of them. Yet he felt the people here as if he could see them, cold and wretched, huddling here in the wind. He swallowed; the world bulged suddenly around him, ominously full.

He went up to the side of the nearest pen, and laid his hand on it. There had to be some way on from here, but he could not see it.

"Corban!"

He wheeled around. Down the shore Grod was running toward him, his face hung with the broadest smile Corban had ever seen on his face.

"Well," Corban said, relieved. "Well, there you are."

The old man slowed and walked up to him, strutting a little. "Got yourself lost, didn't you? Got into trouble. At least I managed to find you again." He reached out and twitched Corban's cloak. "I saw this."

Corban wrapped one arm around him. "I'm glad you did. Do you have anything to eat?" Grod smelled vaguely of cheese.

But he shook his head. "No. I don't. But I have—" he took the coins out of his shirt "—I still have the money."

"The King took mine," Corban said. He turned, and looked back at the slave pens. "She was here. She must have been."

Grod's forehead crinkled. They stood on the river shore, below the high embankment where the King's hall stood; the path led away back into the city, but Grod turned the other way. "Come along," he said, and went back past the ships on the beach, toward the foot of the bank, where a little fire burned, and some men sat around it cooking fish.

Corban slowed his steps, recognizing more of Eric's men. But Grod went straight up to them, and talked for a while in dansker: asking about the last people in the slave pens.

Corban looked away. He felt as if she stood by him, unseen, cool in the air against his cheek.

Grod came back to him. "Those people went to Hedeby, they said."

"Hedeby. Where is that?"

"On the far shore of the sea. In the Danes' march. The whole load was bought at once, they said."

Corban stood where he was, too heavy to move on. Mav was out there, somewhere, but whenever he thought he might catch up with her, she turned out to be farther away than before. It was a curse, part of his father's curse. There was no use in even trying.

Grod said, "Come along. I'm willing to break my usual custom now, for your sake, and buy some bread."

In a flash of anger, Corban remembered how he had lost his money. "I could buy my own, but for the King."

"You're lucky he didn't take your head," Grod said. He shook his finger at Corban, and with one hand on his arm got him turned and walking back toward the city. "Did you do as I told you? You must have made a mistake. I had no trouble at all. You big fool, you can't do anything without me, can you?"

Corban said, "I can't do anything." He trudged on up the street, his eyes on the ground. Grod led him through crowds of people, but he paid no attention; he felt as if the road had disappeared before him and left him standing at the end of the world. He thought of Mav, and of what must have happened to her, what happened to her yet, and his mind went blank.

He could not save her. He could only plod along one step at a time, going nowhere.

He stood at the back of a little crowd while Grod took money to buy them bread. The smell of the bread was maddening and he kept swallowing the water in his mouth and wishing Grod would get back. He lifted his eyes and saw only a few feet away the red-bearded gape-mouthed Viking from the King's hall, staring back at him.

"Looking poor, Irish," the Viking said, and put a hand on him and shoved him.

Corban stood. The terrible gloom evaporated from his mind and left him pure with anger. When the Viking shoved he leaned against it, and when the Viking drew back, startled, and cocked his arm back and went to push him harder Corban caught his arm by the wrist and held him.

The Viking's eyes blazed. He jerked at Corban's grip on him, and Corban tightened his hold; he put all the strength of rowing across the sea from Ireland into holding the Viking's arm exactly where it was. Their eyes met.

The Viking smiled. He stepped backward, relaxing his arm in Corban's grip, and Corban let him go. The redbeard said, "What's your name again?"

"Corban," he said. "Corban Loosestrife."

Grod had come up to them. Wide-eyed, he stood watching as the Viking put his hand out and Corban clasped it. The Viking said, "My name is Sweyn—" and then some muddle of sounds Corban did not know. He turned abruptly and went off into the crowd.

Grod had three loaves of bread in his arms, flat wheels studded with onion and sprinkled with cheese. Corban took one and broke off a chunk and stuffed it into his mouth. The taste of the bread made him almost light-headed. Breaking off another piece, he looked around for a fountain.

"What did he say? His name." He turned back to Grod, walking beside him. "Why did you get so much? Who is that other loaf for?"

"Oh, someone," Grod said. "He said his name is Sweyn Eelmouth."

Corban laughed. "He has a very lamprey look to him."

"How do you know him?" They were walking downhill, toward the street where Corban knew there was a fountain; he swallowed bread in great chunks.

"He took me to the King. Yesterday, when they stopped me at the gate."

"Don't trust him," Grod said. "All these—" He straightened, looking up ahead. "There she is. Come on."

"Who?" Corban followed him down the street; they turned into a steep, wood-planked lane leading down to a big oak tree.

There the street widened out, and opposite the tree on the corner sat a woman in a welter of clay pots. Grod strutted down toward her. Corban went along after, more slowly. The woman sat with her head down, doing something before her with her hands. When Grod pranced up before her she startled, and flung her head up.

Grod danced like a little cockerel before her; she was only a girl, really, looking older for the way her dark hair was drawn back and covered under a white cloth. Hastily she was bundling something away under her apron, as Grod told her that now he could pay her back, and she would be glad now she had helped him— see how her humble gift had been returned to her manyfold. He held out the third loaf of bread to her, with a flourish of his hand, as if he gave her the crown of the world. Corban could understand almost everything he said, words and gesture.

The girl seemed not so grateful and impressed as Grod deemed she should. She smiled at him, and with a murmur of thanks she took the bread, but Corban could see she believed Grod was only giving her something due, and that she thought him funny, her eyes narrow in amusement, and her smile a little sideways.

Then she saw Corban, and the smile curved into a frown. "What?" she said. "Now there are two of you. I knew this would happen."

Corban backed up, raising his hands; he said, "Not me." She

gave him another hard look, pushing him off, and then turned to talk to someone who was looking over her collection of pots. Corban started away up the street again, and Grod trotted beside him.

"You would like the sister much better. She has two sisters, and one is an angel."

"I doubt that matters since she doesn't much like either of us."

"The sister, I tell you, is much better."

Corban was thinking of the girl's little crooked smile. He wondered where they were walking to so fast. They had nothing to do, nowhere to go but back to the church. There Grod promptly got into a gambling game in the shade of the church wall. Corban loafed around in the square, listening to people talk around him; he understood more and more of the words. Late in the day a wagon rolled by and the man on the seat looked around, saw Corban and beckoned. He went after, and with a few words got to work unloading the wagon into a nearby house. For this he got a bit of a silver penny.

He got more bread with it, and he and Grod slept once more in the back of the church, bundled together against the seeping cold. It snowed again during the night. When they woke there was nothing to eat. Grod went grumpily away toward his gambling; he did not offer to use any more of his silver money, and Corban guessed he had lost it in the game. Alone, Corban went over to the fountain to drink his belly full.

As he stood there, wondering how to find more work, something thumped him on the back. He wheeled. Before him stood Sweyn Eelmouth, holding out a jug.

"Here, Irish. Only poor drink water."

Corban took the jug and tipped it to his mouth; it was ale, so thick it left a rim of foam on his upper lip. He gave a groan of pleasure, and his head whirled, airy as a cloud. When his mind settled, he was walking along with Eelmouth and his men down the street past the church. Reluctantly, he gave the empty cup to the redheaded Viking, who turned as he strode along to talk to him.

"Make money. Two pence."

"What?" Corban said, startled. The ale softened his head, too muzzy for Eelmouth's Irish.

"You make me money. Two pence." Eelmouth spoke as distinctly as he could, blowing spume through the gaping hole in his face with each word. He held up his two fingers. "Because of King take two." He laughed, an erupting maw.

Corban tried using his new learned dansker. "I have no money."

"Aha." Eelmouth eyed him a moment. They turned into the street that smelled deliciously of bread, and he stopped. The other two men drifted up toward them; one had gotten an apple somewhere and was eating it. Eelmouth led them all into the first bakery.

Here they filled the whole shop; the baker came out and shouted at Eelmouth, his face red, as the Viking picked up a loaf from the shelf. With the baker still yelling, they all filed back out to the street, and Eelmouth tore pieces off the loaf and gave some to everybody.

Corban's mouth watered. He didn't want to take this bread, but his stomach growled. He remembered when he had stolen whatever he could. Eelmouth shoved a big piece of the bread into his hand; it was still warm, and he began to eat. Eelmouth gave him a sideways look, and they went off down the street again.

When they had gone down toward the river, Sweyn turned and called Corban to him. He said, "No one steals here except us." He spat out the words, and laughed again through his hollow face. "You owe me two pence, hah? What is this, you have no money? And now you speak dansker."

"You took all my money," Corban said.

"Einar Ship-Farmann gave you money—what did he tell you to do, here in Jorvik?"

"What?" Corban asked, startled. "Nothing."

"Hnnnh."

Eelmouth veered off suddenly again into another bakery. They had swung back up around the northern edge of the city. Corban hung back, not so hungry now. The others walked in after their leader and came out carrying more bread. Corban looked away down the street; there on the corner, across from the big oak tree, sat the woman with her pots.

She was bent over something in her hands. He frowned; he had seen her do this before, and he wondered what she did. He remembered that crooked little secret smile.

Eelmouth brushed by him, going up the street. "You say you are not Einar's man—why not then come up to Eric's Hall? We have meat there every night, and good ale."

Corban remembered that hall, where they had feasted, and he had gone hungry; he said nothing.

Eelmouth said, "Are you Christian?"

"No," Corban said, without thinking.

But it was the right answer; Eelmouth twisted toward him, smiling wide in his dripping beard. "That's good. I thought so. I am Thor's man also. It was my father's way. Good enough for me."

Corban kept silent; that monk, all across England, had thought there were only two ways also, and he saw some refuge in that. Now they stopped in the street again and Eelmouth went into a brewery, and this time the other men stood around outside in the street with Corban. One squinted up at the sky.

"More snow. We'll be glad for the fire this night."

"You take the fire," the other said. "I'll take Hilda." They both laughed; they glanced at Corban, and he laughed also, dutifully, and they nodded happily at him.

"She's a good woman," one said, and drove his elbow against the other's ribs. "Good for what a woman's good for. Right, Gorm?"

Eelmouth came out, carrying the wooden drinking cup level in one hand, full of ale. They stood there and passed it back and forth; Corban took a full drink of it. When it was empty Eelmouth went back into the brewery and brought it out again with ale to the brim.

The ale swelled up inside Corban's head, fluffy and warm; he felt a great rush of gratitude for Eelmouth, who was feeding him so well. Connected to it a little pointed jab of fear that this might end. When they had all drunk, and the cup was empty again, Eelmouth sent the other two men off to harry the gamblers alongside the church wall. Corban stirred, uneasy, thinking of Grod. Eelmouth led him off across the plaza past the church.

"So, we're fools, you think? We'll believe Einar gives you money, but you aren't his man."

"It's true," Corban said. "I have no more money anyway."

"Well, you still owe me two pence, which I would have had, if you hadn't yapped to the King."

Corban laughed, more at the strange word than any wit of Eelmouth's. They had gone down past the church, and the street to the river opened on their left; on the right was a twisting lane, overhung with oaks, so that even now, with the sun high, the way was dark. A scatter of low buildings and withy fences lay on either side. Eelmouth glanced down the lane way, and turned to go toward the river.

In the street ahead of them was a large wagon, drawn up before the same house where Corban had unloaded a wagon two days before. He saw something blue in the doorway, and looked close; it was the man in the blue coat, whom he had seen at the King's right hand.

"Who is that?"

Eelmouth gave a look that way. "Oh, that's the Lord Arinbjorn." He frowned at Corban. "Another friend of Einar's."

"Who is he?"

"A buyer and seller. He takes what Eric takes, and turns it into gold, so he is the King's best friend, most of the time."

"A farmann," Corban said, understanding. "A ship-farmann—"

"Is a trader over the sea," said Eelmouth. "How do you know Einar, anyway? An Irishman like—"

Behind them a yell went up. Eelmouth wheeled around. The yell rang out again, a screech, sounding down the shadowy lane up the hill from them, and Eelmouth strode that way, holding onto his sheathed sword to keep it from getting between his legs.

Corban followed him; ahead, several people were now shouting and screaming, and a horse neighed, a frantic frightened blast. Eelmouth broke into a run across the lane to a closed gate and pulled it open.

Corban followed him into a horseyard. Even as he stepped inside, a loose horse galloped up toward the open gate and he wheeled around and slammed it shut. When he leapt forward again the horse was shearing off, whinnying, and past the flogging mane and high-flung tail Corban saw a man in the middle of the yard laying around him with a quarterstaff.

Half a dozen other men were shrinking back toward the fences on either side, out of the way of the quarterstaff and the rampaging horse. The loose horse skidded to a halt against one wall of the yard and wheeled and galloped back across it, neighing; the man with the quarterstaff dodged away and a man sprawled on the ground rolled over and struggled to his hands and knees. The horse, bolting past him, sprayed him with sand and pebbles. The man with the quarterstaff reared back, the long stick cocked in both hands, and rushed at the man on the ground.

With a yell Eelmouth leapt forward, in between the man with the staff and the man on the ground. He caught the staff as it came down, wrenching it half out of the other man's grip. The two men wrestled over the stick. Corban saw at once what to do; he bounded around behind the other man, and jumped on his back and wrapped his arm around his neck. With Eelmouth leaning on him from the front, they bore him swiftly down to the ground.

Corban scrambled away and stood up, dust sifting down from the front of his shirt, his cloak straggling down around his knees. Eelmouth straightened, the staff in his hands.

"What is this about? Who started this?" He wheeled, looking behind him at the man he had defended, who was getting groggily up onto his feet. Somebody had caught the loose horse.

"He—" The groggy man staggered, blood dribbling down his chin. He thrust out his arm toward the other, who was sitting in the dust at Eelmouth's feet. "Sold me a lame horse."

"She was sound when she left here," said the man at Eelmouth's feet. He was panting. "You're the cheat, not me."

Eelmouth lifted his head, scanning the yard; there were other men standing around watching, but when the Viking's gaze fell on them, each one turned away, shaking his head. Corban could see they would give no honest answers. Eelmouth looked from the man at his feet to the other, swaying as he stood, his hands dangling; blood leaked steadily down from his hair.

"Take the horse and get out of here," Eelmouth said to him.

The man with the blood on his face twitched all over. His mouth twisted bitterly, and he looked down at the horse trader, who was getting up off the ground. "He cheated me!"

"You want me to bring you to the King?" Eelmouth said. "I'm saying take your horse and get out of here!" He cast a look at the restive horse. "She looks mettlesome enough to me."

"Too much for him," someone among the onlookers said, and there was a rumble of laughter. The bloody man lowered his eyes. His hands were trembling. Unsteadily he walked over toward the horse; in front of Eelmouth the horse trader, still slumped in the dust, scrubbed his hand over his face. In silence everybody watched the bloody man take the horse and lead it up to the gate and out. It did seem to favor its off foreleg. Corban folded his arms over his chest, frowning; he wondered how Eelmouth had known who was cheating.

When the gate shut Eelmouth turned to the horse trader, and thrust his hand out. "Two pence," he said.

The horse trader coughed, as if somebody had poked him in the belly. He stared at Eelmouth's hand. "Why?"

"Shall I bring you to the King?"

The horse trader's head rose an inch, and his gaze drifted away, as if he would see some alley of escape opening up before him. But his hand moved slowly to his belt and took out a purse. A moment later, Eelmouth was leading Corban out of the yard, two silver pennies in his hand.

They went back up to the main street, which led down toward the river. Corban said, after a while, "How did you know that the one man was the cheat?"

Eelmouth hooted at him. "I didn't. All I knew was, he didn't likely have any money, but Alfric there—Alfric's the horse trader—he would have two pence." He clapped Corban on the arm, grinning at him. "I told you, here nobody steals but us," he said. "One for you, one for me. That was good work, what you did, back there." He tossed the silver pennies into the air and caught them in his hand, watching Corban, grinning, making no move to give him any. "So you only owe me one pence now, you see?"

Corban nodded at him. The muzziness of the ale had worn off. "I see, yes."

"Good," Eelmouth said, and started off back down the street toward the river.

Mav sat in the closed-in bed in the front wall of the Lady's hall, wrapped in a blanket, and sang. When she sang such colors and sounds rose up around her that she was dizzy with them and hardly knew where she was. She saw Corban, walking, winged in blue and red, and then she saw Corban standing before a blaze of purple light, and voices sounded in her ears and she sang them out, true and clear, like veins of quartz in dull, dark rock.

Out in the hall, at their tasks and chores, the other people grumbled; they muttered that she was too loud, they could not sleep, or think. Their looms clattered, their jugs and pots rattled together, ringing like bells, and she gathered them into her singing, with everything else.

The Lady sat with her and listened, held her hand, and listened to all of it.

When the song swelled in her she could not keep still; it fountained from her in sparkling streams of music, but sometimes Mav did not sing. She sat quietly, trying to struggle some order out of this, trying to understand. All the while her mind overflowed with knowing. She felt as if the hinges of her mind had loosened, and everything went flowing together, in and out and top to bottom. She could not move, then, it all tugged her in every different direction.

The Lady sat with her in the morning, every day. They ate bread and drank mead and the Lady gave her clothes to wear, stroked her head, kissed her forehead. At first Mav wanted to lay herself on the other woman's breast, but within her the baby grew that the Lady had wanted to kill. She clasped her arms over her middle, and sat up straight, struggling to stack all the pieces of her mind together again.

The Lady was there, was real, constant; who always smiled, who fed her, sheltered her, kept her from any harm. Who desired something back for those kindnesses, something Mav did not understand.

Once the Lady bent and tried to kiss her lips, but Mav saw her mouth open and imagined herself, like a little wisp of breath, drawn in, and turned her face away.

"Have you no name?"

The Lady gave a chuckle, pouring the thick foamy mead. "My

name is legion, for we are many. Why do you love this baby, who
came from such pain?"

"Such pain," Mav said. Under her clasping arms the baby
stirred, beloved.

She saw: the baby. Herself around the baby. The house around
herself. The city of Hedeby around the house. The sea around the
city, the sea at the center of the world. Rays of light flickered
around the corners of her memory and music swelled up within her
and poured out her mouth in a high wild lust.

Somewhere else the Lady sat, before her the cold King Bluetooth. He wore a gold fillet on his hair, and gold rings on his arms.

He said, "Harald Fairhair brought Norway under him, and that
I can abide, because easier to overthrow one king than many. But
the wrong son has taken his crown, and now that has led to all this
trouble."

"Harald had too many sons," said the Lady. "Which I think
you could take warning from. Bloodaxe is unlucky, and a fool
besides. I never saw why Harald chose him over all the rest of
them, save the rest were such a shabby lot. All but Hakon, and
now Hakon has proven it."

She chuckled. The King before her, another Harald, sucked at
his teeth and shook his head.

"A man's sons are usually his undoing. Hakon is lucky, and
no fool."

"True enough. Mark me, all this turns in your favor, ultimately,
if you will lie in wait. Even Hakon will not hold Norway, the men
of the Trond will break him over the White Christ. And better him
than you. When they have bled each other dry, then you will be
there to pick up the crown."

"Yes, yes, so you tell me, but I thought it better done when
Eric was King of Norway."

"Pagh. Eric is very useful where he is, if we can but influence
him in the right ways."

"You and your influences. This girl, here, this is another of
your tricks, isn't she? And where have you gotten with her?"

"Where the brother walks, she sees. Through her I have seen
Eric in his high seat, with Gunnhild ruling him, as always."

Bluetooth gave a harsh humorless bark of a laugh. "Is this supposed to impress me? This everybody knows."

"Ah, you are a stone. You see only what is in front of you."

"What else is there to see?"

"And so it is. I shall have now what you promised me, when you asked me to do this."

"Asked you! I never asked you anything, you crone." The King bent into the glow of the lamp. His voice kinked. "What did I ask you?" In his long smile, one dogtooth shone dark.

"Why," the Lady said, with delicate surprise, "to find you a spy in Jorvik, to watch out what Eric does."

"I see no spy. I will pay you nothing, you are an old fraud, as they say all over my kingdom. I am a fool for coming here and I am leaving." He drew back suddenly, out of the light, and stamped away.

The Lady smiled. She leaned over her lamp, cupping the light in her hands. "Yet Gunnhild is worse than you, King, she does not even see what is in front of her. He stood there before her and she let him go. When you come back, King, the price will be higher."

Mav knew this, as she knew all things, slipping in and across her mind in all directions, streaming with colors and sounds. The Lady was seeing what she saw, and to some end, some long purpose beyond even the cold hunger of the King Bluetooth. Sometimes Mav thought she put on the Lady's knowledge, when she sang; sometimes she saw it all blindingly clear, for a flash of time, so plain she could have named it—and then event and name were gone again into the entwining streams of light and shapes all around her.

Sometimes all this failed. Sometimes all around her was only a featureless grey emptiness, and she wandered there alone and freezing, too sad even to cry.

Always, in one layer of her mind, she saw her brother. But now he was not coming after her, he was sitting, doing nothing.

CHAPTER EIGHT

All the rest of the day, trailing after Eelmouth, Corban collected food, carrying it along in a lap of his cloak, so that when he met Grod he would have something for the old man to eat. But when he went to the church Grod was not there and he did not come. Corban finally ate it all himself, and sat in the back of the church, not even waiting any more.

He was as alone as a star in the night. No one knew him, no one wanted him. He had lost Mav—even Grod had abandoned him. He remembered what the woman in the High Seat had said, "He is nothing. Nobody." His heart had leapt then to hear it, thinking it freed him from the King, but now he thought she had seen him true, and condemned him.

He dozed off, and finally morning came. He went out of the church and washed at the fountain, and went down through the town on the steep little street toward the oak tree.

On the opposite corner the potter woman was just setting her pots out, taking them from an old box-cart, and beside the cart stood another girl, and Grod. Corban stopped, angry, and Grod saw him.

The old man called out, and waved, cheery as a bawd, and came toward him; Corban stood where he was. Grod gave him a sharp look. "I told you to come there," he said. "What, you slept in the church again?"

Corban grunted at him. "I waited for you. These people are poor—why take from them?"

"I help," Grod said, looking indignant. "Their father is old and feeble. They have no man to do heavy work." He started back toward the pottery. "Come meet Arre, you'll like her."

Arre was laughing; Corban liked her already, with the width of the street between them. Only half-willing, he followed the old man back to the corner, to the company of these other people. The black-haired woman sat in the midst of the pots, looking as if she wished them all away. Grod told Arre Corban's name, and the girl smiled at him; she was very pretty, sweet and open as a running brook.

But she was leaving. She said, "I must go back to Papa. Benna, I will come in with the nones bell." She waved to Grod and rolled off with the empty cart, her long loose russet hair straggling over her shoulders, her strong round arms pushing the cart along.

Grod said, "Well, I'm going to church." He gave Corban a wide, happy stare. "Come with me?"

Corban snorted. He had no interest in Eelmouth catching him among the gamblers. He glanced at the black-haired woman among her pots, looking steadily away; he knew she wanted them gone.

"Good-bye," he said to Grod. "I'll see you later." Grod went off up the street, his step jaunty; clearly these poor girls were feeding him also.

"I'm sorry about him," Corban said, to the black-haired woman.

She said, "He's an old beggar and a stealer, too. I knew it when I saw him first." She glanced up at him, her head tipped sideways, a look crooked like her smile. "Thank God you have not tried to come in along with him. You look as if you eat too much."

He sat down on his heels next to her. "I can feed myself. I could have fed him last night, if he had come."

"Arre will take in anything helpless. She brings in baby birds and nests of orphaned field mice." She got up; a farm wife in a tattered shawl was poking around in the front row of her pots, and she went to talk to her. Corban sat where he was. He did not want to be alone any more. He picked up one of the pots, smooth and heavy in his hand, wondering if she had made it. Maybe that was what she did with her hands, when she thought nobody was watching. He put the pot down; under the straw mat where she sat was a shard of a broken dish. There was something on the inside of it. He picked it up and turned it over, and there was a tree on it.

He sat there and stared at it, amazed. The tree was made of a few dark lines across the clay surface, yet all the tree was there, somehow, even what the lines left out. He lifted his gaze toward Benna, who was talking to the woman in the shawl, and put the bit of clay down carefully where he had found it.

She came back, carrying a bowl full of dry beans, which she

stowed in a leather bag. His gaze went to her hands, her thin strong fingers, stained with dark color. He felt suddenly skin to skin with her, as if he had looked into her soul.

She said, "What are you staring at?"

"Nothing." He got up suddenly, knowing she wanted him gone. Looking down at her, he said, "May I come back, sometime?"

She gave a little, startled laugh, blinked, glanced away. "I suppose so. Yes." Now she looked at him again, straight. "Sometime."

"Good," he said, and went away to find Eelmouth, and join his foraging.

He did not find the Viking in his first cast around the town, and tired of looking for him. He took his sling and went out the gate and walked north, into the narrowing valley along the river.

The path followed the western bank of the river, past fields patchy with melting snow and the sodden, crumpled hummocks of dead weeds, rumpled in long lines from the plow. Through the snow and the moldering old growth new grass shot up here and there in startling green lances. The path was busy. For a long while, as he walked, he put his feet down on the prints of others, and he stood aside to let a cart pass, and went around slower people who appeared ahead of him. He saw men hauling wood in out of the trees along the river's winding course. On the high riverbank across the way a man sat hunched over a pole tilted out over the slow-flowing water. A hunter's liver-spotted dog came over to Corban and sniffed at him, trailing along with him a while until a shout from behind called it back.

The sky was blue when he left Jorvik behind but turned steadily grey, although he doubted it would snow before nightfall. He strayed away from the river, following the land steadily higher, and came at last to a broad snowy slope where nothing had run ahead of him but birds. Taking out his sling, and five or six stones he had been collecting, he went out quietly over the snowfield.

The wind was rising, and he moved until he was walking straight into it. His cheeks stiffened with the cold. The sky was like beaten metal. In his lungs the air was pure and heavy, like cold water. He was very hungry; he felt thinner for it, airy, open to the cold and the pure air and the wind, part of the winter.

He went on down the long slow bend of the land, seeing deer

tracks, very fresh, cutting across his course. A deer was too large
to take with a sling but later if he found someone to help him, he
could run these deer and get a lot of meat all at once. He cupped
one stone in his hand, already loaded, ready for whatever the snowy
land gave him. He loved the silence, the cold clear air in his lungs,
even the blankness of the snow. It seemed a blessing not to think.
The snow-covered grass gave springily under his feet and made no
sound.

Ahead of him a hummock of the grass exploded, and a piece
of it bounded away, a blaze of white through the grey air, each
long leap an impossible arc over the snow, and he whipped up his
arm and the sling spun open, whirled two times and fired. Halfway
through one long gliding arc the hare jerked upward, went rolling
head over heels through the snow, its head erupting a bloody blos-
som, a red spray across the snow. Corban ran toward it, caught it
still kicking, trying to get its feet under it to run, although the stone
had broken its head; one eyeball lay out on the snow, perfectly
round. He sank his hands into the hare's long thick fur, creamy
white and yellow, a few longer, pale brown hairs mixed in. The
body went limp under his hands.

If he had been home, he would have given the skin to Mav. If
he had a home. His mind teetered on the edge of some other, larger
thought he had no strength to consider.

He gutted the hare, and pulled out its heart and liver and ate
them, toothsome even raw, still hot on his tongue. In spite of the
winter there were little yellow bits of fat under the hare's skin and
he ate them too. He cast the rest of the innards into the snow. He
linked the two long hindlegs together, one foot through the other
ankle, and went off across the moor again.

As he went he watched for signs of ducks and geese, he noticed
the paths of the deer, and studied the curious tracks of birds different from the ones in Ireland. The cold bit his toes and fingertips
but he felt better, even though he was still very hungry. Out here
everything came down to a track in the snow, the feel of the wind,
and his skill with the sling, and all those things he understood. The
world shrank down to the cold and the snow and himself, walking
through it, moment by moment. He ambled slowly down toward a
river in the distance, and on a slope spooked a second hare, this

one brown and white, a darting fleck in front of him, which took two stones to kill. In the cold his hands moved like lumps and he had to force himself calm enough to fire the second stone, but he brought the hare down at last, and gutted it and ate of it and bound its hindlegs together, and took it back with the first.

By sundown he had worked his way back across the valley and down, on the other side of the river from Jorvik. He knew that the potter woman and her sisters lived on this bank, opposite the city, and he could see some little huts crowding there above the water. He went through a shabby little wood eaten down to nubs and dead leaves, a great bramble between him and the riverbank, a snarl of branches. It seemed like a midden, and now he saw the trickle of smoke coming up from it, and out from the edge of it came the girl Arre.

He stopped, his jaw dropping. This was their house, then, this wretched hovel, which his father would not have kept cows in. He stood rooted down, unwilling to go closer, and then Arre saw him.

She waved, with a flash of her smile; he had to go on forward, he had to meet her. He held up the hares to her, glad of something innocent to say.

"I brought you something—for Grod."

"Meat," she said, her eyes widening, and gave him the full blessing of an admiring look. "You are God-sent—we had nothing today but some nuts—come in, please." She swept out her hand, beckoning him on as if to a king's hall.

He stooped down to get in through the door. Ahead of him, Arre straightened up in a half-darkness, holding the hares up, and crying, "Look! We have food—God be thanked—and Grod's friend here—what is your name?"

"Corban," he said, blinking, half-blinded in the gloom, and smiling stupidly at people he could not see. The ripe stink of goat reached his nose, and smoke, and many people in a small space.

"Corban!" Grod cried, and came up out of the settling hazy gloom around him, reaching out to grip his hand. "You did come. I knew you would."

Corban looked around, his eyes more used now to the dim light. The hovel was a round dome, high enough in the middle, where he was standing, that he did not have to stoop his head. The underside of the dome was of laced willow branches, fuzzy with cobwebs. He was standing almost in the fire circle; Arre had taken the hares around to the other side of it, where a wide flat stone lay, and she knelt down and laid the hares on the stone and began to cut them up.

Off to his right, against the wall, was a pen of withies, stuffed with goats. An old man sat between them and the fire, a blanket draped around him. In the back of the room, quiet, her hands covering something in her lap, was Benna.

She was watching him; when he saw her, their eyes met, and they both looked quickly away. He lowered his gaze, his cheeks hot.

"You killed these?" Another girl, with wild wooly hair as pale as sunlight, had come up by his elbow. "How did you do that?"

"With his sling, Gifu," Grod said, strutting, his hands on his hips. "I told you he is a mighty hunter."

Corban grunted. "Yes, a great murderer of squirrels and hares." But the wild-haired girl gave him a long look.

"You must be good."

He said, "The one thing I am good at." He could not meet her eyes; he watched Arre neatly dividing up the hares.

"Is that it?" Gifu asked, pointing at his belt. She was bold as a boy, he saw; she looked nothing like Benna or Arre.

"Yes," he said, taking the sling from his belt. "Would you like to try it?"

The girl's blue eyes blazed. "Yes. Could I? Yes."

"Come outside."

He led her out to the evening air, sweeter and freer outside, easier to breathe. He had a few stones left and he slung them one at a time and knocked down branches from the dying trees in the meadow around them. "See that one—the crooked one, there?" He launched a stone that clipped it neatly in half.

"Let me try."

He showed her how to load the stone, how to whirl it, and to snap with her wrist when she loosed it, so that the stone hurtled spinning through the air. The cool clear evening settled over them. Yet he kept looking back to the hut, his eyes turning that way, his mind.

The girl Gifu fired off several stones, running off into the meadow to scrabble up new ones; she started off shooting wildly, but soon she got the knack of it. Arre came out the door.

"The meat is cooking."

"Wait—" Gifu was fitting another stone to the sling. "Wait—one more—"

"Bring it in when you're done," Corban said, and went back into the reeking warmth of the hut.

Benna was spitting chunks of hare and laying them across the fire, amd turning them as they cooked. Corban's belly rumbled. He went to sit by her, and said, "I can help you."

"Don't you think I can do it?" she said. She threaded the spit neatly through the hare's backstrap.

He said, "You do it better than I, but still, I want to help you." He turned the chunks of meat already cooking over the coals. The girl's long slim fingers, stained and deft, drew his eyes.

She said, quietly, "Thank you for bringing this."

"I owe it to you," he said. "For Grod."

She glanced at him, sideways, with her small crooked smile. Arre came, and Benna gave her some of the cooked meat; Grod was right behind her, his hand out, as always. When they had taken food away Benna said, "Will you not eat some, Corban? You brought us this meat." Her gaze followed her own hands, neatening up the bloody stone.

He reached for a bit of the hare. The other people close around them made him edgy; he wanted to talk to her, he wanted to ask her about the drawing of the tree he had found on the pot. She took some of the meat and chopped it and went over to the old man, woke him with a gentle hand on his shoulder, and sat down to feed him. Corban watched her through the corner of his eye. It angered him that they lived so low, these girls; he wondered why nobody in the city came to help them.

He thought of who would ward them, in the city, up in the King's Hall, and saw the other side of that, and maybe why she stayed here in this hovel; why she struggled to keep her younger sisters here.

He ate another piece of the meat. The girl Gifu came in with his sling, downcast.

"I can't do this."

"You need to do it more, is all," he said. He shifted, to make room for her. "Eat some of this." He moved backward a little more, which put him nearly to the rear wall of the hut, and he put his hand down on a broken bit of pottery.

"Ouch." He picked up the shard. Benna swung toward him, her eyes wide.

"No—Don't look—"

He lowered his eyes to the piece of clay in his hand and saw that on it she had drawn Arre's face. He let out a wordless sound, amazed. Benna sprang across the space between them and snatched it from him. She gave it a single quick, angry look, and wheeled, and smashed it down against the rock by the fire.

"Stop! Why did you do that?" Corban scrambled toward the fire, trying to find the pieces. "It was beautiful."

Benna turned away from him. She mumbled something; stoop-shouldered, she went back to her father. Corban found one bit of the clay, and then another, but most was dust. Gifu and Arre were watching him; he lifted his eyes to them, and said, "Why did she do that?"

Arre shrugged. "She breaks them, almost all."

Gifu said, "It doesn't do any good. We can't eat them."

Benna was leaning on her dozing father. She said roughly, "It's a sin. I should not. I keep trying not to do it, but I do it anyway." To his amazement he saw she was crying. She wiped at her eyes with the back of her hand. "I'm sorry."

He said, "It was beautiful."

Grod said, in the shadows, "What are you all talking about, anyway?"

Corban cast a look at him over his shoulder. He laid down the two broken bits of the clay. "I think it was beautiful," he said again, and straightened up. "I'm going. Thank you for cooking my supper for me."

Grod leapt up. "No, stay! You can sleep here—why go to the church—"

"I don't live here," Corban said. "You don't either." He could not abide the stink, he thought, but did not say that. He could not abide that these three girls should live in such a den. The church was cold but better than this. "Good-bye," he said. "Thank you."

Benna had composed herself; she rose, and went to the door with him. "We must thank you, who brought us the meat." Her eyes were red. She would not look him in the face. He guessed she knew he could not endure the hut and was ashamed. She followed him outside, where he gathered the cool damp night air into his lungs, sweet and clean. Snowflakes drifted down past him. The dark was a thickening gloom.

She said, "Do you know how to cross the river?"

"I will find the way," he said.

"There are stepping stones. Let me show you."

She walked along side by side with him, down to the riverbank. Neither of them spoke. From the high bank he looked down through the drifting snow and saw the wide flat stones that spanned the river.

"Why did you break it?" he said, at last.

"Ah, God," she said. "Such a poor, pitiful thing—they never come out the way I want them to—" She gave a shaky little laugh. "It's wicked and vain and I can't even do it well." She turned around suddenly, going back. "Thank you, Corban."

He watched her walk away, back to the tangled heap of brush that was her home. He watched her until she was gone back inside, out of sight, and turned and went down and crossed the river, and trudged up toward the church to sleep.

His steps dragged. The city lay cold and empty around him, the houses shuttered up against the dark. In each a dog barked as he passed, heralding him up the hill. The street was slippery with the snow and he shortened his steps. He thought of the church, lonely and cold, and for a moment wished he had stayed behind in the hovel across the river.

He stopped by the fountain, looking down the street, the dark steeple looming up over him; few but steady, the snowflakes wandered down around him. Grod could crawl in under the hem of the girls' rags but he would not. Yet he thought he could not endure to sleep in the church any more.

He remembered what Eelmouth had said, and went on past the church, down the long wide street toward the river, which flanked the hill on which the King's Hall stood. It shone with torches, up there, and he heard the thrum of voices, and a burst of laughter. It drew him like the warmth of a hearth. He turned up the steep hill, his feet slipping and sliding along the muddy, slushy path. Eelmouth had said he could come in there. There was meat every night, he said. He had praised what Corban did, in the fight in the horseyard. He could make a place there, with Eelmouth's word for him.

He went up toward the loud and light-filled house on the hill, and into his mind came the thought that this was what his father had wanted of him, all along; to serve a king.

He stopped. He was close enough now to see through the open door, the crowd and thrash of many people inside, moving back and forth. The smell of meat reached his nose. He heard a woman give an unfrightened, artful shriek. He knew he would never go in there, to be Eric's man.

Behind him on the far riverbank lay another house, where he also could not enter; he was suspended between them, caught in the middle, hanging above an endless nothing, ready to drop. He turned, his feet stumbling on the steep slope, and went on down the hill and back to the cold, empty darkness of the church.

<hr/>

Benna chewed the meat first for her father, who had no teeth left. He sat nodding his head as if he heard music somewhere. He never asked where the meat came from, and he never thanked her for feeding it to him. While he chewed, she looked for his shoes and socks, which he had taken off, and put them on again. His feet were horny and knobbed and black with dirt, the toenails warped into lumpy little claws. She snugged his socks up over his legs to keep him warm.

He said, "Tell Gifu to come. I want to see Gifu."

He loved Gifu best, who hardly ever even gave him a look.

Benna sat beside him, waiting with another bite of the meat. She wanted to believe she cared for him from a daughter's love but she also knew she needed him. She claimed her place in the market in his name and the right to mine clay from the riverbank. Without him they could not go on living even here.

Only a few years before it had been so different; they had lived in a house in the city, and her father had been known all over the country for his pottery. Then her mother died, and her father lost his sight, and then his mind, and the King took the house. Now they clung to the edge of Jorvik like weeds growing in the chinks of a wall.

She fed her father some chewed-up meat. His eyes were milky and running and she wiped them with a rag.

Gifu should do this, she thought, in a seethe of resentment. Gifu, whom he loved so much. Now sitting there giggling by the fire, head together with her sister's. One fair mop of crinkly hair, one russet brown, fire-gilded, bubbling up gusts of laughter.

They seemed still babies to Benna: Arre who would give away everything they had to anybody who needed it, who laughed and sang even on days when they had nothing to eat; and Gifu, who without a mother or a father was growing wild as an animal.

She should marry, she thought, but who would take her? Who would take any of them, who had nothing, no dowry, no family, not even decent clothes? There were often men around, looking at them, but for bad reasons. Arre said she loved Euan, that Euan loved her, but Euan's widowed mother, who was an apothecary, forbade him to see her. He might sneak across the river whenever he could, but he would not marry her.

The stranger Corban, who had just brought them the first meat they had eaten in days and days, when he saw how they lived, his face had fallen, all aghast.

She fed her father the last of the meat. Off across the river, the church bell rang, and she lowered her head and crossed herself and said an absentminded prayer. It did no good to fret; she had gotten through the day, again, and perhaps that was really all what mattered.

He had said, not once or even twice, but three times, he had said three times that the thing she made was beautiful.

Her father was snoring, slumped down where he sat, his chin on his chest. Gently she laid him down on his bed and pulled the blanket over him. Grod was already asleep, curled up by the wall, snoring. Her sisters also were going to their beds, and even the goats were quiet. In the stillness Benna crept in by the firelight, groping in her apron pocket for a piece of broken pot and her paintbrush.

———

"She is dying," Bluetooth said. "I have wasted a whole winter here waiting for you to make something of her and all she is becoming is a corpse."

The Lady clenched her teeth, angry—with him, with Mav. She kept her back to the hall, where she knew her people watched and whispered. Before her, in the little cupboard bed, the Irish girl lay like a rock, her eyes closed, her arms wrapped around her swelling belly. She was gaunt; they had been forcing food through her jaws, and yet she wasted away before them.

And she did not sing. She gave up nothing to the Lady, not a word, not an image. Something terrible had happened; perhaps the brother had died.

"How long has she been so?" asked Bluetooth.

"Nearly a month," the Lady said. She sat on the edge of the bed and reached out to stroke the girl's cheek, but Mav's skin was icy cold, and the Lady pulled her hand hastily back. A thrill of alarm went down her spine. On Mav's cheeks tears lay hard and pearly like frost. Even her hair was cold. Yet she breathed; and her eyelids fluttered.

Bluetooth grunted. "Hakon daily grows stronger. Soon he will have all Norway under his command, and then he will attack me, and the great struggle will begin. I need someone to distract him and weaken him and Eric is the obvious choice. You told me you would help me and instead you have led me down this path to nowhere, this dying girl. You owe me something now."

The Lady said nothing, the iron taste of failure in her mouth. She wondered if the girl's own power had somehow killed her, or decayed her mind to uselessness.

She wondered if she herself were fading. She should have drawn this girl entirely into her by now. But Mav resisted, holding fast to herself, and she had that wretched baby to keep hold of. The Lady wished again she had managed to get rid of it. The baby bothered her; something unknown, unmeasured, unquiet there, as if it watched her malevolently from the safety of the womb.

The baby kept Mav from yielding to her.

"Kill her," Bluetooth said. "It would be a kindness."

His mouth twisted, loose and lustful, as he said that. In Bluetooth, kindness was a lie.

The Lady stood. "Well, perhaps." She drew shut the cupboard door on the girl's bed.

Bluetooth watched her narrowly. He wore light-bending jewels in a great collar around his neck. Abruptly the Lady boiled with a heat of rage against these kings and their hungers, and against the girl who had filled her with hope and then dashed it. She thought of the flask hidden in her bed cupboard, a long thin tube of Byzantine glass, with its drops of green poison. One sip of that, and in the morning the girl, the baby, would both be on the rubbish heap.

He was watching her, unblinking. He enjoyed her failure. He wanted her to fail, which would give him power over her. She fought down a sudden sickening panic, and collected her mind, struggling back to the calm unmoving center of herself.

"I will send for you," she said. "When I have something more. Go, now." Her voice was shrill with uncertain command.

He stood a moment longer, watching her, smiling. Showing her what he thought of her commands. But then, he obeyed her; huge and heavy-footed, he went away toward the door.

She went back to the cupboard where Mav lay. The girl was strong, even now; just standing here beside the bed, the Lady could sense her unwakened power. Her gorge rose, an upsurge of her will. She would not lose Mav, she needed her, she ached for that power sleeping in her, so close and yet utterly out of reach. Let Bluetooth talk of his great work, the fool. He knew nothing of how great a work there was.

She pulled open the cupboard. Calling sharply to one of her slaves, she sent him for a cup of milk and honey, and sat down on the bed by the girl, to force food down her throat again, and keep her alive.

⸺⸺

Corban went out of the church in the morning thinking he would
hunt again. The day was dark and blustery, although the snow had
stopped, and in the street people hurried along, bundled into their
clothes like sausages. He went to the fountain and broke a skim of
ice on the pool of water. As he was washing his face somebody
thumped him on the shoulder, and he turned and saw Eelmouth.

Without a word, the Viking held out a cup of ale to him. Corban took it, and soon he was walking down along the street with
Eelmouth, foraging from shop to shop, and not going hunting any
more.

They ate bread and apples and sausage, leaving behind a trail
of angry shopkeepers. Corban went along just behind Eelmouth's
shoulder, one of several men in this band, more than usual, and as
they went, Eelmouth picked up other men, until he had a dozen or
more. Corban saw that the redheaded Viking had some purpose in
all this, and drank less of the ale than he wanted.

From the riverbank they turned back up the hill street, past the
King's Hall, going up toward the church. Heavy clouds covered
the sun, and the wind blew raw, booming around the steeple, and
the bell began to toll. In the square before the church, Eelmouth
turned his head and spoke to the men behind him.

"Stay somewhere around me, all of you. Don't go anywhere
alone. Watch me for a signal, if anything happens."

Corban's neck prickled up. He wondered what was happening,
what he would have to do now. With the rest of Eelmouth's men
he moved off to the edge of the square. The bell clanged steadily
overhead, and presently out of the church came a procession of
people.

A young man in a black gown led them—a priest, carrying in
both hands an elaborate wooden box, which he held high so that
everyone could see it. As he went along he called out a long string
of church words.

"Dommmm—" He sucked the sound out long and humming
"—in—oos vohhhh—bis—cummmmmmm—"

After him, in twos and threes, the wide church doors gave out
a steady parade of people, stepping together and praying. The first
to appear were townspeople, men in jerkins and cloaks, bareheaded,

women in long gowns, their hair smoothly wrapped up in white cloth. They answered the priest, their words jumbled and fumbled out.

"Et cumuh sprituh-um-usto—"

Corban said, "This is just some Christian matter. Why do you want to see it?"

Eelmouth was staring sharp-eyed at the growing crowd. "I keep watch every time there are many of them together. They hate us, and there are more of them than us."

"Hunh," Corban said. "Isn't Eric a Christian?"

Eelmouth grinned at him. He wiped drool off his beard with his hand. "He took the water when he was first king. But his father lies in a howe in Norway, water can't change that."

Still more people were funneling out of the church, a steady stream, marching steadily off down the street after the priest with his relic. Many turned their heads and shot curious and angry looks at the Vikings, but most of them were praying, and paid Eelmouth and his men no heed.

Corban wondered what they prayed for—good weather for spring planting, a strong crop of lambs. For the Vikings to leave them alone. The meat and bread and ale that sustained him this day lay uneasy in his stomach. He drew back among the others, folding his arms over his chest.

As the crowd was still proceeding out of the church, the sky darkened, and wet snow began to fall; quickly it turned to a hard frozen rain. Corban pulled his cloak up tight around him, cold.

"Come on," Eelmouth said. "Gorm, Ketil, those of you, go around the other side. The rest of you come with me." With Corban at his shoulder he went along down the street, shadowing the procession.

The priest was leading them all in a long slow circle around the city. Corban trailed along after Eelmouth, watching the people nearest him. He knew many of them, especially the shopkeepers among them, near the front, and their wives. After them came farmers, in from the country, dirt-colored men with broad, heavy hands and shoulders lumpy with muscle, as if they could be hitched up to their own plows.

Eelmouth was tramping along the side of the street, holding

his scabbarded sword still with one hand. Corban licked his lips; he slowed down, letting the procession and the rest of the Vikings go on by him, until at last he saw Benna and her sisters, walking near the very end.

Arre was praying; Benna walked with her head bowed; Gifu strolled along, her hair wild, her eyes searching. Grod plodded after them, looking bored. The rain was falling harder now, spreading icy puddles across the street. Benna walked past him, not seeing him, her face pale in the gloom, her neat-fingered hands before her, rain on her cheek. Corban went into the procession and wended his way up to her. As he reached her, the crowd began to pray out loud again.

"Orrrr—ray—moooos—"

"Pada Nostre, quest in chelly—"

"Benna," he said, his mouth dry, and she turned toward him, her eyes widening. He held out his cloak. "Are you cold? You can use my cloak."

On her far side, Arre's head swung around, and her smile widened. Benna said, quietly, "Thank you." She walked in under his cloak, into the arc his arm made with his body. He held his arm out stiffly above her, sheltering her under a roof of the cloak, not touching her. She was so close he could have put his whole arm around her. She walked along beside him, chanting in a high, uncertain voice.

He did not chant. He went along, protecting her from the rain, struggling with a sudden wild urge to throw his arms around her and carry her off, out of the crowd, off to somewhere dry and quiet. His outstretched arm began to ache. They were walking along the riverbank now, the rain falling thick and fast.

A child's voice behind him said, "Will there be a feast?"

He looked down at Benna walking beside him, her hair smoothed under the damp edge of her headcloth, the tender slope of her cheek, and his chest swelled. She looked up at him, and smiled.

"There will be something," a woman said. "We can't have a procession without a feast."

Corban lowered his arm down around her shoulders, the cloak all around them both, now, and she stepped closer and walked so near beside him her shoulder brushed his chest. He felt as if he could not breathe. She was warm against him, warm and alive. He shut his eyes. He would build her another house. He would take care of them all.

"In the old days, the King would have put on a feast, damn him," said a man, harsh-tongued. "Or the Archbishop. And here it is the middle of the winter and Lent almost on us and we're already starving."

"Not this King."

They were walking up toward the church again. The procession was over. In the square people milled around, talking in the steady freezing rain. Arre disappeared and came back with an armful of bread, giving out loaves as she passed; she came up to Corban and Benna.

"There isn't much," she said, and handed her sister the last loaf. Rain glittered on her hair; she smiled at them, like the sun gleaming through the rain.

Benna broke the loaf, and made to give Corban a piece. He stepped back, drawing away from her; her sister's steady attention made him shy. "No—you take it. I—" Everybody was watching him now, it seemed. They would know he had been with Eelmouth. He nodded to her, moving away from her. "Good-bye," he said, and went quickly out of the crowd. He wondered who else had seen him. In the fringe of the crowd he stood and searched the square with his eyes. Eelmouth stood on the far side of the square, under the eave of a building; Corban turned and went the other way down the street.

CHAPTER NINE

The day after the rain stopped, Benna took a stack of her best pots up to the King's Hall, and there sold them to the cook for three silver pennies. Then she went down to her market corner, and spread the rest of her wares around her.

The procession on Saint Hillary's Eve had drawn in many people from the countryside, who had brought things to sell; a woman with a flock of little children hawking gatherings of nuts and mushrooms; men with loads of wood and bundled withies. A tinker with a grindstone had set up just across from her and was sharpening knives and tools. She settled down in the middle of her pots, the silver pennies carefully tucked into her pocket, and drew out a piece of broken pottery and her drawing kit.

This was a good big piece, which she had been saving for a while, loathe to use it for anything small. She had made the ink from hawthorne berries, and chewed the ends of twigs for her brushes. Now, setting the shard on her knee, she dipped the brush into the ink, and drew Corban's face.

She left off his beard; she drew, not merely the surface of him, but what she saw under the surface. She concentrated on the strong, square lines of his brow, his eyes, the jut of his nose. People drifted by, talking to her and looking at her pots. Up the street the baker woman carried her rolls and loaves before her on a tray, calling out her wares; she waved, and Benna waved back to her. A dog from the shambles edged over toward her, sniffing at the pots. She looked for a stone to throw at it, but the dog scooted away before she could find one. Beyond, she saw Corban coming.

She went warm all over. Quickly she tucked the shard away under the edge of her mat.

He came up, unsmiling, his red and blue cloak slung over his arm; he gave her a single, quick, direct look, and then turned his head away, as if even his look might blister. He said, "May I sit down here?"

"Of course," she said. She slid sideways on the mat, to give him more room. He sank down on his heels beside her, still not looking at her. Neither of them spoke for a while. She was remembering how he had suddenly appeared in the crowd, the day before, and swung his cloak over her, warm and sheltering.

He said, suddenly, "I'm sorry I haven't brought more meat."

"Oh," she said, "we have enough—I sold some pots at the King's Hall." She showed him the pennies. "We shall eat well enough for days and days, and soon the goats will kid, and then we will have milk and cheese."

"Good," he said, and gave her a quick sideways look. "Then you don't need me, I guess."

"You are always welcome among us," she said. "With me, especially."

He stirred, at that, and she saw him smiling, but he still did not look at her. He picked furiously at the dust before him, his head bowed. There was a little silence. She felt, between them, the beginnings of another kind of speech.

Finally, for want of anything else, she said, "Are you going hunting again?"

"Maybe." His head bobbed up and down. He said, "Have you made any new images?"

She saw his glance flick toward the edge of the mat and knew he had seen her hide it. "No," she said, her stomach fluttering.

He turned his face toward her, laughing. "I saw you. Why do you lie? Let me see it." He reached for the edge of the mat, to lift it up, and she caught his hand.

"Oh, please—"

"Why can I not see it?" He was facing her directly now, laughing at her, his eyes merry. She leaned toward him, into the warmth of his attention. "I love what you make. Let me see them."

She gathered in a ragged breath. His hand lay still under her fingers. She said, "All right."

"Thank you." He smiled at her, and lifted the mat and took out the shard. "I don't understand why you want—"

He turned the piece of clay up, looking down at it, and his voice stopped in his throat. She watched him, startled, as he went pale as ash, his mouth falling open.

"Mav," he said.

She licked her lips. He lifted his face to her and his eyes were wild.

"How did you know? Did you see her?"

"Who?" she asked.

"My sister—you drew her—" He held out the pot and she saw how his hand shook.

"No—No—" She caught hold of his trembling hand. "It's you, Corban. It's your face."

He shuddered. Her hand slid away from him. He was staring at the pot again; he never looked back at her. She sat with her hands in her lap, shut out. Suddenly everything had changed between them. Two women were looking over the pots at the far side of her display and she got up and went over to them. Her eyes were burning; she was about to cry.

⸙

Corban sat with the piece of pot in his hands. From the curved pale surface his sister looked up at him with wide eyes.

He had forgotten. He had come all this way and then somehow he had forgotten.

He had not forgotten. He had given up.

He lifted his head, blind to the people and bustle and noise around him. He knew he stood at a crossroads. He could decide now to keep on forgetting. He could stay here, with Benna, with her sisters, with Grod, and build the house he could already see in his mind, with straight solid walls of withy, a byre at one end for the goats, a real thatched roof. A warm snug place in the winter, a family's place.

Or he could go on, alone, and look for Mav.

Mav was far across the water. He had no way to find her. He would never find her. He would trudge on down the long and lonely road forever, seeking her.

He could stay here. He could betray his sister, and stay here.

He felt himself riven down the middle like a split log. He wanted to be here more than he had ever wanted anything else. He wanted Benna, he wanted what he could build here.

He would know, always, that he had abandoned Mav.

He clenched his teeth together. Benna had come back from dickering with the women, her hands full of withered apples and old nuts. She looked deeply into his face but he could not speak, he could not even raise his gaze to hers.

She sat down heavily next to him, and sighed. Only a hands-breadth divided them, but somehow they were far apart; he knew she would not reach across it. He looked down at the shard in his hands.

"You are very good at this, Benna," he said. "It looks just like her."

"It's you," she said, quietly. Then her voice changed, tighter and rougher. "Here come the King's men. At least I have something to give them."

Corban looked up the street. A brace of Vikings was moving down from the top of the hill, stopping at each shop and stall. Eelmouth came first, his wild red hair standing up on his head like a cock's comb, with his brawny friend Gorm on his heels. They came on the baker woman, and took the last of her bread, in spite of her glowers. Ahead of their progress, the shopkeepers scurried quietly around, hastily removing their best wares out of sight.

Corban said, "What does he want of you? He can't eat clay."

"Money," she said. "He takes money from me."

Corban grunted, and stood up. A dull raw rage pressed up through his chest into his throat. Benna said something; he made no answer, but watched Eelmouth sauntering down the muddy street, Gorm tramping slouch-shouldered and bent-kneed in his tracks. The thought ran through Corban's mind that if he died, he would not have to leave Jorvik.

Eelmouth saw him, and his eyes narrowed. He tramped straight up to him, his chest out.

"Well, Irish. I looked for you this morning. What are you doing here?"

"Keep going, Sweyn," Corban said. "She has nothing for you."

"Oh, really." Eelmouth wiped the back of his hand across his slobbery lips. His eyes glittered. He glanced beyond him, at Benna. "And who says that?"

"I do."

"Well, now. I don't remember you standing before the King

to hear his orders." Eelmouth reached out and shoved Corban hard in the chest.

Corban leapt on him. They grappled together; Corban wrapped his arms around Eelmouth's chest and bore him hard down to the ground. People were shouting around them. He gripped one of Eelmouth's wrists and pinned his arm down under one knee, and he was struggling to get hold of the other arm when from behind him hands clutched him by the hair and the shoulder and dragged him back.

He wrenched at the grip, but Gorm had him fast, a hot breath in his ear and one arm wound tight around him from behind. Eelmouth, drooling bloody down his front, surged up off the ground and strode two steps toward Corban and backhanded him hard across the face.

Corban's sense flew off; he staggered, dazed. A hand fisted in his hair jerked his head back. He gasped for breath. Eelmouth faced him, snarling.

"You never do that! You never dare do that!"

Benna leapt between them. In her fingers she held silver, and she waved it in Eelmouth's face. "I have money! I will pay you!"

Corban took a deep breath, his strength and his sense flowing back into his body. Behind him, Gorm said, "We can kill him."

Benna cast a wild look over her shoulder. She held the silver up before Eelmouth's nose, crying, "No—I'll pay—I'll pay—"

Eelmouth stepped back. He swiped his tongue over his lips; his gaze drilled into Corban's. "No." He plucked the money from Benna's fingers. "I'm not afraid of you, Irish. Try that again, and I will kill you. Without help." He wheeled and went across the street, toward the man with the grindstone.

Gorm let go, and sauntered after him. Corban sagged, his knees loose, his rage fading away; he rubbed one hand over his face. The Vikings went off across the street, and he turned to Benna.

"I'm sorry," he said.

"Are you all right?" She had collected herself, her white face smooth and blank. She put a single silver penny back into her apron.

"Yes, yes." He sat down again, watching Eelmouth drift away

down the street. His jaw hurt, and his eye. A slow anger burned
in him. There were people moving up around him; he lowered his
eyes, humiliated.

"I'm sorry. I cost you something."

She said, "Yes, you did."

He punched his fist against his thigh. Everything he did turned
out wrong. He fixed his mind on what he had to do now.

"Benna," he said. "I have to tell you something."

Grod said, "But you can't leave. Not now. Everything is going so
well."

"I have to," Corban said.

The old man's cheeks sucked hollow, his eyes cloudy, and he
glanced around him at the hut, as if looking for help; the girls sat
there watching, a row of unsmiling, accusing faces. Arre had put
her arm around Benna.

Gifu said suddenly, "Well, that's the end of the meat."

Benna straightened up, her face taut. "Don't be selfish. He must
go. You have to see that. He has to find his sister. If one of us was
lost, the others would never stop looking."

Grod said, "I'm not going with you."

"No." Corban reached out and gripped the old man's arm. "I
didn't think you would. You got me this far, and that was the
bargain."

"Grod, you can stay here, with us," Arre said. "It's almost
spring. You can help me with my garden."

Grod leaned toward Corban, intent. "How will you get anywhere without me, though? You'll put yourself in terrible trouble.
You can't even get out of Jorvik, without my help."

"I'm leaving Jorvik tomorrow," Corban said. "I went down to
the river, after I talked to Benna. There's a ship leaving that needs
a rower. It's going first up to Orkneyjar, but then it goes to Hedeby."

"Tomorrow," Grod said, and his face quivered and twitched
and tears gathered in the corners of his eyes.

"I'd like to stay here tonight," Corban said. He was looking at Benna. "Could I do that?"

"Of course," she said.

"Will you come back?" Arre said. Her smile had vanished.

Corban said, "I don't know. I will if I can. But every time I think to find her she is farther off than before."

Arre said, "I'll pray for you," and crossed herself. Beside her Benna lowered her head and looked away. Gifu wrapped her arms around her raised knees and glared at him.

"Thank you," Corban said. His throat had thickened and he did not try to say anything more, but busied himself getting ready to leave. His shoes were splitting along the sides and he had borrowed Arre's awl to sew them up again. When that was done he shook his cloak out, and looked it over: he had thought there were some rips in it, along the edge, but now he could not find them. He thought one of the girls must have mended it.

In the gloom of the evening he went out and helped Gifu and Arre bring in firewood, and they hardly spoke to him, would not look at him. He saw they were angry, in spite of his protests and apologies, and his heart twisted. He told himself he should have slept in the church. He saw the way before him dark and cold and fateful, and himself too weak and small to endure it.

He went inside, sat down, and shut his eyes and thought of Mav. He would never find her. Perhaps she was already dead. He was looking for a ghost. He could give up looking.

Deep in his mind, like a drowned star, his sister burned.

He slept ill, busy with dreams. Before dawn he woke, and gathered himself. The girls were just stirring. The old father snored happily on his bed and Grod also still lay fast asleep, wrapped in his blanket, his hand under his cheek. Corban did not wake him, but went out into the cold blue air of the morning.

Up in the tops of the trees along the river, a flock of birds brawled and flapped and screeched in raw voices. The cloudless sky was whitening toward day. He stood a moment, breathing the air in, willing himself to go on. Benna came out of the hut and came up to him.

"Here," she said, and gave him the broken shard with his face on it.

He took it in his palm, grateful; he saw she had forgiven him. "I wish it were your face," he said.

"Ah," she said. "But I don't know what I look like. I can draw Gifu and Arre but not myself."

He held out the shard to her. "Then keep this, to remember me." He took her hand and put the shard into it and held onto her hand. "Don't break it. I will come back, Benna, somehow, I promise." Her face tipped up to his was pale in the dawn light and the eyes bright and dark. He reached out suddenly and put his arms around her.

She leaned on him, lifting her head, and they kissed. He held her so tight he heard her gasp. She was so slight, and yet so fierce, and all in his arms now, and so soon left behind. He could not let her go. But he had to. He opened his arms, and stepped back.

She lowered her arms to her sides. Tears streaked her face. She said, "Do what you have to do, Corban. Good-bye."

"Good-bye," he said, and lurched off away from the hut, his legs stiff as a stork's, across the muddy meadow.

Benna stood watching him go; she thought he might turn at the riverbank and look back, but he did not. He stepped down onto the log ladder there and was gone down over the rim.

She looked down at the shard in her hand. She hurt all over, as if her body burned. She told herself she had been wrong to be happy. Now she was paying for it. And even with the picture on the shard, she had failed: she had not taken him well, only the line of his cheek, the shape of his nose, not the quick glint in his eyes when he laughed, not the joyful sound of his voice, not the pleasure of his touch. She shut her eyes to keep from seeing what she had done, and all that she had left of him, and stood there crying quietly in the bright dawn light.

Mav climbed up from the cold place, the grey place, into a blaze of red and blue. She woke, in the deep of the night, already singing in her mind.

Corban was coming. She saw him moving again, coming over the edge of the world. He rose and fell like the sea, he walked on the water like Jesus, he went into the sea like a ship sailing away.

She kept silent, although the song wanted to burst out of her. She swung open the cupboard door, and put her feet out of the bed. They had thought she was asleep and could not hear them but she had heard them. "Kill her," he had said, and the Lady had nearly done it.

She slid down out of the bed and stood up, her legs wobbly. Up and down the hall, on the wide benches, the Lady's slaves slept, each meshed in a frightened little dream; the iron of the Lady's will caged them, each one. The Lady meant something like that for her. And she was using Mav to bring Corban here, to do it to him too.

She yearned for him, an ache all through her. And yet she was bringing him into a trap.

All she wanted was to hold her baby in her arms. She had no interest in the Lady's schemes, Bluetooth's schemes, the Kingdom of Norway, or the Empire of the North, whatever they called it, their world-ring. Whatever power the Lady thought she had was nothing to Mav; hardly a power, anyway, just the great floppy seething world around her, and she knowing it. She had no mastery of it. It came and went through her, she only endured it.

Now she was bringing her brother into the Lady's web.

She reached the door, and pushed it open, so that the blue-white moonlight washed across her face. The thin light painted the yard before her, every stick in the fence laying a distinct black line of shadow against the next. The great city slumbered around her, all but a few—a late drunk, a sneaking wife, an old one-eyed cat, stiff in every joint, looking for a safe place to sleep.

She could not leave, even if she could have walked much farther than the gate; already her legs were bending, wanting to drop her onto the threshold. If she left he would never find her. She slumped against the doorway, her eyes aching.

She wanted none of this. She wanted nothing but the child, stirring and mewling in her womb.

She roused herself. She was here for one reason, which was the song, and perhaps now she should master it. If she could not save herself and Corban, then at least she could deny the Lady what she wanted. She had no notion how to do that.

Corban was coming. She had to learn.

She pulled the door shut and went back through the hall, looking for food like a mouse in the night, a crust, a half-eaten apple, or a chunk of cheese; as she went along she dabbled her fingers in the dreams of the slaves, so they stirred and called out. When she went by the Lady's cupboard bed, all woven around with spells like layers of smoke in the air, she kept her feet soft on the floor, and her eyes turned away, and breathed lightly. Finally, exhausted, she went back to her own bed, and drew the door shut, and tried to think how to do this.

⟶⟶

In the morning she was singing again, helplessly, spilling it all out. The Lady looked on her, smiling, patted her cheek, and brought her milk and honey, triumphant.

CHAPTER TEN

The ship was a little trading craft, half the size of the big dragons drawn up on either side, rounder in the belly and higher in the freeboard. She had no deck, only the open hold, loaded now with bales of fleeces and woolen cloth, and several barrels of whiskey, lashed down and covered with hempcloth. On their benches, the rowers had just enough room to stretch their legs out.

The captain's name was Ulf, and there were five other oarsmen besides Corban, three to a side. By the time the sun was well up over Jorvik, they were rowing away down the river toward the sea.

Corban had forgotten how hard this work was, and he leaned into the oar, trying to keep rhythm with the other men, his back and shoulders already sore before they had gone around the first river bend. The high banks of the river slid by, curtained in willows just turning fuzzy with new buds. He remembered what Arre had said, that spring was coming: he might never see the spring here, he might never come here again. Grimly he leaned forward, dipped the oar in, and pulled hard. After a while, the soreness went away.

Jorvik's river wound south a while through fenlands and moor to a larger river, broad like a bay between its banks. The wind was picking up and the wide stretch of water danced with whitecaps. Across the water there were other ships along the shore. The captain, Ulf, ordered the oars in and raised the mast, and Corban helped them rig the sail up. Under his feet the ship grew light and eager, leaning before the wind.

Ahead, the yawning mouth of the river met the sea; Ulf brought them over nearly to the northern bank to pass through the river's mouth, and Corban, wrapped in his cloak against the biting, salty wind, saw how the rough chop of the waves broke white in the center of the stream and guessed why Ulf avoided it.

Ulf, one hand on the steerboard, his eyes squinting straight ahead, swung them neatly through the rippled water of the channel and turned at once to the north, to follow the coast.

"How many days to Hedeby?" Corban asked him.

Ulf shrugged. He was much older than Corban, a short square block of a man with shaggy dark hair on his head and chest and arms, and a coarse, hard laugh. He said, "We have a way to go before we come to Hedeby. I told you that." He reached down beside him and picked up a wooden bucket. "Bail."

Corban bailed. The little ship, heavy laden, pitched and wallowed over the waves, and he began to feel his stomach rolling too, a queasy heave and jerk around his rib cage. On their left hand the dark coast slipped by, bleak and windblown fens, with no sign of any human settlements.

They sailed along the coast all day long. In the late afternoon, Ulf craned his neck, peering toward the shore, and began to edge the ship in toward the land. Before the sun went down, he had run them neatly through the offshore rocks into a little tree-shrouded inlet where they could shelter for the night. They took down the mast and rigged up the cargo cover as an awning over the midships, ate cold bread and bad meat and beer, and slept, tucked in among the casks of whiskey and the bales of fleece and cloth.

So they went on, for days and days, Corban so seasick most of the time that he didn't care. They stopped once in a rivermouth where there had been a village, but only the burnt shells of the houses remained. Ulf grumbled, looking around, and said, "Damn Eric."

Corban said, "What did you say?"

Ulf flapped his hands at him, turning away. "No, no."

In the morning it was raining, warm and gusty. Ulf groaned and swore, tramped around along the beach staring up at the sky, and finally ordered them all to their oars. "There is another place to haul in," he said. "Farther up the coast, maybe there will be some people. Better than this."

He stood in the bow piloting them and they rowed back out through the rocky mouth of the river and into the open sea. There he ordered the mast set up again and the sail rigged, and he came back into the stern and lowered the steerboard into the water, and they sailed away north along the coast again.

Corban went to find a bailer. The air was blustery and warm, so that he was sweating under his cloak. In the stern, leaning on the long arm of the steerboard, Ulf was muttering to himself. He looked up into the sky and Corban saw his brow furrow and his lips purse. Corban sat just forward of him and bailed steadily; whenever he stopped his stomach began to heave, so he kept himself working. The other men crouched together amidships in the narrow space where there was no cargo and played dice and dozed. The rain pelted down, and the wind rose.

The rower in front of Corban twisted to look over his sunburnt shoulder. "Ulf, take us in! Something's blowing up!"

Ulf snarled something under his breath. He cast a look landward, where white waves crashed against the shore. He caught Corban watching him and said, "We should have stayed where we were last night." The sail fluttered abruptly, and the wind fell out of it. Ulf leaned on the steerboard and the ship creaked and heeled over and the sail filled again, but now they were headed straight away from the land, out to sea.

Corban gave up fighting his stomach, and bent over the side and threw up.

The rower in front of him was big and brawny, his shoulders humped with muscle, so that his head looked too small. He twisted his head around again, and again he shouted at Ulf. "Take us in! You're a damned fool! Take us in!"

"We can't go in," Ulf said, under his breath. He cast a look up into the sky again.

The rain pounded them, and although it was hardly midday the sky turned dark, and the wind rose, keening off the rigging of the ship. The ship churned along, driving through the waves. Dark and splashed with foam, the seas were mounting steadily higher, slapping up over the bow and pouring down into the hull. Corban bailed; the other men bailed; Ulf clung to the steerboard, keeping the ship before the wind and bow to the waves. Nobody spoke. The land was out of sight now, far behind them.

The wind was rising. The ship thrashed and struggled up the lifting flanks of the waves, lurched and thrashed down the other side. Corban was sick again. The ship was taking on water faster than he and the other men could bail it out. The brawny man began to shout at Ulf again.

"You fool! You're no captain, Ulf! You got us into this!"

Ulf bit his lips, his eyes narrowed, and said nothing. Corban, exhausted and sick, crept into the bow and curled up on a heap of fleece to sleep for a while.

He woke in darkness. The ship was pitching under him so that he could not gain his feet; hanging onto the side of the ship, he dragged himself aft. As soon as he got out of the shelter of the bow the wind blasted him, icy and salt-laden. The ship was lumbering along before it, the sail taut and all the rigging singing; he saw the next wave rise before them like a snow-capped mountain and the breath went out of him. He clutched the gunwale and shrank down and the ship rose, climbing the wave's steep face, until it seemed to stand on its stern. He heard someone screaming. Clinging to the gunwale he pressed himself to the curved hull of the ship, desperate for its scant shelter. The wave topped over them and broke and dark water thundered down into the ship. The torrent wrenched and hauled at him and he buried his face against his arm and held on, his fingers biting into the wood of the gunwale, his arms aching, and the ship dropped suddenly, pitching forward, shuddering all its length, and he lost his grip and slid feetfirst back into the bow again.

He got his legs under him, sobbing, every muscle quivering. Overhead, the sail swelled out in a great taut drum full of wind; knee-deep water sloshed back and forth in the hull. At the far end of the ship he could just make out Ulf, his beard and hair streaming, clinging to the steerboard. The other men were huddling by the mast. The ship angled down into the trough of a wave and the bucket came floating up the hull toward Corban. He began to bail again, scooping with the bucket and flinging the water over the downwind side.

Then they were laboring up the side of a huge wave and the ship drove its bow into the side of the wave and Corban's breath stopped; he felt the sea beating them down, bearing over them, ready to plunge them like an arrow down to the bottom of the sea. But the ship broke free, shipping dark water over either shoulder, thrust its bow up into the air again, and staggered on.

A cold fear clutched him. He was going to die and no one would ever know. Benna would never know. Mav would never know how he had searched for her. The wind shrieked past his ear like horrible laughter. His fingers were numb; as fast as he bailed he was still to his knees in icy water. The ship bucked and threw him hard against the side, and he nearly went overboard. He could hear somebody praying, or cursing. A wave broke over him and clubbed him down against the bottom of the boat. Water closed over his head. He wrenched himself up again, gasping for breath. The ship was wallowing, helpless, broadside to the waves; overhead, the sail streamed out from the yard in tattered ribbons of cloth.

Ulf was shouting in the stern, calling orders and waving his arm. Corban crept toward the mast, clinging to the gunwale, and found an oar, stowed against the ship's planking. There seemed fewer of the other men than there had been. Two of them were struggling to get their oars out but he saw no sign of the brawny man, and some others also were missing. The roar of the wind and the sea together made a sound so huge it was like no sound at all, as if he were deaf. The ship yawed and pitched under his feet. They were broadside to the waves; when the next one rose it rolled them over onto the starboard gunwale. Corban, braced on the rowing bench, ran his oar out and dug the blade into the sea and leaned all his weight on it, trying to swing the ship to meet the waves; he braced all his strength and weight against the sea itself to turn the ship. Water pounded down over him, slamming against his head and back like a hammer. The other two men had thrust their oars out. The ship answered, heeling slightly over, and labored bow first up the next towering cliff of the sea. Corban flailed with his oar; one stroke bit so deep into the sea it nearly tore the wood from his hands and the next swished through the empty air.

Night came, or he thought it was night: so dark he could see nothing, the rain pelting him, the oar jerking and wobbling in his hands. The sea burst in his face. He got a mouthful of water and choked and coughed. His eyes burned and ached, full of salt, unbearable. He was drowned already, he thought wildly, he was dead and this was hell. Beside him another man groaned and swung at his oar. He could see no one else. Icy water swirled around his ankles. His teeth chattered so hard his jaw hurt.

All that night they rowed, and the storm roared over them. Dazed and weary, he thought he heard voices in the wind, demons or gods, calling out to one another. He strained and heaved at the

oar. If he stopped rowing they would all die. The salt crusted on
his face, and his lips cracked and bled and his eyes hurt, and he
could see nothing, although now there was light; he could see that
much, the pale light filtering through the screaming wind. He
hauled at the oar, his muscles cramping, his legs like stones.

"Stop," a voice said, in his ear. "You can stop now."

"No," he said, or thought. "No." And leaned into the oar again,
reached for the sea with the blade.

"Yes," Ulf said, with a grunt of a laugh. "Yes, stop. We're out
of it—for now, anyway. You have to rest."

Corban shuddered; he lifted his head, blinking. He could see
nothing. But the ship was quiet under him. The wind had stopped.
He let go of the oar with one hand and rubbed at his eyes. The
touch was an exquisite agony, his eyeballs throbbing, and he lowered his hand and shut his eyes tight for a moment and then forced
them open.

The day had come. Above him the sky was a cloudy blue.
They were lying on the breast of the sea, riding long, slow waves.

He rested on the oar, too tired to move. Ulf handed him a
chunk of water-soaked bread.

"Eat."

"Where are we?" Corban asked.

"I don't know. Way west of where we should be." Ulf held
out a wooden cup of beer.

"Water," Corban said; his throat was raw, and the thought of
pouring beer down it made him choke. Yet the bread was so salty
he could barely eat that either.

"There is no water," Ulf said. "Eat the bread, Corban. I think
there's another storm coming up."

Corban stuffed the soggy bread into his mouth and took the
beer. Ulf nodded to the east, and he turned and saw the sky there
walled up with clouds, grey towers into the peak of the sky. With
some effort he swallowed the bread.

"It could at least be blowing us toward Hedeby."

Ulf laughed. "Storms never take you where you want to go."

Corban was trembling with weariness. A lot of the cargo was
gone, he guessed swept overboard in the waves. By the mast, two

men were curled up sleeping, their heads on their arms. He looked around the ship, and then again, startled.

"Where are the others?"

Ulf shook his head, and shrugged one thick shoulder. "I should have stayed inshore, that other morning."

Corban swallowed through his dry and swollen throat. He looked suddenly out over the water, as if he could see their heads bobbing, swimming after them through the long sweeping rollers.

Ulf said, "I need your help."

"I'm tired."

"Yes, you should be. None pulled so long or so well as you, no one else. You rowed us through that, do you know it? But now I need your help. These two aren't much use even in good times."

Corban gathered this in. He could not remember anything of the storm but the buffeting, screaming wind and the sight of a tall sea climbing and climbing up over the ship. His arms ached. He levered himself up off the bench, and scrambling over what was left of the cargo followed Ulf to the forecastle, where the captain broke out another sail.

The eastern sky was black with clouds now. As they took the sail to the mast the first drops of rain struck Corban's back. The rising swells of the sea were pocked with splashes.

He said, "Water."

"Oh, aye," Ulf said. "You're a shrewd one, there, Corban."

They ripped away what was left of the old sail. Ulf was for throwing it overboard, but Corban rolled it up and stuffed it under a rowing bench. They bent the new sail to the yard; the wind was running across the sea toward them, the long swells breaking into sharper, higher rises, curling over at the tops with foam. Beneath the great black cloud to the east, a flicker of lightning showed.

They hauled the sail on its yard up the mast, and Ulf leapt back to the steerboard and got them around to run before the wind. Corban took the old sail, tore off the biggest whole patch he could find, and hung it in a pouch across the converging wales of the forecastle to catch the rain.

The ship pitched and bucked across the seas. Behind them the storm crept closer, drowning the sky, driving the sun away, and the rain fell steadily harder. It filled up the hollow of the sail across the bow and Corban scooped it up with his hands and drank and washed his face off, groaning in the pleasure of the fresh water in his throat. The other men saw and sprang on him, pulled him away, and wailed to see the water gone. He made his way back to the stern, to Ulf, so they could use the rain as it collected in the sail.

Ulf's beard was stiffened to a wedge with salt, his eyes blood-shot, his lips peeling. He said, "What did you do, up there?"

"There's water," Corban said. "I can do this. Tell me what to do."

The captain grunted at him, frowning, and glanced forward, where the other men were splashing up the rainwater. He thrust the steerboard bar into Corban's hands.

"Watch the sail. Keep us headed straight ahead, but if the sail starts to luff, get her around so she's true to the wind again." Ulf slapped him on the back and plowed away up the ship toward the bow.

Corban sat down, clutching the wooden bar of the steerboard; it jerked under his hands, as if it wanted to break free and send the ship crashing back to the storm, and he tightened his fists on it. The ship was leaping across the sea like a deer, bounding and jerking along the waves. Even in the rising chorus of the storm he could hear the water singing past the hull. Overhead the dull roaring storm pressed down over them, but far off on the horizon was a streak of blue sky shot through with streamers of sunlight, and he aimed the ship toward it. He hunched his head down into his shoulders, and pulled his sodden cloak up over himself. Ulf came back and took the helm again, and Corban climbed back to the space amidships and lay down and was at once asleep.

⸺⸻⸺

The wind blasted fitfully and violently up out of the southeast, and now they were caught in some current of the sea that bore them on steadily northward. With so few rowers they could not move the ship against the wind and the current. Ulf doled the bread out to them and they caught water in Corban's water trap and fished, and waited for a wind that would take them east again.

The other two oarsmen whined and griped and fought whenever they weren't rowing. The bigger of them was named Floki; his eyes looked in two different directions at once, one seeing and the other just wild. The smaller, straw-haired and wiry, was named Gisur. He was the one who fished.

He caught a big lump-jawed cod, and they divided it up. Corban chewed the raw meat carefully, picking the bones out of his teeth, trying to make the taste last. Floki gobbled his down, and said, "I didn't get as much as everybody else."

Gisur was gnawing on the fish's head. Ulf, beside him, said, "You got what everybody got."

Floki's lips curled back from his teeth; he drew his head down into his shoulders. His wild eye glared out to sea but his good eye was fixed on Ulf. "You lie. You shouldn't eat anything. You're the reason we're lost. We should eat you."

Corban looked away, his nerves sore. His mouth was dry; they had been out of water for over a day and he scanned the horizon for clouds, for rain. Ulf was ignoring Floki's jibes, staring off across the waves, his mouth twisted. Gisur collected the gnawed fish head and the guts and bones of his catch and flung them out over the gunwale, and baited his hook again with some saved bit of offal. Floki was still glaring at Ulf.

"You got my brother drowned, Ulf, I won't forget that. One of these days I'll—"

He froze, his eyes bugging out; a gurgle escaped his throat. Corban whipped around to look where he was looking, past Ulf, and jerked his hand back off the gunwale. Gisur whispered, "Blessed mother—"

Higher than Corban's head a great dark fin was gliding by the ship, so close he could have reached out and touched it. He sat rigidly still, not breathing, his belly locked up in fear. The tall fin went slowly the length of the ship, and then silently dropped down below the surface of the sea. For a moment, Corban, his breath stuck in his throat, could see a vast dark shape down in the water, larger than the ship, and with a whisk of its forked tail it dove away.

Gisur whispered, "God have mercy on us—"

Floki shoved an elbow into him. "Shut up! Shut up!"

Tears slid down his cheeks; he turned away, his shoulders slumping. Nobody spoke for a long while.

Another storm was overtaking them. Late the next day Corban went to sleep with the clouds towering black up over the whole sky and woke some while later, soaking wet, in the dark, with rain pouring down on him. The two other rowers were lying huddled up against him, asleep, and they did not waken. He straightened up onto his knees; he could see nothing, only feel the ship pitching forward down the slope of a wave and then catching up sharply, lurching around, and driving forward. Rain sluiced down his face. He began to shiver. His mind locked onto the thought that there was either too much water or not enough. The ship shuddered down another ranging wave and heeled over, and he grabbed for the gunwale. When something touched his shoulder he jumped.

It was Ulf, streaming wet. He shouted, "Take the helm. I have to sleep."

Corban groped his way back to the stern; Ulf had lashed the steerboard bar down, and the ship was falling off the wind; he wedged himself into the shelter of the high curved stern and brought her back on course. Looking forward he could just make out the swell of the sail stiff as iron in the blast of the wind, and the prow of the ship, first rising up toward the impenetrable black sky and then down into the high-climbing seas. By the mast Ulf had kicked and shoved Floki awake and made him bail and he sat on a rowing bench listlessly heaving water over the side.

Corban was shivering, his fingers numb on the steering bar; his teeth began to chatter. He wrapped his hands in a fold of his cloak, and pulled another fold up over his head, tucking himself as far as he could back into the shelter of the high curved stern.

The ship drove steadily on before the storm. Twice Ulf woke up and made the other men bail, but when he went back to sleep they quit at once and lay down again by the foot of the mast. Corban could hear Floki sobbing and screaming. The wind was swirling, gusting, now softening down to a whimper, and then bursting up with a roar, and suddenly like a blow from a fist it struck the ship and heeled her over on her beam.

Corban's head slammed into the stern, and he almost lost the steering bar; dazed, he caught himself sliding down into the hull, and braced his feet and hauled on the bar, but the ship would not answer. Steeply alist it wallowed dead in the water; a huge wave carried them up and up, the ship groaning, and at the peak of the wave Corban saw, against the sky, that the sail was gone.

He heard screaming. The mast had broken off, leaving a waist-high jagged stump; the sail lay all over the sea beside the ship, a mess of ripped cloth, dragging the ship over onto its flank. He let go the useless steering bar and staggered down amidships.

Floki and Gisur were heaving at the sail, which lay half over the gunwale and half in the sea like a great anchor pulling them down. Floki abruptly gave up and sank down on his knees. Ulf reared back, an axe in his hands, chopping at the rigging that held the broken mast and sail all fast to the ship. Corban got his frozen hands under the edge of the mass of icy cloth.

"Wait—wait—" Under Ulf's axe the rigging snapped apart; Corban and Gisur and Ulf all shoved together, and the sail slid away and the ship righted itself.

"Get the oars out," Ulf screamed.

Corban and the other men unshipped oars and sat down side by side and began to row. The wind was a breath of ice, the seas mountainous, but the rain had slackened. Around them the day was coming, the air shot with fresh light. The ship struggled up another wave and down the far side. Corban settled into a long even stroke, poling the ship through the water. The rain stopped.

They were going west. The sun was rising behind them. They were going away from Hedeby. Between him and Hedeby lay the storm.

All that day and most of the next they rowed steadily west, trying to get away from the weather. The sky cleared, and the wind slackened. At night the stars shone. They ate the last of the soggy bread; they had run out of water again. They huddled together trying to get warm.

"This is all Ulf's fault," Floki murmured to Corban. His odd eye looked away over Corban's shoulder as he talked.

Corban glanced up toward the bow. Ulf had a notched stick, which he used to judge where they were on the sea. Now he was standing in the bow, holding this stick at arm's length, and trying to get the measure of the North Star.

"This is Ulf's fault," Floki said again. Gisur, beside him, nodded gravely.

Corban wheeled around toward him. "What does that matter? Does it get us out of this?"

The two men blinked at him like startled stupid cows. Ulf stamped down toward them from the bow. "I can't get a good sight," he said. "The sea's too rough." His eyes were narrow. Corban saw he had overheard. He spoke to Corban but with sideways eyes he watched the other men. "I'm sure we are too far north, though. Tomorrow we go south. Maybe we can get to Iceland before our food runs out."

"Iceland," Floki and Gisur said, together.

"East," Corban said. His tongue hurt when he talked. "We should go east."

"South first," Ulf said, and shoved past him, going to the stern.

They turned the lee side of the ship to the rising sun, and rowed. Once Gisur, stretching his arms out, slunk up beside Corban and whispered, "Ulf is a bad one, he won't save you, you know." His eyes were bloodshot, swollen and pink. "We should all stick together, you and me and Floki."

"Shut up," Corban said.

He thought of Benna. She would wonder what had happened to him, surely she would think of him, for a while at least. He wondered if she would pray for him. He knew she was not one to pray with much attention but he hoped she did anyway. He hoped she looked at the picture of him. It eased his mind to think of her and he remembered every time he had seen her, every word they had said, over and over, like a child taking favorite things from a box and putting them back again.

Thinking of Mav wore him down. He had failed her; he was not good enough. She was always farther away, no matter how hard he struggled after her. He had to get them going back to the east. Yet Ulf headed the ship steadily south. And when, a day and a half later, the land appeared, it was to the west.

Ulf saw it first, and let out a yell. Corban stood up on his bench and shaded his eyes from the sun. Over there along the western edge of the sea lay a long dark line, with a row of clouds like airy mountains rising above it.

"Iceland?" Corban asked, uncertainly.

Ulf said, "I don't know. I don't think so, Iceland is all cliffs." He bent them toward it and Corban sat down eagerly and took up his oar again. The other men sat slumped over their oars, their jaws slack and their eyes glazed. The smaller one's lips were bleeding down into his matted blonde beard.

"Pull," Corban said. "There's land."

They leaned to the oars. Corban was so hungry he could not straighten; he felt he might break in half. His eyelashes were crusted with salt that glinted in the sunlight. All the rest of the day they rowed in toward the seam of the land. A seagull glided past them, surveying them with a cold red eye. The sun arched over them and dropped down ahead of them, and sank behind the long dark horizon. As the air cooled and the night fell, they saw ahead of them a rocky beach with low, tree-covered rises of land mounting beyond it.

"Take us in," Floki cried. "Take us in—" He lurched up from his bench and stretched his hands out beseeching toward Ulf.

"No," Ulf said. "Look—" He flung his arm out, pointing. "Sea reeks—who knows what other—we'll go south."

Corban looked where he pointed and saw the black lips of the monsters just breaking the waves off the shore. The hair tingled on the back of his neck. He leaned on his oar, exhausted. The sea was wild and full of storms but this unknown land could be worse. Creatures beyond nightmare could dwell in those shallows, in those dark trees. Yet he could not drag his gaze from it; long after the night swallowed it up he stared that way, trying to make out the beach, the trees.

They rowed all night, one sleeping while two swung the oars, and Ulf always in the stern cursing and shouting them on. When dawn came Corban was too tired to row anymore. His arms were quivering and cramped, and his belly hurt and his dry throat would not swallow. They were drifting into a wide bay, with flat marsh-land on the west and a sandy shoal to the east. Ulf steered them in toward a long, flat, pale stretch of beach beneath grassy dunes. Here there were no signs at least of sea reeks. The waves rolled up unbroken to curl softly against the beach. Ulf ran them into the surf; the ship's keel crunched on sand, and the next wave lifted them and carried them high onto the slope of the shore. With a cry, cock-eyed Floki, who had been rowing beside Corban, flung his oar down, leapt over the gunwale and ran up onto the land. Staggering a few steps, he fell to his knees sobbing. Corban shipped his oar, and stood, and on trembling legs walked out onto the beach, which heaved and bucked under him like an ocean of sand.

CHAPTER ELEVEN

The recent rain had left pools of standing water on the sloping ground just above the beach. Corban still had his sling; when he had filled his belly with water and washed the salt from his eyes, he set off inland, looking for something to eat.

At first he walked through a soggy black swamp, where the ground squished under his feet, and the broken husks of last year's reeds stood straight up out of the muck like giant hairs, but on the far side of that he came on a little stream, and beyond the ground rose, rocky and thick with trees. Most of the trees were scrubby cedars but above their low fringe he could see stands like islands of taller, leafless oaks. He went along through the trees, watching for tracks, and listening for birds. As he went, he picked up good stones for the sling.

He was still tired down to his bones, but he thrust that off. He was ashore now, his feet on solid ground, and he felt stronger and safer. The strange country absorbed him. After the rain the forest was black and dripping, and yet he felt the freshness of the air on his cheek and knew spring was coming here as in Jorvik. He fought his way through tangles of brush where new buds were just popping open on the branches, where tiny sprigs of green poked up through the soggy rotten leaf clutter on the ground. For a while he stood listening to a bird singing, somewhere ahead of him; he had never heard that song before, and he could not see the bird.

He made his way up a narrow little creek bottom, where moss grew thick as green fur on the heavy boles of the trees. Slimy clumps of frog eggs floated in the still pools of the creek, and on a muddy patch of shore he came on strange paw prints, like a long-fingered dog's. In the naked trees above him he saw the dark shapes of old bird's nests like hats caught in the branches. Everywhere, now, he could hear birds singing, a wild racket all overhead.

Up somewhere before him suddenly the woods rang with a wild cry, a throaty outdrawn bellow. He stopped still, the hair rising on his neck. The sound faded, and he made himself push uphill, away from the stream, toward whatever it was he had heard; but the bellow never sounded again.

At the top of the hill a huge oak tree sprouted, its top broken down in some ancient storm, its great trunk humming with bees, still stupid from the recent cold. The huge rotting trunk was torn open half its height, gouged open—some bear, he thought, and wondered if these were honeybees. He could see nothing inside the hollow but the slow churning of hundreds of crawling bees.

The wind rose, rustling the trees above him. He thought, God is here, too, and was comforted; the place felt more one with what he knew. He went on back down to the stream, following the curve of the land, which was not land, really, but great jagged grey rocks, with some soil in between, and all half-buried in drifted dead leaves.

As he came back to the stream again, in a stand of scrubby trees he saw something moving in the thin brush. He crept up cautiously, expecting to flush it—through the brush he could see a great brown furry creature—but it made no move. He reached the brush and looked down and saw, like a great moving mound of long stiff hair, the largest hedge hog he had ever seen. It ignored him, snuffling and snorting at the ground—eating shoots, he saw, the new green shoots of the brush.

The beast paid no heed to him at all. This warned him; it seemed harmless enough, yet it had no fear. He drew his knife, and put out his left hand cautiously to touch it.

It snorted at him, a grunting pig noise, and the stiff spiny hairs all over its back stood up, but it still made no move to run. He touched its fur, and pain shot up his fingers.

With a yell he jerked back his hand, the three middle fingers each sprouting three or four of the creature's spiny hairs. He staggered back, gasping, and went to his knees. The pain made his eyes water. He plucked out a few of the spines but several were deep and well-lodged and he had to work them out with the tip of his knife. His fingertips throbbed. He got back to his feet and went and looked into the clump of brush again.

The creature was still eating. It flourished its spines at him again, and he went back a few steps, and circled around it.

It was large enough to feed them, if it was meat. Exhaustion was creeping over him; he had no strength to hunt for anything else. He had to kill it.

The brush made the sling hard to use. He went around him in the forest and found a stout stick as long as his arm, and went back and clubbed the beast over the head.

It squealed, grunting, terrified, and now shuffled deeper into the brush. He pursued it, beating it across the head and body. The dense underbrush scratched and clawed at him; he got a vine around one leg and tripped and nearly fell into the creature's spines. Under his blows the beast shuddered, its spines flaring up, and then sank down, and lay still. Corban was gasping for breath, his body shaking from the effort.

Surely it was dead. He reached out the stick tentatively and poked at it, and the stick came away studded with spines. The problem now was how to skin it.

He sat a moment, spent from the effort. After a while he used the stick to push and manuver the creature out of the brush onto a patch of open ground under a tree. It was not as big as he had thought at first. The claws of its forefeet were caked with fresh dirt, from digging up the shoots. Its little spiny head was bloody.

He wiggled the stick under it and tried to turn it over, which took him several attempts. The smell of blood made his stomach rumble. Finally he got the creature onto its back.

Its underbelly was soft and hairless. He put the stick down across its hindlegs and set his foot on it, meaning to hold that end of the body down.

A dagger of pain shot through his foot; he yelled and leapt backwards through the air. A spine had pierced up through the sole of his shoe. He sat down and yanked it out, and sat a moment staring at the thorny body in front of him, his mind clogged with fatigue.

The blood smell brought him up again. He had to get to the meat on this creature. He found more sticks, and with them managed to hold the carcass still so he could cut off the head and paws, spreadeagle the animal onto its back, and slice it open down its underside.

The insides looked like every other animal he had ever killed. The heart looked like a rabbit's heart, and he ate it. He pulled the skin back off the creature's body and drew the meat up out of the spines. There were globs of yellow fat around the meat and he ate them too, although his stomach heaved.

He thought of building a fire right here, and eating it by himself. But he needed the other men, he would not get home to the right side of the sea without them. He slung the meat over his shoulder and started back.

When he crossed the stream again, he stopped to wash his hands. As he squatted on the bank he looked across the little water and saw in the mud on the far shore the deep forefoot print of some huge deer, bigger than any deer he had ever seen, less than a day old.

The carcass of his creature was heavier with each step. He walked back to the beach and found the other men there sitting on the sand. They had gathered some wood and made a fire; Gisur was putting on a piece of driftwood when Corban came up. Floki was staring away down the beach, where Ulf walked up and down. Corban came up and flung the dead thing down.

"What is it?" Gisur poked at the dead thing.

"Whatever it is, we're going to eat it," Corban said.

They quartered Corban's creature and put it over the flames to cook. Floki watched the meat hungrily, his lips moving.

Ulf came back. His gaze went at once to the fire, to the thing cooking. He said, without looking away, "There are trees, over there. We could cut a new mast."

Corban was turning one piece of his creature over on the fire. He had no intention of letting it get too much more cooked than it already was; the smell of the flesh cooking was driving him wild. He said, "Where are we?"

Ulf shrugged. "Somewhere in Ireland, I suppose."

Corban gave him a long startled stare. He had no idea where they really were but he was sure they weren't in Ireland. He pulled his piece of the creature off the fire and cut it up and gave everybody a chunk.

The others sat there with the meat in their hands, staring at him, and he saw that, hungry as they were, they would not eat first. He realized they thought the meat could be poison. He wondered briefly if it were; but the heart had not killed him; and he thought it would be better to be dead than hungry anyway. He sank his teeth into the chunk of meat in his hands.

Juice spurted across his tongue. It was delicious. He gave a low, lustful cry of gratitude and appetite. At once the others began to stuff their mouths full. Squatting around the little windblown fire, they growled over their food; Floki was weeping, great tears rolling down his face, as he chewed up the half-raw flesh. Ulf wiped his lips.

"More," he said.

Corban took off another of the sizzling quarters. "Is there anything on the ship? In the cargo? Anything we can use?"

"The whiskey," said Gisur, breathlessly. He clutched at Ulf's arm. "Give us the whiskey."

Ulf sat slumped, his long arms draped over his knees. "All right," he said, with a nod. "Go get one of the casks."

The two rowers leapt up and ran down toward the ship, leaving Ulf and Corban sitting there. Corban chewed up the little bones of the creature; he was still hungry.

Ulf said, "I can take a better sighting on the stars, when the sun goes down."

Corban nodded. He was tired, and wanted to sleep. The two men lugged a cask of the whiskey up to the fire and one of them pried up the lid with the tip of his knife. Greedily Floki plunged in his hands and scooped up the liquor and drank it from his cupped palms.

At once he spat it out, spraying a gust of drops that made the fire sizzle. "Salt," he cried. "The sea got into it," and kicked at the cask, furious. He and Gisur lumbered away toward the ship again. Corban stuck his aching left hand into the cask of salty whiskey and left it there until the many little wounds stopped stinging.

⁓

He woke in the dark. The fire fluttered and snapped in a cold wind off the sea. The six whiskey casks were tumbled around on the sand nearby, all broached, and all empty. They had all been fouled. Overhead the sky glittered with stars, like a scattering of white ash across the flat coal black of the night.

Ulf was standing a little way away, with his stick outstretched in his hand, reading their position. Corban got up, stretched, and went down the beach to make water. From the dark he turned and looked at the fire, its tiny shell of yellow light, the men slumped around it; he thought for an instant he could walk away and leave them, go into the dark forest, and live there.

He thrust off that idea. Somehow he was going to get back to the right side of the sea, to Hedeby. He started back toward the fire, and as he walked toward them the other men began to shout, a sudden, loud outburst of voices in the windy darkness.

"You did this, Ulf—You got us cast away—"

Ulf was arguing with them, his hands raised, but suddenly the two other men sprang on him, one from either side. Corban saw a knife blade flash in the firelight.

He broke into a run toward them. Before he could reach them the three men went down in a tangle of thrashing bodies. He leapt on them, seized the upstretched arm with the knife, and wrenched, and kicked out at the other men rolling and snarling on the sand.

"Stop!" He flung cockeyed Floki down on his face on the sand and tore the knife out of his grasp. Ulf and Gisur were thrashing around on the ground, locked in each other's arms, growling and shrieking, and Corban walked into them, driving his feet into their bodies, until they broke apart, whining. He grabbed Ulf by the shoulder and yanked him up onto his feet, and aimed the knife in his hand at the other man.

"Harm him and I'll kill you. He's the only one who knows how to get us back home."

The little blonde man was panting. Sand smeared the side of his face. He showed his mottled brown teeth in a snarl. "Home. We'll never get home. It's all his fault. Tell him, Ulf."

Corban still held Ulf by the shoulder. The captain stood docilely in his grip, his head down.

"What?" Corban said.

"We're way far south," Ulf said.

"You said we were north."

"I made a mistake." Ulf's eyes glittered. "The sea was rough when I took the other reading. It wasn't my fault, nobody could have read it well."

"Kill him," Gisur snarled. "He's got us all dead. We'll never get home—We're all going to die here—" He lifted his hands like claws. "Kill him, at least."

"Ah, you're mad," Corban said. He tucked the knife into his belt. "Ulf, you said we could rig a new mast. What about a sail?"

"The cargo cover," Ulf said.

"Is there enough rope?"

"There's rope."

Corban swung around toward the other men. "Stop acting like sheep. We're going home. All of us. All together. Understand?"

They stared at him, their faces sagging. Floki turned and glared at Ulf. Gisur said, "We're going to die here. I don't care what you say."

Corban grunted, angry. "If you're right you can tell me so in Hell." He moved over beside Ulf, so that the cockeyed man was staring at him too. "Tomorrow we're cutting the mast." He put his hand on Ulf's shoulder. "Can we do that in a day?"

Ulf nodded. Corban turned to the other two again. "We'll carry water in these casks—"

"They all leak," said Floki, with a groan.

"We'll patch them. There's moss, there's pitch. I'll go hunting again. There's a lot of game here, we'll take meat with us, and we can fish." He looked each one in the face, nodding to him. "We'll leave as soon as we can put away some food."

This silenced them but did not stiffen them. They went back to the fire and sat around it without talking, without looking at each other. At least they had stopped fighting. Corban went away down the beach again, to get away from them, and steady himself.

Now that he was on solid ground again the idea of sailing out onto the sea, of crossing that open ocean, filled him with a sick sense of panic. He thought of Mav, and of Benna and her sisters. He wondered again why it was he, Corban, standing here, alive, trying to get home, and not those other men: like Floki's brother, swept overboard in the storm and drowned in the sea. He wished he could think that meant he would not drown in this crossing, either. He wanted to believe that it meant something, anyway.

He settled himself. The other men had no heart as it stood; if they saw him afraid they would give up. Being afraid did no good anyhow. Sometimes thinking just got in the way. He wished he could see Benna, and he longed for his sister. He went back to the fire, to the poor cold company of the other men.

—⟐—

In the morning Ulf went to work with the axe, and Corban walked off into the forest again. He followed the same stream he had found and traced before, picking it up where it wound into the black mucky swamp at the foot of the rising ground. The day was bright and fresh; he plucked some stems of reeds and chewed them as he walked. They had no real taste, but he swallowed some and did not get sick. He watched the trees for more of the creature he had found the day before, but saw none. Twice he saw owls, high in the trees, too far away to shoot with his sling.

In a clearing he found strange droppings, like bird droppings, but saw no tracks. He overturned rocks in the stream, looking for lizards or frogs, and found nothing. The stream wound back up a narrow rocky ridge. He watched for birds with nests, for the prints of deer—remembering that huge forefoot print, that strange bellowing cry. He began to think that was a tremendous deer, whose meat would take them all the way to Hedeby. He wondered how to kill it, and began imagining trapping it, somehow; clubbing it down. He turned over a rotten log and found a swarm of white grubs, and ate them without even thinking much about it.

The day wore on. Around him the forest rang with a racket of birdsong. He came on a meadow, and circling through it came on the forked prints of deer—but smaller, like the deer he knew. He quartered over the meadow, looking for more tracks. A mouse bolted away almost under his feet and dove into the grass. He saw just the tail of a snake vanishing.

From somewhere downstream a flock of birds took flight, and rose up over where he stood, in such numbers their passage shadowed the whole grassy meadow.

He wandered on, circling back, he hoped, toward the stream. There were big red mushrooms in the heavy shade below a rock, but the color put him off. In a stand of great barreled oaks he came suddenly on an enormous bird, scratching and pecking at the ground like a giant chicken, but looking like no chicken he had ever seen.

It saw him at once, and took off running with a hair-raising warbling yell; he whirled the sling around and fired at it. Just as he loosed, the bird took flight, lumbering into the air, and the stone sailed wide. He ran after it a little way, trying to see where it went, but the bird disappeared at once into the forest.

He went away down toward the stream again, following a narrow game trail, and striding along around a twist in the way, he came on a full grown deer, a doe, hanging upside down in the air.

He jumped. His skin went cold. His gaze traveled up, up from the doe's body, following the long length of rope, up to the top of the tree. It was a snare. His mind seemed to swell, taking in the implications of this. His nerves quivered, as if someone watched him.

He had to get out of here.

He could not leave so much meat. He grabbed for the doe, cut her down, and hacked her quickly into quarters. The feeling would not leave him that someone was watching him. The day before, today coming here, he had left tracks, all through these woods, he had left plenty of signs. It had never occurred to him, until now, there might be people here.

Certainly whoever had made this snare knew that Corban had come into his country. He got all the meat up on his shoulders, and ran toward the beach.

⸺⸙⸺

Ulf had cut down a good tree for a mast, and Floki and Gisur had dug mussels and cockles out of the beach. Corban did not tell them about the snare, but in the morning he drove them to work, moving faster than any of them so they would have to keep up. They heated pine logs in the fire, to drive out the pitch, and sealed the whiskey casks, and he sent Gisur to fill them at the stream. He cut up the deer into chunks and stuffed them into one cask, and filled the spaces with sea water and seaweed.

When Ulf had trimmed the tree trunk they stepped it into the ship. The cargo cover was in two pieces, which meant it had to be sewn together. While they did this Gisur made a hook of bone and fished in the bay, and caught two huge flatfish.

Corban kept looking toward the trees; he saw that Ulf noticed this, but Ulf said nothing. Corban knew that someone was there, watching them. They used an extra oar for the yard, and bent the sail on. By midafternoon, they had the water casks mended and filled, and they loaded the ship.

Ulf said, "Should we go tomorrow morning?"

Corban straightened; they were all watching him. His stomach tightened. They had looked to Ulf before, and Ulf's mistakes had gotten them here. He turned and looked inland again, toward the dark forest. In the night, what might come silently out of those trees and fall on them? He faced the other men again.

"No," he said. "We'll leave now."

Without a word they obeyed him. They drove the ship out through the waves and into the sea, climbed aboard, and rowed toward the open water. The wind was foul for the end of the bay, but the tide was ebbing, and they all rowed, even Ulf, with the steerboard lashed down. No one spoke. By sundown they had reached the open sea. The stretch of white beach was already out of sight behind them, only the forest showing, a prickly dark line against the sky. They raised the sail, and caught the wind to the north and the east.

⸺§⸺

The wind backed around out of the west and they were still well south of where Ulf believed they should be; they started rowing north. The food went bad, and then the food ran out entirely. Corban ate the seaweed, chewing patiently. Gisur fished but caught nothing. Ulf took a reading one night and decided they were far enough north, and they turned east and ran up the sail.

That was worse even than rowing, because there was nothing to do. Gisur dozed as he sat with the fishing line trailing out between his fingers, and Floki moaned and, occasionally, cried. Ulf sat in the stern, the steer bar in his hand, his gaze aimed eastward as if he could pull them back home on the force of his will. Corban thought of his sister; he remembered one day he had forgotten for years, maybe since it happened, when they were little children, a day spent hidden in the byre cracking nuts and telling each other secrets. He longed for Mav as if for food; an aching hopeless hunger. He remembered the smell of the byre, the new-mown hay and the cattle, and the sound of a cow stamping its hoof. Mav leaning toward him saying, "Promise me you won't tell."

He had laughed, startled that she needed such a promise, when he talked to nobody but her.

The memory was so sharp it was as if the whole scene lay before him, everything except the fact. Corban shut his eyes. He was exhausted, half-broken, a bad man who had failed. He had forgotten how many days they had been at sea. The wind blew steadily from the west, fair and true, and the ship drove along before it, muscling along over the long ocean swells; at night the stars blazed from the sky in a white splendor. Corban chewed on a corner of his cloak, watching Ulf take another reading of the stars with his stick.

The captain spoke suddenly, low-voiced. "You see these notches? You put this notch here on the North Star—" He held the stick out at arm's length, toward the north; squinting one eye shut he moved his head a little, and put out the other hand and gripped the stick, and lowered it and showed it to Corban.

"See—this notch is what we want." He nudged his thumb into the indentation on the stick. "Sail on this heading until we strike land, then follow the coast southeast. You see?"

Corban realized suddenly that Ulf thought he was going to die, that someone else would have to read the star. He looked at the captain sharply, whose face was haggard and drooping, blood crusted on his lips. Corban swallowed; he could taste blood in his own mouth. He nodded to Ulf.

"I see it. Thank you."

The captain snorted at him. They said nothing, only sat there in the stern, watching the dark water rise up and then slide away past the ship. Ulf's head sagged between his shoulders, his body slumped down a little, and he dozed off. The wind drove the ship on into the east. Finally Corban got the bucket and began to bail.

They sailed on for days, Corban had no idea how many, the men
lying around in the ship, too spent to talk. Gisur's fishing line
trailed along behind them, but Gisur slept most of the time now.
Then, one morning, he caught a fish.

He had wrapped the string around his wrist, and the jerk of the
hook setting woke him. Floki had to help him pull the fish in. It
was another cod, and they hacked it up with their knives and cut
the scales away skin and all, and devoured the meat raw. Corban
scraped tiny bits of flesh away from the skin with his knife, sa-
voring each little stab of a taste. A while later a seagull slid by
them, looking them over, and around midafternoon they saw land.

Ulf let out a yell, flinging his arm out to point, and croaked
and whooped, and the others looked and laughed, and cried, and
staggered up onto their feet. They were coming up on a low sandy
island. As the ship headed in toward the beach, a boy standing
there turned and raced away up the low grassy hill where some
sheep grazed.

Floki and Gisur were still laughing and hugging each other.
Ulf croaked out something to Corban; the ship's keel crunched
against the sandy shore, and the captain leapt over the side and
splashed through the shallowing wave, stumbling to his hands and
knees. He waddled up onto the beach, headed after the fleeing boy.
Corban got out of the ship, and took hold of the gunwale. For a
moment he was too tired and weak even to try. Gisur and Floki
tumbled out to help him, their hands on the ship, and looked at
him. A big wave came, and he said, "Now," and the wave lifted
the boat and carried it in and they walked up beside it, light as
wind drift, until the wave laid it down sweetly on the land. Floki
went up on the sloping sandy beach and dropped to his knees and
bent over, his forehead to the sand, his hands behind his head.

Ulf came back, with the boy and a man, who lived over the
hill at a farmstead. They went back to the farm and there ate cabbage soup and mutton until their bellies were like drums. In the
morning Ulf had them drag what remained of the cargo out of the
ship so that he could look it over. Most of the remaining cloth was
soaked and matted and ruined, but a few lengths somehow had
stayed dry, and the fleeces were good enough, if a little salty. Ulf
traded the remaining good cloth to the farmer for two bales of

fleeces and some cheeses. They packed up mutton and some bread and a great jug of the soup and sailed off to the south, keeping that island to their right hand, and the next, too, when it appeared, slightly south and east on the hazy edge of the sea.

Ulf knew where he was now. He sat happily in the stern steering them along and drinking cabbage soup from a wooden bowl. At night, he put them in to coves and inlets, and they slept the night on dry land, with fires and cooked food. One day Corban thought he recognized the coast; they were sailing down past Jorvik, he thought. He thought of Benna, and kept his mouth shut.

His eyes followed the familiar coastline as it slipped by, thinking of her, of Grod, of her sisters. The warm little family in that hut. Finally he turned his face forward again.

They rowed south, against the wind, and Ulf took another reading, and turned them due east. They went out of sight of land, and Floki began to curse and sob again, but before sundown they had raised a low coastline to the southeast. The next few days they sailed past white shelving beaches, slowly giving way to swamps and fens, until the land bent around abruptly northward.

Ulf stood up, looking toward the coast, his hand shading his eyes. Abruptly he pushed the steer bar over and headed them in toward land. The coast was flat, indistinct, reeds poking up out of the water, water lying in behind patches of sandy shoal. In all the flatness there was a single little hill, even and grassy, just to the south. They took down the sail and put out the oars; Ulf came down from the stern to row in the second pair.

"See there?" He bobbed his head forward. "That earthworks? Follow that to Hedeby." He leaned into the oars, and Corban swung forward again, and they rowed down into the swamp of interlacing waterways. To the south the hill lengthened into a steep-sided grassy ridge, a great wall, that ran straight away to the east. Ulf called out directions through the swamp, following a thread of current inland. They were catching up to a flat coaster boat, and he swung their ship to follow into the mouth of a slow-moving river. Pulling against the current, they followed a train of ships and boats paddling slowly up the river.

Over the grassy banks Corban could see broad fields, cattle, and once, someone plowing, far away. In the evening, they came finally to a wharf, with a little wooden town behind it.

There were ships already along the wharf, and Ulf after some snorting and groaning steered them to still water off between the wharf and the ridge of the earthworks, visible to the south. Here he fished a floating mooring out of the water and tied them up. At once, a little boat took off from the shore and stroked quickly toward them.

Ulf said, "This is the end, Corban."

Corban stood up, looking at the little wooden town. "This is Hedeby?" he said, surprised; it looked smaller than Dublin.

"No, no. This is only Hollandstadt." Ulf plunged his hand casually back into the stern and pulled out a sack of leather, which jingled. The other two men drew closer. Gisur licked his lips. Ulf said, "Hedeby is at the far end of the road. Follow the earthworks. If anyone stops you, say 'Hurrah for King Bluetooth.'" He dug his hand into the sack and took out money.

Floki pushed forward. "I should get Odd's, too."

"Ah, you scum," Ulf said. "Here, I have the pay for all the crew, divide it evenly." He began to count out English pennies to each of them. The little boat had arrived beside their ship; a fat old woman sat in the stern, watching them expectantly.

Gisur got forty pennies, and Floki forty, and Ulf counted forty into Corban's hand. When he was done, he lifted his face, and said, "You got us through that, Corban. Maybe these two will go and brag in the alehouses about how brave and strong they were, but I won't forget you."

Floki grunted out something. Surprised, Corban saw all three watching him with cow-eyes, like women. He stammered something, not knowing what to say, uneasy under their looks. Gisur reached out and gripped his arm.

"I will sail with you anywhere."

Corban felt his cheeks glow hot as sunburn. He shook Gisur's hand, and then Floki's, and finally Ulf's, and the captain held onto him. He lowered his voice.

"They would have killed me. I mean it, Corban. I won't forget."

Corban laughed. "I think you're too tough to die anyway, Ulf."

"Are you coming, or not?" the fat woman barked, from her

boat, and they got into the tippy round-bottomed craft and she rowed them in to the shore. Ulf and the other men went straight to the alehouse, but Corban slept that night in the high grass at the foot of the earthworks.

In the morning he set out along the road that led eastward out of the little town. It felt strange to walk. The road still rocked gently under his feet as he went along. All around him as he went on there were other people; after being so long with only Ulf and Floki and Gisur he could not take his gaze from the faces of strangers. He swung around a big wagon, laden down with casks and bales, behind a team of wide-rumped horses, also going east. Other wagons rumbled past him in the other direction, raising fogs of dust. He kept to the side of the broad road, where the air was better. The high, even ridge of the earthworks ran along parallel to the road; the wind rippled the tall grass growing on it.

Ahead, now, a smudge of brown hung in the air, a gathering of old smoke. The rattle and creak of the wagons banged in his ears. He walked along among a great milling of hoofs and wooden wheels, with other men calling out, and now and then the snap of a whip. The road was taking him straight beneath the brown smudge.

Ahead the earthworks abruptly met another high grassy ridge, with a gate through it.

Remembering the Jorvik bar, and that other trouble, Corban stopped a moment, feeling like a rabbit. He had the money Ulf had given him tied into the corner of his cloak; he slung the red and blue wool around him and hitched his belt up. With long strides he set forward again, thinking what Ulf had said, to hail King Bluetooth.

No one stopped him. He walked right in through the gate past a crew of guardsmen, a line of wagons stopped and waiting, and into the city beyond.

The din and the smell struck him at once. He walked out of the gate onto a wooden path that led between solid rows of buildings, made of woven wattle thickly dauted with mud, their chimneys spouting smoke up into the broad brown canopy above. Every few yards another walkway crossed the wooden path Corban followed, and these walks were full of people.

A big man in a hat made of fur bellowed something in a language he had never heard before, and all around him people burst
out laughing. Corban smelled garbage and shit and the rotten seaweed stink of the beach. Swinging wide he passed two women
screaming at each other nose to nose, their long yellow braids bristling. The crowds of people pressed thick around him until he
thought it hard to breathe. He walked on, gawking around him. At
a wide place in the wooden path, a man in a red jacket was leading
a big black bear on a leash; as Corban passed by the bear stood
on its hind legs and waved its arms and lifted its feet up one at a
time, like a dance. The watching crowd shrieked with delight, and
the bear gaped its jaws, its tongue lolling.

Corban went by a market with cabbages and onions piled up
like mountains, with rows of ducks hanging by their yellow feet.
In the great buildings teetering up on either side people screamed
and laughed. Music spilled from a window high over his head. He
could not stop walking. The city was enormous; he had been inside
the gate for half the day, it seemed, and had not seen the same
place twice.

He came suddenly out from between buildings and stood before the water, a bay or inlet or broad river, maybe, lined with
wharfs and ships. All along the wharfs there were goods piled, like
the cargo Ulf had brought here: fleeces and cloth, stacks of leather,
kegs and chests and bags, some being taken out to the ships, and
some going into wagons lined up beside the wharfs.

He walked on and on, along the rattling wooden path, past
mountains of goods. At a long wooden wharf lines of slaves were
unloading a ship, throwing sacks of cargo from one set of hands
to the next, until they landed in a growing heap on the side of the
path; one of the sacks had split a little, letting a trickle of yellow
grain run down. Next to it stood a girl in a long blue gown, with
a sleek black bird on her shoulder, which screeched at him.

Slowly, he began to hear something else, under the roar and
crash of the city. He strained his ears to make it out, and his steps
quickened. He thought he heard a voice, a single voice, singing.
He thought it was his sister's voice.

A surge of excitement went through him. He turned his head
this way and that, trying to hear it better. His feet carried him

rapidly along, into a sidestreet, down another path, the song steadily louder and louder. His heart began to gallop. He broke into a trot. Her voice thrilled in his ears. Mav, he thought. Mav. He was blind now to the city, deaf to its sounds, caught on that thread of song. It led him up from the harbor, down a narrow path, to a high gate in a wall not of withies but of posts driven into the mud, and from behind that fence skirled out the wild music of his sister's voice.

He screamed, "Mav!" He backed up and ran at the wall and leapt, caught the top in his hands, and hauled himself upward. His heart was beating so hard he thought it would break out of his chest and soar along ahead of him. "Mav," he cried again, and dropped down into a courtyard, where people turned to gawk at him, dropping the work from their hands to stare. He plunged across the yard to the hall, whose double doors stood open.

Tears were sliding down his face. He rushed into the hall, into the sudden dimness, and turned, toward the closed doors of the cupboard against the wall; he knew people were gathering around him, watching and murmuring, but he hardly noticed them; in the great whirling chaos around him only her voice mattered, and he pulled open the doors of the cupboard, and through the opening she flung herself forward, into his arms.

CHAPTER TWELVE

She was thin, light as smoke, her face hollow, her eyes huge, brimming over. She would not let go of him, her arms wrapped around him, pressing herself against him as if he could absorb her, take her in to hide away. Her arms like sticks, her wrists so thin he thought he could have bitten off her hand.

In the middle of her, round and growing, the baby gave off a great heat, like a fire in a cauldron.

He held her; she cried and cried, and he held her and rocked her and said her name and stroked her hair, stunned and grateful. Presently he became aware of the woman standing beside them, watching him.

He lifted his gaze to her. In the dim light he had trouble seeing her clearly; he could not make out if she were old or young, fair or plain. Her face seemed to float upon her like a mask.

She said, "Welcome, Corban."

"You know me," he said, stupidly.

"She has been singing to me of you for months, now." Her eyes never left him. She sat down on a stool facing him. "I know you very well, I think."

A ripple of fear passed down his spine. He clung now to his sister as much as she clung to him. He said, "What is wrong with her?"

"Her mind is broken," the woman said. She seemed older than he had thought, a moment ago. She said, "Was she not strange, before?"

"Strange. She was deep-minded." He held her; suddenly it overcame him again, that he had found her at last, and he shut his eyes and laid his cheek against her hair and felt her body all against him; her weight, her touch, there again, that had been torn away. He yielded himself up, whole again.

The woman's voice brought him back. "She knows much. I imagine she has always known more than she let on to you bumpkins around her. But now her mind is broken, and what she knows runs in and out like the tides of the sea."

She reached out her hand to touch Mav's cheek. Mav recoiled from her, flinched down against Corban's shoulder, and turned her huge dark eyes on her. The woman chuckled.

"She knows, you see. She knows too much." She stood up, gathering her skirts around her, slithering cloth that glinted although there was no light. "We shall talk, you and I, Corban."

"No," Mav said. "You can't have him." She began to weep.

"Oh, well, then, you too," the woman said, smiling, and went away toward the far end of the hall. Corban stood up, with Mav in his arms, and followed her.

⇌

"I tried to help her," the woman said. She sat down on a stool covered in painted leather. They sat at the far end of the hall, out of the sunlight; she had a place of her own there, beside the cupboard of her bed. Although there were no walls the space seemed cut off from the rest of the hall. She touched her fingers to the wicks of lamps around them and they lit, but there seemed no real light from them, only a faint glow that slicked over the surfaces around them. The woman now seemed very young, and very beautiful, no older than Mav herself.

The floor was covered in a cloth of fantastic design. Corban sat down on it, his sister in his lap. "Who are you?" he said.

"I am the Lady of Hedeby. You need know nothing else."

"There is a King," Mav said. Her voice was hoarse. The words came from her in fits and jerks and horrible grimaces. She curled her arm around Corban's neck.

"There is always a King," said the Lady. She took a round bracelet from her arm, and tossed it onto the floor between them.

Corban leaned forward to see it. Lying on the multicolored cloth the golden ring grew larger, round, shining in the dim directionless light, and within its circle he saw water leaping, and the rough dark shape of lands.

"This is the ring of the world," the Lady said. "In the middle is the Sea, over which we sail from place to place, and all the world's places lie around it. Hedeby is here. Here is Jorvik." She pointed; he thought he saw, for only an instant, the whole city tiny and distinct under her hand, with its miniature church, and even Eric's hall, small as an ant on the embankment. "Here Iceland. Here—" her hand moved northeast, and he saw under it a coastline of countless islands and inlets "—is Norway."

He wished for an instant she would hold her hand over the western edge, so that he could see what was there. In her ring, nothing lay past Iceland but the sea. He lifted his gaze to her face. "Why are you showing me this?"

The Lady lifted her face. For an instant she was wizened and old, and then suddenly beautiful again. She said, "Do you think I will let you walk out of here with her in your arms, and get nothing in return?"

"I will give you anything. I have money."

"I have more money than you will ever know exists. What I want from you is a task."

Mav said, "No."

Corban gave her a long look. She was shockingly thin. Her face was pale as the moon. Only the fat rounding belly of her seemed hale. She laid her head on his shoulder and closed her eyes.

He faced the Lady again. "I will do anything."

The woman before him nodded her head, smiling, as if she had always known this would happen. His throat closed up; he was afraid, he had no power, his sister had the power of them—and his sister was dying in his arms.

He had found her too late. He had not saved her. His heart cracked with pity and dread. She was a wraith already; she could not speak to him, except in wild bursts of sounds, with twitching of her hands and eyes begging him to understand her. Her belly full of the child of a Viking, one of them who had murdered their family.

The Lady said, "You see the world ring, here. Now, heed me, I must make you aware of some things. You have come before Bloodaxe, and know of him somewhat."

Mav shivered in his arms. She seemed asleep. He said, "Yes."

"Bloodaxe was once King of Norway. He was the favorite son of his father, Harald of the Horrible Hair, who brought all the little kings of Norway under his sway, whether they willed it or no. This was some years ago. Of all his sons, and he had many, Harald loved Bloodaxe best—who knows why—and so made him king after him, but unknown to him, he had a better son, a love child, whom he had sent to England to be fostered there. That was Hakon Aethelstansfostri. And when Harald died and Eric Bloodaxe became King of Norway, Hakon came and drove him out, and now he rules there."

Corban thought of the fat greedy king in Jorvik. "He seems no fit lord. Probably he deserved it."

"Well," the Lady said, and her eyes flashed. "However you see him, I want you to go to him, and convince him he should be King of Norway again, and induce him to make some progress toward that end."

"I," Corban said, startled. "How can I do that?"

The Lady smiled at him. Her eyes gleamed. They reminded him suddenly of the purple jewels on the breast of King Eric Bloodaxe's wife. "You will go as my man, to buy and sell for me. That will give you a place there, at court. I will give you cargo, and money. I have a house in Jorvik, which you can use." She leaned forward suddenly and scooped up the bracelet, which shrank back to the size of her arm as she put it on.

"I can't do it," he said. "I don't know how."

"You crossed the trackless sea to find your sister," she said. "I doubt you knew how to do that when you started out. To save your sister now, you will find a way to obey me." She nodded. He could barely see her in the darkness. One by one, the little lamps were going out. She said, "I will keep her here. Through her I will know everything you do. When you come back, and have done as I wish, I shall let you take her away."

Mav whimpered in her sleep. He tipped his head against her hair. Holding her, touching her, he could not bear to think he must leave her.

He said, "I will do it."

"Very good," said the Lady. "Come, now, you must be hungry, and maybe she will eat, too, with you here."

⸺⸱⸺

He was ordinary, she thought, just another man, like any other—
well set up, surely, broad-shouldered and strong, with his thick
curly dark hair and bony, open face—even handsome, but he was
ordinary. And yet there was some quality about him she could not
place. He seemed clear as water, clear as nothing, which was how
he had escaped Gunnhild.

He would not escape Gunnhild again. When he came back to
Jorvik, Gunnhild would suspect him at once.

The cloak had some small virtue, too, which had protected him.
The Lady wondered where that came from. Like him, it seemed
common, a little garden spell, simple as a mother's love, perhaps,
or a good deed.

She watched them sitting together, in the sunlight of the courtyard. Mav would not let him put her down, but sat always in his
lap, her arm around his neck, and he broke bits of bread from a
loaf and daubed them with honey and fed them to her. She was
not singing now. What she knew was closed up and folded over
and around her brother, this innocent, this simple, ordinary man.

The Lady shook off a sudden unease. There seemed nothing
of him she could take hold of, no ambition, no pride, no lust, only
that sweet strange clarity.

She would make something of him that she could manage. She
watched him feeding his sister a morsel of the bread. The girl
laughed, and for an instant she was well again, her eyes shining in
the skeletal pallor of her face. The Lady found herself tensed,
poised, like a hawk ready to stoop.

His coming had changed how she saw this. Through the sister,
she had taken the man. When he obeyed her, she would have power
over him, whatever use he might be to her. When he did as she
bade him, when he became what she would make of him. Then
through him she would take Mav, who had resisted her so inex-
plicably, and who was so much the greater prize. The Lady stroked
her chin, delighted.

⸻

The Lady gave him a red coat that reached down to his knees, very
fancy, with gold stitching in fanciful designs, and fur at the

neck and on the cuffs. She talked to him of buying and selling, gave him keys, tally sticks, a rack of beads she called an abacus.

"See if you can make anything of this. It came from the east, far away to the east, I have no interest in it, but there are those who find it useful."

She gave him a purse full of money, saying, "I doubt you will need more than this." She talked of a ship.

He said, "I have a ship."

She blinked at him. He saw he had surprised her, somehow. He said, "But to use it I will have to send back—to the west end of the road, to Hollandstadt."

"Do so," she said. "Hollandstadt, of course, you came through there. Then you will need wagons, to haul the cargo. I will give you iron. Eric always needs iron. And some other things."

At that she took him around behind the hall, to a room set off from the rest, with a great door and a lock. She opened the lock with a touch and they went in, and she made a light between her hands and hung it up on a rafter.

"First you must present yourself to Eric. Do that in the daylight. Then," she said, "find a man named Arinbjorn."

He started, "I have met—" and stopped, and she turned to face him, frowning, surprised again.

"When I saw Eric," he said, trying to explain. "He was there. Maybe Mav didn't know."

"No," she said, thoughtfully. "All that mattered then was Gunnhild."

"Who is she?"

The Lady took down a box from a shelf, and set it under the light. "She is a princess of the Danes, of a very old and noble house, very powerful. When she was young they saw the power in her, and sent her to the Finns, to learn sorcery—the Finns know sorcery in their cradles that the rest of us have long misplaced, if we had it at all." She turned the lid of the box up and the light shattered and danced on a litter of jewels. "Then she married Bloodaxe, whom she rules."

He shivered; he remembered Gunnhild, watching him. He thought of this woman here, and his sister—he wondered if there were a web of such women, all around the world, a female caul of knowledge over all the doings of men. He looked up, and found the Lady watching him, smiling.

She said, "Give these to Gunnhild. It will blunt her anger with you. She has a great fondness for baubles." She lifted a dozen chips of colored light and flowed them into his cupped hands. He felt them cool and fiery on his palms, like a thousand icy stabs.

"How can I deal with her?" he said.

"You will find a way. She is quick, and shrewd, but she is young still, and very vain."

He was afraid; it trembled on his tongue to tell her he had no power, but she was watching him again, amused, and he said nothing. He felt as if everything he said she had heard in her mind the moment before he said it. He turned his head, looking toward the hall, where Mav lay sleeping.

She said, "Send to your ship at Hollandstadt. I will find a wagon for the iron, and your other goods."

He sat with his sister, taking comfort from her. Sometimes it was enough to have found her. Mav slept. She seemed easier, now; she no longer flew into a terror if she woke and he was not there. While she was asleep he put on his new coat to go out into the city.

The coat was heavy and warm. He took it off, stowed it with the other things the Lady had given him, and swung his old cloak around him again. Then he went out onto the wooden pathways of Hedeby.

Almost at once he was lost. He walked along the booming walkway between two rows of houses whose pitched roofs leaned down almost over his head. On the peak of one roof sat a row of buzzards, stretching out their white-tipped wings to soak up the warmth of the sun. The next lane was a shambles, full of bellowing cattle, and the stink of hot blood. The crowds of people made him shy. In his ears their voices sounded, speaking languages he had never heard. But the vast throng slowly began to make him feel easier. If they were all strange he was no more strange; no one would notice him here no matter what he did.

He watched three men in tight bright clothes toss a dizzying whirl of balls into the air; they leapt, spun themselves in the air like balls, stood on their hands. The watching folk cheered and laughed and threw money at them—Corban tossed one of his silver pennies at them, feeling very fine in doing so.

At the harbor he saw ships rowing up into the quiet water, and watched slaves unloading the cargos. Rotten fruit bobbed in the scummy water of the harbor; he saw some dogs fighting over something at the water's edge and recoiled, his stomach heaving, when he saw it was the body of a newborn baby.

He walked away, his heart thundering; that was a bad omen, he thought. He thought of Mav's baby, planted in her belly by the men who had murdered his family, and his bile rose. He wondered why she loved it. He would have thrown it into the harbor, like that poor baby back there.

She loved it. He knew that; he let go his anger against it. Nothing he could do anyway. He would love it too.

In the next street, a woman in a red gown and a face painted over her real face came up and blocked his way. She put her head to one side, smiled at him, said, "Well, then, handsome one, will you come with me?" and added something that popped his eyes open like cracked nuts.

She hooted with laughter, seeing him blush to the hairline, and reached out and grabbed him by the crotch. He bounded back, out of her reach, and stared at her, while she laughed and pointed her fingers at him. For a moment he thought of going with her, and she saw that, and her dark eyes gleamed, but he remembered Benna suddenly, and turned away.

She hooted after him. He went off, looking back over his shoulder at her. Under the cover of the cloak he slid his hand down over his man's part, still throbbing from her touch. He wondered what it would be like, to handle a woman he did not know, would never see again, to whom he could do anything he wanted. Under his hand his part throbbed, hungry.

He should have gone with her. He was glad he had not.

Fretting on this, he went into the nearest alehouse, and got a stoup of liquor. The man who gave it to him had another, tiny man sitting on his shoulder, covered with hair, and with a long curling tail; Corban's jaw dropped, seeing this, and the ale-man laughed and reached up and patted the tiny hairy man, which chattered in an alien tongue. Corban drank the ale off in a single draught.

He thought, It isn't that the world is strange. It's that I know nothing.

That made him feel better. He realized that the idea of knowing always betrayed him. He had known there were no tiny hairy men with tails, until he saw it. What he actually did know was a tiny rock in the middle of a great sea of unknowing. The ale sweetened his mind; he looked around him now for more interesting sights.

He drifted through the markets, past bolts of cloth, woolen stuff as thick and coarse as his cloak, and fabric so fine he thought it would fall apart at his touch. Under awnings that flapped in the wind were heaps of nuts and combs of honey and a thousand shapes and kinds of bread; he bought a round loaf, studded with bits of fruit, whose sweet taste delighted him. In the next street under a broad green awning was a woman selling toys, dolls and balls, necklaces of clear and amber stones, carved bits of bone and horn, and a chess board with pieces of smooth stone, one side black and one white. He was afraid to ask how much these things cost, but their shine and glitter drew him.

He thought of Benna, of her sisters, who never had such things. Here was a good use for his money. He found a necklace for Gifu of bright colored beads, and a painted wooden hair comb for Arre. Benna was harder to suit. Nothing seemed good enough. Then he saw a tray of disks of shining silver, rimmed with painted metal flowers; when he picked one up to see, his own face appeared reflected in the silver circle.

He recognized himself from Benna's drawing. From Mav's face. The old man behind the display said, "Those were made in Miklagard the Great, those looking glasses."

Looking glass, he thought, pleased. Benna should have a looking glass. The price was almost everything he had left, but he paid it gladly.

"Take care with it," the old man said. "They are full of luck, but if you break it, all the luck will disappear." Corban wrapped up the looking glass in a corner of his cloak and went back to the house of the Lady of Hedeby.

⸺⸙⸺

He was her brother, and he was not her brother. She sat watching him pack up his things, the clothes the Lady had given him, the little glittery charms he had bought for those other people. Her old brother had been a windblown reed, had leaned on her, always, since they were babies, had spoken loud and said very little. This new brother was strong, and nothing bent him.

She had leaned on him, she had gathered up some of his strength, enough that now she could see him going, and not fall into despair. But it was hard. She had so much she wanted to say, and somehow she could not make him understand.

In the middle of her, the hot coal that was her baby stirred. It grew bigger, every day, revelling in its growing, in its newness, its feet thumping up under her ribs, pushing out her belly impossibly round and taut.

She folded her arms around it. Little fool. The Lady had said nothing about it lately, but Mav knew she would kill it, if she could. She curved herself around it, a fortress around it, as she watched Corban close up his pack. She had to protect them, the man going out into the world, the child within her, and she had barely enough strength to stand.

Corban came over to her and sat beside her, and took hold of her hands. "I am going."

"Ah," she said. She freed one hand, and fisted it in the cloak. A wild rush of things flooded at once into her mind—too many. She could not give tongue to all, so she spoke none. "Ah, Corban." She lifted the cloak and buried her face in it, breathing his scent out of it.

He put his arms around her. "You must take care. Eat, and drink, and sleep—" He held her tight against him, and she began to cry. Watch out, she thought, seeing thousands of enemies around him, knives in their looks. Walk straight. Say nothing. Her tongue locked; she could not speak.

"I will come back," he said, and let go of her, and took her face in his hands. "I will come back."

Be careful, she thought. She ran her fingers down the front of his shirt, her eyes full of tears. You came, she thought. You came for me.

Then he was gone. The pack gone, the cloak, the hall empty,

huge, hollow, cold. She sat there on the bed, feeling the space around her stretch and thin toward nothing, as if the world fell away from her, and left her hanging.

She shut her eyes, dizzy. As he went away her mind stretched toward him, following on his shadow. He was gone into the kingdom of their archenemy, and she was powerless to help him—she would even betray him, when she sang, give up everything he did and said. A wave of nausea swept up into her throat. She shook herself. Then she opened her eyes, seeing the hall, the upright columns, the horizontal beams, all still and even and solid.

In front of her, smiling, stood the Lady of Hedeby.

CHAPTER THIRTEEN

He dreamt of the dark forest, far to the west; that he walked up that stream again into the forest, with its thunderous birdsong, its fabulous creatures. He walked along the little stream through the trees. He was looking for someone, someone was ahead of him, in among the dark trees, waiting for him—

"Corban."

"Unhh." He stirred awake, out of the dream; his limbs like waterlogged wood after the lightness of the dream.

Ulf said, "We're almost there. We're almost to Jorvik."

Corban muttered at him. He straightened up out of the bow of the ship, where he had been sleeping; he did not row, now, Ulf had hired other men to row. Corban was only part of the cargo, too bored even to stay awake. He stood, stretching his arms out, and looked eagerly up the river.

They were gliding strongly upstream, past thickets of willow, trailing branches like long green hair into the brown flowing water. The spring had come and gone here; deep summer lay on the land, the trees heavy-headed and full of bees, the fields overgrown with brambles. Ahead the river curved around to the right; Ulf had gone back to the stern, to steer the ship past the root end of a great tree half-blocking the channel. A turtle basking on the downtilted trunk of the tree plopped into the water at the ship's approach. From the shoal behind the tree root a long-legged bird lifted up into the air. Then, as the ship swung around the broad curve of the river, there came into sight the spire and the rooftops of Jorvik, strung along its embankment like a great thatchy crust, overhung with smoke.

He wondered again at what the Lady wanted him to do here. He knew nothing of buying and selling; she meant that, he knew, to get him close to Eric. He remembered how the mere mention of another farmann's name had gotten him out of hanging, when he first came to Jorvik. The traders had power, but he did not understand how.

They were coming up to the shore at Jorvik. He went back to

the bow again and dug out his pack. He took out the fancy red coat, unfolded it, shook it hard to get some of the creases out, and put it on. His old red and blue cloak he balled up and thrust into the pack, down below everything else.

The oarsmen were shouting and leaning out to see ahead of them, the ship wobbling under their unsteady strokes. Ulf roared at them and they settled to the work again, but still their voices babbled up. Corban took the little leather sack of jewels from the pack; he had thought a while about how to present these to the Queen, to buy her favor. He had found a piece of black lambskin, before he left Hedeby; he took this out of the pack also, and quickly poured out the jewels onto the wooly side of the lambskin and rolled it up.

The ship was nosing in toward the west bank of the river; he glanced up, hoping they would find room among the crowd of other ships, and stood straight, surprised. There were no other ships along the shore, not even the dragonships of the King.

Ulf shouted, Corban grabbed hold of the gunwale, and the oarsmen leapt over the side and ran the ship up onto the gravel beach, below the steep high bank where the King's Hall stood. Corban straightened up again.

The shore was almost empty. The slave pens were falling apart. Below the sheer wall of the riverbank where the crews of visiting ships had passed their jugs and kept warm around firepits, the ground was cold and sodden. A few men loitered around by the foot of the street up to the city. He cast a quick look toward the east bank, but he could see nothing there except wild trees.

Ulf came up to him. "Looks as if we're the only people here. That should make your trading easy."

"Why did they leave? There were always ships here."

Ulf shrugged. "I don't know. That's your job. Shall I unload all this?"

"Do you know where the Hedeby house is?"

"Up there, on the right hand of the street. There, the long one in the middle."

Corban looked where he was pointing. The street climbed the bank and went into the town; on the high ground just above the river sat three houses in a row, the middle one longer than the others, the roof higher. "I see it." He took the ringed key from his belt and handed it to Ulf. "Open it, store everything there, and wait for me."

He gave another quick look at the east bank, veiled in a tangle of willows in the green deep of the summer, and went up the street toward the King's Hall.

The red coat was heavy and hot, but surely it had some charm; he needed to wear it now, to face the King. To face Gunnhild. The Lady had said almost nothing to him about her, except that she was powerful, and vain. Corban remembered her sharp, cold eyes, the dry crackle of her voice. His feet were heavy, trudging up the street, the fur under his arm. He thought of Mav, which put some iron back into his legs; he walked harder, striding out. Get this over with. He lifted his eyes, and above him rose the long gable and green thatch of the Hall of King Eric Bloodaxe.

⇒⎯

Ragnar let out a yowl, and gripping little Leif by the shoulders heaved him up off the ground entirely. Along the table a roar went up. Most of the men were off with Sweyn Eelmouth, and they had pulled out the extra tables to make room for the wrestling.

"Bite him, Leif!"

"Kick him in the stones!"

Leif writhed in Ragnar's enormous hands and then abruptly twisted his legs up and booted Ragnar hard in the chest. The big man staggered and Leif bounded free, his yellow hair flying.

"Catch him, Ragnar! Catch the little bastard!"

Eric reached for his cup. Beside him in the high seat, Gunnhild was not watching the wrestling, one finger twisting and twisting a hank of her long, wheat-colored hair. He slid one hand up against her and stroked her hip.

She glanced at him, that narrow sideways look that always reminded him of a snake, as if she struck at him with her eyes. She was angry with him, had been for days, part of this long argument about England. He smiled at her, hoping to jolly her out of it, and rubbed her hip again. She curled her lip at him and turned away, pressing herself against the far arm of the high seat, showing him the back of her head.

Eric snorted. He would get her later, in the dark. He turned toward Arinbjorn, sitting on his right hand.

"I have sent Eelmouth out to raid. When he comes back, we shall have some goods for you to sell, I hope."

Arinbjorn leaned back, not looking at him, pretending to be interested in the fighting. "I shall have to send them all out of the country, to get a good price."

"Whatever you need to do," Eric said. A slave was coming up, bowing and cringing before him.

"My lord King—"

"Yes, what?"

"Corban Loosestrife is at the door."

Eric said, blankly, "Who?"

The slave bobbed up and down, as if dodging a blow. "He says he is from the Lady of Hedeby."

Gunnhild looked around. "Tell me that name again."

The slave hung his head down, to avoid looking her in the face. "He says his name is Corban Loosestrife, Queen."

Eric glanced at Arinbjorn, and saw him interested in this, too, looking up, his eyebrows arched. Eric wondered what he had missed. He struggled to remember the name. Gunnhild struck the table with her hand. "So he is come back again."

"You know this man?" Eric asked. Out in the middle of the floor, Ragnar threw Leif down with a crash; the other men all screeched and cheered. Nobody liked Leif.

Gunnhild was frowning at him. "He was here in the winter. He was then only a simple countryman, passing through, in a cloak that was not King Kenneth's colors, with money from Jedburh that was not from the archbishop."

Eric grunted. "I don't remember."

"Bah."

"Why should I remember every bumpkin who comes before me?"

"He is back again, and with her name on him," she said. "And so he is not a bumpkin and never was." Her fingers drummed on the arm of the high seat. She stared at him, hard. He disliked it when she stared so at him, as if she wanted to see someone else in his place. She turned to the slave. "Send him in."

Eric lifted his head. Ragnar was dragging Leif up and down the hall while the men on either side yelled and stamped their feet and threw bones at them both. Up past them, past the pushed-aside tables, came a man in a fine red coat, a broad-shouldered young man with dark hair, whom Eric did not remember.

He wiped his fingers on his beard. If this Corban were important he would have remembered him. She made a lot out of nothing sometimes. Of course she and the Lady of Hedeby got along like two cats in a sack. He leaned down toward Arinbjorn.

"Who is this?"

Arinbjorn smiled, but his eyes never left the man in the red coat. "Who knows where she gets these people?"

Eric sat straight again. He wished he knew what was going on. He glanced at Gunnhild, who sat with her head back, looking down her long Danish nose at the newcomer, her hand on the thunder-stones around her neck. The man in the red coat came up before the High Seat, and flexed at the waist. Behind him, the brawling stilled, with even Ragnar now watching him.

"My lord," said the man in the red coat. "My lady." He straightened, looking from one to the other. "I am Corban Loose-strife. I offer you the greetings of the Lady of Hedeby, who has sent me here to trade on her behalf."

Eric slouched in his side of the High Seat. "I hope you brought us something to prove her love for us."

Corban stood up closer to the table. Under his arm he had a parcel of black fur, rolled up with the tanned-skin side out.

He said, "For the King of Jorvik, I have six rods of iron, which my men are unloading now, a present to you from my mistress. For the Queen of Jorvik—"

He laid the fur down on the table. Gunnhild leaned forward, eager in spite of herself; she loved presents. The men around the table half-stood to see, and a little murmur started up among them. With a flip of his wrist the newcomer unrolled the fur.

Against the dense blackness the jewels glittered like living eyes. Eric muttered an oath, and reached out to touch them, and Gunnhild caught his wrist. He drew his hand back, out of her grip.

She bent forward, over the jewels, and picked up the biggest, the size of an egg, and red as heart's blood, and held it in her long fingers.

Her gaze lay on Corban Loosestrife. She said, "You have changed your coat, innocent. How did that happen?"

If the Irishman feared her he did not show it. He bowed his head again to her, but straightening he looked her in the face. He said, "I serve the Lady of Hedeby, Queen Gunnhild. She gave me the coat."

Eric slouched against the arm of the High Seat. He was feeling much better suddenly. He needed iron, and now here was six rods, for swords, for helmets, for studded armor. He needed a lot of other things, too, but cold iron would get him those. He said, "Welcome to Jorvik, Corban Loosestrife. You can trade here."

Gunnhild gave him the briefest of glances. One by one, she was picking the jewels out of the fur, holding each in her hand, turning it in the light, and then transferring it to the other hand. Eric saw she would not gainsay him. He turned to the Irishman again.

"Just so that you know. Whatever you trade, here, you must pay me half."

Corban's eyes widened; he was looking full at Eric now, ignoring his wife. He said, "Half, my lord."

"Whatever you buy, whatever you sell, I get half," Eric said.

He waited, expecting some argument, but the man in the red coat only shrugged. "I am here to trade," he said.

"Good," Eric said, relieved. "You may go, then. We have accepted you. I hope you do a lot of trading in Jorvik. You are staying in the Lady's house?"

"Yes," Corban said.

"I'll send my men there, every day," Eric said. "For my half."

⸻

Corban said, "Ulf, are there taxes in Hedeby, for trading there?"

The captain's head swiveled toward him. They were standing just inside the door of the Hedeby house, to which Ulf and his crew had brought all the cargo from the ship.

Ulf said, "Of course. King Harald Bluetooth rules there. Everybody pays him tax."

"Do you know how much it is?"

"Depends on what it is you're selling," Ulf said. "One penny of ten, usually."

Corban looked around him; he saw the barrels from the ship stowed along the wall, and the bars of iron in their special handtruck. "Well, Eric wants half."

Ulf made a sound in his chest. "So that's why no one is here to trade."

Corban went a little on into the long cavernous room. The house was dark, and smelled stale, but it was clean, and a welllaid, banked fire burned in the hearth. Ulf came after him, saying, "There were some people here. I threw them out."

"Ah," Corban said, not surprised. The house had been empty for a while, and anybody could have moved into it. Yet it seemed in good condition. His gaze traveled along the wide sturdy benches on either side, now piled up with their blankets. On the heavy rafters overhead, there were oars and crates and planks of wood stored. He wondered if the Lady maintained it under some spell.

His hands rose to the front of the red coat. He should take it off, to go across the river. Yet he liked the way it made him feel: rich, and important. It would impress Benna and her sisters. He thought how excited they would be to see him, how pleased he would make them with his presents. He went to his pack, got the things he had for them, and left the house.

The sun was lowering into the west. He walked down the hill street to the river's edge. The city seemed quieter than he remembered, the streets empty. Many of the houses he passed were shuttered up. He passed some people arguing in a doorway, and a peddler went by him the other way, carrying a basket of savory pies; his voice rose in a long, plaintive wail. Corban thought maybe he was just more used now to Hedeby, with its crowds and uproar; maybe Jorvik had always been this way, quiet and dull. Off somewhere he heard the clang of a hammer. In between two houses, several people were working with hoes in a long furrowed garden. He reached the river and went northward, to the crossing stones.

There he hesitated, his hands on the coat. Perhaps he should not be doing this. This was too fine a coat to wear jumping from stone to stone. He himself now was too fine a man for that. He lifted his eyes to the far bank, shrouded in willow and wild grass, to the rough log ladder there, and up on the top of the bank saw Grod.

The sight wrenched a yell from him, and he flung up his arm. Heedless of the coat, he ran swiftly along the stones over the river, and on the high bank there, in the grass, Grod looked around and saw him too.

"Corban!"

The old man leapt down the ladder, nimble as a cat; Corban reached the far bank. They came together like two hands clasping, arms around each other. Grod said, "Corban! You came back!" over and over. Corban lifted him up and swung him around and dropped him on his feet again.

"I'm glad to see you," he said. "Are the girls up there still?"

"Of course. But—" Grod's face settled, mournful, his cheeks drooping. "It's very sad. Their father is dying. They are so sad."

"Oh," said Corban.

"Come, though," Grod said. "Although there's nothing to eat." His eyes travelled down the red coat, and his brows arched up. "You look well fed."

"I am," Corban said. He followed Grod up the log ladder.

"Did you find your sister?"

"I did."

Grod swung toward him, surprise in his face. "Where is she?"

"Still in Hedeby." He shrugged off Grod's questions, not wanting to say any more about any of that, not to any of these people. He was glad, though, that Grod obviously admired his coat.

They walked up through the trampled meadow toward the low brushy hovel. It seemed more sunken in than before, with weeds growing all over it, as if the green things would drag down the hut to the level of the ground. Corban looked for the goats, but did not see them—Gifu would be taking them to good browse, he knew, so she might not be here. But ahead there, surely that was Arre, stooping in a garden patch, pulling weeds.

Grod cried out, "Look who is here," and went on ahead.

Arre straightened, and tossed back her reddish-brown hair. A smile spread across her face. "Corban," she said. She came out of the garden, her apron mud smeared, her smile wide, and came up to him with her hands held out. "You came back."

He clasped her hands. "I said I would—but your father—Grod said—"

At that the smile slid down off her face, and her gaze went toward the hut. "Everything is terrible, now, Corban," she said. "You should have stayed away." Shaking the worst of the dirt off her apron, she led him to the hut, and the stooped down to get through the door.

Inside, the hut was steaming hot. A single goat was tied up in the pen, a heap of thorny brambles before her. Corban blinked in the dim light, trying to see better. The old man lay on his mat, his eyes closed and his mouth open. He groaned when he breathed. Beside him, Benna lay, curled up asleep.

Corban swallowed. He wanted to touch her, yet she seemed somehow out of reach, sunk in her sleep. The old man was much thinner, his skin yellow, his lips crusted. The hut stank. And it was empty; no chickens, no pots, only the two people sleeping, the old man, the girl, the one lone goat.

He could not bear to see this; he turned and went outside again. Grod and Arre followed him. In the healthy air he stood, breathing deep.

"Where is Gifu?"

"Off in the woods," Grod said. "She has learned to hunt. Not as well as you, but she's getting better. She'll have something for us to eat."

"Where are the goats?"

"The King took them," Arre said. She twisted her hands in her apron, staring away across the river. "First he came and took half, and then he came and took half of what was left, and so on." She tossed her long tangled hair back. Her voice was steady and even, as if she were bored. "Now when he comes, we hide the one we have left under a blanket."

"What about Benna's pots?"

The girl faced him. Her dark eyes were wide, and clear, and brimming with tears. "There's no sense in making pots. The King takes all she earns."

He swallowed. He felt like a fool in his red coat. He had imagined them running to meet him, glad for his return, grateful for the
stupid little presents he had brought.

Arre said, "She will be happy you're back, when she wakes
up. She needs to sleep—she was awake with him all the night, he
raves sometimes." The tears spilled down her face in shining
streaks.

He said, "I'm sorry."

She said, "You're back, anyway."

"Yes." He reached into the pocket of the coat and took out the
gaudy trinkets he had brought them, all in a heap, the beads, the
comb, the looking glass. "Here. These are for you." He thrust them
into her hands, and turned, and walked back toward the river.

Grod went along beside him. "Where are you going?"

Corban said, "I'll do something."

"Should I come with you?"

"Yes," Corban said, and gripped the old man's arm. "Come
along."

⸺⸺

Now he understood better why Jorvik was so quiet. He went back
over the river, and up the market street. The church bell rang, and
an old woman leaning out a window crossed herself. It occurred
to him that once there had been pigs and chickens all through these
streets, and dogs, but there were none now. The shops were closed
up, even the bakery. He thought: the King takes it all. There was
a ringing in his ears, an insect trilling. He turned to Grod.

"Where can I find bread?"

Grod watched him mournfully. "You have to have real money,
and lots of it."

"Take me there."

Grod trotted off up the street, toward the wooden spire of the
church. Corban walked along beside him. "Is everybody starving?"

"Some," the old man said. "We are not, actually, because of
Gifu, and Arre's garden, and the last goat, who gives milk. But the

father dying—" He shook his head. "Benna is dying along with him."

Corban's heart jumped into his throat; he said, "She is sick too?"

"No, no." Grod shook his head. "I don't mean she will die, really, but her spirits—she is so low, she may give up. Arre is more worried about her than the father, even." He nodded. "There, that baker sells. He always has flour, people say he gives the King a bribe."

He led Corban past a string of shops. Most were closed up, except for a cobbler, who sat at his bench in the sunlight, cutting up a piece of leather, and the bakery, marked by its wooden loaf hanging in front. Several men were sitting against the front wall. As Corban came up, one called out, "Mercy, good sir—have mercy—" and thrust out his cupped palm. The others said nothing, but watched him, their faces lean.

Corban thought: I cannot feed them all. He wondered if he could feed even himself. The coat felt too small, hot and burdensome, and he pulled quickly at the sleeves and the collar. He went into the shop, which smelled deliciously of freshly baked bread. Grod trailed after him, sharp-eyed. The baker came out of the back, and seeing Corban in his red coat bowed.

"My lord. Let me serve you."

"I need bread," Corban said loudly. He took his purse from his belt. "I am opening up the Hedeby house, I shall need bread, every day, for me and my men."

The baker's eyes glinted. "Three pence a loaf."

Corban grunted. In Hedeby, he knew, good loaves of bread went for a farthing. "I will need you to bring bread to my house, every day. Six loaves a day." He opened the purse, and began to put money down on the counter.

The baker's jaw dropped, and his eyes followed the coins, which Corban began to pile on his table in stacks of three. When he had made ten stacks of coins the baker said, "Stop, I have no more bread than that."

Corban nodded. "This is for tomorrow's." He went on making stacks. "And the day after."

"If I can get the flour. The miller too must pay the King."

Corban was staring at the money, and realizing that the purse
was as heavy now as when he had started. Slowly he counted out
more money, the baker gawking at him.

"This is to pay the King," he said, pointing to the second pile.
"Tell the miller to come to me, at the Hedeby house." He weighed
the purse in his hand, remembering what she had said: he would
need no more than this.

He resisted the temptation to turn the purse over, and pour the
money out onto the floor, and see how long it kept coming.

The baker went around the table, and brought up a basket. In
it were half a dozen flat round loaves. Corban could not see himself
carrying an armful of bread around. He said, "Put them in a sack."

The miller went into the rear of the shop and returned with an
old flour sack, into which he stuffed the bread. Corban shoved the
money at him. Grod was watching with round eyes.

When they turned to go out, he said, "Where did you get all
that money?"

"I serve one who has more money than anyone here has ever
seen," Corban said. He stuck the purse carefully back in his belt.
Grod goggled at him, properly impressed. Grod always followed
money.

They went out the door, into the street. The three men were
still slumped against the front of the bakery, and the one again
stretched out his arm, saying, "Mercy, sir—" Corban took a loaf
out of the sack and gave it to him.

The man yelped. He bounded up at once and dashed off, and
the others scrambled up, rushing at Corban.

"Give us—Give us—"

"No, I meant that one for all three of you," Corban said. "I
need the rest. Get yours from him."

One of the men wheeled and ran after the first, who was has-
tening away down the street with his loaf clutched to his chest.
The third man planted himself in front of Corban. "He won't give
it to us. You have to give me one."

"Get it from him," Corban said. "Share it, or you'll all die,
damn it." He brushed past this man and tramped down toward the
street where his house was.

Grod danced along beside him. "Who is your master? Are you a prince now?"

Corban kept the sack tucked under his arm; the meeting with the three beggars had shaken him, as he saw he had done little good, there. Grod bothered him, with his greed, his questions. For an instant, he wondered if he could trust the old man. He pushed that feeling off, and dug up another loaf out of the sack.

"Take this to Benna."

Grod took it and hid it away under his shirt. They stopped at the crossroads; to Corban's left ran the street down to the river. Grod started off that way, and then turned back to him, sharp-eyed. "I'll take this to her. But then I should come back to you, shouldn't I? I'm your man, after all."

He was the money's man, Corban thought. He wondered why he had been glad to see Grod. But there were the girls. "My house is up ahead, that long one, with the high roof, do you see it?" Corban pointed. "Bring them back too, if they'll come."

He doubted the girls would come. He wondered if they even should, in the long run of things. They might be better off where they were. Grod bounded away, off toward the river, and Corban went back to his new house.

⸻⸱⸻

Bluetooth said, "So he's come near to eating up Jorvik, as he did in Norway. The man's a fool. He has no gift of husbandry."

"But he must move soon," the Lady said. "Which gives us the opening. We need only nudge him toward the right direction."

She sat with her head turned slightly toward Mav, who was at the far end of the hall, singing as loud as a brass horn, her voice resounding through the rafters. In the benches the slaves all grumbled against her; she had been singing all night, and kept everyone awake. The slaves, like Bluetooth, had no entrance to the song, to the beauty of it, the stream of meaning; it was all just noise to them.

She turned toward Bluetooth. "I suggest you offer him some ships, since it sounds as if he has few ships."

"He cannot keep a great hall, and so the men leave," Bluetooth said. "Likely they're in Orkney. He can make swords now, but will the men come back to carry them?"

"Men always flock to him."

"Not when there is no plunder, and you say he has stripped Jorvik bare."

The Lady grunted at him. These were all only minor details. She said, "You see, it is going as you wish."

Bluetooth snorted at her. "I am less than convinced that you have anything to do with it."

She shrugged. He had brought her gold, two little ingots, like two little bricks of a wall. It was a wall she meant to build much higher. "You shall see," she said. "Now, go, I have much to do."

"You don't dismiss me," he said. But he was going anyway, obeying her, which was better than the gold. She stroked her hands over the front of her gown, pleased.

Let him rule the world-ring. She would rule him.

Mav was singing of a forest somewhere, flocks of birds, and monsters in the trees. Her voice was as loud as a clarion; she sang all day. Her brother had poured some new life into her. The Lady brushed off a rash of annoyance. In the line and tenor of the song she sensed that the girl was trying to master her gift, to steal it away for herself, shut the Lady out of it somehow. Better it had been when she sickened, her voice softer but still readable, her will failing, needing the Lady more and more.

Now Mav was resisting the refuge offered her, and she was as strong as ever. She found a center in the baby, and folded herself around that. The Lady hated the baby, anyway, its maleness like an insult, an invasion, and she thought that Mav should hate it, too, for its father's sake. When it was born, the Lady would see that it died; that would take only a moment, while the girl was distracted, helpless in her pain. When the child was dead, in her grief and loss the girl would turn to her, and the Lady would breathe her in, and have her to herself, forever.

All her long life she had taken in the minds of women, of knowing women, had sought for them and courted them and gathered them into herself, so many now that she had lost count. Soon Mav too would give up resisting, and join her power to theirs, and the Lady of Hedeby would grow and prosper.

If Mav still did not yield, then there was always the brother. She had seen how they were together; she could use the brother to control Mav. Whatever happened, she would come out well. The Lady picked up the two little gold bars, and went around to her treasure house, to put them away.

CHAPTER FOURTEEN

Benna lifted her head. The hut was dark, except for the little flickering fire, and full of smoke. By the door Grod and Arre and Gifu were all gathered, talking and eating something. Benna got hastily up off the floor.

"What do you have? Did you save some for me?"

Grod turned toward her, smiling wide. "There is plenty. Here. Corban is back." He thrust a chunk of bread into her hands.

"Corban!"

"And he is rich now," Grod said, "and serves some great prince, and we can all move into the city to his palace and live there."

Benna tried to eat slowly, and not gobble, but she was so hungry she bolted it all. Grod gave her another piece of the loaf. She had forbidden herself to think of Corban; now it was hard to let herself do it again. The little bit of food in her hand would be gone at once, never enough. Cautiously, she said, "Where is he?"

"In the city," Arre said. She had sat down by the fire, Gifu beside her.

"Is this all?" Benna sank down by them, the second piece of bread in her hand. She glanced at her father. "Have you tried to give him some of this?"

"I tried to feed him some milk, just before Grod came," Arre said.

Benna chewed the bread. Her father had lain sleeping now for days and days, and would not wake; they struggled to feed him but the milk dribbled out of his mouth. She swallowed a sudden lump in her throat. She caught Arre watching her, in the dim red fireglow, and their eyes met. Benna could not speak; but she thought, He is dying, and as she thought it, Arre nodded at her. Arre reached out and put her arm around Benna and hugged her.

"You do all you can," she said. Then her head went up. "Oh. Corban brought us things. Here."

"What?" Gifu said. She sat by the fire with her arms around her updrawn knees. "You didn't tell me that."

"I forgot," Arre said. She was rummaging in the overflowing pockets of her apron, bringing out onion tops and nutshells and rags, and finally, a heap of bright little objects which she laid down on the ground.

Gifu whooped, and snatched up a string of beads, which glittered in the firelight. "Oh, I want this!"

Grod sat on the other side of the fire. He said, "He didn't bring me anything. He was my friend first."

Benna picked up a wooden comb, with stars and moons carved along the handle. "This is very pretty. I've never seen anything like it before." She watched Arre take up the other toy, a little round disk.

"Oh," Arre said, at once. "I think this is for you, Benna." She held it out.

"What is it?" Benna took it in her hand. Suddenly, there in her hand, was the fire, reflected in the shiny metal. She tapped it with her fingernail: it was not metal, but something else. Arre took hold of her hand, and turned it, and into the disk came a face, wide dark eyes, a small, round chin.

"Didn't you tell me he asked you for a picture of you? And that you said you didn't know what you look like?"

Benna started. She realized that the face in the disk was her own face, and quickly hid the whole thing away under her skirts. Arre had taken the comb. She sat running it through her hair, using her fingers to work out the tangles, her deep, bold profile lined with the red firelight. Her hair glinted. Gifu hung the beads around her neck, and lifted the strand up to the light to admire it.

"Well," Benna said, loudly. "I'm glad he's back. Did he find his sister?"

"I think so," Grod said, "but she isn't with him. I'm going back to his house now." He got his feet under him. "You all can come, if you want. He said so."

Benna said, "We have to stay with Papa."

Grod said, "We can take him. He said I was to bring you."

She shook her head; she knew they could not. She knew her father would not leave this hut again. A familiar heavy weariness

began to collect in her chest, as if she were breathing stone instead
of air, turning breath by breath into stone. "Tell Corban thank you.
Tell him—" She bit her lip. She was still afraid to think of him.
"Tell him thank you."

Grod said, "I will bring you more bread tomorrow." He went
out the door.

"I'm going hunting again tomorrow," Gifu said. She crept into
the back of the hut, where her sleeping rags were. "I'll get something tomorrow, I know I will." She lay down, pulling the rags
over her, and was asleep.

Arre had smoothed her hair with the comb until it was long
and flowing, curling at the ends, glossy and fine. She said, "Now
that Corban is back—"

Benna said, roughly, "He won't come here again, surely, if
he's a prince now. He didn't like it much here before." Her head
turned toward her father, lying like a lump in the dark by the goat
pen. "Will you help me?"

Silently Arre crawled with her over to the old man; they managed to turn him. His arms were gathered close to his body so tight
they could not straighten them. He had shit himself and they pulled
up his shirt and cleaned him. There were bruises and sores all over
him, and Benna got some water and washed him. To touch him
this way, when he was helpless and did not know, seemed evil to
her. He was the father, and should rule over them, but instead they
handled him like a great baby. Arre stroked his face.

"Good night, Papa."

They got his clothes back on, as much as they could. He
breathed harshly a few times, sucking the air in and out with a
sudden vigor, and then subsided into barely breathing at all. His
hands were cold. Benna got her blanket, and threw it over him,
and lay down beside him to try to warm him. Arre lay on the other
side of him.

Benna could not sleep, for all her stony weariness. She said,
after a moment, "How did he look?"

"Corban?" Arre said. "He had on a very nice coat." She
paused, and then went on. "There was something strange about
him, though. He seemed smaller."

Benna bit her lips. Beside her lay her father, dying; she ought to think of nothing but him. She crossed herself, and said some prayers. Presently she could hear Arre snoring gently on his far side, and she got up quietly and went to the back of the hut, where her potter's wheel was, and her things for drawing.

She had stopped drawing, shortly after he left. There seemed no point in it, with all else so overwhelming around her, her father dying, and the King's men coming every few days to take more of what they had. Her hands longed for the brush and ink, and she still saved shards; but what use were her poor counterfeits—no use at all. She made herself not do it. She would never do it again. But now she found the shard on which she had drawn Corban.

She held the curved piece of pottery in her hands, and looked at his face, and wondered what he would think of her now, when she was ordinary. Looking at the drawing, she remembered him better: the merry glint in his eye, and the way he smiled, even the little music of his voice.

She went back to lie down again by her father and slept. In the morning when they woke up their father was dead.

Arre realized it first, touching him, and said, quietly, "He's gone." None of them said anything. They had all known this would happen. Benna laid her hands on his cheeks, and touched his forehead; he was cold and stiff. Inside her was only a kind of dull ache, as if he had been dead for years. Gifu said nothing at all, but went off to the city to fetch the priest down.

Arre and Benna sat by the banked fire, empty, tearless. Benna took a stick and poked at the coals. The ash crumbled, giving up thin feathery flames that died at once. Arre said nothing, her face gaunt. The fire struck deep russet lights from her hair. There was nothing to eat. Benna poured some water from the jug into a cup; she saw something bright on the ground, and picked it up.

It was the shining disk that Corban had brought for her from Hedeby. Her back tensed, alarmed. But the bright surface drew her. She took the disk in her two hands and held it so that it showed her face to her. She stared into that stranger's face, as if she might see there what she must do, and who she really was.

She thought: I am ugly. Yet she was not; she was good enough to look at. A sort of calm settled over her. As she studied her own face, the old habits rose in her. She saw how to draw herself, the line of her jaw and her nose, and the desire to do it overcame her. She went back to her corner, and found a piece of pot and her brushes. Nearly all the ink had dried up but she put a little water in one pot and stirred it, and got color on the brush.

"What are you doing?" Arre said.

Benna did not answer. She went back to the fire, and sat, the shard in her hand, and drew.

Now that she had the brush in hand she did not draw herself. She drew her father, as he had been when he was strong and hale, master of their house in the city, the finest potter in Jorvik. He flowed out of the tip of her brush onto the shard: his broad smile, the shape of his chin, the line of his eyebrows, and as she worked the hot tears began to run down her cheeks. Arre leaned on her shoulder and watched, and cried also. At last she finished the drawing, and laid it down, and turning to her sister put her arms around her, and the two of them leaned on each other and wept until their eyes were dry.

—⇥—

The miller said, "I can only make flour if I have corn, and corn is very scarce. I tell you, there is no bread now in Jorvik, and there will be none tomorrow, or the day after, or the day after that. No bread at any price."

"I will sell you corn. Not today, but soon."

"In the meanwhile there is no corn, and therefore no flour, and therefore no bread." The miller tossed his hands up, the meaty slabs of his palms grimed with old flour. "And who will bring it here to sell, when the King takes so much? Where will you get corn?"

"I will pay your tax to the King, also. I can get corn in Hedeby."

"You will lose much in travel. It molds, carried in ships. There are rats. And it won't come soon. And at such a ruinous cost when it does come that no one can pay." The miller pulled up his apron over his belly. "I could make us both rich, if you could find me corn today. But I think not even the King has corn, there is nothing growing in the ground for miles around Jorvik."

Corban threw his hands up. This matter of trading was past

him, he could not do it. He had a purse full of money and he could not buy anything. "I will send to Hedeby. In the meanwhile, if you find anything—"

"I have no money."

They were standing in the middle of Corban's hall. Ulf lounged by the fire, his legs stretched out, drinking ale, while his crew packed up the fleeces Corban had just bought to take back to Hedeby. Even the fleeces had cost far more than Corban had expected, and they had come all the way from Scotland. Now here was this miller, wanting money, without even having anything to sell. Corban dug into the purse, and took out a handful of pennies and gave them into the man's hand.

"Tell me when you find some corn. And pay the King from that."

The miller bowed to him and left. Ulf came up to him. "I will sail tomorrow."

"Yes. Tell the Lady to send corn, all she can; another shipload too, if she can. You have those tally sticks for the fleeces?"

"I do."

"Tell her also to send more gifts for Eric and Gunnhild."

"I will."

Corban weighed the purse in his hand, and then thrust it into his belt. In all of Jorvik there was nothing to eat. For all the weight of the purse in his hand, he could not buy a single loaf of bread. His mind swung lightly above some black knowledge. There was a knock on the door.

"See who that is." He went back toward the hearth, for a cup of the ale, which was the best he had ever tasted.

"Corban!"

He wheeled. Grod came strutting in, with Arre just behind him, and the tall thin boy Euan, who followed Arre around.

"Look who I have brought here," Grod said. He went straight toward the hearth, and the jug, whose virtue he had immediately discovered when they came on it in the cupboard by the hearth. Arre came up to Corban, and her face bloomed with her smile.

"Thank you," she said. "You see?" She turned her head this way and that, so that he could admire the comb, which gathered her hair at the back. "Thank you. I like it very much."

"I'm glad you do," he said, pleased; he glanced quickly past her, toward the door, but she had only brought Euan. Tall and gangling, his cap pulled down hard over his forehead, he lurked behind her, meeting no one's eyes. Grod had told Corban about him: his mother was an apothecary, and he was not supposed to see Arre at all.

Corban looked back at Arre, standing in front of him. "Grod says that your father died."

That wiped the smile away. She lowered her eyes. "It was a good thing," she said, under her breath. "He is with God, now. But a sad thing, too."

"Come sit down."

She followed him toward the hearth, where Grod filled the cup with ale and passed it to her. She sat down on the bench before the fire and smoothed her apron over her knees. Corban's pack was open on the floor, there, with the tally sticks half falling out, and he reached down to move it out of the way of her feet. She looked around her, eyes bright. "This is a very fine house, Corban. Grod says you are a prince now."

"No," he said. "It all belongs to one I serve, it is not me or mine. But it is a fine house."

She drank some of the ale and gave the cup to Euan, who sat on the bench, looking elsewhere. "Gifu loves the beads, too," she said. "She has gone off hunting again, or she would come and thank you herself."

"Grod told me that she hunts." He wanted to ask about Benna. It startled him how they had sorted out the gifts exactly as he had intended, without any word from him. He said, "Does she use a sling?"

"I don't know. I think she throws rocks." Arre tossed her hair back; unruly, it was spilling from the comb in reddish-brown curls around her cheeks. Beside her, Euan drank from the cup, and put it down, empty. Grod took it at once and filled it again.

"Benna sends you this," Arre said. She dug into her over-flowing apron pocket and brought out a piece of a pot.

Corban took it from her and held it into the light. There on the curved surface, arising somehow out of a few black lines of ink, was Benna's face, as if she stood before him.

He thought, This is a good power. He said, pleased, "May I keep this?"

"Of course." Arre tucked her hands into her lap. "She keeps the looking glass on a string around her neck. She likes it very much, I think. Thank you also for the bread."

"I will send more, if I can find any." He wanted them to come here, but he guessed the whole city would disapprove of that. He should leave them as they were. With their garden and Gifu's hunting, they might eat better than he would. Behind Arre, Euan suddenly reached down by her feet into the pack, and took the abacus out. Corban turned back to Arre. There was another knock on the door. Grod went importantly over to answer it.

"Is—Have you buried your father?"

Arre nodded her head. Her smile drooped. She took the cup from Grod and drank, and passed it on to Euan. "I don't know how we will live, Corban. It is very bad."

He said, "I will help you," although he did not know how. He laid the shard down on his knee and looked at it again. Grod came bustling back.

"Someone for you," he said to Corban. "He says he will see you alone."

"Hunh." Corban rose, and went off toward the door.

Just inside stood Arinbjorn the merchant, the King's farmann, in his elegant long blue coat. Corban stopped short a moment, surprised, and then went over and bowed to him. "My lord. I am very glad to see you."

"Yes—good it is to see this house lived in again." The dansker lord glanced past him, toward the hearth, and turned a little away, so that his back was to the rest of the room. He smiled. He had the sleek, mild look of a man who did nothing for himself, who had only to nod to have what he wanted. He said, "I must talk to you privately."

Corban led him toward the far end of the hall, where an open smoke hole in the roof let in some light. Ulf's men were carrying out the last of the fleeces; the captain waved to Corban, and followed his crew out the door. In the edge of the light coming in through the hole in the roof, Arinbjorn turned, and asked, "You serve the Lady of Hedeby?"

"Yes, I do."

"And you are sending off a ship to her today?"

"Yes—you saw my captain, just now."

"I need—" Arinbjorn cleared his throat, glanced past him, and then turned his eyes to him again. "I need a favor of you."

"Ask it," Corban said. "You saved me once, I remember."

"I think now I had less to do with that than it seemed at the time. I have something that must leave Jorvik. Will you give it to your captain?"

"Certainly," Corban said.

"The King must not know."

"Ah."

Arinbjorn said, "If you are loathe to run the risk—"

Corban thought this might be a test; Arinbjorn seemed to him to live in the King's ear. Maybe they were trying him, to see if they could trust him. But Arinbjorn seemed real enough, and sweating now over something. And if he did Arinbjorn favors, he could get favors back.

He said, "You are sending something to my Lady?"

"A letter. She will pass it on. I have had dealings with her before; she will know what to do with it."

Corban nodded. "I will do it then."

"Thank you." Arinbjorn slapped his arm. "I shall deliver it to your ship, very soon."

Over by the hearth, there went up a gust of laughter. Corban glanced that way, and swung back to Arinbjorn.

"Will you have a drink with me? We can sit back here, if you don't want them to see you."

"Certainly." Arinbjorn sauntered deeper into the hall, past the shaft of dusty light. Corban beckoned Grod for the jug and followed.

"I need to ask you about something," Corban said, carefully.

Arinbjorn smiled at him, his eyes narrow. He set his hands on his belt. "You want to know about Eric."

Grod came up to them, with a cup and the jug of ale, and lingered nearby, until Corban shot a hard look at him, and then was gone up the hall. Corban faced the dansker lord again.

"Yes: Eric. What has happened here? When I left in the spring it was a better place."

Arinbjorn shrugged one shoulder, his face bland. "Just after Easter, last spring, Eric raised his taxes. Everybody complained, so he raised them again."

"He's mad," Corban said, thinking of the baker and the miller, Benna and the goats. "Nobody has anything to eat."

"Eric doesn't care about that," Arinbjorn said. "As long as he has what he wants, everybody else can go hang. But pretty soon he isn't going to have what he wants; he's eaten it all up, here, people can only give so much, and he's going to have to move on soon. That's what the real problem is. He's got to move, to do something, but he's putting it off. He's lazy, Eric. Now he's even sending Sweyn Eelmouth off alone to do what he used to lead the way at." He broke off, his eyes keen on Corban. "What does the Lady want with him? I doubt she's only sent you here to buy fleeces."

"I don't know," Corban said, seeing a good time to lie. "I am nothing, I only do as she bids me." He fingered the red coat; Arinbjorn only spoke so openly with him because of this coat, he knew.

"Well, it's Gunnhild who bids Eric. She wants him to take on England, which in my view is fairly mad." His lips stretched into a smooth smile. "The Lady, like as not, wants him to go for Norway, which is even worse—Eric was no match for Hakon in the old days, but now that he's fat and old—"

He broke off, looking elsewhere. Corban filled his cup again, saying nothing. He realized Arinbjorn was quicker at this game than he was, knew everything already, and was reciting like a bard from his favorite tales. Probably had some matters of his own interest. Arinbjorn drank the cup down appreciatively. "This is good ale."

"It's the jug," Corban said.

Arinbjorn laughed, as if he had made a joke. "Well, anyway. Something has to happen with Eric, but I can't see what it is. Certainly he's ruining Jorvik, which was the richest city in England. And there's Gunnhild. She's never been content here. His boys are almost old enough to take on the chores, so if he won't do it, Gunnhild will turn to them soon. But Eric won't stand for that, I think—that house breeds old men, old and murderous, and when he gets his back up Eric is still a great warrior."

He held out the cup, and Corban filled it again, and the dansker lord drank. He said, "That's very good ale, but I've paid for it now," and started toward the door. Corban went alongside him.

"You should come up to the hall," Arinbjorn said. "I understand the King is very pleased with you, for the sake of that fine load of iron. He'll give you a place there, although what you'll get to eat nobody can predict. I'll be at your ship in a little while. Good day to you, Corban."

Corban saw him out the door. What Arinbjorn had told him turned slowly around in his head, like something unfolding. He felt the vast churn of some struggle going on around him, but he had no sense of it: who was behind it all, and what they were fighting for. The thought crept into his mind that no one was the master of it, that all these people were only battling for small advantages, while the world fell apart of its own weight.

He reminded himself that usually when he thought he knew something, he was wrong. Holding the jug and the cup, he went over to the hearth, where Arre and Grod were laughing, and Euan was bent over the abacus, moving the beads around.

Grod took the cup and filled it. Arre said, "That jug is never empty."

Corban said, "Take some with you." The wonderful jug, like the wonderful purse, was a useless magic. It did no good, but only muddled people's wits; what he needed was a wonderful loaf, but he had found nothing like that in this house. Now Arre was standing up, her cheeks flushed. "I am going, Corban. I'm very glad to see you." She laughed again, drunk.

Euan said, "May I have this?" He held out the abacus.

Corban frowned. "No, it is not mine to give to you. Do you know how to use it?"

"I think so," Euan said. He blinked a few times; Corban wondered if he were a little short-sighted. He said, "It's very interesting."

"Come in tomorrow," Corban said, "and show me how."

Mav had been singing all day long. The Lady withdrew wearily to her cupboard, and sent a slave for a cup of warm wine. Now at least she knew what she was up against, in working the Danish king's will with Eric Bloodaxe.

A kink of anger tightened in her stomach. Young Eric had looked like the rising star of all the world. He had been magnificent, then, a golden-haired warrior on the verge of mighty deeds. She wondered if he had ever been a hero, or if it had all been only Gunnhild, clothing him with her expectations even then, when he was young and strong.

The cup of wine came to her hand, and she drank some of it. Taking the gold ring from her arm she laid it on the carpet, and watched the little world appear, with the wrinkled sea waves, and the gilded edges of the land all around its edges.

Now she knew also that Corban's ship was coming. He was working, at least. He had learned too quickly about the purse, and he was distracted by the idea of saving the people in Jorvik, which was useless to her, and not possible anyway. Certainly it made no sense to send shiploads of corn there, which he would never get a decent price for. In her mind she saw the little bars of gold in her storeroom turning into money, and the money like a flock of little yellow birds flying away out the window.

Still, there would be more money, and Corban had brought her knowledge, which was better than money: she knew now what he needed. If Bluetooth would not, she herself would send Eric an offer of some ships of hers, if he manned them. Once he accepted the ships she could see that he took them off in the right direction. Gunnhild she could lure into the scheme with something pretty— like the vision stones that she collected, foolishly, the Lady thought; all vision stones bent and twisted truth, gave back mostly what the viewer wanted to see, and some were actively false, especially if acquired wrongfully.

Maybe she could secure a false vision somehow for Gunnhild. She thought that over a while, getting nowhere.

She toyed with offering something for the eldest prince,

Gimle—a boy of ten or twelve years, she knew—old enough to go a-viking, and where better than Norway? That would suit Blue-tooth's purposes, and hers, just as well as sending Eric off to raid. She considered what might happen if she offered Gimle Ericsson one of her ships for his own.

She smiled. That would boil the family cauldron to a fine hot havoc. She had no use now for havoc, but she would keep it in mind. As for the rest, it was done. She would send the cargos straight off to Hollandstadt, to save Corban's captain the trouble of sending overland to Hedeby. The letter from Arinbjorn to King Harald Bluetooth, she knew, would be an offer to mend the long quarrel between them, and she would see that lost; it would not do to give Arinbjorn any place with Bluetooth, although he was only a man, and not even a king. A wise, subtle, rich man, though: keep him on the outs with Bluetooth.

With half an ear she listened to Mav's wild singing, flashing images of Jorvik through her mind. She would send no corn. Let Corban go hungry a little—it would sharpen his wits and teach him how to keep. Picking up the gold ring again, she slid it back onto her arm.

CHAPTER FIFTEEN

Eric's hall was packed, more tables out than Corban had seen before, all jammed with men. On every roof post a torch blazed, sending out billows of pine smoke, and the roar of voices was deafening. Corban went in quietly. He saw Sweyn Eelmouth, at a table near the High Seat, sitting with his head thrown back, laughing. He had heard that Sweyn was off on some errand of the King's but clearly now he had come home again. The rest of Eric's men were all sitting together at the four tables down the west side of the hall.

Across from them, at two other tables, sat strangers—obviously not dansker—men in darker clothes, with trimmer beards and hair, who did not laugh. Corban straightened himself, and was suddenly very glad of the red coat, which was as good as any in this hall.

He looked for Arinbjorn, and found him, but not where he usually sat on the King's right hand; he was down the table. In his customary place was a tall man with black hair and a massive gold chain around his neck. Corban walked up between the two rows of tables toward the High Seat.

Eric took up most of the great chair. He seemed grander than Corban remembered him, bigger, with the high head and flashing eyes of a true king. He wore his crown, and his clothes were magnificent. Corban went up before him and bowed.

"Welcome, Corban Loosestrife," Eric said. His voice boomed, resonant. He turned to the black-haired man in the gold chain, and said, "This man buys and sells in Jorvik for the Lady of Hedeby."

The tall man cleared his throat. He looked as if he had bitten into a quince. He said, "We are Christians in England. We do not suffer witches."

On Eric's left side, Gunnhild stirred suddenly, her head turning, her long golden braids slithering down her shoulder, her feet tucking under her, as if she coiled herself. Arinbjorn was watching Corban. Their eyes caught for an instant and the dansker trader nodded to him. Corban said, "By your leave, my lords," and went

around the end of the table, where Arinbjorn was making room for
him on the bench.

As he set himself down, Arinbjorn swung toward him, his eyes
glinting. "You're going to take that? I'd at least insult him back."

"Who are all these people?"

"Talkers from the English king," Arinbjorn said. "Meaning
spies. Morcar there speaks excellent dansker, although he should
know better about the women. But you can thank them for the fine
food; Eric has stripped his storerooms to impress them." He nodded
at the great roast boar sprawled across the table in front of them.

Corban pulled a fat back rib off the roasted pig and began to
eat. He had given the last of his bread to the people in his house;
if he had not come here he would have had no supper, and he ate
with pleasure.

The Englishman, he noticed, did not, but tasted only a little of
the flesh and made a face, putting his hand on his stomach. On the
far side of him from the splendid Eric sat Gunnhild, her hand firmly
on the King's, staring in the opposite direction from Morcar, and
smiling.

"What are they spying out?"

Arinbjorn shrugged. "Nothing that will do them any good, I
think. Here come the skalds. At least we shall have some enter-
tainment."

Up the length of the hall paraded a file of men in gaudy tunics,
with combed hair and beards and gold rings around their arms and
necks. Corban sat back, his belly full. Down at the next table he
could hear Sweyn Eelmouth talking, his voice high and clear
against the general din. Then abruptly the din hushed, and the first
of the skalds began to speak.

The words were dansker, but Corban could make no sense of
them, just grand baffling phrases, which the skald rolled out in a
high-pitched yell that carried all through the room. Corban glanced
at Arinbjorn and saw the merchant lord smiling with delight, his
head nodding along with the words, his eyes fixed on the skald.
Corban struggled after the meanings of the sweeping chains of
syllables, a strange mix of swans and roads and Odin and Thor,
booming out in a harsh cadence that made his hair stand on end.
As the skald cried his song furiously to its close, he began to feel

the huge rhythms of it, the elegance of the phrases; it reminded him of old Irish songs, about a time when men were heroes, and did great deeds.

Except this was not about ancient men, this was about Eric. The song ended with a cascade of praises for the King of Jorvik, who sat with his head proudly high, and the skald bowed almost double and sat down.

"A drapa for the King," Arinbjorn said. "Everybody makes one now." He leaned back so that a slave could fill the cup he and Corban were sharing. "A few years ago, Eric caught an old enemy of his, an Icelander who is as good at poetry as he is at killing. Eric was about to take his head, until the Icelander made a great drapa about him, and recited it right here, in front of the whole of Jorvik. Eric was so pleased he let him go. Nobody can actually remember much of that drapa, not even Egil, probably, who made it up, but now every skald in the world wants to outdo the Head-Ransom. It's a lesson, somehow." He tasted his ale. "I wish you'd brought some of that ale of yours. This is swill."

Corban agreed with that. Another skald was rolling out a tongueful of phrases, his arms carving the air in enormous jerky gestures. Under the steady flow of compliments, the King sat sprawled in the High Seat like a cat in the sunshine. His wife was curled beside him, looking elsewhere, her hand on his arm. Corban eased the collar of his red coat; he felt a little drunk, too hot, and stuffed into his coat like meat into a sausage.

Eric lifted his cup and spilled some of the beer down the front of his magnificent clothes. It was the same Eric, for all his royal looks. Corban drew his eyes away from him, his spirits sagging. He wondered what if any of this was real, and what was only in his mind, absorbing something that Gunnhild gave off like a vapor. Suddenly he felt as if he were somewhere else, separate from all these men, watching them through a window.

Beside him, Arinbjorn was leaning forward slightly, his hands propped before him, his gaze intent on the reciting skald. Down at the next table, Sweyn was talking again, under the louder voice of the poet. "I sailed down the coast all the way to Humbermouth, and there was nothing. Not a field, not a cow."

The words chimed together in Corban's mind. In his memory

he saw a pile of the bloody bones of cows, beside the seacoast. His gut churned. From down deep in his thoughts a terrible knowledge was rising irresistibly toward the surface, something he had actually known for a long time, but had refused to face. He remembered Arinbjorn saying, "Eric sends Sweyn now to do his work." The back of his neck grew hot. Up into his mind like a blinding white blaze of light came the realization that it had been Eric, that day, in Ireland, those bloody bones, that burning house, those slaughtered people. Eric, and these men.

He held himself utterly still. He laid his hands on the table, and stared down at it, while the first rage broke over him: the will to rise, and strike at them, and kill them all where they sat, with all their murders on them.

Around him they talked and laughed, lolling on the benches, feeling nothing of the furnace heat of his anger. The coat half-choked him. He yanked hard at the sleeves.

He thought of Mav, and he cooled. He came back into himself, as if just now he had floated, a red mist, in the air over the hall. He could not kill these men, not even one of them. And there was Mav, all he had left was Mav.

As he cooled, and as the world rushed in on him again like an icy wind, he felt the pressure of the look, and turned his head and saw Gunnhild, down the table, staring at him.

He lowered his eyes, tingling all over. He got up with a mutter to Arinbjorn and went unsteadily down the hall toward the door.

He walked out to the airy darkness. His skin burst with sweat, and his belly rolled, the meat suddenly bad in his guts, the ale sour on the back of his tongue. He wanted to vomit it up, to rid himself of any taint of Eric Bloodaxe. His head pounded. The coat was too small, too tight. He tore at the front of it, yanking it open, letting the cool air reach him. He walked down toward the river; he felt swollen and clogged and he hardly looked where he was going, but let his feet take him. Slowly his mind cleared. He found himself on the street going down toward the river, near where Benna had sold her pots, and he went on down to the riverbank, and stood looking out over the water.

Damn you, Eric, he thought. Damn you all. Puny little words.

He was a puny little man, who had sat among the men who had destroyed his family and not even lifted his hand to strike back.

It was all so twisted and crooked. He loved his sister, he could not fail her. He hated Eric. What was good was evil, or maybe there was no good, only lesser and greater evil. He could not think about it. Everything he did came out wrong. The world was corrupt, too broken to mend.

Not the world, but himself. He felt the cold wind on his face and chest, and the stars rained down their light on him. The rippling of the river reached his ears. He remembered, the winter before, when he was first in Jorvik, when he had gone off into the snowy wildness to hunt. He remembered how he had walked alone looking for hares and deer, and the peace he had felt then. That peace was gone now. Nor could he walk out there again and find it. He was a different man, somehow. He imagined himself trudging along in the snow, the red coat like a wound, like a blood spot against the snow.

He stood staring across the river, trying to make out Benna's hut, thinking of going over there, and then behind him he heard a low growl.

He wheeled around, his scalp prickling up. For a long moment all he saw was the street rising away from him between two rows of shuttered, silent buildings. Then from the dark between two houses there stepped a wolf, her head low, and her eyes green in the moonlight.

He knew immediately who this was. The breath froze in his throat. The wolf paced toward him, staring at him, and the urge flooded into his mind to run.

He forced himself calm. He never took his eyes from the wolf, but watched her slink toward him, her jaws slack, and her tongue lolling out. He felt the ground under him wobble, the path shrink under his feet. An abyss opened up on either side of him. If he ran backwards, he came to the riverbank; if he ran upstream, the foss; downstream, the city wall. She would catch him any way he tried to escape, there was nowhere to hide—no matter how he dodged and doubled, she would catch him at once. He stood where he was, his knees buckling.

She said, "Where do you think you are going?"

"I am—" He cleared his throat. His hands went to the coat, and hastily he pulled it closed around him. In the back of his mind he begged the Lady for a charm. "I am going home," he said. He took a step forward, straight ahead.

She growled at him. She leaked light, all her edges fiery. "You dare to threaten me and mine."

"I have no power to harm you," he said, and took another step straight ahead, toward her, armored in the Lady's coat. "I am only going home."

She sprang at him. He crouched, his arms up, and she passed right through him, a hot blast of wind. He let out a yell, but she was gone. He straightened, trembling, sick to his stomach. The world seemed to have tilted up, and now righted itself under his feet, the road before him solid and wide. Up on the height of the city, the church bell began to toll.

He stood where he was, cold. He felt no easier now. The coat had saved him, but she would try again, some other way. The Lady had said he would know what to do. He had no idea what to do. He walked on down the street toward his house, looking over his shoulder every third step.

⟜

Mav stuffed her fist into her mouth, to keep herself from singing, but the leap of the wolf brought from her a shriek that sounded through the whole house. She panted for breath, she throttled herself again, struggling to keep silent.

Her brain burned. Over and over again she felt the incandescent burst of his rage. The tidal surge of anger sizzled along all her nerves, screaming to be heard; she clenched her jaws against the rising tide of song, stuffed the coverlet into her mouth, but the song was bursting up, uncontrollable.

She dared not sing. Anything she told the Lady now could damn them all. The lady wanted Corban on Eric's side; if she knew then Corban's rage, she might turn on him and Mav both. But the song was prying open her throat, spilling up and out of her in a great thunderous howl, telling the Lady all that happened, all that Corban did and knew.

She could not stop singing. Frantically she sought some other
way to do this. She could think of something else to sing. Someone
else. Her mind gathered, pushing that way. She had always sung
to Corban, closer to her than her own skin. Now there was someone
else she loved as much, and she lowered her head, and wrapped
her arms around the great round womb-home of her baby.

As she did, he fetched her a solid kick against her side, and
like the spring from the rock, the song gushed forth.

The world cracked. Her spirit soared up. Suddenly Corban and
his hate and rage were gone, her mind cooled, wide forests and sea
opened up before her, a flow of incomprehensible images she had
never seen before. All the brighter, the livelier, that she had not
seen them. Under her cradling arms the child turned and thrashed
against her, and she held herself around him and sang out the
worlds where he would walk.

—⸻—

The Lady sat on her stool by the girl's bed, and held her hand. She
had known immediately that this was not the true singing, not what
she wanted, and yet she could not stop listening, her breath catching
in her throat, her mind swept along in this river of dreams.

The music filled her imagination, a great sweep of sound, blazing color, visions as real as if she were there. They rowed past a
mountain of blue crystal that towered up above them; pieces of the
crystal broke off and crashed down into the sea, and the ship rose
on the wave from it. In the icy blue sea there swam great monsters,
and the men in the ship did battle with them.

They went among copper-skinned people, with long black hair.
A girl kept walking toward her, a copper-skinned girl with gray
eyes. This was in a great forest somewhere, and there was a strange
house. Corban Loosestrife stood beside the house, wearing his red
and blue cloak.

She could make no sense of this. It flooded over her so fast
she could scarcely keep up with it, each place bursting upon her
like a flash of dream, then suddenly gone, and another rising.

She saw a little settlement, burning. The towering blue crystal
mountain appeared again, the rolling blue sea. She saw a night sky,

with strange stars. In the gray dawn, blank treeless dun hills rose up above the sea, gaunt as earthen bones. Then the sea was glittering with sunlight, and ships sailed against each other across the green waves. She saw row on row of dragon ships, surging forward on banks of oars like the striding legs of giants.

Opposite them sailed lines of strange ships, with high boxy prows, and eyes painted below the railings. The dragons strode swiftly toward them; it seemed that they would crush the strange ships in a single attack.

Just before the ships closed, from the other fleet came up a steady stream of balls of fire, like suns hurled through the sky, trailing flames and smoke. The fireballs exploded on the dragons, spitting out gouts of burning stuff, and the sea boiled and flames gusted up, and men burned, and rolling black smoke blotted the clear blue sky.

That copper-skinned girl was walking toward her again, speaking of something, something she needed. That was another place entirely.

The Lady took hold of Mav, and shook her a little. "Show me Eric," she said. "Show me Gunnhild."

The girl ignored her. When the images poured on, the Lady yielded to them again, half-drunk on their splendor. She was in the middle of battle, with sweaty, grunting men all around her heaving up their weapons and sagging under blows. Beneath her feet the ship heaved and rocked, she could hardly keep her feet. Men died around her. Many screamed to Jesus.

Even in the song, that name pierced her. She half-turned, fending it off.

Up through some dank and dripping pine forest she climbed, and stood on a headland and looked out over the edge of the world, where the sea poured over into the abyss, wreathed in fog, with a thunder that made the ground shake under her feet. She turned her head and saw the copper-skinned girl beside her, watching her.

On some great western lake a dragon ship set forth, but at the oars sat dark-skinned men, not danskers, their hair like a dog's roach. She watched them row into the west, into the sun's eye, the water golden around them and notched with shadows where the blades dipped.

Then before her, on the High Seat of Norway, sat an old woman, holding a crown on her knee, and it was Gunnhild.

The Lady gave out a hoarse cry. She shook herself from her blissful daze, and seized Mav by the shoulders and shook her. "Wake up! Wake up—"

Mav swung heavily around to face her. Her eyes were bright as lamps, silver as the moon, round and huge. From her open mouth came a deep resounding voice, not her waking voice.

"Do not touch me."

The Lady's body recoiled, but she kept her hands on the girl's thin bony shoulders. "You are telling me of things to come—I command you, by this hold I have on you now, tell me of Blue-tooth, what is to come with him." Still in her mind, like an after-image, she saw Gunnhild, old and worn, on the throne of Norway, holding an empty crown. "Tell me!"

The girl stared a moment from her silver eyes, and then sang, and the Lady jerked her hands away, startled, because in the streams of music she saw King Harald Bluetooth in a white shirt, kneeling, and a man with a cross in his hand sprinkling him with water.

"Ah!" she cried. "Show me no more of that!"

Then Mav laughed, and her eyes dimmed, and she pulled herself out of the Lady's grasp and sank down on her bed and was still, her arms around herself. The Lady stood. She had no more taste for any of this, suddenly, and she went away to her cupboard in the back of the hall.

—◈—

Soon Bluetooth came to her, as he often did, and wanted something bought or sold, and something found or lost, and as always, news of Jorvik. The Lady put him off. What she had seen of times to come with him seethed in her mind. She was helping him toward the end that he would destroy her. In her little sitting place, between her cupboard bed and the long wall, she gave him wine to drink, and let him be comfortable, but she watched him narrowly the while.

Suddenly she could bear it no more; she burst out, "So you are to become a Christian, hah?"

He startled, and his face darkened. He made some fuss with the wine cup. Finally he said, "I have given it deep thought."

"Ah, you fool," she said, furious. "They talk so well, the Christians. Have they poisoned your mind too? What gain will you have of them, for what they will cost you? These archbishops are no better than anyone else."

"Oh, they are," he said. He settled himself again in the chair, and his eyes turned toward her, cold and intent. "They are. I have done some study of it, and I have learned that Christ is the true god of kings, never mind Odin or Thor. Christ, who drives out all his rivals. As there is only one God, so there is to be only one King, you see."

"Bah," she said, frightened. She could fool him easily, when he tried to be clever; but when he was being stupid she had no way with him. "You would uproot all we are, for one little advantage."

"I cannot turn from this, it is a sword of great price." He was getting up. He gathered his cloak around him. "When you have more word of Eric, summon me. I will hear that."

She growled at him. He had just said he would betray her, and still he expected her to serve him. She let him go by himself to the door.

When he was gone she thought it all out carefully. As always there were different ways to look at it. Eric Bloodaxe had been sprinkled with the Christians' water, and had never really turned from the old gods. She stroked her chin, feeling her way through this. Possibly there was an under way and an over way.

But she knew that Bluetooth did nothing as Eric did; and the Christian priests were already much afoot in Denmark.

There was no place for her in the Christian church, which was a matter of faith, of blind belief, rituals and relics, fear and order, not of knowing. Certainly not of her kind of knowing. She wondered if her time here was coming to an end. Bluetooth, like all men, only half-believed in her anyway.

But she had seen Gunnhild on the High Seat of Norway. That seemed to mean she had succeeded here, somehow—with Bluetooth or in spite of him. Then the great work was not lost, after all, but only gone along some more crooked path.

What she knew now made everything different. It mattered less to her now that she have her way with Eric, and bind Bluetooth to her, than that she get the brother back here, so she could force Mav to yield to her. She would go nowhere without Mav, especially now, with her power blooming. Wherever she went, such a power as that would be worth kingdoms.

There was much to be done still, in spite of Bluetooth. She touched the gold ring on her arm, bidding herself be patient, and keep on.

CHAPTER SIXTEEN

The priest said, "God's will be done. It is God's will that makes Eric king over us—"

The score of people facing him stirred, restless. Benna in the back of the group tightened her lips, but said nothing; she was here in her father's stead, and now that he was buried in the churchyard, ought not to be; but no one so far had made any mention of it. At least there were three or four other women here; Euan's mother stood over by the altar, in front of a row of candles.

From the other side of the church a deep voice bellowed, "No, it was not God, it was our good archbishop, wanting to keep the English off us. And where is Wulfstan now?" A ripple of humorless laughter went up.

The priest's hands rose up and down like doves along the front of his black robe. "God have mercy on our archbishop."

"God have mercy on us!" the deep voice bawled.

"We must bear our burdens with patience," the priest cried. "Ask God what he wishes of us—"

He would talk like this forever, Benna saw, and she took a step closer and called, "You must go to Eric, and beg him to relieve us."

At once she put her hand over her mouth; she had not meant to speak out, but now she had, and all around, people turned and stared at her—the bakers, the cobbler, the butchers, all men.

But they were nodding, and agreeing. Voices rose, repeating what she had said. "You must go to the King!"

The priest said, "This is a mere woman here, does she counsel priests and kings?"

Benna flushed, her anger spurred up once again; she had spoken once, she might as well keep going with it. "As I am a mere woman, so I need the protection of my King, and my priest. Will he give it to me or no?"

Now around her everybody let out a yell. To her surprise, the apothecary's widow, Euan's mother, turned around and smiled at her, and nodded.

The priest swayed back and forth, looking in his long black robe as if he had no feet. His face was screwed up, mouth twisted and eyes half-shut. "It will do no good," he said. "God is testing us, and you are failing it, my good people—"

The deep voice on the far side of the crowd called, "Stop hiding behind God! Go to the King! We'll go with you. Or we'll go without you, Father, you can choose."

"But choose wrong," the cobbler yelled, "and you'll see damned few of us at Mass!"

The priest gasped at the oath, but the rest of them hooted and yelled, high-spirited, now that it was the priest they confronted, and not Eric or his men. Benna glanced around at them, her spirits flagging. It was easy to yell and cheer to each other. Making Eric pay heed would be much harder.

They went out of the church into the deep summer afternoon sunlight. As she went along, the cobbler came by and said, "Well spoken, Benna," and around him other people nodded at her. Many more people were gathered in the churchyard, waiting for them, and she looked for Arre.

Her basket on her arm, her sister stood trading quick words with a restless crowd of town boys, Euan's friends. Euan was not one of them. When she saw Benna her face lit with her smile, and she quit the eager mob of boys and came across the yard.

"How did it go?"

"I don't know," Benna said. "The priest has to go up there and beg the King to help us, that's all I know."

At that moment the priest himself came out of the church, and everybody cheered. The priest looked wan as milk. He lifted his hand and blessed them with a limp unhappy hand. Grimly he went off down the street, and the crowd walked after him.

"Let's go to Corban's house," Arre said. "It will take him a long while to get the King to listen, maybe all day." She crooked her arm through Benna's.

"Corban," Benna said, stiffening. She had not seen him since he came back to Jorvik. He had given her the looking glass, she had sent him a drawing, but nothing else had passed between them.

He did not want to see her. She wasn't sure she wanted to see him; she had made a fool of herself over him the last time. "Maybe—"

"Come along," Arre said, firmly. "Look, there's Grod." Calling to the old man, she towed Benna off down a lane toward Corban's street.

——☙——

Euan said, "This is how it works. How much did you pay for those fleeces, there?"

Corban had spent the morning buying fleeces Arinbjorn had brought in from the country; he went through the pile, naming each price. "This was four pence, and that one three." As he spoke each price, the boy's long knobby fingers pushed the beads back and forth along the abacus. When he had gone through all the fleeces, Corban straightened, frowning at him, and Euan held the square frame up toward him, the beads strung out along the wires.

"That is how much you paid for all of them. Four tens, and two—so forty-two pence." He laid the square on his knees again and played on it like a harp, and lifted it up again. "This is how much you owe the King—two tens, and one, so twenty-one pence."

Corban scratched his chin. This did not seem such a great power to him; he marked his tally sticks, and with the Lady's endless money in his purse he didn't see that it mattered much anyway. But he saw that Euan thought the abacus was wonderful. The boy was handling it again now, his fingers dancing on the beads, his pale short-sighted eyes intent. Corban said, without thinking much about it, "Euan, will you come and work for me, here?"

The boy lifted his head, blinking at him. "Doing what?"

"Counting fleeces," Corban said. "Other things, as they come up."

The boy pulled off his cap and stroked his hand over his long brown hair. "My mother needs me. Things are very hard right now, you know."

"I know. Do you have anything to eat?"

"I—" Euan pulled the cap down over his forehead again, and turned back to the abacus. His long fingers toyed with the beads. "We have bread," he muttered.

"You do. Where do you get it?"

The boy would not face him, but pored over the abacus as if it told endless secrets. "A friend of my mother's, from outside the wall."

"I will give you money, if you will buy—"

"No." Euan was shaking his head, and now he did look up. "My mother said I was not to tell you. There is hardly enough now for us, and if you offer, with your money, he will sell it all to you, and leave none for us."

Corban folded his arms over his chest. He saw some hard ugly joke in this. He wondered if all matters of money, everywhere, were not some hard ugly joke. Euan said, "I'm sorry."

"No reason," Corban said. "You have told me what I need to know."

In the door then came Arre, with a basket over her arm, then Grod, and behind them, Benna. Corban straightened; he was walking toward her before he realized it, a great stupid smile on his face. She turned toward him, and as their eyes met, she smiled too, and his heart jumped.

Arre said, "I have brought you some turnips and onions, Corban. Gifu went hunting; perhaps she'll have meat when she comes back." Grod had brought the cup and the jug and she reached for a drink.

"Thank you," Corban said, looking at Benna. "Without you I would starve, Arre."

Benna said, "Thank you for the looking glass." Her hand rose toward her throat; he saw she had the little round glass on a thong around her neck.

"I'm glad you like it," he said. "I'm very glad to see you."

Beyond them, Euan was saying, "What happened at the church? Did the priest offer to do anything? I doubt it much."

"No," Arre said, "he didn't offer, but they got him to go talk to the King, and there's a great crowd on the street now waiting for him to do it. Rogn and Ralf were there, they were looking for you."

Benna said, "You would not come across the river to see me, though."

"I—" Corban looked at the others, Arre and Euan and Grod,

standing there drinking the ale. Abruptly they were all moving toward the door, talking in a rising clamor of their voices.

But Benna stayed, watching him.

"That's a very handsome coat," she said.

He ran his hands down the front of his fine red coat, which fit him so poorly, and was always too hot. Abruptly he shrugged out of it. "You don't understand. There's so much going on—" He turned his head toward the door, where her sister and Euan and Grod had gone out. "Where are they going?"

"The priest has gone to talk to the King," she said. "To get him to help us."

"Ah, God," he said. "What good will that do?"

She gave him a sharp, angry look. "We have to do something, we are dying! What would you have us do?"

"Is there a crowd out there?" He went toward the door, to look into the street; there leapt into his mind the memory of Eelmouth, gathering his men, shadowing the crowd, saying, "I always watch them. They hate us."

He had the coat in his hands, still; uncertainly he put it on, needing its protection. "Come on," he said. "Let's go," and led her out to the street.

⸻

"Turnips and onions!" Eric slammed his fist down on the table. "That's an insult. Let the churls eat what they grub out of the earth. I have to have meat!"

"We have to save the meat," Gunnhild said. "For tonight. For this Englishman, Morcar, so that he will believe us rich. But tomorrow he will be gone."

"Then there will be no meat at all. Where's Eelmouth? He's the one who's failed us. He was supposed to bring back beef, and he came in empty-handed."

Gunnhild curled up in her corner of the High Seat; her eldest son Gimle stood off to one side, tall and scrawny, and she slid a look at him, hoping he was watching all this. He looked half-asleep, his corn-white hair mussed. She wished her little Harald were older, he was more apt. Down at the far end of the hall a black-robed figure skulked fearfully in the shadows, and she crooked one finger at him. "The priest is here," she said. "He wants to talk to you."

Eric leaned forward, his arms on his knees, staring down the hall. "Gimle!" When the boy startled up, abruptly awake, he said, "Go find me Eelmouth."

Gimle went off toward the back door. Gunnhild said, "You should have listened to me when I told you, last winter, that this would happen."

"Bah," Eric said. "You never remind me of all the things you say will happen that don't." He slouched in the great carved chair, his beard rumpled on his chest.

The priest was slinking up the room, his close-set eyes everywhere but on the King. He was terrified of Eric, which Gunnhild thought amusing. Finally he reached the other side of the table from Eric and bowed his head down.

"My lord—O Great King of Jorvik—"

Eric lifted one foot and slammed it into the table, which shut the priest up instantly. "Well," Eric said. "Are you eating?"

"My lord. I had a little bread for my breakfast—"

"I am eating turnips and onions!" Eric lurched forward, shouting the last words at him. The priest quivered. Eric had driven out all the other priests but this one, once the archbishop was safely locked up in Jedburh; this one only stayed because he was too afraid to run. Eric thrust his head forward toward him, and the priest cowered.

"My lord—the people have nothing! They've asked me to come here—to ask you—"

"To ask me for what? Do they think I grub the earth, to feed them? I am King here! They feed me!" Eric slammed his foot against the table again, and slumped back into the chair.

"My lord—if you would lift the tax—then people might bring in food to—"

"You mean," Eric said, straightening again, "that there is food, somewhere, and they're hiding it from me?"

"No, my lord, no—it's only—if the tax were not so high—"

"Damn them!" Eric lurched up onto his feet. Gimle had come back, with Sweyn Eelmouth a step behind him. The priest slid backward toward the shadows, his face and hands floating against his dingy robe. Sweyn came past him, past Gimle, toward the King.

"My lord," Sweyn said, "there's a pack of people down on the street outside. I think they're waiting for this priest, here, to come out and talk to them."

In the shadows, the priest whispered, "Oh, no, no," and shook his hands back and forth. Eric curled his fingers in his beard, his lips pouting. A trickle of sweat ran down his temple.

"What do you mean, a crowd? Get them out of there. That English legate is only over in Arinbjorn's hall, I don't want him to see a mob here."

"They're hungry," Sweyn said.

"Get those people out of there!" Eric said, his voice rising. "Take all the men and run them off, do you hear me?"

Eelmouth was already turning to go. Gimle said, "I'll help."

"Good," Eric said. "Take him, Sweyn."

"My lord," the priest cried. "My lord, please."

"Get out," Eric said. The priest skittered off.

Gunnhild said, "It's come to this, you see. Now you are eating roots and nuts, and fighting off the churls and bonders, and now finally you see that you must do something, or you are no more King."

His head swung toward her, his shoulders bulled up, his brows bristling, and his lower lip out. "Don't get on me about this again, woman."

She smiled at him. "You must make a bold move, now, and London is the direction of it. Edred is weak and cowardly. Why do you think he sent Morcar here, except to find out if you mean to attack him? Let Morcar go back to Edred in London with some fair words, and they will think you harmless, and then take him by surprise. You could seize the crown of England in a season's campaign."

"I have no men," Eric said. "I would need a great army to attack England."

"You had more men last winter."

"I have no men now, when we are talking of it." He hitched himself around in the chair. Outside, suddenly, there was a great yell, a hundred voices rising, screaming. Gunnhild twitched, her head back; the sound of a crowd always made her jumpy. But Eric crowed.

"You see, though, I have men enough for this." He sat back, grinning in his beard. "Sweyn will harry these townspeople. Morcar will see I am master here."

Gunnhild shifted in her place, putting her fingers to her hair. "Why not take your axe down off the wall and go out to lead them? That might convince him even more."

"Bah," Eric said. "Sweyn can handle it." He slumped down in the High Seat as if rooted there, but he was still grinning, obviously now pleased with himself. He reached for his cup with its thin poor beer. Gunnhild turned her face away, biting her lips in rage.

Euan walked back and forth along the wide street that ran along the edge of the embankment, between the King's great hall and the town. Some of the older people were still here, standing in little groups, talking, but many had left already—afraid, he knew, of what would happen when the priest talked to Eric.

He stopped, looking up at the hall there; the lesser buildings on either side of it made it seem even larger. A few of Eric's men drifted up around the corner of the main building. As he stood watching them, Ralf and Rogn, the miller's two big sons, edged up to him.

"Watch out for Eelmouth," Rogn said. "When he shows up— watch out."

Euan wiped his hand over his mouth. With a quick glance he fixed around him several other boys his age, the smith's boys sauntering along, the apprentices from the shambles in a clump at the mouth of the long street leading over to the Coppergate. None of them were drifting off. They were all idle now, with no work, except the constant work of trying to find something to eat. He watched the apprentices' heads turn, as if all on strings, to watch a few more of Eric's men tramp down the embankment path.

Euan clenched his teeth, watching these men come toward him. He hated Eelmouth and Gorm and the others, always taking what-

ever they wanted, sneering at the town boys, beating them up when
the chance came.

He knew they still ate well, too. That brought up his hackles
worse than the sneers and blows. He was half-dansker; his father
had been Danish, not a Viking, but a woodwright who had worked
to build the new church. They should not treat him so, as if he
were beneath them.

He nudged Rogn, beside him.

"There's the priest."

Like a flapping crow, the priest hurried down the brow of the
embankment, past the danskers waiting there. His face was white.
His white hands flew like doves against the front of his black robe.
His mouth worked. Euan could not hear him at first, but as the
priest came running, he saw more of Eric's men appearing suddenly, from all around the hall, and he saw that they carried weapons. He wheeled and yelled.

"Run! Get away—"

A roar went up from Eric's men, behind him. Over his shoulder, as he bolted toward the cross-street, he saw them flooding
down the embankment, and a surge of panic lengthened his strides.
Ahead of him, in the narrow way of the street, he saw Arre, her
basket on her arm.

"Euan!" she shouted, and ran to meet him. He caught hold of
her hand.

"This way!" He ran, Arre beside him, and the rest of the crowd
rushing along with them, along the narrow street that led across
the town to the Coppergate.

Eric's men were swooping after them, swords in their hands,
and as they charged they howled. Somebody screamed. Euan, in
the middle of the rush of running bodies, Arre racing at his side,
swung around into a lane between two houses and looked wildly
around for a weapon.

Arre banged into him, out of breath. She said, "They're coming!" She whirled and looked out of the lane into the street.

Out there Eric's men had caught up with the slowest and weak-
est of the crowd. A wail went up. Casting around the lane, Euan
grabbed everything he could lay hands on, some rocks, a rope, a
long stick of wood, and rushed back out to the street; Arre was

scooping up rocks and stuffing them into her basket.

In the street two big men were kicking and pounding at somebody on the ground, and Euan reared back and flung a rock. He was bad at throwing and the rock sailed wide but the men dodged anyway, saw him and Arre, and roared. Lifting their swords in their hands they charged.

Euan screamed, "Run!" He raced behind Arre down the street, the two danskers pounding after them. Suddenly Grod was there, on Arre's other side.

"This way," Grod shouted. "Go to Corban's house—"

The street was narrow here, the buildings leaning over from either side, forming a dark space like a long cave around them. As he ran Euan heard doors banging shut, shutters closing, as people locked themselves safe into their houses. The two danskers were right behind them, and now abruptly three of Eric's men rushed around into the way before them; they were trapped.

Grod let out a wail. Euan lifted the stick and jabbed with it around him, trying to keep the Vikings back, and Arre dragged Grod after her into a tiny walkway between two houses.

Euan dodged a wild swinging blow from a sword, and a body crashed into him from the side, knocking him flying. He landed on his back, all the wind swooshing out of him. Somebody grabbed him by the arm and pulled him along the ground. A Viking with a club ran down the lane toward him, his sword drawn back to strike. From the narrow walkway just behind Euan a volley of stones pelted the Viking, who staggered, one hand to his bloody face, and reeled down to one knee. Euan rolled to his feet and dashed into the narrow little path and ran, Arre and Grod ahead of him, bounding over the low walls of a garden, down behind a row of houses.

As he ran, he thought, We can hurt them. We can get back at them, if we can only stop running away.

Grod was screaming, "We're going the wrong way! We're going the wrong way!" Arre was red-faced, her hair flying; she had her basket slung over one arm, a stone clutched in the other. They burst out of the alley into a wider place where two streets met and ran headlong into three other town boys coming from the other direction.

They knocked each other down. Euan bounced up; he recognized the other boys, and called them by name. "Edwy! Rogn! Ralf! Come this way—"

He wheeled around, getting himself straight. His eyes were a blur of buildings and running people but in his mind, clear as the abacus, he saw the town around him, and he knew what they had to do.

"Come down this way! They're pushing across to the Coppergate—if we all get behind them—"

"Here they come," Arre cried.

Four of Eric's men surged around a corner into the street right in front of them. Euan shouted, "Everybody together—hit them—" Arre, beside him, reared her arm back and let fly a fistful of stones.

"Here!" She thrust her basket at him, full of rocks. He grabbed handfuls of them and threw them blindly into the street, the two boys around him screaming and throwing. With rocks raining down on them Eric's men flinched back, turned, and ducked into the shelter of a doorway.

Euan roared. He moved to get a better view of them, shouting, "Come on! Come on!" Then from both sides at once streams of Vikings pounded toward him.

Something glanced off his shoulder and he went to one knee. Arre's voice sounded in his ear. She was lifting him up. He was afraid, suddenly, a wild beating terror in his throat, and he flailed out with one arm, trying to catch hold of her. Around him men tramped and groaned, beating each other. He could not see. Grod was screaming, "This way! This way!" Euan got his feet under him and blundered forward, crashing into people. A familiar hand closed on his arm, and he followed Arre down the street and around into Coppergate, and down the hill, slipping and sliding on the garbage littering the way.

At the bottom of the street, by the oak tree, he stopped; they had outrun the fighting, and he turned, blinking, looking up the street toward the shouting and the thud of blows. A woman was screaming somewhere, as high pitched as a pipe. Beside him, Arre lifted her empty apron to wipe the blood from her face.

Euan groaned. "Are you all right?" He caught hold of her hand. "Where are you hurt?"

"My head is cut," she said. She was white, her lips pale, the blood startlingly red against her cheek, her hair matted with it. "I don't know how. Come on, Grod is right. We should go to Corban's house."

They turned from Coppergate to the street above the river. Someone shouted, "Down there!" From the far end of the street men were running toward them. Euan gasped for breath; he hurt all over, his knee, his shoulder. He felt sick to his stomach. All his plans dissolved out of his head; he just wanted to get somewhere safe. Grod sprinted off, and with Arre beside him Euan dodged after the old man into a narrow, garbage-clogged lane and down and around the back of the Hedeby house.

Grod banged on a shuttered window and it sprang open. Grod went through it like a snake into a hole. Arre scrambled in over the sill, and Euan followed her into a room jammed with people, all standing silently in a mass, their arms around each other.

Euan turned to Arre, standing in the light coming through the window. "Are you all right?"

Blood was streaming down the side of her face. She said, "I want to sit down," and sat down, right there on the floor. A moment later, Benna was there beside her.

"Here. Let me see."

Euan turned to the window; Edwy and Ralf had followed them in their flight, and they were climbing in over the sill. They put the shutter up over the opening and the room was suddenly much darker.

"Where is Corban?" Grod said.

"Outside," said Benna. "In the street." She sat with one arm around Arre, who was holding a sodden rag to her face.

Euan moved a little away from them. He ran his gaze over the darkened room. There were many men here. If they all fought together, he thought, they could overcome Eric's men. In his mind, again, the city appeared, like the abacus, a set of lines and beads; put these beads here, and those beads there. . . .

He wiped his hand over his face. It was dark in here and he could not see very well and his head was pounding, and Arre whom he loved more than all the world was sitting on the floor bleeding. He slumped down next to her, drained.

⸺⸙⸺

Corban stood in the street outside his house, his arms folded over his chest; he was wearing the red coat, and he knew the danskers would not harm him. From the next street came shouts and screams, and now Sweyn Eelmouth jogged down the lane, a sword in one hand, blood all over him.

"Hah, Corban! This is like butchering sheep. Have you seen any trouble here?"

"Nothing much is happening here," Corban said. "I think they have all gone up toward the great bar."

Eelmouth stopped beside him, the sword loose in his hand. Slobber dripped down his chin and he wiped his beard with his free hand. "We should burn this place down," he said.

"Don't do that," Corban blurted out. "I have much of value in my house."

Sweyn laughed. "Send to me if you have trouble," he said, and went away up the street. When he got to the next corner, and turned, Corban went inside.

"I think we're safe for now."

Benna came up to him. "My sister," she said. "They nearly killed my sister."

"I think, if you all stay here—" He looked around at the jammed hall, where now most of the people were sitting down, huddled together, their faces grim. "A little while longer. I think this will pass by."

She was watching him with a strange wild look, her eyes wide. "Just now, out there—I saw you—you spoke to him as if he were a friend."

Corban said, "Where is Arre?"

He went by her, into the back of the hall. Arre lay curled up on one of the benches, Euan beside her; the boy had taken off his shirt and laid it over her.

"Arre," Corban said, and touched her, but she did not move. The side of her head was swollen and turning dark.

"She's asleep," Benna said. "Just as my father went to sleep—" Her voice quavered.

"No," Corban said, and put his arm around her; a sick fear jabbed up into his belly.

She moved away, out of his embrace. "You talked to him as if he were a friend of yours." Her voice shook. "Is that what you meant—how confused it all is, whatever you're doing?"

"Benna," he said. "Let me explain."

"No. I don't want you to explain. I want you to help us."

"I am!" he cried, and swung his arm around, toward the hall, the people taking refuge.

She said, "Helping us, or him?" She reached out and flicked at the red coat. "I think this makes you King Eric's man, Corban." She turned and sat down again beside her sister; she turned the back of her head to him.

Euan looked up at him. "That's not true. I know it's not true."

Corban turned away, his belly rolling. He thought again of his father's curse—everywhere he went, he did no good, but only caused trouble. What he did worked the opposite of what he expected. He thought, No, she is right.

Around him, little by little, the people were settling down. Some brought out bits of food, and shared it, and the jug of ale went from hand to hand, with people drinking directly from it. Grod was already very drunk, peddling his usual lies by the hearth, his voice rising in the smoky air. Corban moved away from Arre, from Benna and Euan; he lifted his hands to the coat.

A wash of cold fear went over him. The coat was his power, he needed the coat to fight Eric. He remembered how it had saved him from the wolf. He could not do this by himself. He had no idea what to do anyway. He stood there in the midst of the quiet and trembling people, his hands on the red coat, and wished he were another, bigger man.

CHAPTER SEVENTEEN

"I told you," Eelmouth said, "I sailed all down the coast, into the Humber, everywhere. The villages were empty. There was nothing even growing in the fields, not an ear of corn, not a cow, anywhere. But I heard—" He turned, looking around, to where Arinbjorn was standing. "The Lord Arinbjorn heard that some of these people have taken all their goods and gone up to Aidansby, in the hills."

Arinbjorn, hearing his name, turned and listened and nodded. He said, "They think, if they go far from any river, you cannot touch them."

Eric scowled at him. "Why did you not tell me this?"

Arinbjorn looked surprised, his eyebrows rising. He always managed to be looking down at everybody. Eric wondered why he kept him around, when he never fought. Except that Arinbjorn was rich, and usually made sure that Eric too stayed rich.

It did no good to have a storeroom full of gold when there was nothing to eat. Eric gave Arinbjorn another hard look, and lurched forward, planting his hands on the table. "Then go to Aidansby," he said to Sweyn Eelmouth, "and prove to them that they are wrong."

Eelmouth wiped his hand over his mouth. "I will. But you should lead us, my lord."

Eric snorted. He straightened up, standing between the High Seat and the table, looking down at the other man. "Are you afraid?"

But then behind him, in the High Seat, Gunnhild spoke up. "Yes, Eric. You should lead your men. You don't want them to teach these people a righteous fear of Sweyn Eelmouth. It's Eric Bloodaxe they must learn some proper respect for."

Eelmouth gave her a quick glance. The suspicion rose in Eric that they had planned this, together, his wife and his underling; he frowned from one to the other, trying to sort this out.

Gunnhild caught his eye. "Go," she said, "and show yourself the king you are, my lord. That will do much to get you more warriors for the fall fighting season." She twisted a tress of her hair around her finger. "And while you're at it, take Corban Loosestrife with you, and see he doesn't come back."

"Ah," Sweyn said, "Corban isn't so bad—" and Gunnhild swiveled her head around to glare at him, and froze the words in his throat. He took a step backward, mumbling, his gaze pinned to the floor.

Eric hunched his shoulders. Aidansby was two or three days away in the hills. This would mean riding a horse, sleeping on the ground, leaving his wife behind. He sat down on the edge of the High Seat again, and gave Gunnhild a narrow look; he marked she wasn't talking about doing this herself. "Why should I have to go? It isn't even a real raid."

Gunnhild was watching him with her eyebrows drawn down and her lips pressed tight together. Her gaze switched to Arinbjorn. "They have food there?"

"In plenty," Arinbjorn said. "From what I've heard, they have a thousand sheep alone."

Gunnhild turned her slit-eyed look on Eric again. He saw she meant to have her way in this; she showed her teeth, and the hand in her lap was fisted.

Her eyes flickered dangerously, and she said, "We could let Gimle lead them."

Eric went cold down to his heels. He wheeled up onto his feet; his hand went to his belt where his axe should have hung. "Gimle?" he said. He took a step toward her, lifting his hand. "You think I'm an old man, hah? You think I'm finished? Is that what you're saying? Gimle?"

She watched him, unafraid, her eyes remote. She said, "Then lead them yourself, Eric." Her voice grated, like the crunch of ice. "If you are not an old man."

He clenched his fist. She stiffened, wary, her eyes on his hand, but he knew it would gain him nothing to hit her. He opened his fist, and rubbed his palm over his mouth, struggling with a low nausea of doubt.

He began to get angry. He would prove he was still King here. He glared at her, to show her he was not forgetting this, and turned to Eelmouth.

"Very well. I will lead you. Everybody comes. We'll take horses. Make sure everybody gets a horse. Swords and helmets, don't worry about heavy armor. We can bring some of these sheep back to sell to the people in the city, too, that will make them happy." He glanced at Arinbjorn, sitting impassively at the table, watching. "I'll even lower the tax again, maybe. Have they food there besides sheep?"

"A lot of cattle," Arinbjorn said. "Pigs."

"We'll take it all," Eric said. "I'll show them nobody can hide from me."

"Good," Gunnhild said, and smiled, relaxing. She reached out and laid her hand on his arm.

———

In the early morning, with the fog still lying on the river, Corban went up the hill to find Arinbjorn to arrange to buy more fleeces, which now somehow Arinbjorn had in plenty. When he reached the top of the embankment, where Arinbjorn had a house near to Eric's hall, he found a crowd gathered by the King's front door. Arinbjorn in his fine blue coat was among them; Corban worked his way in through the crowd to the dansker merchant's side, and just as he reached him, the door to the hall opened, and Eric came out.

With him was the emissary from the English king, whose name, Corban remembered, was Morcar. Corban realized what they were all doing here, and stood there beside Arinbjorn while Eric and the glum-looking Englishman said loud good-byes and gave each other presents.

The sun was climbing into the sky; it would be a hot day. Corban was sweating under the heavy coat. Arinbjorn took a step sideways toward him and said, quietly, "I am leaving for Orkney, as soon as I can load my ship. If I were you, I would get out too."

"What?" Corban replied, startled.

"Gunnhild has it in for you, that's obvious."

Corban lifted his gaze from the merchant's face toward the hall; there in the doorway Gunnhild was standing. When his gaze fell on her a wave of dizziness struck him, and he shivered all over. He turned to Arinbjorn.

"Thank you. I hope you fare well, wherever you are."

Arinbjorn stuck his hand out. "I wish you the same, Corban." They shook hands.

The ceremony was ending, with Morcar on a tall red stallion riding away up the road to the great bar in the city wall, his men straggling behind him, some on foot and some riding. The rank of men behind Eric broke up, everyone wandering off in his own direction; but the King turned and tramped over toward Corban and Arinbjorn.

He wore his magnificent clothes, his great collar of gold, and the majesty that somehow Gunnhild clothed him with. His great fat belly seemed to spread him out behind it, as if it rolled him flat, his shoulders thrown back, his legs turned out. Above his beard the skin of his nose and his cheeks was grainy, like tanned leather. He nodded coldly to Arinbjorn, who bowed, and turned to Corban.

"I am taking my men up to Aidansby, in the hills, to do justice there, and I want you to come with us." He pulled his mouth into a humorless smile. "I may need you to buy goods from me."

Corban twitched. He wondered what justice Eric could do. Abruptly he realized this was a raid, overland; they were going to attack Aidansby. Those were the goods he might buy, plunder and loot. Slaves. The King was watching him steadily, as if he knew what Corban was thinking. Corban pried his jaws apart; he had no way to refuse this.

"As you wish, my lord."

Arinbjorn grunted. He started off down the hill, walking fast. The King ignored him, his stare pinning Corban in his place. "We'll leave before noon. I'll find you a horse."

"I'll walk," Corban said. He turned on legs like sticks of wood and went away down the worn path in the embankment, toward his house.

His mind was racing like a rabbit, darting back and forth, looking for a hole to escape through, a place to hide. He hardly noticed anything around him; when he reached his house he went blindly in the door and stood, in the dimness, trying to breathe. He was hot; he put his hands to the coat. All his nerves were jangled, out of order. He jerked at the coat, and for a moment it seemed to tighten around him, as if it might grow on him, another skin.

His temper snapped. He wrenched at it, ripping the sleeve from cuff to armpit, and tore the coat off his body, and threw it down on the floor.

At once he was cooler, calmer, and the thought leapt up into his mind: this was a chance, this raid, maybe the best chance he would have against Eric.

Gunnhild would not go, for one thing. And they would be riding overland, into the rough upcountry, not over the sea, in their ships, where they were strongest. There would be a lot of them. Surely Eric would take all his men. But he had fewer men than usual. This was a chance, if only he could figure out a way to take advantage of it.

He went up the room toward the hearth. Grod was lying on the bench before the steady crackling fire, the jug cradled comfortably in his arms. Corban took the jug and put it away again in the cupboard. He went back down to the far end of the room, to the bench where Arre was lying.

The girl lay on her back, covered still with Euan's shirt, her head swollen under her hair; they had cleaned the blood off, and put on some kind of poultice, a wad of greens and clay. Her hair was spread out in curling waves across the bed.

Benna sat beside her, drawing something on a piece of pot. Euan was dozing on the next bench. Corban stood a moment looking down at Arre, who twitched and trembled in her sleep, her eyes moving under the lids.

He bent down and stroked the girl's hair. Beside her, Benna looked up.

She flushed, her fair skin all rosy. "I'm sorry," she said. "I shouldn't have said what I did, yesterday. When you saved all those people from the King's men—"

"Oh, no," Corban said. "You were right." He smiled at her. "I think your sister is waking up."

"Yes." Benna turned around toward Arre, and took hold of her hand. "She did wake, a little while ago, just for a breath of time, but she knew me." She lifted her gaze to his face. "What will happen to us?"

"I don't know," Corban said. "I need some help. Euan, are you awake?"

The tall boy stirred, and lifted his head. "What is it?"

Corban sat down on the bench beside Arre. "The King is going off to attack someplace called Aidansby. Do you know where that is?"

Euan blinked at him. "Yes, I think so, somewhere up the Westmoreland road."

"I want you and Grod to go out after that Englishman, Morcar, who was just here. He left by the great bar. Go tell him where Eric is going, get him to help us." Morcar only had a dozen or fifteen men. Eric would take sixty at least. Corban's rabbit brain was scurrying around again, looking for a hole, for a path. "Morcar must know where to find more men. At least he can warn the village." There would be more men at the village, maybe a lot of men. He began to see a way to do this.

Euan said, "What about you?"

"The King has ordered me to go with him."

The boy's face quivered. "He means to kill you." Benna murmured something, pale again, her eyes fixed on Corban's face.

"Maybe," Corban said. His stomach was tucked up against his backbone. "I'll deal with that. You get Morcar to help—tell him they can catch Eric in the country, without ships." He laid his hand on the boy's arm. "Do whatever you can, Euan."

"I will," Euan said. He took off his hat suddenly and raked his hand through his lank hair. "I will."

"Take Grod," Corban said. "If you can get him to wake up."

"I will." Euan went away up the hall, calling the old man's name.

Benna said, "What can I do?"

He said, "I don't know. I think—there is something we have to deal with, and maybe only you can do it. We need to distract Gunnhild, the King's wife. I don't know what she could do, but we have to keep her busy somehow."

Benna's jaw dropped. "How can I do that?" She gave a disbelieving laugh.

"I don't know. But I know you have a power, and I need you to use it now."

She gave another, frightened laugh. She seemed small and

harmless, her shoulders hunched, sitting in front of him, but her eyes were steady. "I'll do whatever I can."

"I don't think—" He licked his lips. "I don't think there is much danger in it—for you—not for you especially—" His voice ran out. He looked away, gathering some breath, and brought his gaze back to her; she stood waiting, watching him.

"I love you," he said. "I would not put you into danger unless I really needed it."

She reached out and took hold of his hand. "I love you, too, Corban," she said, and came into his arms.

He held her tight, his face against her hair, glad of her. Unwillingly, he thought of Mav, off in Hedeby, very near her time, now; what danger was this for her—what would become of her now, his sister?

He could not know. He never knew. He had to keep going straight on, doing what he could.

Maybe that was what had saved him against the wolf; not the coat, but going straight on.

He stood holding Benna tight for a moment longer, and then let her go, and stood back. "If I don't come back, remember me."

"Where are you going?"

"With the King," he said. He went back up the hall, to the bench where he slept, and kept his gear, and dug into his pack. In the bottom of it he found his old cloak, the red and blue cloak he had gotten in exchange for the Cymryc boat. Benna had come after him. Up by the hearth Euan had Grod up on his feet, groaning and cursing, but moving toward the door.

"What are you going to do?"

He was afraid to tell her anything; Gunnhild might discover anything she knew. He shook the cloak out and swung it around him. "Be careful," he said, and bent and kissed her.

She flung one arm around his neck, kissing him back, hard. They stood so for a long heartbeat, and then Euan called, "Corban! Someone is here for you."

He straightened. "I'm coming." He looked down at her, and tried to smile. She stepped back, her eyes all glossy with tears. He went up the hall to the door.

Outside, in the street, Sweyn Eelmouth stood, holding two

horses by the reins. "Are you ready?" He had a stiff, strange look on his face.

"I think so," Corban said, and went out into the street.

—⚬—

Euan dragged Grod along, making him walk, all the way up through Jorvik toward the great bar, where the deep main gate cut the wall like a cave and the road led off to the west. Although it was full morning there was nobody around in the street; Euan thought he saw the miller's boys, away down in Coppergate, but all the shops were shuttered and barred. When they reached the gateway, the only people there were two of King Eric's men, sitting on the ground looking bored.

Euan kept his eyes away from them. After the work of the day before, he hated them worse than ever. He and Grod went out onto the road, which wound away through meadows and gardens and stands of trees. The late summer sun hung over everything in a golden haze. Bees hummed in the thick drying grass in the ditch below the wall, and in the tree beside the road, a crow squawked and flapped.

Morcar had left the city only a little while before, and Euan could see a cloud of dust, far down the road, probably kicked up under the hoofs of his train. He chewed thoughtfully on his lip, watching the dust cloud, which wasn't even going in the same direction as Aidansby.

Grod said, "We'd better hurry if we're going to catch him."

Euan was putting thoughts together in his mind, even and orderly. He said, "He didn't help us yesterday, when he was right here in Jorvik."

"Well, he couldn't, then, with Eric—"

"This is Eric again."

"What do you mean?" Wide-eyed, Grod glanced around behind them, toward the gate porters, back inside the bar, and turning intensely back to Euan lowered his voice to a quiet hiss. "Corban said we were to get him to help us!"

"Corban is desperate," Euan said. "He doesn't know what else to do." He rubbed his hands together, excited, and swung around, back toward the center of the city. "I have a better idea."

"Euan," Grod wailed. "No—we have to do what Corban said—"

He wheeled around suddenly, and leapt off the road, pulling Euan with him into the ditch. Out the gate a great parade of horsemen filed. Lead among them was King Eric, massive as a mountain giant, one hand on his hip, talking to the man who rode beside him. Eric wore a breastplate of iron-studded leather and his great battle-axe swung by his thigh, the curved edge gleaming. His army followed after him through the gate by twos and threes, slouching on their shaggy horses, long swords slung behind their saddles or hanging from their belts, their helmets clanging. In among them, with no sword, no helmet, rode Corban, in his red and blue cloak.

He saw them; his head turned toward them. Euan met the Irishman's wide grey eyes, and then he was riding past, crowded alone and unarmed in the middle of the Vikings.

Euan stood straight, his heart thumping in his chest; he watched them progress on along the road, and vivid in his mind he saw what he had to do.

Beside him, Grod suddenly made the sign of the cross over himself. Euan hooted at him. Grod said, "Just for luck, that's all. A man can always use a little luck." In their webs of wrinkles his eyes looked sad and old.

"Come on," Euan said, and ran off back through the gate, into Jorvik again, to look for his friends Edwy and Rogn and Ralf.

—✦—

Benna had seen King Eric often enough that she could draw his picture. She did not make him as he seemed to her, fat and evil, but as she supposed his wife would want him: strong, handsome, a king's son, a king himself. Then she took the shard up to the back door of Eric's Hall.

The cook sat on the back step, buying vegetables from the first of a line of people with baskets and sacks of things to sell. Benna took the last place in the line and watched him buy onions and cabbages, three fresh-killed hares, some fish, and two loads of firewood, and when she reached him got the courage up to ask for Gunnhild.

"What do you want her for?" The cook scowled at her. "What is it about?"

Benna took the shard out of her apron and showed it to him. The cook's eyes widened.

"Jesus and Thor." He reached out for the shard and she drew it back out of his reach. "All right," he said. "Go inside."

She went into the back of the hall, where the empty tables stood, the air dusty and still; the far door was wide open, and the smokeholes let in shafts of light. Through that far door she could hear children yelling. She went forward a few steps along the side of the great room, uncertain, and turned around to look at the High Seat.

There she found the Queen, curled up against one of the lion-headed arms. The peaked back of the chair loomed above her. Her head was propped on her fist, her eyes shut. Benna thought she was asleep, but suddenly the woman's eyes popped open, staring straight at her.

The look was like a blow, a finger pointing, a shout from inside her ears. Benna stood, mute. Gunnhild looked her over steadily, and after a moment said, "You are trying to find me?"

"Lady," Benna said, her mouth dry, her tongue suddenly not working right, "I thought—I would like to show you this, that you might buy it."

"Buy it." Gunnhild stretched out her hand. "Come on, come closer, I won't sting you. Here." Benna went around the end of the table and up beside her, and gave her the shard.

Gunnhild took it, and like the cook blurted out an oath. She stared down at it, turning the shard slightly from side to side. "He has not looked like this for years," she said, and gave a laugh. For a long while she studied it, and then lifted her gaze to Benna, her face altered, her look full of curiosity, and almost kind.

"Who are you? I believe I know you—the potter's daughter? Yes, and now your father is dead, and you should come into our wardship, and we shall find a husband for you." She lowered her eyes to the shard, while Benna considered the prospect of marrying somebody Gunnhild found for her. "You made this?"

"Yes, my lady."

"You are very clever. No, I shall not buy this," Gunnhild said. "I have the man in the flesh, I need no image of him. But—" Her hand rose to graze the side of her throat, and her eyes melted. She seemed abruptly to be only a girl, a beautiful, languid princess of a girl. Her voice was sweet as milk. "Would you make one of me?"

Benna started; she had not thought of this. Before she had felt the Queen's look as a blow, and now it seemed the softest caress. "Yes, my lady—of course—if you wish. I have to go back for my ink and brushes."

"Bring them." Gunnhild sat upright in the High Seat now, her hand on the great lion-arm. "But not—" With one finger she flicked scornfully at the clay. "I will have something for you to place it on. Come back as quickly as you can."

"I will, my lady." Benna bowed down, her stomach watery, wondering if she could do this, and went back out the door.

⁂

Gunnhild thought about Eric a little, pushing him along in her mind; he had to do something, this time, but whatever he managed, even a little sheep raid, she could make into a great victory. Then more fighting men would come, eager for booty, glory, a season of raids and a soft life through the winter, and the favor of such a King as Eric Bloodaxe, and she could get him headed toward London.

Once he had taken London, more men would come. He would be King of all England, and with that wealth of gold and men, he and she could turn then to seize the rest of it, one kingdom at a time. Each one adding power to the thrust. Norway, Denmark, Sweden to the east, perhaps ultimately even Rus—and, westering, Iceland, that nest of outlaws, and the Orkneys, Ireland, Man, all the lands around the northern sea. One piece at a time they would lay the whole world together under one house. Her house. She looked down at the shard of clay, with Eric's face on it, smiling. He would make a king after all, with her to help him.

She could follow him now, in her mind; seeing his face made that easier, somehow, and she went along with him a while down

a dusty road, toward Aidansby. She had lost track of Corban Loosestrife already, which annoyed her.

Gimle came in, his head down, and his face long. He had
wanted to follow Eric on the raid, but the King had ordered him
to stay, with his little brothers, to command in his absence. Which
of course meant nothing since Gunnhild was here and Gunnhild
commanded always, in absence and presence. Gimle went up the
hall toward her, striking the benches with a horsewhip. He gave
her an evil look.

"Well, little man," she said, and put the shard aside. "Why so
sour?"

"I'm never going to get to fight!"

"Oh," she said, and drew him over to her, and stroked his hair
back. He was a very handsome boy, she thought, although little
Harald would be more handsome.

He pulled away from her, angry. "I'm not a baby!"

"Ah, you brat," she said, and slapped his cheek. "Go out, go
fight with your brothers, if you want battle."

"Mother—"

"Do as I say." She turned away from him, and clapped her
hands; two of her women appeared, and she sent them for the
casket with her jewels and her fur cloak. It was a hot day, but she
needed the cloak. "Go, Gimle," she said, when the boy lingered.
"I have things to do." Her gaze drifted toward the shard again, the
image of Eric, a fine and wonderful Eric. A prickle of lust coursed
through her, not for her husband.

She should keep after him, on the way to Aidansby, make sure
that everything went as it was supposed to. But it was such a long,
empty ride, and she wanted to see herself like this, a fine and
wonderful Gunnhild, an everlasting Gunnhild, wife and mother of
Kings. Surely Eric could manage this himself, a little sheep raid,
anyway. She called impatiently to the women, to bring her the
jewels and the fur, and settled herself on the High Seat, and composed herself as she wanted the girl to see her.

Grod said, "I think this is a bad idea, Euan."

"Think what you want," Euan said shortly. He glanced behind him; he had found almost twenty boys and young men from the city to come with him, and they were following him now in a tight pack up the road, under the clear summer sky. In the dust before them Euan could see the fresh prints of King Eric's horses, a pattern of dimples leading away into the distance. He rubbed his nose, which wanted to sneeze. He wondered if Grod was right, and for a moment his will faltered, but then in his mind he saw the order in it, like the abacus, and he stiffened. Abruptly, to his amazement, Arre's little sister Gifu was walking up beside him.

"Where are you going?" she said. She wore a man's shirt, patched and torn and patched again, with a heavy belt around her waist, and a knife through that, and the sling hanging beside it. On her feet were stout boots, her long brown legs bare. She had a string of colored beads around her neck, and her face was dirty.

He said loftily, "We have important deeds to do, Gifu. Go home and tend your goats."

She strode along beside him; her blue eyes ran over him, over Grod, and over the boys hurrying along after them, and at last returned to Euan again.

"I'll help you."

"You can't," he said. "You're just a girl."

"I can help you," she said. "I know a fast way to Aidansby, for one thing."

Euan sneered at her. "That's what you know. We aren't even going to Aidansby."

She frowned at that, but opened her mouth to argue again. He said, "Well, wait." He was thinking now that perhaps she should go with them; he had seen her down a squirrel with a rock, once, at thirty paces, and she had roamed all over this country. He said, "Do you know the Westmoreland road?"

"All the way to Aidansby," she said, angrily.

"Good," he said. "Come along, then. Maybe you can help, after all."

—⊷—

Gunnhild gave Benna a sheet made of hide, scraped and stretched stiff, to draw on; one side was striped with lines of marks in dark brown ink, but the other side was fresh and clean. Benna laid it on the table, put her pot of ink beside it, and picked up the brush.

Gunnhild sat in the High Seat. She seemed much greater now, with a cloak of glossy black fur spread out around her, a collar of jewels around her neck; her hair was sleek as gold, and her face resolute and calm, as if she looked down from some height inaccessible to ordinary folk. Benna stared at the white sheet before her, and suddenly, for the first time in her life, she could not draw.

Nothing she did would be good enough. Her stomach knotted up. The space around her seemed to crinkle. A boy around Gifu's age came in, kicking at the furniture, and the Queen called him over and patted him, and then abruptly sent him away with a push. Benna fixed her gaze on the blank white page, which she dared not touch.

She could not do it. She would not do it well enough; she had never done it well. It hadn't mattered, before, but it mattered now, and she would fail.

It mattered now. It mattered for Corban's sake. For Corban's sake she had to do it.

A calm fell over her. The crinkling faded around her. She looked up at the woman on the High Seat, and reached for her brush. She could do this. To do it properly—to capture her as she really was, that would be hard. But as she wanted to be, that was easy.

She made the image as large as the piece of hide, putting in the fur, the jewels. She left out the harsh lines of Gunnhild's mouth, and let her smile a little, as she had when she was petting her son. Benna's stomach felt evil. She was not doing a good enough job; the hide absorbed the ink differently than clay did, the texture was wrong.

The line of the arm was good, though. The eyes were good. Bit by bit, she made what was good better. She worked all the afternoon, while Gunnhild sat there smiling at her. Finally, as the slaves were going along clearing the tables, she put her brush down and turned the page around.

She felt tight as a drum inside, knowing she had not done it nicely enough; she never could get close to what she saw in her mind. Gunnhild leaned forward to see, her eyes hot and intent.

"Bring it to me," she said, and Benna picked up the drawing carefully between her two hands and went around the table, and laid it on the Queen's knees.

Gunnhild sighed. She looked down at the image of herself, a smile curving her lips. One finger twined in a curl of her golden hair. The other hand played softly over the drawing.

"Be careful," Benna said. "It might still be damp in places."

Gunnhild murmured. She did not take her eyes from the picture, and her fingertips grazed over it, caressing it. Benna waited a moment longer, relieved. She wondered in a corner of her mind if Gunnhild would now buy the picture, but she did not know how to ask, and Gunnhild took no more notice of her. Finally she went out the back door.

CHAPTER EIGHTEEN

Corban remembered that the way west led by the gibbet, where the hanged men had saved him and Grod when they first came to Jorvik, but Eric did not take his army along that road. Instead, soon after they left Jorvik, they swerved off to the north, along the river valley, following a dusty path that led along the low ground west of the river. Off to their left, long sloping hills rose in soft heaps of late summer green and brown, threaded with dark seams of trees. The road went past fallow land, which had been planted once, but now sprouted mats of weeds and brambles. Corban thought of Euan and Grod, who had been standing there in the ditch by the Jorvik bar, and his belly clenched; he fought off a burst of fury.

His whole plan was collapsing, such a poor plan as it was. Euan and Corban would never catch Morcar in time to bend his course to Aidansby. Now Corban himself was riding along in the midst of the men who had murdered his family and destroyed his home, and they were going on to do that to another place, another people, and he was helpless to prevent it.

He thought of Mav, and his whole body seemed to wrench toward her, as if he could propel himself across the sea, and be with her again, one with her again, and out of this.

The sun climbed in the sky, baking the valley floor, so that the distant hills wrinkled in the shimmering heat. Around him the danskers groaned and complained about the horses, shifted and stirred around in their saddles, trying to get comfortable. Corban stayed well back in the pack, away from Eric, who rode next to Sweyn Eelmouth, talking in a loud voice.

"You have to ride hard on these people, or they get presumptuous. Never let them get their faces off the floor, that's what my father told me. I'll drop the tax, at harvest time. They'll be so glad, they'll kiss my feet in gratitude."

He laughed, and the other men all guffawed along with him. Corban glanced around toward the empty land beside the road;

there would be no harvest here. He thought Eric was blind, or crazy.

Sweyn Eelmouth said, "Harald Fairhair was a great King, I've heard."

"You've heard, have you?" Eric growled. "Let me tell you, my father was the greatest man who ever drew a sword to hew down his enemies. You should get down and pray thanks you weren't his enemy, I tell you."

Sweyn laughed. "These days, who you pray to is what makes you enemies."

The man riding next to Corban murmured something. Somebody else said, "The whole god thing is getting too confusing, that's for certain."

Eric said, "My father was as close to god as I need."

Nobody had anything more to say about that. The road wound around the foot of a hill; up ahead, they saw, far down the low ground, three or four sheep hurrying away. Eric flung his arm out.

"Take them."

"Too far," Sweyn said, making no move to obey him. "They'll get into the bog down there, and we'll never find them."

"Well," Eric said, "when we come to Aidansby, we'll have plenty to eat, anyway."

Corban bit his teeth together. Their horses plodded on through the heat of the day. They went through a stand of trees, where all the trees had died; their barkless white trunks stood like ghosts among the green veils of vines and brambles growing up over them. The men straggled out along the road; he thought they could have walked there faster.

"I've done a lot of wrong, in my life, but one thing I can say," Eric was saying, "I never turned against my father. I wonder how long it will be before this oldest boy of mine turns on me."

"Oh, he's a good boy, Gimle," Eelmouth said.

"He's all Gunnhild's," Eric said. "And none of mine."

Another of the men said, "That's the way of sons, that's all. They strut off thinking they can do so much better than their fathers, and they all end up just wishing they could do as well."

"I never left," Eric said. "I never had to. I did everything he told me to do. Some of my brothers defied my father. He sent me to deal with them, and that's where I got the name Bloodaxe. And so will I deal with Gimle, if he doesn't watch out."

There was a little silence after this. Finally, Sweyn Eelmouth said again, in a thready voice, "He's a good boy, Gimle."

They followed the road up into the hills, and stopped for a while by a spring, in a copse of trees. Corban got stiffly down from his horse. The men around him called out loudly, and stamped around, and laughed; he went quietly out of their midst, to the edge of the little wood, and looked out over the yellowing hillside.

He leaned against a tree there, and remembered the forest in the far western land, with its fabulous creatures. He longed to be back there again, where this evil could not reach. A dank black mood dragged at him. He thought of Mav, whom he was betraying, and for no real good: he wondered what the Lady would do to her, when she found out he was trying to destroy Eric. Another murdering brother. He thought of Benna with a hurtful, tender sadness.

He had put her in danger, too, and all for nothing.

Benna was strong, she would wend her way out of whatever he got her into. He remembered thinking once that there was a web of women's power, like a caul over the world; Benna was part of that web, Benna and Mav, the Lady and Gunnhild. He laughed, remembering how Benna had broken the pot shard, spurning her own gift.

Abruptly, he thought, I am doing that.

A thrill went down his spine. To Benna and Mav, what seemed strange and potent to everybody else was only their way of knowing; was it not the same for him? In his mind the web of power widened, and he was part of it, one little part, with a little power, and yet real, and necessary; he felt himself taking a step up, as if on a great stairway, a rainbow bridge winding into the sky—

"Corban!" Suddenly Eelmouth was beside him, slinging an arm around him. Corban jumped, startled almost out of his skin. The stairway vanished from his mind. He felt tumbled down to earth, and he turned, angry, to snarl at Sweyn, and saw on Eelmouth's face a strange, stiff look he had seen once before.

He shut his mouth, seeing also, over Sweyn's shoulder, Eric Bloodaxe tramping away toward the spring. Eric had been just behind him, while he dreamed of his rainbow staircase, his own little conceit of power, Eric and his axe.

He gathered in a long shuddering breath, his back cold. He reminded himself again that thinking he knew anything was dangerous. He nodded to Eelmouth. "Thank you."

Sweyn drew his arm away, not smiling anymore; he cast a quick look over his shoulder. "I didn't do anything," he said. "And I can't do it again. Come on." They went back to their horses, and rode on.

⚓

They rode up through meadows of blowing grass, and down again through stands of oaks, their great crowns heavy with dusty green leaves. The road wound along the shoulder of a hill, and then turned steeply down a slanting cut in a bank, close grown with willows and brambles, which led onto the fording of a river. The water spread out four inches deep and one hundred feet wide across a gravel bar, and the road ran straight across it and up the far bank, higher than this side, with masses of tree boughs hanging over.

Corban was thinking that if they stopped for the night, he dared not sleep; Eric would fall on him like a wolf.

They went out across the ford, the horses crowding together out of the deep water, and Sweyn Eelmouth suddenly raised his head. "Do you smell smoke?" Corban sniffed, and caught a whiff of smoke. Then, Eelmouth screamed, "Helmets! Helmets—" and the bushy trees on the far bank exploded in volleys of stones.

Corban shrank down over his horse's neck; stones struck him in the head and the shoulder and the back. A rock the size of a cabbage struck the man in front of him on the head and he sank down sideways out of his saddle. Sweyn Eelmouth roared an oath. More stones rained down on them. Ducking down out of the way, Corban rolled off his horse, holding onto the mane and the reins, and the horse reared up and its hoofs battered the air over him. He let go of the rein, and the horse in front of him shied up against Corban's and knocked it stumbling and splashing to the ground.

Rocks pelted down around him. All he could see was the massive thrusting hindquarters of the horse directly in front of him, whose rider slumped down, blood spurting from his hair. Relentlessly stones showered around him. He held his hands over his head, and shrank away to one side, trying to see through the milling horses. A rock bounced painfully off his hand. He floundered into water up to his hips.

Over there, at the river's edge, something blocked the path up the bank—brush, a tree trunk—Eelmouth was up there, trying to fight his way through. No one was helping him. Half the men in the ford were out of their saddles, struggling to get out of the way of the floundering animals; the other half were trying to rein in horses that leapt and bucked and reared and screamed. Corban's horse, down in the middle of the ford, was lashing out wildly with its hoofs, and now another horse went to its knees, throwing its rider. Two of the Vikings jumped to help the thrown man, but before they could reach him a panicked horse galloped straight over him, knocking the other men flat.

Another barrage of stones thundered into the tangled mass of men and horses. Corban stood to his waist in the river, downstream of the ford, out of the fall of the stones. He looked for Eric; if he could find Eric, maybe he could kill him, now, no matter what happened. A man staggered past him, blood streaming from his head, and blundered into the water and lost his balance and fell. In twos and threes, the horses were bolting away, up out of the ford, back the way they had come.

Behind them Eelmouth was shouting orders, pulling men up onto their feet, waving them up out of the shallows where they were crouching. "Come on—there aren't very many of them— Take them on! Let's go! Come on—run!" He charged the high undercut bank, with its veils of willows, from which another volley of stones pelted down.

Corban stooped down in the sweeping water, rocks pelting the river around him. Up on the far bank, above the heavy brush, he thought he saw a mass of wild curly fair hair. The brush rustled furiously and more stones rattled down. But the Vikings were answering Eelmouth, who was waving his sword and shrieking, and they rushed headlong at the bank and started scrambling up the sheer clay face, grabbing hold of roots to pull themselves along.

Corban saw no sign of Eric; he stayed where he was in the river, watching Eelmouth's charge.

On the top of the far bank now, smoke was rising. He could see people running up there, back and forth, as the Vikings surged up the bank. Flames licked through the brush, and black smoke rolled out under the trees. At the head of his charge, Sweyn Eelmouth clambered hand over hand up the bank and into a crackling sheet of fire.

He shrank back, and the men behind him slid back down and fell into the river. Eelmouth jumped down into the water again and wheeled. His eyes blazed; slobber erupted through the great hole in his teeth, and he roared, "Come on! This way!" He jammed his sword back into its scabbard, swung the scabbard back over his shoulder, and leapt downstream into the river.

The other men followed, throwing off their armor and their helmets. Corban pushed off from the bank to join them. The current took him. Eelmouth led them, swimming strongly along, his head cutting through the water like a dragon ship. Corban, swimming behind him, looked around him at the other danskers, watching for Eric. On the top of the river bank he caught glimpses of people running through the brush, and now clods of earth and burning branches showered down on them.

Corban slowed. He let the other men pass him, swimming after Eelmouth down the long cavern of the river, under the looming banks and the crowding branches of the trees; none of these men was Eric. When they were all past him, he paddled over to the near bank, where the water was only waist deep, and stood up.

He walked back toward the ford, striding against the solid push of the river, his feet sliding on the rocky bottom. He knew he had not seen Eric, in the men following Eelmouth. A body floated past him, face down. Clinging to a branch in the busy current, a man bleeding badly from one eye called out to him for help, and Corban got him by the arm and hauled him to the bank and left him there, sprawled on the mud vomiting.

He waded on up to the ford. The broad sun-dappled gravelly shallows were littered with dead and wounded men. The flames had died on the bank, but smoke still rolled down into the gorge of the river and the air stank. The horses had run back up the path;

he could see them stirring restlessly back and forth under the trees. From down the river suddenly there rose a shrill scream, and the roar of several voices.

A curved shadow sailed across him. He looked up; in the narrow space of sky between the dense canopy of the trees, a stream of black birds circled. At the foot of the far bank a man with one arm dangling pried himself suddenly up out of the gravel, took two staggering steps, and fell face first into the river and began to float away. The birds were settling down into the overhanging branches, onto the high bank, with noisy flaps of their wings. In the shallows of the ford, blood pooled red among the stones. Next to a bloody trampled body lay a sword, the blade half buried in the water.

Corban stood in the middle of the ford, and now he saw King Eric Bloodaxe, crawling out from under the lee of the bank.

Corban went cold, all over; he straightened, his hands at his sides. The King saw him and stood upright.

"Get me that horse." Eric pointed to the nearest horse, standing where the path went up the riverbank behind him.

Corban said, "You killed my father."

Eric blinked at him. He had a bruise on his forehead, and one of his hands was bloody. In the great greying mat of his beard his mouth worked, red as a wound; he looked toward the horse again, and said, again, "Bring me that horse."

Corban's voice rose. "You killed my mother, my baby sister. My brother. You killed them all."

Eric's lips pulled back in a snarl. "Now I'm going to kill you."

He hauled his axe out of his belt and charged across the shallow water. Corban dodged him, jumping to one side, his own hands empty. Eric rushed at him and he flinched back and the axe whistled past him and struck the ground with a clang.

Eric stumbled to one knee. His breath whistled through his teeth. He wore a leather breastplate, studded with iron; he would be hard to kill. A sword. Corban knew where a sword was. He lunged past the King, found the sword in the river, gripped it with both hands, and wheeled to strike. His first blow swung wildly in the air, and the weight of the sword nearly carried it out of his grasp. He heaved it awkwardly around again, and the blade caught fast on Eric's upraised axe.

With a coiling heave of his shoulders the King tore the sword from Corban's grasp; it hurtled through the air and splashed into the river.

Eric snarled, baring his teeth. His face was red. He prowled toward Corban, swaying from side to side, chopping the axe up and down in front of him. Corban backed away, his eyes on the moon-shaped blade of the axe. The water rose to his knees, the current tugging at him. Eric came at him in a sudden burst, slashing down, and Corban staggered back. Losing his footing, he saw himself going down helpless at Eric's feet, and flung himself backwards, into the deep water of the river.

He swung around in the water, scraping his knees on the bottom, got his feet under him. Eric thrashed out into the water after him, the axe lifted over his head, and Corban barreled up out of the river, up under the King's raised arms, and crashed headlong into him.

Eric went down hard on his back in the shallows. Corban slammed down on top of him. With one hand he grabbed the wrist that held the axe and pinned it down under the water, against the stony ground. The King heaved up under him, roaring, scrabbling at him with his free hand, and Corban butted him in the mouth. Blood spurted across him. Still clinging tight to Eric's arm he swung himself up, knelt on the King's chest, and planted one foot on the King's free arm.

Eric cried, "Ransom—I'll ransom—"

"No, you won't," Corban shouted, and now, suddenly, he saw the knife in Eric's belt.

He howled. "This is for my father—" He wrenched the knife out of its scabbard, put the tip of it between two of the iron studs on Eric's leather armor, and drove it to the hilt into Eric's chest.

The King shrieked, his body arching upwards. Corban swung the knife up again and stabbed it down into Eric's body.

"This for my mother—" He jerked the knife free and hacked it down again, over and over, the straining body under him shuddering, and then softening, falling back inert on the gravel, mere meat now. "This is for my sister—this is for me—for me—for me—"

He ran out of breath. For a moment he hung, dazed, above

what he had done, and shut his eyes. Some terrible weight he had been carrying around with him since his family's fall now seemed to lift and float away. He stood, leaving the knife buried in Eric, and a sound above him brought him abruptly around, looking up at the overhanging bank.

Up there in the trampled brush, Euan and Gifu and Grod were standing, watching him. Corban wiped his hand across his chest; he realized he was covered with blood.

"Where are the rest of you?" he asked.

"Scattered," Euan said. "Going home. Eric's men are chasing them. We have to get out of here. They'll be circling back through here soon."

"All right," Corban said, and staggered up the path toward the horses.

—❦—

Grod's hands were bloody. He had carried stones, all the while; they had not let him fight, but he had to carry baskets of stones to them. He had run back and forth, lugging stones, and his fingers were pulped and aching from the effort. Now he clung to the saddle of the dansker horse and longed for the jug, as they jittered along the dusty road home.

This was all Corban's doing, he thought, and groaned.

But he thought of Corban, stabbing old Eric to death, and a reluctant little laugh worked its way out of him. Corban was a hero, he supposed. He glanced at Corban, riding along beside him, his red and blue cloak wrapped around him, and felt a sudden leap of pride. His Corban.

It didn't last long. He was hungry and thirsty. He clung to the saddle; he hated horses, he wanted to get down and find his nice jug and lie down and sleep. Corban rode right in front of him as they trotted along. They were coming to a copse of trees, a shady place. He opened his mouth to call to Corban, to make him stop for a while and let him rest.

Before he spoke, Corban was straightening in his saddle, twisting around to look over his shoulder. He jerked his horse to a halt; Grod's horse ran up alongside, its head across the neck of

Corban's, and Corban grabbed his reins from him.

"Somebody's coming. Quick! Euan! Somebody's coming." Corban wrenched his horse around, dragging Grod behind him, and veered off the road into the viny brush alongside it. Euan and Gifu crashed in after them, pushing through a dense thicket, deep into the shadows under a straggly tree.

Grod slumped down in the saddle, panting. His chest hurt suddenly. The Vikings would catch them. He bit his lips together. The Vikings would catch them yet. The air was full of dust. He strained his gaze back toward the road, visible through the masking branches of the trees around them. For a long moment there was nothing. He glanced at the others; Euan was blinking toward the road, Gifu was picking a splinter out of her hand. Then out on the road came a drumming of hooves, and through the gap in the branches Grod saw streaks of brown flash by, several horses, at the gallop.

The pounding hoofs faded away. Corban said, "Eelmouth. Gone to tell Gunnhild."

Grod groaned in relief. Euan said, "We have to get off the road." He turned to Gifu. "Is there another way?"

"Longer," she said. She was taut, strung like a bow, her eyes dark. All through the fight she had been at the front of it, heaving rocks and branches down, shouting to the others, leaping like a mad thing when she hit her targets. Now she led them up out of the thicket, and they started off down the slope into the valley.

Maybe they were all heroes, Grod thought, with a start.

He longed for the jug. His hands were sore and he bounced on the saddle, bruising his old bones. But the Vikings had not caught them. He was beginning to feel better. Now he saw that he was definitely a hero, just like Corban and Gifu, and Euan, who had figured it all out, told them what to do. He clutched the front of the saddle and followed Corban down onto the floor of the valley, going back to Jorvik.

—⚬—

Mav shrieked with delight. She could not keep this in; her voice rose in scream after scream, triumphant.

The Lady came and stared at her, but Mav only laughed. She flung her head back against the cushions of her cupboard bed and laughed, and screamed, and sang of Eric Bloodaxe's death at the top of her lungs.

The Lady stood staring at her coldly. She said, "You may gloat now, girl. But you will not keep me from doing as I wish." All her layered faces shivered like grass in the wind. "Your brother will come for you, and when he does, then you will both suffer, you and he." She swung the cupboard door closed, and Mav heard the bolt being thrown.

She lay back, her eyes shut, her teeth gritted together. She had to be alone now anyhow. She was already suffering, which she had been striving hard to keep the Lady from realizing. Her body twisted, her womb tightening around the baby, forcing him down, forcing him out. She bit her lips to keep from screaming again, her hands on her great belly, hard as stone now under her palms. She had to do this alone, and in silence. She shut her eyes, and steadied herself for the work.

CHAPTER NINETEEN

"And now all the young men gone. It's an evil wind," the baker woman said. "No good will come of it."

"Amen," the other women murmured.

"At least they're trying to do something," Arre said.

The baker woman sneered at her. "What can they do? That fool Euan! He will only draw the King down on us."

From the other women there rose a sigh and a wail. Arre folded her arms over her chest, uncertain, and full of dread. They were standing under the big oak tree, several women, having nothing else to do. Her head hurt. Euan had been gone all day, Euan and the others. She glanced across the street at the corner; even Benna had disappeared.

"That boy Euan is a bad one," the baker woman said, behind her. "Mind me, this is all his doing, and when the King is cutting our throats we can blame Euan for it."

Arre set her teeth together. She could not argue with them, and turning her back on them she walked swiftly up the Coppergate. Maybe the priest was right; it was God's will, and they were striving against the very will of God, who had set Eric over them.

Her head began to pound again, a relentless throbbing ache, as if some iron garland tightened on her skull.

She remembered running from the King's men, the fear acid in her mouth. Now out there somewhere Euan faced them again, Euan and those other boys, their fists against swords and axes. She quailed from the sudden blinding vision of a blade slicing down on bare hands. Her stomach lurched. Without God's help they couldn't hope to stand against Eric.

She walked up through the shambles, empty and silent, its gutters stained with dried blood, and came to the church. The priest was standing outside, his hands folded in front of him. She stood a moment, staring at him, morose, knowing what he would tell her.

He turned toward her, and caught her eye, and when she was

slow to dip herself to him, he frowned. She went on past him, feeling torn in half.

She went on up to the great bar, where the road pierced the city wall. Two or three men lounged around in the deep shade of the gate: old hangers-on of the King. All the danskers who could carry a sword had gone with Eric.

She fought off that vision again, that sword descending. Going up the wall a little way, she came to the steps cut into the earthworks and climbed up onto the top of it, wide and flat, where a narrow dirt path was worn through the green grass. God favored kings, she thought, in a sudden rush of anger. That was ungood of God. She crossed herself, afraid.

She turned her gaze away from the city, looking north and west, along the Westmoreland road. Out there in the baking afternoon nothing moved.

If God was good then surely Euan would win. Her breath shuddered in her throat, she saw the abyss that thinking opened up before her. She had to submit herself to God, whatever happened. Her head was aching so she could scarcely think. She tried to pray, to beg God for some sign that Euan and the others were right and the priest and the baker woman were wrong.

God's will be done, and Eric was their King, by God's will.

She wondered where her sisters were. Even old Grod was gone, she was alone. She stared away through the golden sunlight of the late afternoon, her head aching in dull waves of pain.

She walked up and down the top of the wall all the afternoon. In the late part of the day, she began to see something moving on the road. Someone was coming.

She straightened and shaded her eyes. Her heart leapt. Horses coming, fast. She went back to the steps down from the wall and ran swiftly down, and went to the edge of the opening of the bar, where she could listen.

She pressed her hand against a wild fluttering under her ribs. Leaning against the wall she strained her ears.

The horses pounded into the bar, their hoofbeats suddenly louder, hollow, echoing. She heard the blast of their breath. One of the porters called, "Sweyn! What is it? Where's the King?"

The riders made no answer. One gigged his sweated foaming

horse on through the gate, past Arre, and turned into the street across the town. She caught a glimpse of his face, the gaping toothless maw: Sweyn Eelmouth, the King's captain.

He was going to the King's Hall, she saw, excited, and he was going in a great haste. She turned back toward the bar, where the other horseman had dismounted.

His voice rose, keen with aggravation. "I'll never do that again! My arse is—"

"Where's the King?" one porter cried, shrill, rushing up to him, and the other joined him. "Where is the King?"

"The King is dead. We ran straight into some huge army coming down from the north."

Arre gave a yell, and as the men all swung around toward her she turned and ran. The pain in her head was gone. Her feet skimmed the wooden pathway of the street; she let out another yell of triumph, and skipped into the air.

What Eelmouth was going to tell the Queen, everybody in Jorvik should know. She knew one way to tell them. She ran down the wide empty street toward the church, bunching up her skirts in her hands.

⁓

Gunnhild jerked up out of a half-sleep; she was in the High Seat, with the painted image on her lap. She struggled to remember what had wakened her. Some deep dread coiled in her belly like a worm, and she looked down at the image and thought, suddenly, that she had been tricked, and stood up.

Eric, she thought, and the worm turned and turned in her belly. She went down the empty hall. As she reached the door, she heard the church bell begin to toll.

The hair on her head all stood on end, and her belly heaved. The ringing of the bell lashed her nerves into a rising quiver of panic. Something bad had happened.

"Gimle!" She strode back up the hall, shouting. "Guthorm—Harald—"

The door behind her slammed open, and she whirled, her hand on the knife in her belt. But it was Sweyn Eelmouth who stumbled in the door, his face streaked with old dried blood.

"Lady, don't you hear the bell?" he shouted. "Eric is dead. The mob is gathering in the city. They will come here, and there's no one to stop them. You have to run, lady—"

"My sons!" She flung her hands up to her head, and stabbed him with a hard look. "Eelmouth, are you with me?"

He straightened; she saw he was tired, and hurt too, but his eyes gleamed. He said, "I will follow you, lady."

"Get my jewels," she said. "The casket—there—" She strode back toward the High Seat. Gimle had come in the back door, Guthorm behind him.

"Mother, what is it? Why is that bell ringing? Is something wrong?"

She gripped him by the arm. "Yes. Get your brothers, we have to get out of here." She stooped and picked his little brother up in her arms. "Eelmouth will attend us—Sweyn! Is there a ship?"

Gimle cried, "Father—is it my father?" The strokes of the bell rang relentlessly on.

Eelmouth came up the hall, the jewel casket in his arms. "Three ships," he said. "We'll have to raise oarsmen from the loafers down by the river. We have to be quick, though."

"Go ready the ships. I'll bring the others. Hurry." She plunged around toward the back door again, and the rest of her boys came running in.

"Mama!" Harald rushed toward her, his arms out. "Mama, there are people coming—they're shouting that Father is dead—"

"Hurry," she said. Little Sigurd was crying, and she picked him up and shook him. "Stop crying, you brat. You're a king's son." She reached for Erling's hand. As they went by the High Seat, she stopped, and letting go of her little son for a moment, took up the painted image of her, and cast it into the hearth, among the banked coals; it took fire at once.

She stood a moment, watching her own face melt in the flames. She said, under her breath, "You think you have ruined me, but you have only set me free upon my course. I shall not falter, and I shall have my revenge." Then, with Gimle and Guthorm leading the two middle boys, she strode out of the King's Hall of Jorvik.

⎯⊶⎯

Dark was falling; Arre, out of breath, wound her way through the mass of people loitering in the street, her gaze on the Hall of the King on its embankment above them. Someone behind her called, "What happened? What happened?"

"The King is dead!"

A roar went up from them all, and the crowd surged a little closer to the embankment. Arre started forward, eager. Then the baker woman was at her elbow.

"It wasn't Euan, you know," she shouted. "It was some army of Scots come out of the north—"

"Look!" Arre thrust her arm out, pointing.

From the crowd another huge gust of a cry went up. Out the door of the hall, into the last light of the day, came a stream of people. Leading them was tall Gunnhild, the Queen, the witch, her yellow hair streaming out behind her. She paid no heed to the mob rushing and roiling in the street, but hurried away down the hill toward the river.

Arre shouted, "Now! They're going—" She rushed forward, driving herself straight up the steep embankment, toward the hall.

She knew, not caring much, that most of the others followed her, knowing better than to chase Gunnhild. She had no interest any more in Gunnhild. It was the King's Hall that drew her, the place of power, the High Seat. She scrambled up the hill, her breath sawing in and out of her throat. Pounding feet followed her, shouting voices; she stretched to go faster, to be the first through the yawning door into the gloomy darkness.

The hall echoed with her footsteps. A single torch burned, up near the High Seat. She ran to it. In through the door behind her the townspeople flooded, and fell on what was nearest: the rugs and furs on the benches, the pots and kettles, whatever they could lay hands on. Arre stood on her toes and reached up and dragged the heavy smoky torch out of its bracket on the wall.

In the dark around her people were breaking open chests and fighting over their loot, their voices a babble. She turned to the great High Seat, all carved with beasts and crowns, and empty now.

She said, "This to your power," and cast the torch into the High Seat, and stepped back to watch it burn.

⚓

Corban and the others did not reach Jorvik again until after dark. Gifu led them across the valley, through a bog, along the riverbank, sometimes in the river. Well before they reached the city they could hear the church bell ringing, and see the red glow in the sky, and when they rode up to the wall the noise of the celebration going on inside echoed out over it. They rounded the wall to the open, empty gate. Just inside, Euan dismounted stiffly from his horse.

"I'm going home to see my mother," he said, and walked away, leaving the horse standing heavy-headed and exhausted behind him.

Grod was slumped over his horse's neck, groaning. Gifu reached out and took Euan's dangling reins; she had taken to riding as if she had done it forever. She said, "We can keep them, can't we? The horses?"

Corban said, "If nobody recognizes them. They could be more trouble than they're worth." He rode beside her through the gate. Over the rooftops he could see Eric's hall blazing like a torch on the embankment. The steady clanging of the church bell grated on his ears. He wondered what had happened to Gunnhild and her children.

They rode down the wide street into the middle of the city. In the open square at the top of the Coppergate, two rings of boys and girls were dancing by the light of torches. In the dark alleys on either side, boys and girls were doing other kinds of dances. Red-faced and laughing, men and women thronged up and down the streets, shouting and passing jugs out to one another from hand to hand. There were no danskers anywhere. All the houses were open, with people spilling in and out of the doors, and clapping their hands and whooping.

Down by the oak at the low end of Coppergate, some people were cooking a pig over a great fire. They had been hoarding food, all along, he realized. He wondered if Eric would have starved before they did.

He turned into the street where his house was; he slid down from the saddle of his horse and tossed the reins to Gifu. His legs throbbed from the long riding, and he felt as if he walked hoop-legged. Grod hurried past him across the threshold; Corban knew he was going for the jug.

Corban thought, I have to get out of here. He went cautiously over the threshold. But the place looked solid and good, everything straight and square, the fire blazing on the hearth. He looked around for Arre and Benna, but they were gone. Then up from the hearth end of the room came Ulf, yawning.

"There you are. Where have you been? Did you hear? Eric's been killed."

"What?" Corban said. "When did you get here?"

"Around noon. A little after I'd hauled in, Eelmouth came charging through and collected Gunnhild and the brats into a ship and made off downriver." Ulf looked him up and down, frowning. "You're a mess. Where have you been?"

"Looking for trade," Corban said.

Ulf reached out and plucked at his sleeves, which were stiff with dried blood. "Hard trade, I guess."

"What are people saying about Eric?"

"Oh, he's dead for sure. Gunnhild wouldn't have taken off like that. She's witchwise, but that won't help you when a mob comes up the hill with torches. What I've heard, he was going up north to raid, and ran into a great army of Scots."

"That's good enough," Corban said. He pulled his cloak off; he was tired to his bones. "I have to leave right away," he said to Ulf. "Make the ship ready, will you?"

Ulf shrugged. "As you wish. I don't think we ought to be here if the Scots decide to keep coming, anyway."

Corban laughed; he had not considered that. Grod appeared, carrying the jug and an empty cup, looking very downcast. Ulf went by him, going out, and the old man came sadly up to Corban.

"Nobody will believe me," he said. "I'm a hero, I killed Eric Bloodaxe, and all anybody talks about is about some army of Scots." He lifted the jug to fill his cup.

The thick foaming ale ran steadily into the cup, an amber ribbon, and then, abruptly, the ribbon folded down into the cup and
was gone. Grod gave a devastated cry. Lifting the jug, he peered
into it. "It's empty!"

Corban's back tingled. He said, "She knows." He paced down
the hall, working off the abrupt jolt of fear. "I have to go get my
sister from her. And we should get out of this house. Let's go."

"Where?"

Corban got him by the arm and towed him toward the door;
he looked up into the dark rafters of the hall, expecting them to
crack and sag. The fire was dying on the hearth. The place was
utterly quiet, and cold. He hauled Grod out the door.

"Where are we going?"

"To Benna's," Corban said.

⟨⟩

Mav bit down on her fingers, trying not to scream. Her body
twisted up like a knot around the hot stone of the baby, butting his
way out through the narrow places of her body; she clawed at her
face, whimpering. The pain subsided, and she slumped down in
her soaking bedclothes, gasping for breath.

It was the dead of night. The Lady would be asleep now. If
she could bear the baby without anyone knowing, then maybe she
would be strong enough, when they did find him, to keep the Lady
from taking him away. The next great backbreaking spasm came
on her, and she buried her face in the stinking covers and sobbed.

Through the night she labored. As every mounting pain began,
her heart clenched in dread, and then she bit her lips and wept
while it wrung her like an old rag that must be squeezed of every
drop, and then slowly relented, so that she could fill up again, and
be wrung once more.

She had helped deliver babies, at her old home. She knew what
to expect. In the darkness before the dawn, she squatted on her
bed, grunting and snorting like a sow, and reached down between
her legs and drew him out, wet and slick. She laid him down on
the blankets and felt for the great twisted cord that tied them together.

In the darkness she could not see him. He gave a little whimper, and she could feel him struggling, arms and legs milling. She brought the cord up to her mouth and bit through it, the blood spurting over her lips. She ripped cloth from the hem of her dress and tied his end of the cord fast, and picked him up.

He gave one frightened wail. No, no, she thought, make no sound, they must not hear. Then through her body another rippling pain squeezed out the great flopping afterbirth.

She kicked that away, and lay down in the filthy sodden blankets and brought the baby to her breast. He was warm, heavier than she had expected, and he nuzzled at her and caught hold of her nipple and began clumsily to suck. With her fingers she traced the contour of his little cheek; she felt the pulse beating in the top of his skull. A surge of mother-love welled through her so strong it made her shake. Deep in her body, her empty womb clenched painfully again. Still in utter darkness, unable to see him, she gathered the blanket around him, and he nestled into the curve of her arm.

She floated on a warm glow of happiness. She had brought him forth by herself. The horror that had started him was only a long ago moment that didn't matter anymore; Eric was dead now, and this child was hers alone, who had made him from nothing. Later she would name him, guide him, urge him, all hers, all the rest of their lives.

He was suckling strongly now, unseen in the dark, warm in her arms, her son. She cupped her hand over his head, feeling the soft crinkle of his hair against her palm. Her sense of triumph was fading. Their lives might not last very long, when the Lady found him—when Corban came. And Corban would come, but she saw nothing he could do. She curled herself around her child, afraid.

—⚬—

In her own cupboard, the Lady lay awake, hot rage bubbling in her mind.

She hated them. Mav had defied her, and foolishly thought now she could hide the baby from her; the brother had betrayed her. She would look like a fool to Bluetooth, her whole plan destroyed with him.

But she knew Corban. She knew he would come for his sister, and when he did, the Lady would have her revenge.

Her anger made her tremble. She felt the edges of her mind loosen and fray, the whispering of those captive voices, whispering she was making a mistake—that was the danger in this, that her grip on them might crack.

She would endure the risk. She would not lose Mav, with her thrilling gift of foresight. With such a power she could make her way anywhere she chose. When the brother was in her grip again, she would barter with the girl—her brother's life for her acquies- ence, her surrender. She knew Mav would accept. Once she had entrapped her, then she would blast the brother, and she would cast the wretched baby into the sea.

She calmed herself. Bluetooth and Eric had failed her; that was a woman's lot, of course, to trust in mere weakling men. She her- self went on. This would be another victory. She fought down the rebellious, doubting spirits within her, and waited for Corban to come back to Hedeby.

CHAPTER TWENTY

Benna said, "I'm going with you."

He held her hands, looking into her face. "I may not come back."

"That's why I'm going with you."

By the fire, Gifu and Arre were watching them; Gifu had one arm draped around Arre. The firelight made a wiry gold nest of her hair. Arre said, "Benna, what about us?"

Benna was looking steadily at him, her eyes wide. "Can they go?"

"I'm not going," Gifu said. "And Euan, Arre—Euan won't go."

Grod said, "I'm not going."

Corban gripped Benna's hands. "You have to leave them. But you will never be alone. If you go, it must be as my wife."

Arre said, "Benna. You'll leave us?"

"I will," Benna said to him. "I will."

He bent his head and kissed her hands. "Thank you."

She turned, and went to her sisters, and they put their arms around each other. Corban got up, to leave them alone together, and went out to the dark. The wind was sweeping up from the moors, smelling deeply of dry heather; across the river he could still see Eric's house, crowning the embankment with a dull red heap of embers.

His guts roiled. The Lady knew what he had done. Yet he had to go back there. He imagined Mav like the bait in a trap, waiting for him.

He could not turn aside; that was the straight way.

Grod came out of the hut behind him. "You'll have to get along without me, I guess," he said. He jerked his thumb toward the hut. "They need me more than you do."

Corban said, "You are a good friend, Grod."

"And you." Grod cleared his throat. "And you." His hand fell on Corban's arm. "I wish I could come with you." His voice thickened; Corban saw that he was about to cry.

Corban said, "I thought you were going to go home."

"Home," Grod said. "What's that but where you're known and loved?"

"What you know and love," Corban said.

"That's what I said," Grod answered.

Benna came out of the hut, carrying a cloak and a bundle. Corban reached out one hand to her, and she took it, and came to stand beside him.

He stood, not moving, enveloped in this moment with her. He was happy now. Once he started forward again, he knew, every step was treacherous. She turned and looked up at him, questioning. He cleared his throat. "Let's go, then," he said, and started forth.

⇨

"It was Euan and your sister and twenty of their friends who saved Jorvik," Corban said, "and will anybody ever know? Already there's this rumor of an army of Scots. The world is one thing, and the way people think of it is another."

She sat beside him in the forecastle of the ship, drawing on a piece of wood. "What does it matter, so long as you know?"

"Better for Euan and those boys and Gifu if nobody ever knows."

"Did you give him the abacus?"

"Yes."

She laughed. Her hands stroked expertly over the piece of wood, and the ship appeared on it, the men at their oars, the lines of the prow.

She said, "Where are we going?"

"To Hedeby."

She leaned on him; the ship thrashed through the sea, England a long dark streamer of land off to their right. A seagull floated in the air before them, white and gray and white, its head turning to watch them.

She said, "Where is your sister?"

"In Hedeby. In the hands of a woman much stronger than Gunnhild. I don't know why she wants Mav, or what she intends to do with her, but it cannot be good. Anyway, she has my sister now, but she is not almighty, as Gunnhild was not—what did you manage with her?"

"I made her image."

"As she is, or as she would be?"

Benna laughed. "I would rather have drawn her as she is." On the wood she traced the shape of a seagull, tipped against the wind, and made the wind visible.

"With the Lady of Hedeby that would be impossible."

"What?" She licked salt from her lips.

"I can't explain. She changes."

"A shape shifter?"

"No, Gunnhild was that; this woman is like water—never the same way twice."

She sat up, reaching for her drawing kit. "What is Hedeby like?"

He told her, spilling himself into her in words. On the flat piece of wood, she drew the seagull, arching through the weather-beaten sky.

They reached the coast across from England, and rowed northward along it. She asked, "How will you save your sister?"

"I don't know. If I don't, you must go back to Jorvik."

She said nothing. It was dark, so she could not draw. He said, "If I do come back—"

He sat quiet a moment. She was warm against him, her head against his shoulder. He said, "When I went away from you the first time, we did not sail straight to Hedeby, you know. A storm blew us west and south—far west and far south. There was a land there, very fair and sweet and rich. I want to go there again. I want to go somewhere far from here, where the priests and kings haven't reached yet. I want to make a life for us free of them."

She said, "I will go wherever you go."

His heart leapt at that; he tightened his arm around her. Yet the closer they came to Hedeby, the more he wished he had not brought her. He could think of nothing to do against the Lady, no way to rescue Mav from her. Now he was bringing Benna, too, within her reach.

On his right was flat fenland. They were coming up to the watery inlet that took them to Hollandstadt. Another sail ghosted along ahead of them past islands of reeds. She plucked some of the reeds, chewed the ends, and saw how they brushed her ink onto boards. They nosed steadily up the river; on the great earthworks, cows grazed.

With the sun going down they reached the mooring at Hollandstadt. The harbor was full of ships and they stayed on board the ship for the night. They lay down to sleep in the bow, side by side, and when Benna was asleep, Corban slipped away from her and went aft, to where Ulf was dozing in the stern.

"Where are you going?" Ulf said, startled.

"To Hedeby. Shut up. Listen to me." Corban kept his voice low. "Do you have any money?"

"A little."

"Pack the ship with food, extra sails, rope, water—everything we need for a long voyage."

"I'll do it." Ulf nodded past him toward the bow. "You're leaving her?"

"When I get back—if I don't get back, take her home to Jorvik. But I have to go get my sister, Ulf."

Ulf slapped his arm. "Christ and Thor both go with you, Corban."

He said, "I don't know if it works like that." He gave one more look back into the bow, and then swung over the side of the ship down into the water, and swam in to the shore.

⸺⸙⸺

Benna asked, "Where is he going?"

Ulf jumped, startled; he had been staring away after Corban, over the dark water. He mumbled something at her. The moon was rising up over the earthworks, lopsided and eaten up like a piece of old cheese.

"To Hedeby?" she said.

"He says you're to stay here."

She said, "I'm not staying here. Turn your face away." She

stood up, pulling off her long dress. Ulf jerked his eyes in another
direction, saying, "Now, Benna—" but he did nothing to stop her.
She bundled the dress and her shoes together and sat down on the
gunwale, swung her legs over, and slipped off into the water.

"Benna!" he called, softly, behind her. She swam away, toward
what she hoped was the shore.

It was hard to swim carrying her shoes and dress. She stroked
with one arm and kicked with her feet, driving herself steadily
along. From the surface of the water she could not see where she
was going. She paddled along past a moored ship; the reflection of
a light on the shore wrinkled toward her, and she followed it. She
passed another ship creaking at the end of its long slanted anchor
line. At last her feet touched the ground. She waded up out of the
cove, her clothes weeping around her, into the edge of the light of
a flaring torch set above the door of a building.

There was a cluster of houses here, and a crowd of people,
many going in and out of the one with the torch. The earthworks
loomed up in the dark to her right; a broad road spilled off along
the foot of it. She wrung her dress out and put it on, and started
uncertainly toward the road. From the house with the torch over
the door came a burst of wild laughter.

Maybe he had gone in there. She turned toward the road, and
saw nobody. She looked around the torchlit house again, frowning.
Most of these people were drunken men. She had to get out of
here, before someone noticed her.

She went down the road a little. Ahead of her, pale under the
moon, it stretched empty toward the horizon.

No. Far down there, someone walked, alone.

Her heart lifted. She knew that was Corban. She set off down
the road after him.

After the long ride in the ship, the walking felt good. Her skirt
was heavy with water and she wrung it out as she walked. She
thought perhaps she would catch up with him, and make him take
her with him, but it was hard enough just keeping him in sight,
down the long moonlit road.

She hitched her skirts up under her belt. The night wore on,
kicking by under her feet, every stride sliding more of the night
past her. She was tired—she had not slept—and hungry, but she

could not let him leave her too far behind; she might never see him again. The sky whitened. Her feet aching, her legs sore, she followed him toward the haze of dust and smoke in the distance, getting closer and closer.

They were coming to a gate; even so early in the morning people clustered around it, some on foot, and one with a big wagon. She hurried her pace, afraid of losing sight of him in the crowd.

He disappeared into the gate, and she rushed in after him, walked in through a mass of people, and fought her way through. She went out the other side, into the teeming city. Frantically she searched the crowded ways before her, and saw him, saw the red and blue cloak, bobbing along through the streams of other people. She plunged in after him.

She kept her gaze pinned to the red and blue cloak; she saw only glimpses of the city around her. She had never been in a place with so many people. She wound her way through groups of women, by peddlers and a crier and three men playing pipes. The wooden walkways boomed under the constant stamp of feet. She smelled a harbor, like the river at Jorvik.

He turned into a side street, and broke into a run. As she watched helplessly he ran up to a wall and leapt up, caught the top of it, and vanished over it.

She looked wildly around. The blank wooden wall stretched away down the side of the street. She went up to it and looked up at the top, impossibly out of her reach, and started off along the foot of it. Reaching the corner she turned into a narrow gap between the wooden wall and a withy fence and fought her way down through knee-deep marshy reeds.

At the far end of this wall she came out on a canal, stinking of rot. At the foot of the wall a little sluice came out, draining water from the space within. She got down on her hands and knees and crawled in through the sluice.

She stood up in a yard still quiet from the night, dark from the high wall around it. In front of her was a hall, deeply thatched, with walls of split planks, as big and fine as the King's Hall in Jorvik. She went slowly toward it, her heart thumping.

Midway up the long wall a door stood open; she stopped dead, seeing two people there, crouched furtively by the edge of the door, peering into the hall.

They did not move, they did not see her. She went cautiously nearer, reached the doorway, and stood there a moment. The two people were staring fixedly into the hall, and neither paid any heed to her.

Then a voice reached her, harsh and high. A woman's voice, angry.

"So, you see, you did exactly what I wanted of you. I wanted you to come back here, and you came. Everything you do, I will of you. You are my thing."

Benna went quietly in over the threshold, into the hall; the benches on either of the long sides were full of people, cowering in the corners; she saw their eyes glinting in the dark. The hall stretched dark around her, save for a white glow of light, at the far end.

There a lamp burned, shining on the floor at the feet of a tall, tall woman, but the light of the lamp was nothing to the white blaze of light from the woman's face. She stood with her arms outstretched, barring the way, and before her, small and dark, stood Corban.

Benna hung back, in the shadows, with the onlooking slaves of the hall. This then was the Lady of Hedeby. Behind her and her blaze of white light she saw cupboard doors, cast open. That was where Corban was going, and now, he said, "I've come to take my sister."

The Lady blazed up a little, so that all the watching people flinched back, and laughed.

"You have come to your destruction, little man!"

"No—" From the darkness of the cupboard bed another voice cried. "Me. Take me."

"I will, don't doubt it." The woman laughed in her rippling of the white light, shedding beams of color into the air; yet she lit nothing else. All else fell in shadows.

Corban took another step toward her. "I'm coming, Mav!" He lifted his arms, ready to shove the Lady out of his way, and strode forward.

She swung her arm up, and her hand fell on his shoulder. He

stopped in his tracks, held fast as if he were nothing. Benna gasped. He was crumpling, struggling to keep his feet under him, but still driven down under that touch, his knees buckling, his back bowed. The woman towered over him, screaming in triumph.

"Did you think you could betray me with no cost? You stupid little man."

Benna crept forward. She was shivering all over. She had to do something, now, before this woman noticed her. She remembered how Gunnhild had fallen in love with her own face. She couldn't even see this woman's face for the glare of the light streaming from it. Corban had said it would be no use, she could not draw her anyway. Certainly she had no time.

Corban was now collapsed at the witch's feet. She gave a shriek of derision. "Not so strong now, hah—Kill a king, will you—" Without looking back, the woman thrust her other arm out behind her, fending off someone else.

Faint in the lamp light, there was Mav, come out of the bed. She was thin as a twig. She wobbled on her feet, but she stretched out her arms.

"Me—take me—"

The towering light-struck figure whooped, delighted. "I will, girl, but I will have him first—watch him die—" She reached down her hand and gripped him by the beard, to turn his head up. "Look into my eyes, Corban!"

"No," Benna cried, and ran forward, fumbling around her neck. The looking glass. The looking glass would have to do. The woman in her streaming light swung toward her. "Look into your own eyes, witch," Benna shouted, and reaching Corban's side she held the looking glass out before her.

The wash of light struck Benna; her sight blanched, and she winced back, blinded, her arm thrown up before her eyes. With her other hand she held out the looking glass, a shield against that gaze.

The woman shrieked. Benna blinked her eyes, trying to see again. Corban brushed against her, straightening up off the floor beside her, and his hand gripped her hand with the looking glass, holding it steady.

Benna's vision was a white fog, in the center of it a tall, swaying shape. She blinked, and more of her sight came back, a shadowy counterworld floating in the glare. Before her the Lady jerked her face away, her hands rising, fumbling in the swelling, surrounding dark.

She was shrinking. The white light around her was fading. Mav brushed by her, staggering toward her brother, and at her touch, the Lady slumped down to her knees. The flame on the lamp blew down. Corban murmured under his breath. The Lady knelt down before them. The last light of the lamp showed her face collapsed into a thousand wrinkles, her hair hanging lank and long and white as sea-spume down her shoulders. Her gown was shredding into dull black rags that hardly hid her old white flesh.

"Mav," Corban whispered. "Bring the baby—run."

Benna moved closer to him and he put his arm around her; her legs were shaking. Mav tottered off back to the bed. "Is she dying?"

"I don't know," Corban said. "I doubt it. We have to get out of here."

"Wait," Mav said. "Look."

The lamp flickered, its flame a blue bead on the surface of the oil. The first sunlight was coming into the hall. The old woman knelt down before them, bowed over her clasped hands, her eyes shut. From her nose a tendril of smoke curled.

Benna's fingers tightened on Corban's arm. The smoke drifted up into the sunlight, spreading and swelling into a wraith of a woman. Her long hair swirled in the smoke and her arms rose like columns of the smoke, and she threw her head back, laughing, rising away from the Lady of Hedeby. Behind her another curling vapor slipped free, swimming up after her, and another after that, and another, until Mav had lost count of them.

They rose up into the dusky air, riotous and silent. One at a time they paused above Mav, and hovered over her, only a moment, bending toward her. Then each one floated away and was gone. They left behind only a little old white-haired woman, waxen faced, hunched forward over her knees, and fast asleep.

"Now," Mav said, and started toward the door.

Before they could reach the door the hall around them erupted. All the frozen, frightened slaves came suddenly to life. Their voices rose in a panicky babble. Flinging on clothes, snatching up blankets, hauling sacks onto their shoulders, they made for the open sunlight. They swept up Corban and Benna and Mav in their midst and out the door and across the yard; the front gate burst open under the first pressure and they pitched forward onto the wooden boardwalks of Hedeby.

—⚬—

The first sunlight was climbing into the sky. Corban clutched Mav by the hand; she could hardly keep on her feet. She was thin as bone, her skin like whey. Her eyes shone bright with life, and in her arms the baby, wrapped in a filthy scrap of blanket, let out a sudden, lusty yell.

Corban turned to Benna, beside him, who had come up suddenly from nowhere beside him when he faced the witch, and put his other arm around her, and kissed her. He looked down into her face. "You saved us, Benna. You saved us. Where did you come from? How did you get into the hall? How did you find us?"

"I followed you," she said, and brushed her hair back. "Did you think I would let you go again?" She nodded at his sister. "She's about to fall. I'll hold the baby, if she wants."

"Yes, take him." He picked Mav up in his arms, a bundle of sticks in a bloody, tattered gown. Benna lifted the baby out of her arms.

"Where are we going?" She raised her gaze to his.

He pulled his cloak around Mav, to shelter her; she leaned on him, and shut her eyes. He was too tired to think. But all he had to do was what he had been doing. He had only to keep on, going straight ahead, doing what he could do. He gathered up the last of his strength, his sister in his arms, and his wife beside him.

The slaves had run away, leaving the boardwalk all but empty. The sun was rising over the rooftops, hot and bright. He turned into the long stream of its power.

"West," he said, and started off. "Into the west."